CERTAIN TRUTHS

A Novel

STEPHANIE WYLER

PAGE PUBLISHING, INC.
Conneaut Lake, PA

First originally published by Page Publishing 2021

ISBN 978-1-6624-5154-6 (pbk)
ISBN 978-1-6624-5155-3 (digital)

Printed in the United States of America

CHAPTER 1

"Nine one one... What is your emergency?"

"My wife has been shot! She's dying! For God's sake, send help!"

"Okay, sir, try to remain calm. Tell me, where is her injury? How do you know it is a gunshot injury?"

"She's been shot in the head!" The caller started sobbing, unable to put words together. Finally, he screamed into the phone, "I know... because I shot her! Send help! Now!" The sobbing resumed while the dispatcher, in a professional and dispassionate voice, assured the caller she would stay on the line with him until first responders arrived. The caller, again without the ability to respond with words, alternated between mournful cries and breathless gasps.

*****

The silence in the courtroom was deafening. The jurors, the court staff, and the onlookers who packed the courtroom every day of the trial, even the judge, were all holding their collective breath as the recording of that emergency call was played, the words and the emotions echoing throughout the marble columns and brocade drapes of the magnificent courtroom. The caller's words and emotional hell were still resounding in every listener's ears. The horror and pain in his voice pierced them to their very core. As they listened, they fixed their gaze on the caller; he was seated next to his attorney. Dressed impeccably in a navy Armani suit and a cherry-colored tie, the caller was hunched over the table, his head in his hands, trying with all his might not to break down in tears. He failed. Several jurors hung their heads in a futile attempt to contain their own emotions.

It was the trial of the century in Cincinnati, but it would only hold that distinction until the next trial of the century. For the past two weeks, Allen Mills had been on trial for the murder of his young wife, the mother of his little girl. Allen Mills was a notable presence in Cincinnati, a successful restaurateur who owned three high-priced locations frequented by those who want to see and be seen in local society. He was also known as the son of the governor of Ohio, Richard Mills. Governor and Mrs. Mills were seated in the front row of the courtroom gallery since the first day of their son's trial. They let tears of grief flow while the sounds of their son's most horrific experience echoed throughout the courtroom.

Public life has been an integral part of his childhood and adolescence. Allen and his wife were featured on the society page regularly, attending or sponsoring charitable events.

Celeste Davenport Mills, despite her beauty and talents, was a deeply depressed and jealous woman. She regularly accused Allen of being unfaithful. He constantly denied it. Allen had never cheated on his wife and had never even harbored the thought of straying despite the many temptations that came his way. She had become so consumed with jealousy and mistrust that she had regularly hired a string of private investigators to follow Allen, hoping to catch him in a compromised position. However, every investigator had reported back to her that there was nothing, absolutely nothing clandestine in his activities. Always dissatisfied and unaccepting of their findings, she would hire yet another snoop in the hope of getting a better result. A deeply conflicted soul, Celeste was not sure what she would do if she ever received the report that confirmed her suspicions. Would she stay in the marriage, or would her pride prevail and lead her to divorce?

Almost a year ago, Allen came home late from his flagship restaurant in the downtown business district. He had entertained some college fraternity brothers in town for an informal reunion. Dinner, wine (lots of wine, in fact), and cigars with friends made for a very late evening. It was almost two o'clock when he tiptoed into the house and upstairs to the master bedroom. So as not to awaken Celeste, he undressed in the dark. He slipped into bed and settled down to sleep. He was just drifting off when he heard a quick clicking sound. Although he had never actually heard the sound before, he knew in an instant what it was. At virtually the same instant as the click, Celeste snapped on the lamp atop her bedside table. After Allen's eyes adjusted to the light, he saw what he intuitively knew to be the source of the clicking sound—his .25 caliber revolver, which he kept in the drawer of his bedside table. Celeste, kneeling next to him on the mattress, pointed the gun inches away from his face.

Celeste hurled accusations at Allen, screaming she knew he was with his old college sweetheart, Abby Scofield. She continued her grip on the gun. The barrel was pressed against his chest. His heart was beating so fast and hard he feared he would lose consciousness. Despite every effort to calm her, anything Allen said only seemed to make her angrier and more hell-bent on bringing this confrontation to an irrevocable and tragic conclusion. In his last desperate attempt to bring an end to the standoff, he reached for the barrel of the gun. They struggled for a few seconds, which seemed, to Allen, an eternity. The gun went off, the explosive sound reverberating throughout their bedroom suite overlooking the river. The bullet lodged in the crown molding of the ceiling but not before it had passed through Celeste's brain, killing her instantly.

With blood and brain matter speckling Allen's face and chest, he placed the frantic emergency call the jurors had just listened to with rapt attention.

Allen's attorney, Jackson Berman, rose from his chair at counsel table and approached the jury. "Ladies and gentlemen of the jury, the prosecution played the 9-1-1 call for you in its case in chief. They wanted to persuade you that my client confessed to murder in that phone call." He turned toward the judge. "Thank you, Judge, for allowing me to replay it for the jurors." He returned his gaze to the jury panel. "In the recording, you heard Allen Mills in his own words and in his own unimaginable emotional hell, describing what was the most dreadful moment of his life. Did it sound like a man who had set out to take the life of his wife, the mother of his child? No, I submit to you it happened exactly as Allen told you when he testified. There is no question that he shot his wife. But you have to decide if it was murder. Consider the emotion in his voice, the raw terror, while you also consider the evidence presented to you throughout these two weeks of trial. The gun went off in Allen's right hand, but Allen is left-handed. Would a man who had intended to kill his wife do so with his wrong hand? Why would he risk missing his target? Remember the friends of Celeste who told you, while they are still grieving the loss of their dear friend, Allen was correct when he testified about his wife's quick and fiery temper and her all-consuming jealousy. What about Allen's old girlfriend, Abby Scofield? We established through her closest friend's testimony that, tragically, Abby lost her life two years ago in a boating accident. Allen Mills and I thank you for your service as jurors. We both know it has been an exhausting two weeks for you. But multiply your exhaustion a hundredfold, and maybe you can begin to appreciate the agonizing experience Mr. Mills has suffered for the past year."

He gathered his notes from the podium, gave one last knowing look at the jurors, and returned to counsel table to take his seat next to his client. Although he had been in this situation many times before, there was always a sense of panic, knowing there was nothing else to do now but wait for the jury's verdict. The panic had never diminished despite having tried more than a hundred cases in his career—so far.

*****

The mammoth wooden doors of the courthouse pushed open, and Allen Mills emerged with Jackson Berman flanking him. They descended the stone steps to street level and into a sea of local and national members of the media.

"Members of the press, Mr. Mills will not answer any questions at this time. He is grateful for the jurors' attention, service, and careful consideration of the evidence. We were confident Mr. Mills was not guilty, and the jury's verdict confirms our position. The death of Celeste Mills was a heartrending accident. It has been a grueling two weeks and an even more grueling year for him. He requests you honor and respect his family's privacy, so he and his daughter can finally grieve the loss of Celeste together. Thank you." The two sharply dressed men made their way through the crowd to a waiting vehicle. Jackson's hand was on Allen's shoulder as he shepherded him through the crowd of reporters and onlookers. The driver whisked them away while reporters continued to scream questions and while photographers and videographers continued to preserve the moment for posterity and profit.

Jackson, "Jax" to his friends and family since childhood, turned off the television broadcasting the press appearance. It had taken place hours earlier. After the driver delivered Allen to his home, he transported Jax to the Manor Hotel. Jax settled in and watched coverage of the verdict on local news programs and national cable news networks. He took a sip of Scotch he poured from the bar in his hotel suite, leaned back on the sofa in the living area, and reflected on this latest chapter in his professional life. He thought about Allen and his little girl, wondering what they were doing right now. It would be the first night they were spending together since the tragedy. Allen had spent more than ten months in jail, awaiting trial, and his little girl had lived with Celeste's parents during those months. Thankfully, little Aubrey slept through the entire nightmare that unfolded in her parents' bedroom. She had awakened in the morning to be told by her grandparents that her mommy had died and that her daddy was away in jail. Aubrey, at age six, had been too young to visit Allen while he languished in the county jail, waiting and preparing for his judgment day. What do you say to your child, your only child, after being separated so long under those circumstances? How do you just pick up where you left off and carry on as a family? God only knows what the grandparents had been telling Aubrey for these past several months while they cared for their only grandchild, their daughter's daughter. Allen had been holding the gun when it fired into Celeste's skull. No two ways about it; he did kill her. But did he commit murder? The jury said no. However, there was no denying he killed her. It was the absolute truth. It was a truth Jax had successfully convinced the jurors to ignore. In his profession, Jax learned early there were times when he could not let the absolute truth get in the way.

He sipped his cocktail and tried to find logical solutions to such a horribly illogical situation. He found it ironic that Allen was spending the night with his little girl while he himself was a resident of this hotel suite, not spending the night with his own daughter.

He rose from the sofa and, cocktail in hand, walked to the large bay window, and he watched the barges and pleasure boats ambling past him on the muddy waters of the river. While he was considering these questions and trying to decide what to have for dinner, his cell phone buzzed. Jax reached for the phone, and a smile automatically came to his face when he saw the "Home" displayed on the screen.

"Hello, Princess."

"Hi, Daddy. I wanted to call you. I saw you on television."

"How did you know I would be on television?"

Olivia gave a righteous sniff only a ten-year-old girl can do to perfection. "I've been following your trial on the Internet. Naturally I knew you would be on TV today."

"You do always pay attention to what I'm doing. Forgive me for questioning you." Jax never tired of conversations with his daughter.

Olivia giggled and said, "That's okay. I wanted to tell you that I thought you handled yourself really well with those reporters. Congratulations. I'm proud of you."

It was all Jax could do not to laugh, but being the father of a princess, he knew the repercussions of a laugh could be severe. Nobody laughs at a girl who is dangerously close to adolescence and walks away unscathed. Olivia, being an only child, had been surrounded by adults in her preschool years; it was no wonder her vocabulary made her seem years older than she was. Jax had to constantly remind himself, despite her witty observations about life, she was still very much a little girl in so many ways. "Thanks, Princess. Your opinion always means a lot. You know that. So how about dinner with your old dad tomorrow? I could pick you up after soccer practice."

"As long as Mom says it's all right, it's a date. Wait a minute. Mom wants to talk to you."

"A perfect end to a perfect day," Jax grumbled to himself while he waited for Catherine.

"Hello, Jax. I suppose congratulations are in order. You managed to keep another violent criminal roaming free among us."

"Catherine, I'm going to take that as the most heartfelt congratulations you could ever muster for me and my career. Let's not belabor the point. I would like to take Olivia to dinner tomorrow after soccer, unless you already have plans."

"That's fine with me so long as you have her home by eight. She has homework to do. You're welcome to have her this weekend since you haven't spent much time with her during this trial."

Jax, as always, was uncertain whether her comment was genuine concern or the latest in a never-ending series of criticisms and caustic remarks. He swept the question away, thanked Catherine, and terminated the call.

Jax returned to the window. He watched the sun setting over the city, casting an amber glow on the river traffic. He had spent every evening of the last six months looking out this window, surrounded by the luxury of his suite: the heavy upholstered furniture in the living area displaying rich golds and reds and the spacious adjoining bedroom with a sitting area looking over the skyline. A notable figure due to his success in high-profile cases in Cincinnati as well as other nearby cities, he had no difficulty rounding up friends or business associates for drinks or dinner or both. He enjoyed a steady diet of camaraderie since he had become a resident of the Manor Hotel. But he would give just about anything in the world to be able to peaceably coexist with Catherine, to resume their marriage, and to raise his precious little girl together under the same roof.

Enough, he thought to himself. *Stop wallowing, you idiot. You just scored another major coup in a string of coups in the courtroom. The verdict will be on national media cycles for the next twenty-four hours. Relax and enjoy it. Have another Scotch on the rocks, Jax. Don't mind if I do, Jax.* He put his empty glass on the bar, changed into his favorite jeans and a sweater, and headed for the elevator to have his second cocktail of the evening with his new best friend, Frank, the hotel bartender.

CHAPTER 2

Jax closed the hotel bar with Frank while they bantered over scintillating topics ranging from Frank's latest girlfriend to politics and horse racing. The next morning, he waltzed into his office promptly at seven-thirty. This was not unusual; Jax made it a point to get into the office before the phone started ringing and his first client of the day arrived. He made an effort to, at least, try to get there before his office assistant. He could count on fewer than the fingers of one hand the times he actually had arrived before her.

Today was no exception. Marion Anderson was working away at her computer, the light from the screen casting an almost ephemeral glow on her face. It was the only light on in her office.

"Good morning, Marion. Tell me what's on the schedule today."

"You're full up today. You have three pretrials and a motion hearing in Judge Manning's courtroom, plus an arraignment in room A in municipal court. Five appointments this afternoon, two are new clients. I've got the preliminary info on them waiting on your desk, including a copy of their charges plus the details of my phone conference with them. Then a haircut at five with Angela."

"Okay, it sounds like a fun day any way you look at it." He turned to leave but then came to an abrupt halt. "Wait a minute. I didn't make a haircut appointment."

"No, you didn't. I did. I saw you on the news yesterday standing there with Allen Mills. Trust me, you need a haircut. You don't want people mixing you up with most of the clients you represent, do you?"

Jax chuckled and patted Marion on her shoulder. "You do take good care of me. I will give you that."

She couldn't help but smile back at him and reply, "Well, Lord knows somebody has to do it."

She had been doing it so well for the past decade. When he left his first job as a trial attorney with Lamping and Jacobs ten years ago, Marion joined him. She was a seasoned veteran when Jax joined the firm as its newest associate, fresh out of law school and an almost record-breaking score on the bar exam. Despite his successes in law school, he had much to learn about the real world of practicing law. This was especially true when learning the art of practicing criminal law. Marion had been just the person he needed to mentor him on the finer points of dealing with a difficult client. To add to her talents, she was a true master at getting clients to pay his fee.

Marion had been with the firm for fifteen years when Jax entered as the newest associate. Persuading her to leave and take a chance with him in his new office was not easy. Lamping and Jacobs was a family for her. In many ways, it was her only family. She had only worked there for a few months when she and her husband were involved in a car accident that took her husband's life. A carload of teenagers had blown through a traffic light, striking the vehicle on the driver's side, sending it spinning into a telephone pole. Greg Anderson was pronounced dead at the scene. Marion suffered a fractured leg, which required three reconstructive surgeries in one year. Her most grievous injury was a miscarriage. Marion was five months pregnant with the couple's first child.

A tall, slender brunette with impeccable fashion sense, it was not surprising that, over the years, Marion had many men approach her in the hope of starting a relationship. Marion, however, showed no interest. Her warm memories of her husband and the love and deep friendship they enjoyed in their short time together made it unthinkable to start over with someone new. As time passed, her office friendships filled her time and her heart.

When Jax met Marion on his first day at the firm, she greeted him with a cool politeness. She had seen her share of bright-eyed young lawyers come into the firm with enthusiasm but whose polish were tarnished quickly by the grueling schedule and high expectations of the senior partner, Malcolm Lamping. She saw too many young lawyers gasp, inwardly or outwardly, when they realized Mr. Lamping expected or rather demanded every member of his firm work, at least, sixty hours a week. Perhaps more accurately, the demand was not so much to the lofty profession of the law but instead to the firm and its bottom line. She had seen almost two generations of lawyers come and go from the firm. She never became attached to a rookie lawyer, for who knew just how long he or she would last?

When Jax had been with the firm for a few months, she developed a cautiously optimistic feeling about his future. He didn't balk at working late nights and weekends. He didn't tremble and shake when, only six months after joining the firm, Malcolm Lamping gave Jax his first case to try solo. Before then, he had tried a handful of cases, sitting second chair with Malcolm as the lead counsel. Malcolm liked what he saw in Jax and gave him his first solo case far earlier than any of the other very capable attorneys he had hired over the years.

So why in the world, thought Jax, *would there be any purpose to be served by debating whether or not I needed a haircut?*

Leaving Marion's office, he walked past the conference room to his office, a massive corner location with two walls of glass. He had a panoramic view of downtown. It was his sanctuary. He had spent countless hours contemplating the next trial, the next strategic move, or just pondering life while keeping watch over the activities on the river and the streets. He spent hundreds of evenings watching the sunset and the lights of the city spring to life. Antique paintings of riverboats, collected over the years, dotted the walls. In recent years, they had become quickly outnumbered by Olivia. There were photos from school, sports, and vacations and photos of Olivia being Olivia.

Picking up a file from the corner of his desk, he went to his chair to relax for a few minutes before leaving for the courthouse. When he eased into the chair, he heard a loud and angry screech.

"Sorry, girl. But you don't need to yell like that."

Sitting upright in his chair, with a look of disdain mastered exclusively by the feline species, was Bailey, his office cat. A sleek, muscular silver tabby with piercing green eyes, she stretched and hopped onto his desk. Jax could resume his original plan of sitting at his desk. The cat started grooming herself then settled on the desk for her first nap of the morning.

This had become a daily routine Jax and Bailey counted on to begin their day. The routine was deeply rooted in a trusting bond between them. Despite her notoriously feline personality, Bailey displayed a quiet love and gratitude for Jax. He rescued Bailey from certain death at the hands, or paws, of a pack of dogs prowling in his parking lot late one evening. He had been in the right place at the right time. As he was walking to his car, he heard growling and barking. Turning in the direction of the noise, he saw the dogs circling a petrified kitten. Grabbing his umbrella from the back of his car, he ran toward the dogs, shouting and waving the umbrella at them until they scattered. The kitten, still too frightened to move, crouched in the lot, trembling. Jax picked her up and took her into the office. After he had calmed the kitten, he left her for only as much time as it took to dash to the nearest pet store to buy everything a cat needs and wants. He brought it back to the office, arranged food and litter box and toys in the room next to his office, and fell asleep with the cat lying on his chest. The next morning, when they both awoke, they were already lifelong companions.

Stroking her head while he read the file, he thought to himself that the past year with Bailey had added a new dimension to his life. He never had a pet as a child. His mother was allergic to pet hair, or so she claimed. He never questioned it or anything else she told him.

Stella Berman was a stern and unforgiving woman, who hadn't smiled a genuine smile since the day Jax's father walked out of their lives. Jax was in kindergarten when his homelife was permanently altered. Ray Berman always worked hard and provided for his family, but he couldn't decide whether drinking or gambling was his favorite pastime. What he did know was Stella and Jax interfered with both. He couldn't figure out how to balance family life, drinking, and gambling, so he narrowed it down to just drinking and gambling.

For the first year, Jax saw his father weekly, but eventually, it dwindled to a monthly occasion. By the time Jax was eight years old, Ray was only a hazy memory brought to the forefront with a birthday card and a Christmas card every year. Sometimes there was a little cash in the card; most of the time, it just contained his scribbled signature. The cards stopped before Jax was in high school.

It was a stark contrast to his relationship with Olivia, Jax thought while looking at the photos of his daughter. Jax hadn't really felt the void left by his father, thanks mostly to the devotion of his mother. Although she was strict and expected Jax to obey her rules, she supported him in everything he set out to do. She was his most ardent fan when he was involved in sports or his real passion—music. He fell in love with the piano when he was a toddler. Unlike his friends in kindergarten and in later years, he didn't indulge in toy guns and war games. He was much happier playing his piano or any other instrument he could persuade his mother to buy. His bedroom became an eclectic collection of percussion instruments, a guitar, keyboards, and a glass flute he found at a museum gift shop. The glass flute was displayed on the polished wood bookshelf in Jax's office, next to one of the last photos of his mother.

Jax had never been a loner. He loved his friends at school, and he hung out with them as he got older. But music was and would always be his best friend in good times and in bad. In high school, his music made him a hit at many parties where there was a piano for him to entertain his friends. It also earned him a lot of invitations to parties in college.

Before court this morning, Jax reviewed the documents waiting for him in preparation for his afternoon appointments. Thanks to Marion, as always, he had everything he needed to make sense of the trouble awaiting today's two new clients. Copies of their pending charges as well as vital information about them made the initial appointment more efficient and shorter too.

The name of the first new client seemed oddly familiar, but Jax couldn't figure out why. He reread the file Marion had put together. Michael Sanford was charged with driving under the influence and resisting arrest. Nothing very complicated, but there was something about the name.

It struck him. Could this new client be related to his first client when he was with Malcolm Lamping? Is he connected in some way to Blake Sanford?

Blake Sanford is and always will be permanently etched in Jax's memory. Blake's was the first trial Jax handled without Malcolm. More importantly, Blake taught him the first lesson a criminal defense attorney must always remember: *don't believe a word your client says.* There is truth, and there is the client's version of the truth. The client, over time, may have more than one version of the truth. The attorney must ascertain which truth is most reasonable and which will be most convincing to the jury. No wonder attorneys are notoriously bad at math, which is the epitome of truth, isn't it? Numbers are numbers; equations have one solution. Two plus two always equals four. Criminal law is not so simple. The truly great criminal lawyers learn this lesson quickly.

It had been almost fifteen years since the Blake Sanford trial. Blake was a relatively successful building contractor, building upscale homes in trendy Cincinnati neighborhoods for nouveau riche clients. On his way home from work one Friday evening, he stopped at a local tapas bar for a little food and a lot of beer. His server, a bright young college student named Amy Wilkens, took care of him all evening. At closing time, Blake was still there, working on his tenth beer of the night. He offered Amy a ride to her apartment, and she stupidly accepted, contrary to the restaurant's rule against this. With Amy being the last to leave because it was her turn to close up for the night, nobody was around to hear her cries for help in the wooded area next to the parking lot. Nobody heard her screaming when Blake threw her to the ground, tore off her skirt, and sexually assaulted her. At least, that was her statement to the investigating officers when she showed up at the police station the next morning.

Blake denied Amy's version of events. He painted a picture of an evening of innocent banter while Amy served him beer after beer, but the banter became a little less innocent as the evening went on. Blake testified at trial that it was fully understood between him and Amy that there was to be more than just a ride home to her apartment. But the situation heated up so quickly that they made love right there in the grass next to the parking lot. He delivered his testimony in a convincing manner, thanks to hours of preparation with Jax.

It was while the two of them were together in the spacious marble hallway outside the courtroom, waiting for the jury to reach a verdict, that Blake laughingly confessed that Amy's testimony had been right all along. While Jax was reeling from this revelation and trying to sort through his own emotions and moral values, the jury announced they reached a verdict. Jax still had only a hazy memory of entering the courtroom and sitting next to his client when the judge read the not-guilty verdict to the crowd. Seated in the courtroom were Amy, her parents, and her twin brother. Jax could still hear Amy and her mother crying while her father and brother shouted their dismay at the jury's decision.

Jax was still in a fog hours later at dinner with Malcolm. He had taken him out for a night on the town to celebrate his first solo victory. After his second glass of wine, Jax told Malcolm about Blake's courthouse confession and sought Malcolm's advice. Malcolm gave him advice but not the advice he anticipated. While he was hoping for words of wisdom, instead, the advice he received from his mentor was, "No shit. You didn't really believe his story, did you? Look, if we only represented innocent clients, we would need a second job to pay the bills." Malcolm flagged down their server and ordered another round of drinks, his gold Rolex watch emerging from the cuff of his custom-tailored shirt.

More than a decade since that conversation, Jax still let those words ramble in his mind whenever he was in an initial interview with his most recent wrongly accused and totally innocent client. With the aid of his apprenticeship with Malcolm, he developed an artful way of asking the right questions but, more importantly, of not asking the wrong questions. Sometimes the truth is viewed as an inconvenience in a criminal case, especially when the view is from the side of the defense.

It would be no different today with his new clients, including Michael Sanford. He finished feeding Bailey and rubbing her on her head, picked up his briefcase, which Marion had loaded with the files he needed for court that morning, and went to court.

CHAPTER 3

The following morning, Jax's cell phone rang. It was a phone call he received virtually every morning while driving his black Porsche Carrera to the office.

"Good morning, Chief. What's happening?"

"You're what's happening, Rick. As for me, I'm just living the dream."

Rick snickered and said, "This call will keep the dream alive for a little while longer. I have a big-money client who has just been slapped with a domestic-violence charge by his future former wife. His third future former wife."

Rick Meredith and Jax had been friends since their first day of college, when they were assigned to be roommates. They were paired up because they were on a football scholarship. In addition to sharing a room in the dorm reserved for scholarship athletes, they spent countless hours together during football season. They attended practices, meetings, and games, and they endured regular fitness training during the off-season. They still found time, probably more often than they should have, to hit one of the local college taverns near campus. Many evenings were spent listening to local bands pounding out the latest hits, drinking beer, and dancing with pretty sorority girls.

Graduation did not interrupt this bond. They attended the same law school and shared an apartment during the three-year journey toward the coveted license to practice law. Football activities were replaced by countless hours of classes, study groups, and reading, reading, and more reading. Despite the grueling demands of law school and their part-time jobs, they managed to find one or two evenings a month to spend at their favorite neighborhood tavern for a dose of liquid therapy.

After graduation, Jax and Rick both landed promising positions with law firms in Cincinnati. Jax served as tour guide and mentor to Rick, who had spent his childhood in a small farming town in northern Ohio. Jax joined Lamping and Jacobs to practice criminal defense law. Rick entered a mega firm with more than a hundred attorneys as well as hundreds of paralegals and support staff. He started in and stayed with the family law division. He quickly earned a reputation as an aggressive but ethical divorce lawyer and was annually listed as one of the premier family law attorneys. His clients were almost exclusively big-money divorces. He represented old money, new money, and local sports celebrities. None of whom were especially committed to the notion of keeping their marriage vows till death do they part.

Rick's good looks, wry sense of humor, and substantial income were all attractive to an unending stream of eligible women. Rick had added a few pounds to his frame after leaving the world of football behind. It somehow worked for him. His sandy-blond hair and piercing blue eyes were accentuated by the added flesh to his face. Rick seemed to have always been in a relationship with someone, either for the short term or the long term, but he always stopped short of walking down the aisle. He had been engaged or engaged to be engaged so many times Jax lost count. Rick once pronounced, "I'm great at getting into a relationship, but not so great at staying in a relationship." He was also unwavering in his complete lack of interest in fatherhood. Despite his aversion to having children of his own, Olivia spent countless hours with him and adored her uncle Rick. The feeling was mutual. Rick was known to attend the occasional soccer game or school event.

"Have your client call Marion for an appointment."

"Will do. Hey, how about drinks tonight? It's been a month since we have caught up with each other."

"Got a date with Olivia tonight. Meet me in my hotel bar tomorrow evening, and the drinks are on me. Consider it a referral fee for the new case."

"Tomorrow at seven o'clock. Over and out."

Jax smiled as he disconnected the call. Winding his way through the downtown morning rush hour, he indulged himself in a stroll down memory lane. He began with the first time he saw Rick. Riding up the elevator of the dorm on move-in day for freshman athletes, they walked down the hallway together, not knowing they were roommates until they both stopped at room 617. Having developed a great rapport by dinnertime, they hung out together constantly. They were prelaw majors. They shared many classes together. Add to that a shared love of draft beer, and it was the perfect recipe for a lifelong friendship.

Rick was a great referral source for clients who needed Jax's help. It was amazing how many people got themselves in trouble with the law either before, during, or after their divorce. Sometimes their crimes led to the divorce; other times, the divorce sparked their crimes.

He entered the back door of his office building and headed to Marion's office.

"I just got off the phone with Rick. He's sending a client our way."

"Already done, Jax. Dr. Harwood is coming to see you at three o'clock today. He sounds like your perfect client. He has money, and he has a lot to lose if he gets convicted."

"You're right, Marion. That combination usually means he'll follow my advice. And he'll pay the fee. I'm just not sure which of those is the most important." He smiled, and she returned his smile with a laugh.

"Rick already sent an email with some good info on Dr. Harwood and his wife. This should make your first meeting short and sweet." She handed him a copy of the email.

Closing the door to his office and having moved Bailey out of his chair without incident, he perused the email. Bailey was preparing for a nap on top of Jax's desk. Reading Rick's message renewed Jax's stroll down memory lane.

He recalled not only the beginning of their close friendship, fostered by the fact that neither of them had a brother, but also the good times and bad times that forged an impenetrable bond. The worst of the times came roaring back in his head, although it happened twenty years ago.

Returning to their apartment after a late-evening lecture on taxation law, the light was flashing on the answering machine. Jax played the message as he was taking off his coat but immediately put it back on and streaked down the stairs. Rick followed close behind.

"This message is for Jackson Berman. This is Dr. Nelson at the emergency room at university hospital. Your mother, Stella Berman, has been admitted as a result of an automobile accident. It is urgent that you come to our emergency room as soon as possible."

The message was recorded thirty minutes before Jax and Rick heard it. Rick drove while Jax fidgeted nervously in the passenger seat, trying not to hyperventilate during the ten-minute drive to the hospital. Rick dropped Jax off at the emergency room entrance and parked the car in the nearest lot after weaving through a line of ambulances. He entered the emergency room to see Dr. Nelson consoling Jax with the news that his mother had succumbed to her injuries minutes earlier.

The driver who crossed the center line, hitting Stella's car head-on, had a blood alcohol content three times the legal limit. He was so drunk he probably did not feel the impact of the collision that killed him instantly. It had taken the paramedics almost half an hour to extricate Stella from the mangled wreckage that was her trusted Volvo, her transportation for the past twenty years. That Volvo had taken Jax to countless games, practices, piano lessons, and recitals during his childhood and teenage years.

Although he was in his mid-twenties, nearing the end of his education and preparing for a career in the law, he felt incredibly childlike at that instant. He was an orphan. His mother had been taken from him, and his father might as well be dead. He was consumed with feelings of lonesomeness. Before the sensation brought him to his knees, Rick draped his arm around Jax's shoulder and shepherded him home.

Jax was Stella's only surviving next of kin, which made him the sole beneficiary of the wrongful death settlement. Jax was able to pay off his student loans from undergraduate school and graduate law school with no debt and purchase a modest four-family apartment building. He and Rick moved into one unit, and Jax deposited the rent checks from his tenants into an account that had become fairly sizeable when he finished law school and passed the bar exam. He still owned that apartment building, and he still deposited the rent checks into that same account. Over the years, he and Rick purchased other apartment buildings, earning them substantial money over and above their incomes practicing law. They considered it an additional retirement account. It was a convenient fund for buying the occasional sports car or taking an exotic vacation too.

Hours later, Jax was comfortably decked out in jeans and a sweatshirt, on his way to pick up Olivia for their dinner together. He pulled into his former driveway; Catherine was walking to the front door, having just retrieved the daily mail from the mailbox—Jax's former mailbox. Catherine in no way acknowledged Jax's arrival. As he exited the car, she opened the front door, entered the house, and shut the door. This meant that Jax had to ring the doorbell of his own home or his former home, as Catherine liked to call it. He never let her petty comments or actions get a rise out of him, and he would be damned if he would start now, especially with Olivia present. He took a deep breath or two or maybe three, rang the doorbell, and waited almost a whole minute before she opened the door.

"Oh, you're here," she drawled.

"Yes, I'm here. You're looking lovely today. New dress?"

"Actually, yes. I decided to indulge myself and do some shopping yesterday."

"Well, you are certainly entitled, what with all the stress you're under having lunches with friends. And then there's the tennis too. How do you ever manage to keep score accurately? How does it go again—love, 15, 30, 40, game?"

Catherine gave him a haughty look, one she probably had been storing up just for him. "I'll get Olivia. There's no need for you to come in. She's been waiting for you." She closed the door, his former door, in his face.

Thankfully, Olivia came bounding out of the door before Jax could really muster up an unhealthy level of anger. Any anger that had formed was dissolved the minute Olivia threw her arms around his waist and gave him a big bear hug.

"Hello, Princess. Your carriage awaits. Where do you want to go for dinner?"

Walking to the car, she suggested, "Actually, Daddy, I was thinking that we could have dinner near your office. I haven't seen Bailey for ages, and I thought she might be missing me."

"Sounds like a great plan. Why don't we visit Bailey after dinner so we can take some leftovers to her? And on our way to dinner, we can stop at the pet store and pick up some new toys for her."

Olivia smiled her sweet, innocent, and genuine smile. It is a smile everyone has during childhood, but it gets eroded by one's travels through adolescence into adulthood. "Great idea!"

Their evening together, as well as with Bailey, went happily and smoothly, as always.

Jax was driving away from his former home, delivering Olivia in time to do her homework and get ready for bed. Once again, Catherine shut the door with purpose, not even acknowledging his presence when he kissed Olivia goodbye. Driving down the highway toward his hotel, his current home, he dialed his phone.

"I thought you had a date with Olivia tonight," Rick said when he answered the phone.

"I just dropped her off. I'm calling about drinks tomorrow evening."

"I thought we were meeting at the bar in your home away from home," replied Rick.

"We still can. But I think we need to start with a meeting at your office. I need to retain your services."

There was a lengthy period of silence before Rick spoke. "Are you talking about filing for divorce?"

The question rattled him. Although the notion of divorce had been swirling in his head for a while, hearing the word had a jolting effect. "Probably. I'm not completely sure at this moment. I'm not thinking about filing right away. But communication between

Catherine and me has been going from bad to worse. I need to know where I stand, what my rights are concerning Olivia, and everything about the wonderful world of busting up a marriage."

"Okay. Meet me in my office at five o'clock tomorrow. I'll wear my professional hat and give you a quick education on divorce. Then we'll go as planned to your hotel bar. Trust me, you will really need a few drinks by then."

Jax laughed out loud, probably the first genuine laugh in a long time. "I can't wait, Rick. Over and out."

CHAPTER 4

Drinks with Rick—presided over by Frank, the bartender—turned into many drinks. Drinking also leads to bad food choices. At the time, it was a great idea to have a gourmet pizza, with every topping known to man, delivered to the bar. It was an even better idea, at the time, to devour the entire pizza, except for the piece Frank indulged. Alone in Jax's hotel suite several floors above, his stomach offered its own critique of the evening. He stretched out on the sofa and listened to John Coltrane on the sound system.

The drinks and the pizza were not the best idea, but Jax attributed his current stomach distress to the eye-opening and equally depressing conversation with Rick in his office earlier. The thought of property division, custody and parenting time, spousal support, child support, and holidays and vacations with Olivia being divided between him and Catherine were overwhelming. While the information from Rick was helpful and necessary, it put a cold, distasteful spin on the current state of his marriage.

Look on the bright side, he told himself. *You're still young. You have a steady income stream. You actually make more money every year. And it's just money. The only asset of the marriage that matters is Olivia.* Whatever it takes and costs, the bond between Jax and Olivia could not suffer. This was nonnegotiable.

Alcohol and late hours make for wise and considered decisions. At least, that is what every person convinces himself. Jax knew better than to expect any realistic and reasoned answers would be discovered at this hour. Instead, he contented himself with a stark reflection of his marriage—how it was now and how it used to be. Maybe the marriage didn't disintegrate after all. Maybe it was doomed from the start.

*****

Jax and Rick drove to Chicago for a weekend of rest and relaxation. They had been working nonstop for more than a year in their positions with their new law firms. Many months had been spent in courtrooms, conference rooms, and partners' offices—each of them learning their own specialized practice of law. Jax was grasping the subtleties of client control. Rick was learning how to develop a bedside manner with a client whose home, marriage, and life were imploding. While they were both learning the human side of their business, they were also developing their own style in court. But now it was time for a weekend recess. What better place than Chicago for some relaxation and recreation?

They checked into a small hotel off Michigan Avenue, threw their suitcases into the room, and hit the Magnificent Mile in search of the perfect cocktail. Jax had not been in a relationship or had even had a second date with anybody since the death of his mother. Rick had just ended a brief romance with the latest perfect girl to come his way. The weekend in Chicago had not been intended to be a search for love in either the right or the wrong places. But things happen when you least expect them.

Jax and Rick entered an art-deco bar overlooking the Chicago River. The lights were turned down low, and the music was turned up high. It was clearly a hot spot for the young professionals who lived or aspired to live on Michigan Avenue. As luck would have it, there were two empty seats at the far end of the bar.

A second round of drinks was on its way when Jax's phone rang. Recognizing the number as one of his current needy clients, he left the bar to take the call. When he returned, he found Rick deep in conversation with a young and well-jeweled woman. The conversation was apparently so fascinating Rick did not notice the woman's companion, an equally well-jeweled lady, had taken Jax's seat at the bar and was ordering a drink. Having been drilled on proper etiquette by his mother, Jax did not challenge her for his seat. Instead, he reached past her to retrieve his freshly delivered cocktail.

"I am so sorry," exclaimed the beautiful stranger. "I took your seat."

Jax replied while gazing into her dark-brown eyes, "You look much better sitting in it than I did." He had never seen such brown eyes in his life. The chestnut curls that ringed her face were the perfect complement.

"Wow, flattery and a seat at the bar. I'm a lucky girl."

This was Jax and Catherine's first conversation. They went through the preliminaries. Catherine was born and raised in the Lincoln Park area of Chicago. College at Indiana University was followed by a career in Chicago working for various private nonprofit organizations. Her job description officially was raising awareness, which translated into raising big money. Jax knew, looking at her clothes and jewelry, she had more income than her salary. There must be some big family money.

The conversation continued as they strolled down Michigan Avenue, with Rick and Catherine's companion following behind. They found a quiet Italian restaurant perfect for a late dinner. Jax was so intrigued by Catherine and her beauty, her brains, her wit, and her story, he was still quite certain he never learned the name of her friend. Since Rick never saw her again after that weekend, it didn't really matter if he knew her name. Rick might not have known her name either.

The weekend flew by in an instant. Jax and Catherine spent every waking moment together. They shared every meal and an afternoon Cubs game at Wrigley Field. Rick and the woman with no name were always there too, but Jax and Catherine plunged deeper and deeper into their own world with each conversation and laugh.

Jax and Rick returned to Cincinnati, and they resumed life in the real world of clients, court hearings, conferences, and phone calls. Jax was still preoccupied with Catherine. He had dated plenty of girls and had his fair share of serious relationships in college, but this was different. Catherine was infused into everything he said or did. Every plan he made, including work and social plans, was with her in mind. He found himself calling her first thing in the morning and the last thing at night. He called her a couple of times during the day while rushing to court or to his office.

Less than a month after their weekend in Chicago, he was back in the Windy City for another weekend with Catherine. They spent every moment together, not only the waking moments. This confirmed Jax's theory that Catherine had more income than just her job in the world of charities. Her brownstone in Lincoln Park was tastefully decorated from floor to ceiling. There were more than a few expensive works of art adorning the walls. Her brownstone was the only one on the street with a rooftop terrace.

Jax was scheduled to leave Sunday morning to drive home and review some files before court on Monday. But he was still comfortably stretched out on the sofa in Catherine's gathering room at four o'clock on Sunday afternoon. It didn't take much effort for Catherine to convince Jax to stay just one more night and leave early Monday morning. Jax discovered that another of Catherine's talents was in the kitchen. The dinner enjoyed by candlelight on her rooftop was a delectable contemporary French cuisine. That sealed his fate; Jax was officially in love. But he wasn't going to say those magic words to Catherine yet.

The following summer, after a year of daily phone conversations and weekends shared in Chicago and Cincinnati, Malcolm Lamping summoned Jax to his office. In what seemed to be a sign from above, Malcolm pushed a file across his desk.

"Big, big case, Jax. Complicated issues too. The client is suspected of having ties to organized crime. He owns several legitimate businesses, but the FBI has been circling the waters for years. They have him indicted on multiple counts of tax evasion. That's the best they could do. But it could still mean years in federal prison for our client. The case is in Cook County, Illinois."

Cook County? Illinois? "Chicago, Chicago, is my kind of town…," sang the voice in Jax's head.

Malcolm interrupted the daydream. "I think this would be a good case for you. It will be your first major case outside Ohio."

Malcolm smiled. "I'm sure you have someplace to stay while you're there. Trial is in three months and is scheduled to last six weeks."

Jax paused before asking, "How did you know I have a Chicago connection?"

Malcolm leaned back in his chair, folding his arms over his chest. "I pay attention, Jax. I simply pay attention. Take the file back to your office and feel free to come to me for any help with trial preparation."

The rest is history, as the saying goes. The trial lasted six weeks, culminating with ten hours of jury deliberations that produced a not-guilty verdict on all charges. Jax wasn't sure who was more elated, his client or him. After enduring many hugs from his client and his wife, he phoned Malcolm to deliver the good news. The phone call ended with Malcolm inviting him to his office early Monday morning.

"Until then," he said to Jax, "you've got the weekend in Chicago. Celebrate your win. Celebrate your future with the firm. Big things are coming your way."

With a little luck and a crisp one-hundred-dollar bill discretely pressed into the palm of the maître d', Jax and Catherine celebrated his courtroom victory with a bottle of the finest champagne at Chicago's trendiest restaurant. Sipping the champagne while watching the sunset over Lake Michigan from their window table, Jax thought life couldn't get any better. Caught up in the moment and in his alcohol-induced musings, he reached across the table and took Catherine's hand. "Marry me."

Catherine put her glass on the table, having downed its entire contents in response to Jax's declaration. "You can't be serious, Jax. We've only known each other for a year."

He emptied his champagne flute in one long sip and looked into the eyes that melted his heart last summer. "I couldn't be more serious. We've known each other for only a year, that's true, but we're not high school kids. This isn't puppy love. We're both old enough to know what we want and what we don't want. I know I want you. In my life. Till death do us part. I don't want a life without you."

Catherine knew him well enough, if only for a year, to know he was deadly serious. "Well," she drawled with a sly smile emerging. "I do want you too. And I don't want to be without you."

Jax sat back in his plush chair. "If I take that as a yes, do you want to shake hands, or can I kiss the bride?"

"A kiss seems to be in order. And you can take that as a yes."

Late the next morning—actually early in the afternoon—they awoke after having two bottles of champagne at the restaurant. When the maître d' realized there was a marriage proposal going on at their table, he brought a second bottle of bubbly "on the house." He announced it loudly enough for the other diners to hear. The restaurant erupted in applause.

Following a light brunch, the newly engaged couple wandered the Magnificent Mile in search of the perfect engagement ring. They shopped at Cartier, Tiffany, Neiman Marcus, and every other jeweler on Michigan Avenue. Jax had never shopped for a diamond ring before. He learned a whole new vocabulary, such as *color* and *clarity*. He had never before given any thought to the variety of *cuts*—another new word. By the end of the afternoon and after countless rings that were slipped on and off Catherine's finger, she made her selection. "The perfect ring," Catherine proclaimed.

Arm in arm, they made their way to the Oak Street Beach. As daylight was leaving, so were the swimmers and beach volleyball players. The beach became virtually deserted. It was the perfect place for Jax to officially propose and place the perfect ring on Catherine's finger. The ritual completed as daylight turned to dusk. They were back to Michigan Avenue for a celebratory dinner. At a much-less pricey restaurant than the previous night, he was now the proud owner of a diamond ring.

Turning off the light in his hotel bedroom suite, he wondered how his life would have turned out if he had lost that trial instead.

CHAPTER 5

The door to Jax's office flew open. Bailey jumped from the corner of the desk and landed unceremoniously on the Persian rug. Confident his office was not being overrun by terrorists, he looked up from his file. "I always enjoy your subtle arrivals, Leo. Bailey's glad to see you too." The cat was giving her best feline glare.

Leonard Kurtzman chuckled and seated himself across from Jax. "Just reporting for duty, boss. Pissing off the cat was a bonus."

Leonard, a retired lieutenant from the Cincinnati Police Department, had been Jax's private investigator for the past five years. A seasoned veteran with almost twenty years' experience as a major-crimes detective, he had the knowledge and connections to do his job very well. He seemed to have had no trouble crossing over to the dark side of criminal defense. While he believed in his mission of searching for the truth, whatever the truth might be, he also owed a debt of gratitude to his boss.

After he retired, Leonard opened a private investigation firm. He was the sole investigator, with a handful of office workers. During the early months in business, he worked part-time as a private security officer for the largest nightclub in the downtown entertainment district. He had been there for only a few months when the nightclub burned to the ground after hours. The state fire marshal determined it to be arson. Review of the security cameras on the adjoining buildings showed Leo was the last to leave the club, and it was only fifteen minutes later when a passerby called 911 to report smoke billowing from the roof.

Leo was charged with arson, which could send him to prison for twenty years. At the time, he was in his early fifties. A twenty-year sentence would see him released when he would be an old man, if he would live long enough. Prison is a lonely and dangerous place for an inmate who used to be a cop. He sought out Jax for his help.

It had taken a week to seat the jury; many potential jurors knew about the case due to the nonstop media coverage. When twelve seemingly impartial jurors were seated, they listened to ten days of testimony. A lot of it was very technical. The jury sat through testimony of the state fire marshal as well as experts for the prosecution and the defense offering their conflicting opinions as to whether the fire had been intentionally set. Then there was the issue of Leo being the last person captured on the security cameras.

Jax and Leo were riding alone in the elevator at the end of the last day of testimony. The following morning would be closing arguments—first, the prosecutor and then Jax. The case would be in the hands of the jury by early afternoon. Reality was setting in on Leonard. His fate was in the hands of twelve strangers, and he didn't like it.

Leonard asked, "How do you think it's looking for me?"

Jax paused before answering. "Leo, you know I can't get into the minds of the jury. We have been able to offer counter theories from our experts that hopefully will create reasonable doubt on the arson theory. There's been a lot of technical evidence for them to sift through. I think tomorrow's closing arguments will be crucial."

Leonard, a former college football player like Jax but with a couple more inches of height and fifty pounds of weight on him, grabbed Jax by the collar and lifted him off his feet in the moving elevator. He said, "Then you'd better deliver the most brilliant fucking argument of your life tomorrow. You know what I mean?"

Still dangling in Leo's clutches, Jax gasped, "I'd been planning on doing that all along, Leo. Put me down."

When the two exited the elevator, nobody suspected anything had gone down between the lawyer and his client.

Fortunately for Jax and for Leo too, the jury agreed with everything Jax said in his brilliant fucking closing argument. When they left the courthouse together, Leo, now vindicated, offered to buy Jax dinner. Jax accepted.

The following day, Leonard Kurtzman became an employee of Jax's firm, with the title *investigative specialist*. Leo kept his firm open for business and accepted cases from private clients. But his employment with Jax was always top priority. For almost five years, Leo was an invaluable asset to Jax. His ability to find witnesses and talk to them and his skills at getting background information, coupled with Jax's talents in the courtroom, made them a dynamic duo.

"Do you have a new assignment for me, boss?" asked Leo, picking up Bailey and putting her on his lap. She forgave Leo's intrusion, settling in for a quick nap. It wasn't the first time Bailey had slept in Leo's lap.

Jax slid three files across the desk. Leo picked them up and looked through the meager contents. They were all new clients Jax had interviewed earlier in the week.

"I assume you want me to fill these files for you, right?"

Jax leaned back and replied, "Of course. Just another day where I make my problem your problem."

Leo put the files back on the desk, taking care not to wake the sleeping feline. He had already pissed off Bailey once today. He knew he shouldn't push his luck.

Jax said, "Marion has all of the original charging documents in the file along with my notes from the initial interview. You've got a domestic-violence charge against a doctor from a very vindictive ex-wife. You've also got an embezzlement case and an attempted murder to keep you amused."

"And I get paid to have all this fun. Is this a great country or what?" Leo grinned, picked Bailey up, placed her on the adjoining chair, and slipped out of Jax's office.

Bailey resumed her nap.

CHAPTER 6

After a morning spent rushing from one courtroom to another, like a juggler trying to keep the balls in the air, Jax opened the sunroof and soaked in some sun as he crossed the historic Suspension Bridge over the Ohio River. He saw barges and towboats interspersed with tour boats serving wine and lunch to visitors, plus a few private boaters enjoying the day. He would have traded his right arm—no, he writes with that arm, so he would have traded his left arm—to be on the water instead of driving to another courtroom. The afternoon would be spent in the hallowed halls of the courthouse in Covington, Kentucky. Same shit, just a different courthouse. And a bridge over the river to get there.

With three judges, three assistant prosecutors, and three clients later, Jax traveled across the bridge to his office. Stuck in traffic, he took the opportunity to brighten his day with a phone call to his favorite person.

Unfortunately, just as the three billy goats had to pass the evil troll to get safely across the bridge, Jax had to get past Catherine in order to have a phone conversation with Olivia. He wished Olivia were old enough to have her own cell phone. Not quite yet. He and Catherine did agree on that issue.

When Catherine answered her cell phone, Jax could hear outside noise in the background.

"Where are you?" Jax asked without exchanging any preliminary pleasantries.

"Olivia has a four-day weekend, so we flew down to the beach house last night."

The beach house was a comfortable southern-style home, complete with a large veranda, the family purchased more than a decade

33

ago, situated on the beach in the Sea Pines Plantation on Hilton Head Island. Catherine was pregnant with Olivia when the opportunity fell into their lap. The owners were dear friends of Catherine's parents. They realized their age, physical infirmities, and commitment to their growing herd of grandchildren made the Hilton Head home impractical. Jax was able to negotiate a purchase price that made them happy; saving money on a realtor's commission made Jax happy.

Two years later, when baby Olivia was taking her first steps, Catherine's lavish remodeling project was completed. The home was a showpiece. A sprawling one-floor plan was designed to give a magnificent view of the water from every room. The great room, with its vaulted ceiling, featured a contemporary fireplace that opened on all four sides. The master suite and the other three bedrooms each had a water view. The entire length of the home boasted a sheltered veranda overlooking the beach. Jax was especially fond of the outdoor kitchen on one end of the shelter.

In happier times, Jax and Catherine and Olivia spent every Thanksgiving and Christmas there. Egg hunts in the yard and on the beach were the only Easter memories Olivia had. She couldn't fathom the notion that the Easter Bunny did not live in Hilton Head. Santa Claus living at the North Pole she understood. She had seen enough Christmas shows to plant that seed in her young mind.

"I thought I was spending this weekend with Olivia," Jax said in his coolest tone of voice.

"Sometimes things don't go as you planned. Olivia has four days off from school, and I asked her if she wanted to hang out with you at your hotel or would she rather come down to the beach house for a few days. It was her choice."

"Presented to her in a very objective manner, I'm sure," retorted Jax. "I hope she has a good time. May I speak to her before you disconnect this call, please?"

"Hold on, I'll ask her." Jax waited for what seemed to be hours before Catherine returned to the phone.

"Olivia says she doesn't want to get out of the pool right now." Catherine hung up.

At the very moment that Jax tossed his phone into his passenger seat, trying to keep calm, he questioned whether Olivia really said that or whether it was just one more taunt from Catherine.

Lunchtime at his favorite deli near the courthouse had become, over the years, an oasis for Jax. It was an hour without the courtroom cast of characters—judges, prosecutors, clients, and witnesses—sucking the life out of him. Harold's Deli was a favorite of many lawyers for the same reason. It was a great place to get together with people in the same circumstance. It was its own little support group for beleaguered and bedraggled lawyers. They could vent their frustrations while enjoying the best corned beef sandwiches on the planet. And the pickles displayed on each table in a vintage canning jar were pure kosher heaven.

Harold's wasn't fancy. It probably hadn't been painted in the forty years it had been in operation. The walls were adorned with photographs of celebrities and other notables who stopped by for a meal and a photo op. Some of the pictures had been there so long the original black-and-white gloss was faded into shades of gray. Others were fresh off the digital presses in vivid color. You could find Hollywood personalities and Washington, DC, elite in the photo collection. Two presidents dined there over the years; their pictures taken with Harold were in a prominent place.

Jax grabbed a seat at a table with Rick and a few other family law attorneys. Just like Jax's troupe of prosecutors and defense attorneys, Rick battled in the courtroom with his band of divorce lawyers then socialized with them on his personal time. If attorneys took the legal wrangling with their opponents personally, they would be sad and lonely people with no friends to call their own. When the legal boxing gloves were off, it was just a group of people who had a lot in common, getting together to blow off steam.

"How's your day going? You look like you could use a few beers to go with your sandwich," Rick observed.

"It's just a day like every other," muttered Jax while savoring the first bite of his sandwich. "Too many clients, too many courtrooms, plus an added delight. In the middle of it all, I tried to call Olivia, but Catherine blocked that from happening. It turns out they're in

Hilton Head for some school break, which means no Olivia this weekend."

"Sounds like maybe we need to pick up where we left off in our Divorce for Dummies training. How about dinner tomorrow?"

Jax nodded as his phone rang. It was Leonard. "Talk to me, Leo," Jax garbled. His mouth was filled with his kosher nirvana.

"Jax, do you have time for me later today? I've got some interesting stuff already on the cases you gave to me."

"Meet me at the office at four o'clock."

"Over and out." Leo terminated the call.

Jax returned to his office, walking at a brisk pace after having eaten too many pickles with his sandwich. His thoughts were swirling. This was the first time Olivia and Catherine were in Hilton Head without him. There had been times in the past when trial schedules kept Jax from traveling with them, but he always caught up with them a day or two later. They would spend the rest of the trip together as a family. Whether or not it was as a happy family was open to debate. It depended on Catherine's mood at the moment. For the first time, he was not welcome in either of his homes—Cincinnati or Hilton Head. At least, it was the first time he knew he was not welcome. Maybe Catherine had a different perspective.

There had been arguments over the years. There had been days when Catherine inflicted the silent treatment because of something he did or didn't do. Most of the time, he never knew what it was that set her off. But he was smart enough to wait it out for a calculated time and then show up with a piece of jewelry as a peace offering. The arguments got louder and more frequent as time wore on. The silent treatment lasted weeks and months instead of just days. Eventually, the verbal abuse escalated to physical abuse.

Several weeks before he took up residence at the Manor Hotel, he and Catherine were in their kitchen having an uneventful discussion that morphed into a full-scale screaming match. *Screaming match* is a misnomer; it would suggest both opponents were screaming. A more accurate description would be a screaming attack launched by Catherine. But this one was different. In the midst of her tirade, she picked up the coffeepot and threw it at his head. The coffeepot was empty, but it sailed so close to Jax he felt the breeze as it flew past him. It crashed on the kitchen floor, disintegrating into tiny shards of glass. Jax did nothing to help clean up the mess. Instead, he retreated to the garage, hopped in his car, and drove to his office. He and Bailey spent a very restless but safe night on the sofa.

He learned the hard way one of the truisms of domestic violence. Once your partner threatens or attempts physical harm, no matter how many times your partner apologizes and swears it won't happen again, it will happen again. The next time will be worse. Catherine was living proof. Her emotional, contrite phone call the next morning, the lavish dinner she prepared, her calm and even temperament were a welcome relief. There was tranquility in the Berman home—for a while.

The evening before Jax's move to the Manor, he left the office to watch Olivia's soccer practice. This was always a treat for him. Olivia was developing into a skilled player. She was improving her speed and agility. He loved talking with her friends on the team after practice. This evening was no different. It was a beautiful spring evening. The trees were sprouting bright-green leaves. The daffodils and tulips were in full bloom, and the azaleas were a bounty of reds, pinks, and purples. Jax took this in from the top row of the bleachers.

After taking two of her friends home, he and Olivia pulled into the garage. She gathered her gear and ran up the back staircase for a well-earned shower. Reflecting on the events that followed, Jax was thankful for the noise created by the shower followed by the blow-dryer. Olivia missed the scene that would forever change their family.

While Olivia was bounding up the stairs, Jax entered the kitchen to find Catherine in the early stages of preparing a pasta dish and salad. He noticed a glass full of white wine and an almost-empty bottle nearby. He had never, until that moment, known Catherine to drink wine or any cocktail unless she was at a party or if she and Jax were having a late dinner at home. He had never known her to drink alone. He thought back to the night a few weeks ago when Catherine threw the coffeepot. Had she been drinking then?

Placing his hands on her shoulders, he gave her a quick kiss on the back of her neck. Hunching her shoulders in response to his gesture, she moved away from him without any acknowledgment of his presence.

Sensing a storm brewing, Jax took a glass from the hutch and filled it with water. "What did you do today?" he asked calmly.

"Nothing that would interest you" was her reply. She still made no eye contact with him.

"I'd like to hear about your day, Cat."

No response. Instead, Catherine continued chopping the salad ingredients.

"Cat, obviously something is bothering you. What happened?"

She threw the knife in the sink, causing it to rattle for a few seconds before coming to rest. "Nothing happened today. Nothing is bothering me with the exception of you. Just leave me alone."

This dialogue was unlike anything that had ever passed between them. Jax was concerned about Catherine, and he was worried about his own safety. He drank his water and filled the glass again, but this time, he used the second sink in the kitchen, which put a little distance between them. "Cat, give me a hint. What have I done?"

Now she made eye contact. She turned on her heels to face him and, in an increasingly loud and shrill voice, yelled, "Everything you do is the problem! You are such a big damn deal, and I am nothing more than Mrs. Big Damn Deal. No matter what I do in this shitty town, I am nothing more than your wife. Or Olivia's mother. I was Ms. Big Damn Deal when I was in Chicago. I was me. People respected me. People admired me. When I married you, I didn't expect to lose myself. I pretty much hate you right now!"

Jax was expecting a simple answer, such as "You didn't take out the trash last night…" or "You left the cap off the toothpaste…" or "You left your shoes and socks on the floor instead of putting them in the closet." This conversation was not going to end with a mere apology or a piece of jewelry. "Okay, Catherine. There has to be a way to make this better for you. Olivia is in school all day. She has soccer and other after-school activities. You have much more time now so you can get out there and find your niche. You can be Ms. Catherine Berman. And I can be Mr. Catherine Berman."

The words sounded reasonable to Jax when he said them. He thought his delivery was on target too. However, Catherine interpreted his words and his tone of voice drastically differently than he intended. "You fucking son of a bitch! Now I'm just a joke to you? You think some witty platitudes are going to make my feelings go away? You are the most arrogant bastard." As her words rang in his ears, Jax saw her pick up the wine bottle and raise it over her shoulder. She charged at him.

He managed to put his arms in front of his face. When she swung the bottle at him, it hit his forearms rather than his face, which was her intended target. He retreated from the kitchen, but she ran after him, hitting him in the shoulders and his back repeatedly with the bottle. Jax was able to keep ahead of her, her blows glancing off his back side. Then she slammed the bottle into the back of his head with such force that the bottle broke. The remnants of the wine bottle and the wine still in it sprayed the floor as well as Catherine's pride and joy—the custom handloomed rug in the gathering room off the kitchen. The force of the blow dazed Jax for several seconds. Catherine stood in stunned disbelief, still holding the top end of the now-broken wine bottle. Jax could sense the warm wetness of blood gathering in his hair. He regained his equilibrium, and with his hand on the back of his head to slow the bleeding, he went upstairs, taking the steps two at a time. After packing enough clothes and other items to last him for several days, he tossed the hand towel that he used to clean his head wound into the wastebasket.

Hurriedly descending the back stairs, he rushed through the kitchen. The last thing he remembered was Catherine standing at the kitchen sink, completely silent, and staring out the window with an icy look on her face. She was still holding the jagged-edged top of the wine bottle.

It was nighttime when Jax, carrying his leather duffel bag and matching garment bag, checked into the hotel. The desk clerk did not seem to recognize Jax's name when he gave the clerk his information. The clerk's facial expression revealed he was not accustomed to checking in a hotel guest who had a local address. The last thing Jax cared about at the moment was the thoughts or suspicions of the hotel staff. He needed a room with a bed, a hot shower, and some peace and fucking quiet. And a minibar with ice and Scotch. Just what the doctor ordered after having been assaulted by one's wife.

After a hot shower and a cursory look at his head wound with the use of the mirrors in the bathroom, Jax settled down on the love seat. It was conveniently situated within arm's length of the minibar. Sipping a tall Scotch and water on the rocks, he replayed every moment of the evening. Rewinding it over and over in his mind, he was at a complete loss as to how the conversation devolved into a physical attack. *Why was Catherine drinking wine all by herself? Had she really consumed half of the bottle before Olivia and I came home? How many times has she done this? Did Olivia notice anything before she went upstairs to shower? What did she hear while she was upstairs? Where does she think I am? Oh God, what has Catherine told her? Without question, whatever she tells Olivia will be to her advantage, which means it will be far from the truth.*

Jax then moved to the absurd conversation that led to the attack. *Was it the wine talking, or is Catherine so unhappy in the marriage?* He wondered if she truly meant everything she said. Jax labored over her words. He never had any indication that she felt overshadowed by him and his professional success. He never, for a moment, thought they were in competition with each other.

Jax found himself nodding off, the glass of Scotch still in his hand. He decided to take a break from his in-depth analysis of Catherine's words and actions and go to bed. The answers might be more easily discovered in the light of day following a good Scotch-induced sleep.

The next morning, Jax showered and dressed, just like he did every morning except that he was doing it in a hotel suite instead of his home. He drove to the office and parked in his reserved parking space, just like he did every morning. He entered the office and joked with Marion, who was already working at her desk, just like every morning. He had been in the office for only a half hour when Rick walked in, which was unlike any other morning.

"Good morning," Rick said, setting two cups of gourmet coffee and a bag of pastries on the desk. "Anything you'd like to get off your chest?"

Jax was just twelve hours into what seemed, to him, to be an updated version of *The Twilight Zone*—his wife screaming absurdities at him, his wife breaking a wine bottle over his head, and him having to flee from his own home for his safety. Now, in the next act of this sci-fi drama, his best friend showed up with breakfast. To borrow from the vocabulary of today's text messages, "WTF?!"

Before Jax could respond, Rick leaned toward him and said very quietly, "Your protector, Marion, called me after you got here. She saw the back of your head and was worried. She was especially worried because you didn't mention the bloody bump and how you got it. So here I am. Talk."

Jax talked. He talked and talked. He shared with Rick his worries about Catherine and the wine, Catherine's verbal attack, and Catherine's physical assault. He and Rick had been through so much together over the years. This was not the time to hold back. Jax understood, while he was pouring his heart out, he needed Rick more than ever, even more so than after his mother's death.

CHAPTER 7

"Viva, Las Vegas," Rick announced, lazily stretching his legs in his window seat on the direct flight to the Sin City. Jax and Rick were on their way to the Mirage Hotel, this year's site of the annual American Bar Association convention. "Four nights in Vegas. Gambling and booze. Plus food to soak up the booze. All that and we earn continuing education hours. Life doesn't get any better," chuckled Rick.

"Not bad, Rick, not bad at all," laughed Jax. His heavy schedule of trials and client appointments always meant, when the annual reporting deadline approached, he was scrambling to sign up for seminars and webinars to earn his required hours. It was no secret; every lawyer dreaded these education requirements. Twenty hours each year was spent in a crowded and austere banquet hall at some bland hotel. Hours were spent with lawyers who were equally bored and reading the newspaper online or playing video games on their phone. *Continuing education my ass.*

The conflict with Catherine was escalating. A little time away from the scene would be therapeutic, especially when good food and an endless supply of Scotch were available. Vegas wouldn't run out of Scotch, would it? Could it?

They checked into their two-bedroom suite on the top floor of the Mirage. After quickly unpacking, they inaugurated the minibar. Jax conducted a quick inventory and determined there was enough Scotch on hand for their stay. There was plenty of bottled water too, but who in their right mind would be drinking bottled water in Vegas? There was probably a law against it.

Between their first and second drink, they checked in with their offices and returned a handful of calls. Jax believed his clients possessed a weird sixth sense; they seemed to instinctively know when he was out of town. It was exactly the point in time when they needed him ASAP for one reason or another. Something new had happened in their case, and he needed to know about it right away. Sometimes they called to hear Jax's voice reassuring them their legal predicament would work out in the end. Jax never instilled false hope in his clients. Malcolm had ingrained that lesson into him at the beginning of his career. *Reassure your client you will do everything you can to resolve the case in the client's favor, but don't, under any circumstances, make promises you can't keep.* Jax knew he could only control his end of the case. He couldn't guarantee what the prosecutor or the judge or the victim would do during the course of the case. Hell, he couldn't predict what a witness would say or do on the witness stand. One of the great mysteries of life was whether or not the witness's testimony at trial would, in any way, resemble the initial statement he had given to the police at the scene of the crime. Although Jax made this abundantly clear in his first meeting, the client would make regular phone calls to Jax, seeking, if not an absolute guarantee, then, at least, a solid assurance that his case would have a happy ending.

The problem with criminal defense work is, just like other specialty areas of the law, a victory in a case is not easily defined. While the average person may think a victory is easy to see—a not-guilty verdict or a dismissal of the case—there are other victories as well. If a client was charged with a crime that could send him to a maximum-security prison for twenty years and Jax resolved the case and his client would spend six months in the county jail instead, it would be a win for the home team. Another task in that first meeting was to mentor the new client, whether this was his first criminal charge or he was a frequent flyer in the court system, on this definition of victory. Some clients got it the first time; others needed remedial instruction along the way.

Jax and Rick decided their third round of cocktails should be downstairs in the Revolution Bar. Named after the Beatles' legendary song, the bar was heavily decorated with rock-and-roll memorabilia. Jax always found solace in his music. His piano was his first love, but he spent years amassing an eclectic assortment of vinyl records. He had climbed on the technology train and had thousands of songs downloaded on his phone, but he preferred his vinyl collection. The albums brought back warm memories of his mother. Her album collection introduced him to music of all genres. Mom had Elvis, the Beatles, big bands, classical, and a little bit of country music. When Jax came home from school or football practice, Mom always had music playing on her record player, and she was usually singing or humming along while cooking dinner. She didn't smile or laugh out loud very often, but the music in her soul kept her mood upbeat and tranquil. He thought to himself, *I need to get my turntable and my albums from the house the next time I pick up Olivia.* Perhaps it would make his hotel suite at the Manor feel more like home.

After several rounds of drinks and several bowls of peanuts and olives the bartender kept refilling, Jax and Rick went to the casino to try their luck. They were not novices when it came to blackjack, but they were far from professional gamblers. They chose a blackjack table that, not coincidentally, had an extremely attractive young woman dealing cards to two gentlemen. Jax and Rick soon became lifelong pals with their fellow players. The first thing they had in common was a love of Scotch on the rocks, followed by a mutual reason for their Las Vegas adventure. The two men were partners in a law firm in Portland, Oregon, and they were here with the same level of commitment to continuing legal education as were Jax and Rick. While they played and drank, they swapped stories about clients and trials.

Jax and Rick each opened with a two-hundred-dollar bet. In the first hour, they were both up over a thousand dollars. Feeling pretty sure of themselves, they decided to continue the action. Their luck took a turn for the worst. As midnight approached, they had a little more than a hundred dollars between them. Rather than leaving defeated, they decided to throw their remaining funds in for one last hand to be played by Jax. With Rick cheering him on, within less than an hour, they were back up over a thousand bucks. They split their money, and each of them resumed playing a hand. Their new best friends from Portland had cashed out but stayed to watch the action.

By three o'clock in the morning, not only were the Portland duo watching and cheering them on, but also a sizable crowd of onlookers gathered to witness what turned out to be an amazing run of luck for both of them. Together, Jax and Rick accrued more than twenty thousand dollars. They continued playing until sunrise, even though the sun was not visible inside the neon depths of the Mirage casino.

At seven o'clock, Jax was the last man standing. Rick had been asleep in his chair for the past hour, his head resting near the mound of chips he won throughout the night. As the good-looking dealer was ending her shift and turning Jax over to her replacement, she leaned over the table to him and whispered, "I could get fired for saying this to you, but you have been a blast to have at my table. And you and your friend have been so kind. Between the two of you, you've won, by my calculations, almost as much as my annual salary. Quit while you're ahead, because your luck will probably change with a new dealer. Get out of here. They say quitters never win, but in this city, winners know when to quit." She gave Jax a wink.

Jax breathed in slowly and drained the remaining drops of Scotch from his glass. Before he woke Rick, he gave the dealer a thousand-dollar chip in gratitude for a fun night and her sage advice. It took a couple pokes in the ribs, but when Rick awoke, he, too, thanked the dealer with a thousand-dollar chip and followed Jax out of the casino. On their way to the elevator, they cashed in their chips and left with more than twenty grand. Not a bad night's work.

Alone in the elevator, Rick whispered, "You know, we have to be careful with all this cash. We could get rolled on the way to our suite."

"Rolled? Are we in some James Bond movie here? For God's sake, we're not on the south side of Chicago, you know. I think we can make it down the hall without having to fight off any bad guys."

"All the same, we need to hide this money somewhere in the room."

Knowing better than to argue with his very drunk and very sleepy friend, Jax said very quietly, "Okay, I'm with you. We'll put it in the safe."

Rick thought for a moment, or maybe he dozed off for a moment. He replied, "No. No way. That's the first place they'll look when they come for the money. I say we hide it under the mattress."

"Seriously, man? This is not the Wild West."

"Just do it. For me."

He did. It took them a while, but each mattress had more than ten thousand dollars tucked underneath. Jax and Rick had one more cocktail before heading off to their separate bedrooms. The sun rose over the city as their heads hit their pillows.

Jax had only slept for an hour when he awoke with a headache unlike any he had ever endured. He stumbled to the bathroom in search of aspirin or any sort of pain reliever that didn't contain alcohol. The last thing he needed was more alcohol. Finding nothing in his shaving kit, he searched Rick's bag and found a travel-size bottle of ibuprofen containing four caplets. Deciding his headache needed extreme measures, he downed all four caplets with one gulp of water and went back to bed, leaving the cluttered bathroom behind.

Jax's self-medication did the trick. He was asleep within minutes. He was nestled comfortably among the sheets in a deep, restful sleep when he was startled awake by Rick shouting and shaking him by his shoulders.

"What the hell?!"

Running his fingers through his hair, Rick exclaimed, "I was right all along. You need to remember this. Someone came into our suite while we were asleep. They were looking for our money. You should see what they did to the bathroom. They tossed our bags, looking for the cash."

"You dumbass! It was me! I had a hell of a headache, and I went looking for something to take for it. You had four caplets of ibuprofen, and I took them. Nobody was in here, man, so go back to sleep."

Rick stood there for a moment, trying to take in this information. The night's activities plus the intake of Scotch for the past twelve hours caused him to operate on a five-second delay. He eventually comprehended what Jax said, muttered some sort of apology, backed out of Jax's room, and closed the door behind him.

Jax and Rick never talked about it again. Ever.

Their flight back to Cincinnati was uneventful. Tired and hungover, they were each richer and smarter, thanks to twelve hours of continuing education. They retrieved Rick's Mercedes from the airport car valet and drove downtown. It was only noon; they both decided to go to their offices and see what emergencies needed their attention. Rick dropped Jax off in his office parking lot, helped unload his luggage, and roared off to his office a few blocks away.

Jax entered the office to find Bailey asleep on top of a stack of files at the corner of Marion's desk. Marion was working while trying not to disturb her furry office mate.

"It must be true. Dog is man's best friend, and cats are selfish, fickle beings," chuckled Jax.

Marion stopped typing, took off her reading glasses, and said, "She always misses you when you go away. This is nothing new. I wouldn't say she's fickle. I think she just believes if you can't be with the one you love, then…"

"Yeah, yeah, I know the lyrics, Marion."

Bailey opened one eye, looked at Jax, yawned, and resumed her nap.

Jax laughed out loud. "That's the warmest welcome I've received from anyone in months! Not counting you, of course." Marion also laughed out loud and resumed her typing while Bailey slept.

Jax was in his office long enough to sort through the mail that Marion had organized—an urgent pile and a not-so-urgent pile—when she buzzed him. "I think you'd better come to my office."

Jax entered to find a tall young man, with blond hair and a scruffy blond beard, standing in the doorway.

He stepped forward. "Excuse me, are you Mr. Jackson Berman?"

Jax, sensing this kid needed his help but had barged in without an appointment, said in a rather curt tone of voice, "Yes, I am. What can I do for you?"

The young man answered, "I'm here to give you this." He extended his arm and handed him a manila envelope with Jax's name and address on the front.

"You've been served, sir."

He turned and exited the office.

Jax sat in the chair next to Marion's desk. Having been awakened by the stranger, Bailey decided it was bath time and was concentrating on some imaginary dirt on her paws. Jax opened the envelope, extracted the collection of legal documents inside, and read through them. Marion, knowing Jax as well as she did, recognized the look on his face. It signaled he did not want to be interrupted. She sat silently, not even resuming her work on the computer.

After several minutes, Jax returned the documents to the envelope, stood up, patted Bailey on her head, and looked at Marion. Taking a deep breath, he said, "I've been served with divorce papers, Marion. Could you please find Rick for me?"

Jax was standing in his office, staring out the window, when Rick entered. He took a seat on the sofa and said not a word. He waited for Jax to begin the conversation. Jax sat at his desk, then he decided to sit next to Rick. He took out a bottle of Scotch and two glasses. Rick found ice in the refrigerator.

"I knew it was coming. I thought I would be the one that would have to strike the first blow. But I couldn't do it. I couldn't do it to Olivia. I remember the first time I held her, just seconds after she came into the world. I promised her I would always take care of her, always be there for her. I promised her the most beautiful life. But I let her down. I've been gone for almost a year."

"Whoa, let's stop right there," Rick countered. "You've been there for her every step of the way. You were up for the middle-of-the-night bottles. You changed more diapers than any man I've ever known. You've been there for everything—games, recitals, practices, teacher conferences, school plays, and concerts. You talk like you've abandoned her. Hell, man, you fled for your life. Let's not forget Catherine's role in this melodrama."

Jax took a quick drink from his glass. "Spoken like a true divorce lawyer. You make a lot of sense, but right now, I feel like wallowing in negativity and self-pity while I down this cocktail. Then we'll get down to business."

They downed their cocktails. They didn't need to fill the silence with bullshit. Then they got down to business. The business of divorce and survival—financial and emotional survival.

Jax followed his lawyer's advice to every last detail. First order of business was buying a home. No more temporary lodgings at the Manor. He needed to establish a home. For himself. For Olivia. He found a charming Victorian home, three floors, beautifully appointed with deep oak floors and crown molding. A baroque stained-glass window adorned the landing on the staircase winding from the first floor. High ceilings, bevelled glass, and a beautifully landscaped backyard that featured an oversize slate terrace. He was excited about the prospect of making this his home. It was ten minutes to the office and fifteen minutes in the other direction to Olivia.

The first piece of furniture he moved into his new home was his piano. It was the piano his mother bought for him after his father officially stopped visiting or contacting him. Looking back on it, Jax now fully understood the sacrifices his mom made when she became not only a single parent but also a single parent with no help from the other parent. Mom must have had to really scrimp and save her money for the piano. She did it so he had something to call his own, something he could do for himself. As early as kindergarten, his musical ability was noticed by anyone who heard him play. Despite his talents on the football field, he was known, admired, and loved by his friends for his skills on the piano.

His piano had been in storage from the time he and Catherine moved into their home, now Catherine's home. Catherine refused to have it in the house, complaining it clashed with the decor. Never mind sentimental value; never mind the pleasure the piano gave him. Olivia had only heard him play a handful of times, when they were at someone's house who happened to have a piano.

He and his piano were reunited. What a great stress reliever it would be to come home after a tough day, either as a trial lawyer or as the future former husband of Catherine Berman. Maybe Olivia would be interested in taking lessons.

While he was standing in the living room, contemplating how to furnish and decorate around his musical treasure, his cell phone vibrated. It was Leonard.

"Hey, boss, I've got some updates on a couple of cases coming up for trial in the next few weeks. When do you have time for me?"

This was just what Jax needed to regain his equilibrium. "How about a beer or two this evening? You name the place."

CHAPTER 8

When Jax entered Marion's office, she didn't greet him with her typical witty charm. Instead, she made eye contact with him and nodded toward the waiting room.

"Your nine-o'clock appointment has been here since a few minutes after eight. I reminded him his appointment wasn't until nine. He smiled, said he knew, but he wanted to sit in the waiting room. I've offered him coffee and water, but he says he's fine. He's a kid, Jax. He can't be fine."

"A kid? He's here alone? I know we're getting older, Marion, and most of the population looks like kids to us. What do you mean, he's a kid?"

"His name is Matthew Spencer. Yes, he's from the Spencer family, if you know what I mean. He just turned sixteen. Drove here in a beautiful BMW convertible, compliments of Daddy Spencer, I'm sure. It was Daddy who called earlier this week to make the appointment. I thought he would be here with his son, but the poor kid's all by himself." Jax could tell that Matthew had triggered her maternal instinct.

"Give me a minute or two to get settled, then show him to my office."

Marion retorted, "You may be getting older, Jax, but speak for yourself. I am going to stay forever young."

Jax gave her the thumbs-up and said, "Yeah, yeah, I know those lyrics too."

Matthew Spencer entered Jax's office, and after shaking Jax's outstretched hand, he gave him a copy of the criminal complaints he pulled out of his jacket pocket.

"Underage consumption of alcohol and possession of marijuana, Matthew," said Jax after reviewing the documents. "Tell me the details. When and where did this happen?"

Matthew sat straight-up in the chair. "It happened about two weeks ago at a friend's house. His parents were away for the weekend. You know how it goes. Jason invited a few of us over, but when word spread that Jason was home alone, let's just say the guest list grew. A lot. Next thing we knew, there were almost a hundred kids. Most of whom we knew, but a lot we didn't. More booze and weed came too. The music got a little loud, or maybe a lot loud. One of the neighbors called the cops. They came straight into the backyard, which is where most of us were hanging out. We didn't have time to stash anything away. A bunch of us got busted. They didn't arrest us, but instead, they wrote us up and gave us these papers telling us our court date."

Jax asked, "Where are your parents? My assistant said it was your father who called to make this appointment."

"Dad is somewhere being Dad. He works all the time, mostly out of town closing real-estate deals. Mom is at our home in Naples. She's been in Florida for a few weeks. I don't know when she plans to come home."

"Where are you staying while your parents are gone?"

"At home. We have a housekeeper. She's worked for us since I was a baby. She's like a second mother to me. She stayed on after Dad moved out."

Jax remembered the Spencers settled a highly publicized divorce a year ago. Rick represented his mom. She was awarded a mountain of cash as well as the Naples vacation home. She held onto the sprawling mansion that Matthew called home and a hundred-acre horse farm fifty miles east of the city. Mrs. Spencer had been involved in the horse-breeding business for several years. Despite the generous property settlement, Mr. Spencer landed on his feet. He purchased the penthouse suite in an exclusive high-rise on the Kentucky side of the river, which gave him a commanding view of the city. This made sense because he had been the developer of the building and the surrounding restaurant and retail district. He also held on to the other family vacation home in a small town on the coast of Maine. He kept the eighty-foot yacht docked in the Florida Keys during the winter and in Maine for the summer. The boat, named *Estelle* in honor of his wife, went through major renovations and a name change. Mr. Spencer had christened it *Liberation*. David Spencer had never been described as subtle and understated.

Matthew added, "I have the contact info for my dad's business manager. You're supposed to call, and he'll pay your fee."

"I'm not worried about that right now. But I am concerned about you being on your own without one of your parents at home with you. Do you have brothers and sisters?"

"My sister is working on some fancy PhD in engineering at MIT. My brother is in medical school at the University of Chicago. They're much older, so we really didn't grow up together. They're not home much, and they hardly ever come home because of the divorce. They call me once in a while, but that's about it. Even when they still lived at home, we were never very close. In a lot of ways, I suppose, I'm an only child."

Jax was sitting across his desk from the proverbial poor little rich kid. He had a fancy car, designer clothes, and multiple family houses, but nothing resembled a home or a family life. No wonder he was partying whenever he had the chance. Marion had already done a quick record check. A quick glance revealed this kid had never been in court before. It was either he was very lucky or this was an isolated act of stupidity.

"Tell me, Matthew, honestly, did you drink at the party? Smoke weed?"

After a brief hesitation, he mumbled, "A little."

Jax smiled. How many times had he gotten that answer? "Well, Spencer, either you smoked weed and drank alcohol or you didn't."

"I did. But I wasn't drunk or high."

"How much did you drink?"

"Only about eight beers and a few shots of tequila."

Only eight beers and a few shots, Jax thought to himself. *That's enough to knock seasoned drinkers on their ass.* This kid was not new to the cocktail scene. He was destined for far worse things than this minor criminal charge if something or somebody did not intervene. Jax could feel himself getting more emotionally involved than he should. But this kid needed someone, and he needed someone now.

"Okay, Matthew, meet me in the juvenile court lobby next Wednesday at ten-thirty. Your case will be called at eleven o'clock. In the meantime, I'll get in touch with the prosecutor assigned to your case. I'm hopeful it can be resolved easily. I'll try to get this case referred to the court diversion program."

"What's diversion?" asked Matthew, leaning forward in his chair.

"It's an education and counseling program. If you successfully complete it, the charges will be dropped. You'll have no juvenile court record."

Spencer sat back in his chair while breathing an audible sigh of relief. "Sounds like a winner!"

"Listen to me, Spencer," said Jax. "One of your parents has to be with you in court next week. You're a minor, so a parent must accompany you."

"Okay, Mr. Berman, I'll find out who's able to be here. Thanks. See you next week." Spencer shook Jax's hand and left the office clearly more relaxed and confident than he was when he entered the office.

Next Wednesday arrived, and Jax met Matthew in the court-house lobby. Matthew was alone. Again.

"Mr. Berman, I never could get hold of my mom. My dad can't come back to town today, but he can appear by phone."

Great, thought Jax to himself. *This kid is breaking my heart.* "Get him on the phone, please."

When David Spencer finally answered his son's call, Matthew handed the phone to Jax.

"Mr. Spencer, because Matthew is a minor and this case is a juvenile court matter, a parent or guardian must be here with him."

Mr. Spencer kicked into his power-broker persona and replied, "You said parent or guardian? Can't you be his guardian?"

"Technically, the court could appoint me as his guardian for purposes of this case only."

Mr. Spencer, accustomed to getting his own way, replied, "Fine, Mr. Berman, you have my permission to act as his guardian. Feel free to add this service to your fee. My manager will see to the payment. If there's nothing else, I'm late for a meeting." The call was terminated. And not by Jax.

Leaving Matthew alone in the lobby, Jax went through the back hallways of the juvenile court to seek out the assistant prosecutor assigned to Matthew's case. Juvenile court was not someplace Jax frequented. Most of the juvenile cases were minor matters, and the child and his family either used the public defender or handled the matter without an attorney. The major juvenile crimes seemed to get swallowed up by the public defender. Even families who could afford to hire an attorney often opted for the public defender because, in their minds, it was just juvenile court and not a big deal.

A child like Matthew, with a prestigious last name, is likely going to have a private lawyer to prevent any tarnishing of the family name. This was obviously why Matthew's father, or business manager, sought out Jackson Berman. They were prepared to spend whatever it took to resolve the matter without any publicity or inconvenience. They were not, however, willing to devote their personal time or energy to the cause.

Locating the prosecutor's office, Jax entered to find a dozen new lawyers who staffed the Juvenile Court Prosecutor's Office. Typically, this was where a new assistant prosecutor, fresh out of law school, was assigned. It was only natural that Jax didn't recognize a single face in the office. But most of them recognized him. The conversation stopped. All eyes turned toward him.

One of the young lawyers was a petite woman, with dark hair and matching dark eyes, attired in a very flattering yet professional charcoal-gray suit and matching pumps. She introduced herself as Michelle Dawson.

"I am the prosecutor on Matthew Spencer's case. I assume that's why you're here. We were all taking bets on which top gun the Spencers would hire for their little boy. You were the odds-on favorite."

Jax was taken aback for a moment. "I'll accept that as a compliment. Is there somewhere we can talk about the case?"

"If you really think it's necessary. Let's get down to basics and not waste a lot of time. He's a spoiled little rich kid whose parents are more interested in having fun than in raising a child. The rules don't apply to him, especially when Mommy and Daddy are out of town, living their lives. But I will give your client this, Mr. Berman. The arresting officers report that when they entered the backyard party, most of the kids ran for their lives, and some even scaled the privacy fence to escape. Those who weren't fast enough did everything they could to get out of this jam. One kid even gave a false name, using his mother's maiden name to conceal his true identity. Kids, huh? But your client didn't run. He gave the police his driver's license as identification and was more than polite and cooperative. He won the prize for being the most well-mannered and honest delinquent of the bunch."

"A backhanded compliment, but I'll take it. Matthew has never been in trouble before. Sounds like he's a great candidate for diversion."

Ms. Dawson sighed. "He's exactly who the diversion program is designed to serve. I have no problem referring him and closing the case in six months if he stays out of trouble and completes the program. But mark my words. He'll be back. Then diversion will not be an option. Make sure you convey that to your client."

"Will do, Ms. Dawson. Now there is just one tiny wrinkle, which actually plays right into your very astute observations about my client. Neither of his parents are in town nor were they able to return for the hearing. I need to be appointed as Matthew's guardian for the hearing."

Assistant Prosecuting Attorney Dawson smirked, "What happened? Did they misplace the family's private jet? Sorry, just had to get one more jab in. Don't take it personally, Mr. Berman. It was a pleasure meeting you. I'll see you in the courtroom."

Thirty minutes later, Jax and his delinquent client emerged from the courtroom. With him being Matthew's guardian, he and Matthew signed the necessary forms for the diversion program. The court permitted Jax to remain as guardian in the very likely event that he, and not one of the parents, would accompany Matthew to the family information and education sessions. Through this process, he could discern in Matthew a combination of embarrassment about his family dynamics as well as gratitude for Jax's willingness to step in and help.

"Your first session is in two weeks. You must let me know if you need me to attend. It would be preferable if one or both of your parents were with you, but I am happy to help whenever you need me."

"Thanks, Mr. Berman. I've got your phone number saved in my phone."

There was something about the way Matthew looked at him that tempted Jax to disregard another cardinal rule of criminal-defense work. It was a simple rule: never, under any circumstances, get emotionally involved with a client. It can only lead to disaster. Represent the client to the best of your ability and explore all viable defense strategies, but leave it there. Jax had been faithful to that advice throughout his career. Until now.

"Glad to help, Matthew. Since we are sort of family together, call me Jax. Come with me. I'm buying you lunch at the best deli in Cincinnati. Have you ever been to Harold's Deli?"

Two weeks later, as Jax and Matthew were leaving the first diversion meeting together, Jax bought Matthew dinner, and they made plans to play a round of golf the following weekend. So much for not getting emotionally involved.

CHAPTER 9

Jax's cell phone vibrated as he exited the courthouse. Rick's ID lit up the screen.

"I just got off the phone with Catherine's attorney. She has a new set of settlement demands."

Jax stopped dead in his tracks in the middle of the sidewalk, causing a young couple to step around him in order to avoid running straight into his backside. "A new set of demands? This is the third new set of demands! I agreed to everything in the first two sets of demands. When does this chess game end? At some point, when both parties agree, that's it. Isn't that what we learned in contracts? Meeting of the minds and all that crap? She keeps everything we own together in her last demand. Does she want my health too?"

"That's a good one, Jax," Rick chuckled. "I'll have to use that one. 'Counsel, does your client want my client's health too? She can have the kids, the car, the house, the good china, the car, and a shit ton of alimony, but now she wants his last breath too?' Yeah, I'm going to use it."

"Glad I can be a source of witty comebacks. Seriously, though, when is this going to end? The marriage is over, but we've been getting along when it comes to Olivia. We attend her practices and games without too much discomfort. Olivia seems relaxed when we're together. I've agreed to give her the house and an obscene amount of alimony plus child support. She gets everything in the house too. She's always said she doesn't want the Hilton Head house. What does she want now?"

"She just wants more, Jax. Sorry to be vague, but that's all I'm getting from her lawyer. Steve Barker and I have had a lot of cases together over the years. He's a good trial attorney, but he's a better negotiator. I've never seen him act this way. He's always had much better client control in the past."

Jax started walking toward his office again. "There could be a complication in this case. Maybe I'm just being paranoid at this point. Did you know that Steve and I went to high school together?"

"I had no idea," Rick responded.

"We played sports together. We started out in Little League football. Then middle-school and high school football. We were the running backs for the team, but my statistics were always better than his. I made the city all-star team, he didn't. I made the all-state select team, he didn't. I won a college football scholarship, he didn't. My girlfriend was homecoming queen, the same girl he chased for years. She never gave him a second look."

After a few seconds of dead silence, Jax thought he and Rick were cut off. Rick finally said, "*Wow*, Jax. Interesting background information. I wouldn't bet any money on your theory, but it could explain the stonewalling. I chalked it up to Catherine being bitter and Steve couldn't talk any sense into her."

"Trust me, Rick," Jax sighed. "Catherine may be bitter and obstinate, but she's not stupid. She's not going to pay Steve's ridiculous fee and then ignore his advice. I know her well enough."

"You may be right. I'll definitely keep this in mind when I talk to him. I'll try to pin him down on exactly what she wants. I'll get back to you."

When Jax walked into the waiting room minutes later, his cell phone vibrated in his pocket. He read the text message from Rick: *She now wants the Hilton Head house. And she wants you to pay her attorney fees.* Jax thought to himself, *So she truly does want everything. Before this is over, she will want my health.*

*****

Jax and Matthew Spencer golfed together a few times and grabbed a quick meal after the three diversion meetings they attended. Matthew graduated from the diversion program; his alcohol and marijuana charges were officially sealed. End of chapter.

It was a beautiful sunny October day. The leaves had transitioned into a medley of reds and golds, and the colors reflected off the waters of the river. Olivia spent the previous night at a friend's house. Jax didn't want to be an obnoxious parent and try to cut in on a natural part of growing up—spending more time with friends and less time with parents. Quality time with your child did not include a sulking young girl who was missing out on fun and games with her friends. Jax was on his own this beautiful autumn Sunday.

He called Matthew, who was, not surprisingly, home alone. Matthew eagerly accepted Jax's invitation for a ride on his boat. Jax picked him up and drove to the marina. His thirty-foot motor launch, with a small cabin and kitchenette, was perfect for a day trip on the river.

Matthew learned, with Jax's help, how to tie up the boat at a marina upriver from the city. The Spencer family yacht probably had a crew of five or six permanent members, which meant Matthew never had the opportunity to learn how to tie up a boat or do any of the basic, fun boating activities. The marina, nestled on the river near a small rural town about an hour away from the city, served cold beer and the best chicken wings on the Ohio River.

They munched on their third order of wings and fries. Jax drank a beer while Matthew guzzled down multiple glasses of water.

Jax said, "I haven't seen or heard from you in about a week. Everything okay?"

Matthew took another sip of his water before answering, his eyes looking down at the table, "Yeah, things are pretty much okay."

Jax was not convinced. "Where are your parents?"

"Dad's been on the West Coast for a week or so. Closing hotel deals in Sacramento and Portland. Mom is in Naples, which is where she usually goes. She went on a Caribbean cruise last week with a friend. I don't know the friend's name, but I'm guessing it's a guy."

"When was the last time one of your parents was home with you?"

He thought for several seconds, then he finally responded, "I'm not sure. Maybe around the end of July."

"You've been home alone for two months? That's not right."

"Actually, it is, Jax," sighed Matthew as he drank more water. "It's much better when they're not around."

Jax's first thought was, any red-blooded teenager would find being home alone and unsupervised preferable to answering to Mom and Dad. But Matthew kept talking.

"You see, Jax, it's a beautiful house in a beautiful part of the city. And I drive a fancy-ass car, and I have more spending money than most families earn at their jobs. But there's a price to pay for those things. The car and the clothes and the spending money are Mom and Dad's way of compensating."

"For being gone all the time?"

"Partly," muttered Matthew. "Also for how it is when they are home."

"All right, Matthew. Spill it. What do you want to tell me?"

"It's nothing like *The Brady Bunch*. Or any of those old sitcoms where everyone gets along and life's little problems are resolved by the end of the half-hour episode. Dad rarely speaks to me. When we do have a conversation, he never fails to remind me of my mistakes. My brother and sister were both class valedictorians. They knew when they were kids what they wanted to do with their lives. And they're doing it. My brother always wanted to be a surgeon, and soon he will be. My sister has always wanted to build bridges; that's bound to happen too. But I'm sixteen years old and don't have a clue what I want to do when I grow up. I don't have any deep, burning passion like they did at my age. Dad doesn't know how to deal with a kid who has no interests in life, so he doesn't deal with it." He munched a couple of fries before continuing.

"Mom drinks. A lot. She's always on some sort of antidepressant. I have never seen her completely sober. Ever. When she reaches a certain level of intoxication, she becomes very angry and mean. I'm the one who bears the brunt of it. Especially if she and Dad had just gotten into it over something."

"What does she do, Matthew?"

"It starts out with screaming, lots and lots of screaming. Yelling about everything and nothing. Then when she gets really wound up, she starts throwing things. Sometimes breakable things, sometimes heavy things that hurt when they connect."

"She's throwing things at you?"

"Sure. It's been happening for years. I've been to the emergency room for stitches a few times. I tell the ER staff I fell off my bike or some other innocuous story about how I got cut. My convincing story plus the family name means nobody questions it. I get patched up, Mom and Dad buy me whatever I want, put more money in my account, and we never talk about it again. A few years ago, to deal with the pain of stitches or just the pain of having been assaulted by my own mother, I started sneaking a can of beer into my room at night. Then two beers, and on and on till I started sneaking a Jim Beam and Coke for a nightcap before bedtime. Eventually I couldn't fall asleep without the help of booze. When I started high school and weed was everywhere, I added that to my diet too."

Jax sat in stunned silence while absorbing everything Matthew had confided to him. On one hand, he was overwhelmed and truly touched that Matthew trusted Jax to talk about his life. On the other hand, he was overwhelmed with anger and disgust for the Spencers.

"It's why they split up," Matthew continued. "Dad couldn't take it anymore. The divorce took years because there's so much to fight over. But I'm not anything they fought over. They spent months and months bickering and negotiating about every asset they've accumulated. I'm pretty sure they both view me as a liability and not an asset of the marriage. My guess is, they'll both celebrate, separately, when I'm eighteen years old and out of their hair."

"You've got this year plus another year of high school before college. Surely there will be times when they'll be home with you. Not necessarily together, though."

Matthew smiled. "I wouldn't count on it."

Jax took the final sips of his beer, watching Matthew eating the last remnants of the french fries. He felt himself slipping further and further away from Malcolm's advice about not getting emotionally involved.

CHAPTER 10

Rick slid into the booth. Music was blaring over the speakers in the corners of the ceiling, accompanied by the bells, whistles, and shrieks from video games. He had to shout to Jax.

"You just scored a major win, saved the career of a rich doctor, and we're celebrating here? I was thinking a few drinks at a rooftop bar then dinner and a few more cocktails somewhere a helluva lot quieter than this place."

The jury deliberated for less than an hour before they acquitted Jax's client of domestic violence. Rick was Dr. Harwood's divorce attorney. He sent the doctor to Jax after his estranged wife accused him of beating her. Leonard had uncovered damning information about her past behaviors with other men in her life. She made false accusations of abuse against several past boyfriends. She set fire to her ex-husband's house shortly after he remarried.

Jax smiled. "This is when the confirmed bachelor in you shines brightest, my friend. I haven't seen Olivia since the beginning of the trial. I have her all weekend. I let her pick the place to celebrate my victory."

Rick answered, "You're right. I was seeing this evening through eyes unencumbered by marriage and parenthood. My apologies. You know I love Olivia like she's my own daughter, and I'm glad to spend the evening with her." Olivia ran back to the table to scoop up more tokens for the video game she was determined to conquer. She kissed Jax on the cheek and gave him a quick hug, and she did the same with her uncle Rick before running back to her video game.

During the evening, through another round of beers plus gourmet burgers and fries, they discussed the divorce negotiations. They only talked about it while Olivia was away. When dinner was served and Olivia joined them, the conversation centered around Olivia's school, soccer team, and blooming preadolescent social life. Both Rick and Jax breathed a sigh of relief when Olivia insisted she did not have a boyfriend because she thought boys were idiots.

"Speaking of idiots," Rick said, munching the few remaining fries in the basket, "your good friend Mr. Barker is still stonewalling. I'm beginning to buy into your hunch. The history you and he share seems to be influencing the way he's handling this case. In all the years he and I have been on opposing sides, no matter how nasty our clients behaved, he was always straight up with me. He's always had excellent client control. He's always been willing to settle the case rather than battling in the courtroom. But not this time. No matter how many times I say yes to his proposals, he always ups the ante."

Jax leaned back in his chair and rubbed his hands over his face in a slow massaging movement. "Catherine won't talk to me about anything. We see each other when I pick up Olivia, and we're together at Olivia's games and practices. The conversation never runs deeper than the day's weather forecast or whether Olivia has any homework. I have no idea what she does or how she fills her time."

Rick finished the remaining crumbs in the basket of fries. "I'm going to pull back on this for a week or so. Let them come to us. I'm just going to sit on the latest demand, which now includes the Hilton Head home. We'll see who's better at the waiting game."

"You're the boss," he sighed. "It's not like I'm in a rush to get married or have someone waiting in the wings. But to use another buzz phrase, I would like 'closure' for everybody's sake. That includes my little princess who's trying to win some ridiculous video game that, from the sound of it, is all about death and destruction. Gone are the days when a doll or a stuffed animal was all she needed." Jax finished the remainder of his beer.

Rick laughed. "Hey, man, they all grow up. You just have to go with the flow."

"Words of wisdom from an unmarried man who has no children and no interest in having children either."

Rick smiled. "Olivia is all I need to fulfill my paternal instinct."

"There is no such thing as a paternal instinct."

Rick finished his beer and set his empty mug on the table. "Exactly."

Two weeks later, Jax dragged his tuxedo from the recesses of his closet and pulled a flashy red-and-black bow tie with matching cummerbund from his bottom dresser drawer. He prepared mentally for his first public social event since he and Catherine had separated. He steeled himself for the onslaught of questions from friends and non-friends, who would ask where Catherine was this evening. He rehearsed in his mind the appropriate answer without divulging too much to the inquiring minds.

He had begrudgingly accepted Dr. Harwood's invitation to be his guest at the annual gala benefitting the Cincinnati Children's Hospital. It was traditionally held at the elegant Hall of Mirrors in the city's oldest and most prestigious hotel. Dr. Harwood had also invited Rick as his guest. In years past, he and Catherine had been regular supporters of the event. They purchased a table and filled it with friends who were willing to spend the evening bidding on silent auction items they neither wanted nor needed. He confirmed with Catherine that she had no plans to attend this year. Both of them at the event without being there together would be the height of awkwardness.

Jax flipped the keys to the Porsche to the valet at the grand entrance to the hundred-year-old hotel. He entered the lobby to find Rick waiting.

First stop: the bar. Fortunately for Jax and Rick and most of the other guests, there was a bar with multiple bartenders in every corner of the mirrored ballroom, which was adorned with three priceless and oversize crystal chandeliers. They stopped at the nearest bar.

The trajectory of Jax's life took an unexpected yet miraculous turn.

As he edged away from the bar, his Scotch on the rocks in one hand and Rick's vodka on the rocks in the other, he narrowly avoided a collision with an exquisitely dressed woman. They both gasped. Looking back on it, Jax was unsure if he was speechless at the near collision or if he was tongue-tied because of her undeniable beauty and poise.

Fortunately, Jax made his living, and a damn good one, by thinking on his feet. He quickly regained his composure and smiled his most genuine smile.

"I know I should say something unforgettably clever right now, but all I can say is, can I buy you a drink?"

The woman was dressed in a simple but elegant floor-length navy gown, her neck adorned with pearls, as were her wrists and ears. She paused for a moment before answering. "Not unforgettably clever, but unforgettably generous, Mr. Berman."

"Have we met before?" replied Jax. "If I have actually forgotten meeting you, I need to retire now because I must be sinking into early senility."

"Now that was unforgettably clever. Yes, you may buy me a drink. White wine, please, preferably a chardonnay."

Rick, seeing Jax in conversation with an attractive member of the opposite sex, came to rescue his drink. He did it so smoothly and silently the conversation between Jax and the lady in blue continued without interruption.

Jax took a very discreet look at the mystery woman's left hand. No wedding ring. Encouraged by this discovery, he pursued the conversation. "Seriously, have we met before?"

Jax handed her chardonnay to her. She replied, "No. But I do keep up with local news, and you always seem to be in the headlines with some notable criminal."

"Well then," answered Jax, "allow me to formally introduce myself. Jackson Berman, ma'am. My friends call me Jax."

She smiled, sipped her wine, and said, "Pleased to meet you, Jax. I am Julia Winston. My friends call me Julia." She laughed.

"Tell me, Julia, may I call you Julia?"

Again, she laughed. "Yes, of course, Jax."

"What brings you to this event? I've been attending for years and don't recall seeing you."

"I joined the staff at Children's Hospital six months ago. They hired me away from Boston Children's. I'm in pediatric oncology."

"Impressive," remarked Jax as he and Julia strolled away from the bar and toward a quieter, less populated part of the ballroom. "What exactly do you do there?"

"Assistant head of the department. After I graduated from Tufts University Medical School, I was accepted into the residency program at Boston Children's. I stayed for several years. Then I got an offer from Cincinnati I couldn't refuse."

Becoming more and more fascinated by this beautiful and obviously bright and accomplished woman, he pressed on. "Are you settling into the Cincinnati lifestyle?"

Julia paused for a moment before saying, "I am. Professionally, Cincinnati Children's is one of the best in the country. As is Boston Children's. Both receive patients literally from around the world. The professional challenges are here for me. Cincinnati has really started to grow on me. It has an easier, more relaxed pace than Boston. And the people are friendlier."

Jax ventured forth. "I hope Cincinnati Children's isn't the only offer you couldn't refuse. Will you join me for dinner tomorrow?"

Jax held his breath, awaiting her answer. Julia smiled and said, "I would like that. Another offer I can't refuse." She laughed again. Jax could listen to her laugh for the rest of his life.

They exchanged phone numbers and made plans for Jax to pick her up for what, Jax hoped, was the first of many dinners to come.

*****

Sunday seemed to drag. He checked his watch every few minutes, counting down to the time to pick up Julia. He didn't want to seem overly anxious to please, and it occurred to him it was more than a decade since his last first date. He hoped the rules hadn't changed.

Sunday afternoon was spent with Olivia. Father and daughter rode five miles on the nearby bike trail. They stopped for a quick pizza lunch at a quaint bistro along the trail, then a leisurely five miles back to their starting point. Conversation always lingered between the light and fun, as usual. While Jax was savoring his time with Olivia, as he always did, he kept track of the time. Olivia didn't notice anything different; she kept pedaling and chatting.

Catherine was unloading groceries from her car when Jax and Olivia pulled into the driveway. Jax helped bring the bags into the kitchen. They talked together while Catherine put the groceries away. Jax couldn't tell if there was less tension between them than there had been since the separation or if it was his own upbeat mood in eager anticipation of dinner with Julia. Whatever the reason, a pleasant family conversation took place, and Olivia seemed especially pleased to be able to share some happy time with both parents together in the same room.

Despite their problems, they continued to shelter Olivia from the worst of their conflict. Olivia was not happy her father didn't live with them anymore, but she always seemed at ease when he and Catherine were together at soccer games. In spite of her bitter feelings, she always put Olivia first. While maybe she was not such a great wife and partner, Jax couldn't argue with her commitment to their daughter. Considering how things between the two of them had turned out, her talents as a mother outweighed anything else.

Jax headed home, parked his car in the garage, and took the steps two at a time to his bedroom. He spent an unusually long time, for him, selecting his clothes for the evening. Dress to impress but don't look overeager. He selected the right slacks, sport coat, and shirt. No tie, he decided; that would be overeager. He took one last look at his ensemble, then he hopped in the shower.

Toweling off after a relaxing steam, he was dressing when his cell phone vibrated. He looked at the caller ID; it displayed a phone number instead of one of the names in his contacts. He recognized the three-digit exchange as the hospital district. His experience with his mother conditioned him, not only to the phone number, to answer the call without delay.

"Is this Jackson Berman?" a female voice asked.

"Yes, it is. How can I help you?"

She replied, "Mr. Berman, this is very unusual. This is Jane Atkins, admitting nurse at Children's Hospital. We have a male patient who was transported to our emergency room in critical condition. We found your business card in his wallet. He has his cell phone, but it's locked. So we have no other contact information."

Jax was confused. "Does the wallet have identification information on the patient?"

"Yes, sir, we have his driver's license. His name is Matthew Spencer."

The air left his body. Despite the warmth from his shower, a gnawing chill spread over him. "He's a former client of mine, and we've become friends. Why is he there? Is he sick?"

"No, sir," replied Nurse Atkins. There was a brief silence before she continued. "He is being admitted with a gunshot wound, and I'm afraid his condition is extremely critical."

"I'm on my way. I will try to reach his family. I'll be there in fifteen minutes."

Having thrown on the sweatshirt and jeans he wore on the bike trail, he made it to the emergency room parking lot in twelve minutes. Sprinting toward the emergency room doors, he remembered Julia. He called her, told her briefly what was happening, and asked for forgiveness for standing her up. She told Jax she would pray for his young friend and to please keep her updated.

He tried several times to get Mr. Spencer on the phone, but there was no answer. He didn't want to deliver this horrible news in a voice mail, not until he had information on Matthew's condition. Jax checked into the nurses' station, and he met Nurse Atkins personally. She escorted Jax down the hall to Matthew's room. When they arrived, Jax was surprised to see a police officer standing outside the door.

The officer immediately stood to attention and said, "Mr. Berman, I sure didn't expect to see you here. Has Matthew's family already retained you?"

Jax, confused for the second time in less than an hour, replied, "Nice to see you, Sergeant Williams. I have no idea what you're talking about. I'm a friend of Matthew's. The hospital called me because they found my contact information in his wallet. Why would he need a lawyer?"

Sergeant Williams shook his head. "I'm not saying he does necessarily. Not even sure if the poor kid's going to pull through. But here's what I know. Matthew was throwing some sort of party at his house while his parents were away."

"No surprise there," said Jax. The police officer nodded in agreement. He gave Jax a look that let him know he was aware of the family situation, if only from a law-enforcement perspective. Jax could only guess at the number of times the police had been dispatched to Matthew's home because of partying and annoying the neighbors. This time, it was horribly different.

"The 9-1-1 call from his residence," continued the officer, "was from a young male who screamed that Matthew had been shot. When EMTs arrived at the scene, there was Matthew, lying in the family room, on the floor, with a gunshot wound to the head. The only other person there was the young man who called 9-1-1. The other 'friends' fled the scene."

"How was he shot? Who shot him?" asked Jax, trying to absorb this shocking tale.

"According to the young man, Matthew shot himself. He had been drinking and smoking weed with the rest of the partygoers for an hour or so, then he left the room for a few minutes. When he came back to the party, he was holding a revolver. He told his friends it belonged to his father. Matthew then announced he had put one bullet in the chamber and suggested they should all play Russian roulette."

"Dear God," muttered Jax, reeling at the mental image of a group of drunk teenage boys thinking this was a smart idea.

Sergeant Williams paused. "According to the witness, Matthew was the only one who played. He spun the barrel of the gun, pulled the trigger, and click. He won. He decided to make it two out of two, and when he pulled the trigger the second time, bang. Bullet entered above his right temple."

Jax slumped into the chair next to the one occupied by the officer. The two men were silent for several minutes.

Jax finally asked the officer, "What about the kid who called 9-1-1? Are you going to file charges against him?"

He let out a long, slow exhale before answering. "Absolutely not. He was the only kid there with the heart and the courage to stay and try to do something to help. When I arrived, he was sitting on the floor, holding Matthew and rocking him. Sure, I could charge him with underage drinking, but quite honestly, I was tempted to serve the poor kid a cocktail myself. He was shaken to the core. One of the other officers took care of him and made sure he was transported home safely."

Sergeant Williams stood up, stretched his arms out wide, shook his head, and announced he was leaving. Jax promised to keep him updated on Matthew's condition.

As the sergeant rounded the corner in the hallway and disappeared from sight, a doctor approached Jax from the opposite end of the hallway. He introduced himself as the attending physician on duty in the ER and asked if Jax was a family member.

"No, Doctor, just a personal friend of Matthew," he responded. "I have tried several times to reach Mr. Spencer without any luck."

The doctor sat down in the chair that had been occupied by Sergeant Williams. "I'm afraid there is nothing we can do for your young friend, Mr. Berman. The bullet entered his right temple above his ear and lodged in the brain, causing massive damage. Testing shows no brain activity. It may be minutes, hours, days, or weeks, but Matthew will never wake up. Instead, his body will eventually give up and forget how to breathe."

Tears welling in his eyes, Jax thanked the doctor for the information and resolved to stay with Matthew until his family arrived. When the doctor walked away, he tried Mr. Spencer's phone one more time. Mr. Spencer answered the call. It was left to Jax to break the news about his youngest child.

Hours later, with only the light of the machines and monitors illuminating Matthew's room, Jax nodded off in the chair he moved next to Matthew's bedside. He was awakened by footsteps and a feeling that someone was in the room.

Standing in the doorway was David Spencer. Jax looked quickly at his watch and discovered that it had been more than two hours since he had told him about his son's accident.

"Mr. Berman," sighed Mr. Spencer as he approached Matthew's bed. "What an unexpected surprise to find you still here."

"I wasn't going to leave him alone, Mr. Spencer. Have you spoken with the doctor on duty?"

David Spencer pulled up a chair and sat next to Jax. "Yes, I found him before I came to the room. What a horribly stupid thing Matthew has done to himself. He's been taught to stay away from my gun collection."

He was probably taught to stay away from alcohol and drugs too, Jax thought. *But parents need to be there every step of the way to make sure their teenaged kids live the lessons they were taught.* Jax thought better of voicing his opinion to a man who would soon bury his child.

David rose and walked to the window. He opened the drapes to look out on the lights. "I never could understand that kid," David muttered. "The older ones always had their heads on straight. They knew, even when they were young, what they wanted to do with their lives. They never wasted time with silliness. Always had their eye on the prize. But this one"—he paused and turned to look at Matthew lying in bed—"never had a fire lit under him. He never took anything seriously." He watched the monitors next to the bed, their lights and beeps the only connection between Matthew and life. Looking closely at this father, Jax didn't know if the look on his face was one of sorrow or disgust. Touching his son's cheek softly, David turned away from the bed and returned to his chair. He and Jax sat silently for several minutes.

Jax whispered, "I'm going to step out and grab some coffee in the waiting room to give you some time alone with your son. May I bring you a cup?"

"No, thanks. I don't drink coffee or any caffeinated product. It makes me too edgy. By the way, when I've spoken with Matthew over the past few months, he told me about your outings together. He enjoys his time with you. Thank you for taking an interest in my son."

I was only doing for Matthew what you should have been doing, thought Jax, again swallowing the words. Instead, he merely nodded and exited the room. The only sound in the room was the machine breathing for Matthew.

Jax, returning from the hospital cafeteria, sat down in the chair in the hallway to give Mr. Spencer as much time as he wanted with his son. Matthew's last breath could come at any time, and his father should be there when he leaves this world.

Jax must have dozed off again, only to be awakened by footsteps and the feeling of a nearby presence. Again, it was David Spencer. He was preparing to leave.

Jax quickly regained his composure and asked him if it was over, if Matthew had passed away. For the rest of his life, he would never forget the reply: "No, Mr. Berman, he has not, but the doctors say there's no hope that he'll regain consciousness. They cannot state with certainty when the end will come. I'm afraid I can't stay any longer. I have a meeting in Philadelphia tomorrow afternoon. The doctor has my contact information, and he promised to keep me apprised of any changes."

Jax was speechless. Before he could come up with anything to say to convince this man to stay with his son, he held out his hand to shake Jax's, thanked him again for his friendship with his son, and strolled toward the exit doors. Reflecting on the time they had just spent together in Matthew's room as well as in the hallway, it struck Jax that at no time did Mr. Spencer shed a tear or lose his composure. *How could a parent be so callous in the face of his child's death? How could a parent effectively abandon a teenage boy who would have traded the fancy car, clothes, and the obscenely large allowance for just a little time and attention?* Jax had no answer.

Jax returned to Matthew's room, sat down again at his bedside, held his hand, and waited. Waited for the end.

The end came at daybreak. Jax was still holding Matthew's hand when Matthew's body trembled, and he took a deep gasping breath. Then there was nothing except the shrill alarm on the monitor alerting an emergency. Two nurses came in within seconds and turned off the alarm, and one nurse held Matthew's other hand to check for a pulse. She looked at Jax, who was still holding onto Matthew's hand, gave a sad smile, and shook her head. The other nurse left the room to summon the doctor on duty. The doctor came in to declare time of death. He said he would contact Matthew's father.

Jax moved to a corner of the room while the nurses removed the tubes from Matthew to prepare him for transport to the morgue. It suddenly occurred to Jax that Matthew's mother must not be aware of the situation. She certainly hadn't shown up. Mr. Spencer didn't even mention her. There was no guarantee that Mr. Spencer would bother to tell her. *What the hell is wrong with these people?*

Rick would have her phone number because she had been his client in the divorce. Jax remembered Matthew's comments about his parents' divorce and how he would be a liability instead of an asset. Jax thought it was just a flip remark from a cocky teenaged boy, but now, having met his dad in person, he realized Matthew had been brutally honest and tragically correct in his assessment of his relationship with his parents.

Rick sent back an immediate text with Mrs. Spencer's number. Still sitting in the chair in the hallway outside Matthew's room, he tilted his head back and closed his eyes, trying to come up with the right way to break this horrific news to her.

For the third time that night, Jax was jolted by the sound of footsteps and the feeling that someone was approaching. He sat up, brought his eyes into focus, and saw Julia striding toward him. The sight could not have been more welcome.

She sat down next to him and took his hand, which he gladly offered to her. "Oh, Jax, I am so, so sorry. I checked Matthew's chart at the nurses' station. Have you been here all night?"

Jax nodded, wiped the tears from his eyes, and told her about his night. He told her about Daddy Spencer's brief appearance as well as his fear that Mommy Spencer didn't even know her son had died.

Julia said, "Jax, instead of you buying me dinner, how about if I treat you to a gourmet breakfast in the hospital cafeteria? They make some mean scrambled eggs and bacon."

Taking her hand in his, he replied, "Sounds like a great first date, Dr. Winston. I gladly accept. However, I have one piece of unfinished business. I'll meet you in the cafeteria."

Julia smiled, squeezed his hand, and walked toward the elevators.

Jax sat down again and dialed the number. He slumped into his chair, tears blurring his view of the sunrise emerging through the clouds. The phone was answered on the fourth ring.

"Hello, is this Mrs. Spencer? My name is Jackson Berman. I'm a lawyer in Cincinnati, and I'm a friend of your son, Matthew. We've never met. I am sorry to say I have some terrible news…"

CHAPTER 11

The first date, although it was under tragic circumstances, was a tremendous success. It lasted more than two hours in a hospital cafeteria, not exactly a place known for soft music and mood lighting. When Jax called Marion to tell her what had happened with Matthew the night before, she swung into action. She enlisted other attorneys to cover his court hearings. He had done the same favor countless times over the years. She rescheduled his afternoon appointments. With the exception of catching up on sleep, the only agenda item was breakfast with Dr. Winston. Julia.

Savoring their third cup of coffee at a table in the rear of the cafeteria, they shared the highlights of their childhood. They discovered some common threads in their stories. The conversation was not only a tremendous icebreaker, but it also served to divert Jax's sadness over the death of Matthew. Jax was, in retrospect, grateful he had broken the rule forbidding emotional involvement with clients. Had he not done so, Matthew would have died alone.

Julia was raised in a small seaside town in Maine, the youngest of eight children. Her father was a commercial fisherman and a volunteer firefighter. Her mother worked as a nurse at the regional hospital in the neighboring town. Julia was a good student, loved school, especially science, and played every sport at her high school. Listening to her, Jax knew she was devoted to her family. Her elder brothers and sisters were always looking out for her. She loved and liked her parents. They were her best friends. He thought he and Julia were alike in their deep respect for and attachment to their parents, but Jax just had one parent, while she had two. She continued her story.

During her senior year, her father picked her up one evening from basketball practice. He spent the day fighting a barn fire. Julia knew something was wrong. Her father looked pale. There were beads of perspiration on his forehead, despite it being winter on the coast of Maine. This alone was not uncommon; her father often suffered temporary effects of exposure to heat and smoke while battling a fire. This time, there was something more. He was unusually quiet; he didn't ask about practice. His driving was erratic during the fifteen-minute ride home. When they reached the house, her mother was not yet home from work. As soon as her father opened the door from the garage into the kitchen, he collapsed. Julia called 911. She was frantically trying to follow the dispatcher's instructions on administering CPR when her mother joined the chaos. Her mom took over while Julia paced back and forth, waiting for the ambulance to arrive. Although it seemed like years, help arrived less than seven minutes after the dispatch. The EMTs took over from Julia's mother, continuing to work on him as they loaded him for transport to the hospital. It was the hospital where her mother had just ended her shift. The EMTs all knew Tom Winston. Not only did they share fire and emergency calls together, but they also gathered at a local pub during the summer after playing softball. This emergency run was personal.

Julia's father was pronounced dead on arrival. This unexpected loss to the family meant a revamping of Julia's plans for college. She had been accepted to the University of Maine in Orono. The academic scholarship paid for tuition and books but not room and board. It would have been an unbearable financial burden for her mother to shoulder alone. Tom's life insurance paid for the funeral and helped with the regular household expenses, but college expenses were unmanageable. Julia knew her mother would do anything, including taking on a second job, to make her dream come true. She could not fathom the idea of inflicting more stress on her. Her mom needed time to grieve and develop a new life, a new normal, without her husband.

The end of one dream usually means there is a new dream ready to take shape. The memory of her father's death and her feelings of complete helplessness when she was following the CPR instructions inspired her to work in the medical field. A traditional college education might be out of reach at the moment, but there were other ways to pursue higher education. Julia enrolled in nursing school. She lived at home with her mother, which not only saved money but also ensured her mother would not be alone in the house that was once filled with her husband and their eight active, noisy kids.

After completing nursing school, Julia landed a job at the same hospital as her mother, and they enjoyed driving together when they worked the same shift. Living at home enabled her to save most of her paycheck. She completed her undergraduate degree at the University of Southern Maine while she continued to work as a nurse. Her perfect 4.0 GPA plus her nursing experience earned her a full scholarship to the medical school at Tufts University. The rest, as they say, is history.

Their first date would have gone on potentially forever except for Julia's call to duty on the oncology floor. Before she gave him a quick kiss on his cheek, she accepted his offer of dinner that evening.

When Jax returned home, before he crawled under the covers, he moved the clothes he had set out the previous day for his first date. They would be perfect for his second date with Julia. Drifting into a deep sleep, he vowed to remember his ratty sweatshirt and jeans were a great look for a first date after all.

Their first date, which had been catapulted into their second date, was just as successful as their time together in the hospital cafeteria. Now accompanied by mood lighting and soft music as well as one of the best wine lists in the city, the conversation between them never lagged, except for the occasional sip of wine. Having explored their pasts together, the dialogue covered everything from music preferences to politics. While there might have been some differing opinions on a few minor issues—Jax preferred Motown and blues music, while Julia liked her rock and roll—it was becoming clear they were quickly building the foundation for a meaningful relationship. A very meaningful relationship.

With the exception of his evenings and overnights with Olivia, Jax and Julia spent virtually all their free time together for the next month. Although he was trying his best to keep the relationship on a slow simmer—since legally he was still married to Catherine—the time he spent with Julia made him realize it was a losing battle. He was head over heels about this funny, warm, and genuine woman, who was also a skilled doctor. She just happened to order a drink at a bar at the same time that he, too, needed a drink. *Ah, the mysteries of life,* he mused.

Casting aside his intentions to play it cool, he dropped in on Julia at her office. Jax knew enough about her daily schedule to show up after she finished her rounds. When she looked up from her pile of reports and saw him standing in her doorway, she jumped up and moved in for a kiss. The kiss confirmed he had made the right move.

"This is a pleasant surprise. I hope you're not at the hospital because of more bad news about someone close to you."

"Oh, no, not at all," replied Jax quickly as he sat down on the sofa in her office. Julia sat down next to him, holding his hand.

Jax took a deep breath before saying, "Actually, I'm here to learn something about you that I don't yet know."

Julia leaned back on the sofa. "What would that be?"

Jax smiled, still holding her hand, and answered, "I was wondering if somewhere in that marvelous and disciplined mind of yours there might also be an impulsive streak." He paused as he settled back into the sofa. "Well, is there?"

Julia, looking a bit perplexed, thought for a minute before answering, "It's been known to make an appearance in my life on occasion. Not recently, though. Why?"

"You do have the next three days off, don't you?"

Julia smiled. "You've been paying attention to my schedule?"

"Yes," Jax smirked. "I have been paying attention."

Still holding his hand, Julia asked, "Why are you asking?"

Taking another deep breath, Jax replied, "I was hoping you're impulsive enough to fly to my place in Hilton Head for the next three days. We could fly out tonight or early tomorrow morning."

Julia let go of Jax's hand and rose from the sofa. She walked over to the window overlooking the hospital parking lot. Jax, afraid to speak or make a move, waited for what seemed like an eternity for her to reply. He was mentally kicking himself for making this bold leap so soon into their relationship when she turned and looked at him.

"I'm impulsive enough to go to Hilton Head with you."

Jax jumped up and took in her arms. After several minutes of playful kissing, they broke apart, both breathless.

Julia said, "We could leave tonight. I get off in an hour."

Jax couldn't resist the urge to respond to the double entendre. "Good thing I work out, Dr. Winston," he said with a wink.

After she finished laughing uproariously at his joke, she kissed him again and said, "See you tonight, Mr. Berman. Then we'll see just how effective your workouts have been."

Walking to his car, his almost euphoric state was tarnished by thoughts of Catherine. He had never been at the vacation home without Catherine and Olivia. It was their sanctuary and their traditional holiday venue. Was he rushing this relationship with Julia? Would ghosts of vacations past put a damper on their first trip together? These thoughts persisted as he drove to the office for his afternoon appointments.

Turning off the ignition, Jax remained in his car. After a few minutes, he shook his head vigorously and exited. *The only way to find out is to go on the trip. If there are ghosts lingering, it's time to exorcise them,* he resolved.

*****

Seated in first class, Jax and Julia sipped a flute of champagne, and he gave her a mental walking tour of Hilton Head. Julia had never visited the island.

Parking the rental car in the driveway of his home, Jax unloaded the luggage while Julia retrieved her carry-on bag from the back seat. Jax took the key from his jacket pocket and unlocked the door.

When they entered the house, Jax found everything to be clean and in order. Catherine and Olivia had been the last ones here, when they came down during her school break. The family photos were displayed on tabletops and walls in the hallway. Jax glanced at them as he carried the suitcases to the master bedroom. *So far, so good,* he thought. Memories of time past weren't lurking in the shadows. The photos were reminders of happy times, but there were no feelings of regret. Jax realized, in just those few moments, he could embrace warm memories without having to abandon them in favor of new ones.

Their first vacation together was, in Jax's mind, almost magical. They took long walks on the beach facing the Atlantic Ocean and Calibogue Bay. They bicycled along the maze of bike trails interwoven in and out of the woods, marshes, and golf courses. Watching the sunset from one of the many waterfront restaurants, sharing a bottle of wine, was a perfect end to a perfect day. Three perfect days.

Their first night together was almost magical as well. Although nothing had been spoken between them, they knew this vacation was not going to include separate bedrooms. They had not yet spent a night together, but they both understood they were on the threshold of "the next level" in their relationship. Returning home after dinner, Jax poured a small glass of port wine for them. They took their drinks to the porch and nestled together in one of the oversize lounging chairs. They kissed as they sipped their aperitif. Draining the last of the port from their glasses, Jax rose from the chair. Julia took his outstretched hand, and they walked arm in arm to the bedroom.

Jax undressed first, turned back the duvet on the bed, and slipped under the covers. From there, he watched as Julia slowly undressed, never once looking away from Jax. Stepping out of her lilac laced bra and panties, she joined him beneath the sheets. Slow kisses and caresses gave way to hungry passion. They explored each other throughout the night. It was dawn when the satiated couple drifted off to sleep.

While nothing was stated between them, they were falling in love with each other. They knew it without having to say the words. Not yet.

In the blink of an eye, the vacation came to an end, and they returned to the real world and the real demands of their lives. Julia jumped into her grueling schedule of appointments, hospital rounds, and new-patient evaluations. Her surgery schedule was jammed. Jax returned to a pile of new files. His first two days back in the office were filled with new clients and their new problems. He managed to meet them all, get the necessary information from them, and put their troubled minds somewhat at ease as together they navigated through their criminal case with Jax at the helm.

The evenings and the nights were reserved for the new couple, either at her place or his. The only interruption in this marvelous new schedule was Jax's time with Olivia. Although he freely admitted to himself he was falling in love with Julia—not that he had admitted this to her yet—his time with Olivia was sacred. Another reason why he was so in love with Julia was her ready acceptance of his relationship with his daughter. They agreed Olivia should not meet her yet, especially since Jax's relationship and lines of communication with Catherine were on a day-to-day basis. When Jax would pick up Olivia, he would either be greeted by a friendly and talkative Catherine or a dark and brooding Catherine. There was no way to know which Catherine would answer the door. Catherine's mood was impacting Olivia's mood. Talkative Catherine meant Olivia was talkative, jabbering almost nonstop with Jax as she filled him in on everything she had done since their last visit. But dark Catherine produced a silent and sulking Olivia, at least, for the first hour she and Jax were together. A master interrogator of witnesses in the courtroom, Jax was no match for Olivia if she did not want to answer his questions about her friends and activities.

The second day back at the office, Marion was waiting for him when he opened the door. Jax knew something big must have happened; otherwise, she would be working at her desk.

"Did you see the news?" Jax knew he was right.

"Not yet. I opted for some rock-and-roll music while I drove in this morning. I should have paid attention to current events. What happened?"

As he followed Marion into her office, she replied, "Officer-involved shooting downtown in the West End. White police officer shot and killed a black teenage boy. Details are sketchy, and the press clearly doesn't know all the details because the officer, Kevin Wilson, has already scheduled an appointment with you. He'll be here today at noon."

He pulled up local news sites on her computer to find any details about the shooting. He didn't find anything more than what Marion had told him. White cop. Black teenage boy. One shot to the chest. Victim was unarmed. Two witnesses saw the victim running from the officer, the officer in close pursuit. The victim turned and pulled something from the pocket of his hoodie. Initial report confirmed the victim was unarmed. Jax wondered what the victim was pulling from his pocket.

Marion was still talking while he read the news website. "Kevin Wilson is twenty-five years old. He started on road patrol after completing the police academy three years ago. For the past six months, he'd been working on neighborhood street patrol in the West End, part of the 'one cop, one neighborhood' program. The president of the police union also called. Had lots of great things to say about Officer Wilson and said he has the full support of the department."

"Helpful information. Is the union going to help him with my fee? That's happened in the past, you know, with other cops I've represented."

Marion sat down and answered, "Yes, he made that clear. Officer Wilson himself told me there would be no problem paying your fee, whatever it is. He didn't say anything, but the union president told me Kevin comes from a wealthy family in northern Ohio. The other cops in his academy class nicknamed him "Trust Fund". He donates his entire police salary to local charities serving underprivileged kids."

"Next thing you're going to tell me is he was an Eagle Scout."

Marion smiled and said, "I didn't get that much information over the phone, but I'll bet you ten dollars he was."

"Not taking that bet, Marion."

Kevin Wilson arrived at the office promptly at noon. Five minutes into the interview, Jax gave silent thanks for not having taken the bet with Marion. Yes, Kevin Wilson had been an Eagle Scout. Yes, Kevin Wilson donated his police salary to local kid charities. He seemed too good to be true. There was a saying, "If something seems too good to be true, it probably is." With that in mind, Jax spent another hour getting to know his most recent notorious client. By the end of the conversation, he wished he could have wound back time and spent the hour another way. Despite his accomplishments and his charitable spirit, Kevin Wilson was a freak show.

The upstanding former Eagle Scout, born to a wealthy philanthropic family, learned by example to pay it forward. What he learned elsewhere was a complete disdain for those less privileged than him. He donated his police salary to charity, but writing a check never got his hands dirty. He didn't have to interact with those who benefitted from his generosity. He never had the experience of putting faces and names to the causes he supported. Officer Wilson's words and his tone of voice left no room for doubt. His view of the world bordered on white supremacy.

While this was certainly not the first nor would it be the last time Jax found a client to be offensive, repulsive, and reprehensible, this guy made the hairs on his neck not only stand up but also try to flee the room. Jax made every effort to ensure his facial expressions did not betray his feelings. His phone beeped. It was Marion.

"Jax," she said in a low library-volume voice, "Jim Gaddis is calling about Officer Wilson. Do you want to take the call?"

How in the hell did Gaddis make the connection between Jax and Officer Wilson? Jim Gaddis, chief assistant prosecutor, right-hand man to the county prosecutor John Dawson, essentially ran the office while John was out making public appearances. In other words, John was constantly running for reelection and left the real work to Gaddis. Jim always seemed to have a sixth sense about the details and direction of the big cases, such as a white police officer shooting an unarmed black teenager. Sensing Officer Wilson would be in Jax's office, however, was bordering on creepy.

"I'll come to your office. Give me a minute."

Excusing himself from Officer Wilson's company, making some veiled statement about seeing to an unrelated matter, Jax slipped over to Marion's office and took the call.

"Good afternoon, Jim. To what do I owe the pleasure of this call?"

While Jax and Jim had squared off against each other countless times in the courtroom, they shared a mutual admiration and respect. But they were not personal friends. Although Jax got together with John Dawson regularly for an evening cocktail or two, Jax and Jim never socialized. When one called the other, there was no small talk or friendly banter. It was strictly business.

"Officer Kevin Wilson is the reason for the call. Word has it the cop union is retaining you to represent him."

Jax was truly impressed with the inside information. "You apparently know more than I do. Besides, I don't know there's any need for my services. At least not yet."

"Trust me, there will be a need for your services. Sooner rather than later. We're convening a special grand jury tomorrow."

Jax thought for a moment before asking, "Are you calling to give me a preview of coming attractions?"

Chuckling into the phone, he responded, "Let's just say the witnesses who have come forward are very compelling. We're aiming for a murder indictment."

This really stunned Jax. Murder? They thought this cop intended to kill this kid? Usually in these circumstances, the charge is voluntary manslaughter; the homicide was committed under extreme duress and provocation. Murder? The prosecutor thought he could prove it was a deliberate act? He wondered if his gut feeling about Kevin Wilson's true persona was shared by others, perhaps in the police department or the Prosecutor's Office.

"That's a hell of a preview of coming attractions. Let's suppose the union does retain me. Can you keep me in the loop? There's no need for the media circus that would swirl around an actual arrest of Officer Wilson. We can arrange to surrender him if there's an indictment."

Jim Gaddis was a hard-nosed prosecutor, but he also had a compassionate side as well as a general disdain for the local media. He never missed the chance to kill a good story. "No problem, Jax. I'll be in touch after the grand jury makes their decision."

CHAPTER 12

It had only been a few weeks since their first trip to Hilton Head, but Jax and Julia had been able to arrange their schedules and slip away again for the weekend. Olivia was attending a Girl Scout weekend campout, and Julia switched hospital rotations earlier in the week with another oncologist. They booked a Friday-afternoon flight and arrived in time to quickly unpack and change clothes.

Friday-night dinner consisted of wine and fresh shrimp grilled to perfection with just the right hint of garlic in the butter sauce. They shared more stories and memories, and together they marveled at the setting sun, with its glorious reds and oranges. Nine holes of golf the next morning were followed by an afternoon walk on the beach. Holding hands and running through the rolling waves, they alternated between lively conversation and comfortable silence. Julia regaled Jax with childhood stories about growing up in a large family. An only child, he never experienced sibling rivalry or comradery. With all their physical activity during the day as well as their nights, dinner on Saturday night consisted of steaks on the grill, a fresh tomato caprese salad, and Jax's favorite red wine.

Driving home from the Cincinnati airport on Sunday evening, he called Catherine to arrange dinner with Olivia the following evening. There was no answer. Although this was unusual, Jax didn't dwell on it. Instead, as he and Julia listened to her favorite satellite radio station for rock and roll, they talked about their upcoming week's schedules. They made plans to see each other as often as possible.

Jax delivered Julia to her door. After a lingering kiss and a warm embrace, Jax was back in his car, driving home. He tried Catherine's phone again, but she didn't pick up.

Monday morning was foggy and rainy, a harbinger of late-fall and early-winter weather. Having continually failed to get an answer from Catherine, he decided to go to Olivia's school at the end of the day and pick her up after soccer practice.

Jax made his way through rush-hour traffic. He dashed into the office, had a quick conversation with Marion, picked up his court files, and walked briskly to the courthouse. After a half-dozen pretrial conferences and arraignments, he returned to his office shortly before noon. Marion had a corned beef on rye waiting for him, fresh from Harold's Deli. While he ate his lunch, he returned phone calls and emails. *Just another typical Monday,* mused Jax. In between returning phone calls, he called Catherine. No answer.

The afternoon found Jax spending most of his time on the phone with Kevin Wilson. Police policy requires any officer involved in a shooting to be placed on administrative leave, with pay, until an internal investigation is completed. Jax acknowledged the rationale behind this policy, but he understood it left an officer like Kevin Wilson with a lot of idle time. Like other police officers he represented over the years, Kevin filled his free time calling to talk about the case and to ask Jax's prediction of the outcome. Just like the other police officers who had been Jax's clients, he refused to make any predictions. Whether the case was an officer-involved shooting or any other criminal charge, neither Jax nor anyone could predict the outcome. There were just too many human variables, from the assistant prosecutor assigned to the case to the judge presiding at trial and the twelve ordinary citizens called upon to serve on a jury of one's peers. Somewhere the truth was supposed to emerge, as bright and obvious as the sun shining in the sky. At least, it was supposed to.

Finally able to end the phone call with Kevin, he returned a handful of calls. He changed out of his suit and into his favorite pair of faded jeans and a long-sleeved golf shirt. It was a good choice for dinner with his daughter. Driving to Olivia's school, listening to Julia's rock-and-roll station, he thought about Olivia. He faced the grim reality that she was no longer the little girl he used to coax to sleep with bedtime stories. She was fast approaching her eleventh birthday. She had gone on overnights with her friends and her Girl

Scout troop. Having listened to his friends lamenting over the tribulations of a teenage girl's roller coaster of emotions, he was in no hurry for Olivia to grow up. Jax resolved to enjoy every moment with his not-so-little girl as the clock ticked toward the teen years.

Jax turned into the parking lot of Olivia's school and proceeded toward the rear parking lot adjoining the soccer field. Perfect timing. The team had just finished their practice and were picking up their backpacks and water bottles. Jax walked toward the team. He knew all the girls, having watched Olivia play on teams with them since kindergarten. He exchanged quick greetings with them as they walked toward their waiting parents. When the last one had passed, he realized Olivia was not among them.

He headed toward the coach, who was packing equipment.

"Coach Meyers," Jax called as he approached. "I'm here for Olivia. Where is she?"

"Hello, Mr. Berman. Unusual, but Olivia wasn't at practice today. When I asked the girls, they said she hadn't come to school."

Jax paused before replying, "I had no idea. Olivia rarely misses a day of school. In fact, she's had perfect attendance the past two years."

Coach Meyers picked up the duffel bags and said, "I wish I could give you more information. I don't know if anyone is still in the school office, but you could call and see if your wife phoned in this morning."

"Good idea, Coach." Jax quickened his pace back to his car.

The school secretary was still in the office. Jax learned Catherine had called early in the morning and said Olivia was not feeling well and would stay home for the day. Catherine gave no specific details, but she told the secretary she doubted Olivia would be in school the following day. In her entire, albeit brief, school career, Olivia had never missed two days in a row. Jax was worried. There must be something really wrong with Olivia. Why in the hell had Catherine not let Jax know? Why hadn't she answered her phone?

The sun began its descent in the western sky as Jax drove hurriedly to Catherine's house. No music on his sound system, Jax used the silence to mull over the events of the past two days. There was no word at all from Olivia, not one of her silly phone calls to ask about his day. Catherine would not answer her phone. Olivia, a student who prided herself on her perfect attendance, was not in school today and was not expected to be there tomorrow. Catherine gave no specific details to the school explaining why Olivia was going to miss school, only that she was not feeling well. This had never been enough to keep her from going to school; it was always an argument to convince her to stay home from school even if she had a fever. Olivia would always insist, "It will pass" and "I will feel better by lunchtime." Catherine didn't let Jax know there was anything wrong with Olivia. As Jax thought more about this, he wasn't even certain that Olivia attended the Girl Scout overnight the previous weekend.

He pulled into Catherine's driveway, and the decorative lighting lining the walkway and the front door switched on. It was not unusual because it was monitored by a light sensor, and the setting sun kicked on the lights. The garage door was closed and locked. At the front door, Jax could see through the windows on either side of the main entrance. The front rooms were dark, but there was the glow of a light peeking from the kitchen in the rear of the house. Jax sensed an eerie calm. There was no music, no television, and no background noise that comes from a normal home occupied by parents and kids, especially during a weekday evening. Usually Catherine or Olivia could be seen or heard outside, then in the kitchen and gathering room while together they prepared dinner, talked about their day, and began homework.

Jax didn't have to ring the doorbell to know the house was empty, but he rang it anyway. He waited. He rang again. He waited. He went to the back of the house. Peering in the kitchen window confirmed a single light was on over the kitchen island, but it was the only light on.

Returning to his car and thankful none of his former neighbors witnessed him sleuthing around his old home, he tried Catherine's cell phone once more. No answer.

He needed to get in touch with Rick but not over the phone. The growing knot in the pit of his stomach signaled there was something very wrong. It was only seven o'clock; he knew he was still at his office. Jax was right. *At least, I had been right about something today*, he thought to himself, entering the lobby of Rick's office.

He walked through the dark waiting room and past the empty offices of the paralegals and clerical staff. He reached the corner office and found Rick stretched out on his sofa, shoes off, tie undone, reviewing a stack of papers. Another divorce client, another set of documents detailing the client's marriage—assets, liabilities, and secrets. Jax wondered how big the stack of papers would be to describe him and Catherine.

Only slightly startled by the intrusion, Rick sat up, cast the paperwork aside, and offered Jax a quick beer. They twisted off the tops of their bottles, and Jax updated him on everything following his return from Hilton Head yesterday.

Rick contemplated while he drank his beer. Jax did the same. Rick called Steve Barker. Barker said he hadn't heard from Catherine since last week. He hadn't tried to call her nor had he ever tried to call her because she contacted him almost daily. He said he hadn't really given it much thought; he assumed she went out of town for a few days. Rick asked if he would mind trying to call her, and he agreed.

Jax and Rick hadn't finished their beer before Barker called to say when he tried Catherine's cell phone and home phone, they both went to voice mail. He promised he would notify him immediately when he heard from her.

Jax and Rick left the office and walked around the corner to a small bistro for another beer and a quick cheeseburger. While they ate and drank, they put together explanations, some reasonable and some not so reasonable, for Catherine and Olivia going off the grid. They agreed Jax should get Leonard involved; he was a master at finding people. Jax paid the check, and the two friends walked in opposite directions to their cars.

Listening to soothing jazz in the car, Jax engaged in deep-breathing exercises, a futile effort to calm his nerves. He almost regained his equilibrium when he turned into his driveway. In an instant, his equilibrium dissolved.

Exiting his car, he slowly approached his front door to find the adjacent window broken. Inside, amid the shards of glass on the floor of the foyer, was a cement block. The heavy ceramic pots next to his door—pots he and Olivia together purchased and filled with pansies—were turned over, and the flowers were unceremoniously dumped on the sidewalk.

What the fuck? Who the fuck? Entering the house while dialing 911, he thought today was the worst day of his life. Little did he know that tomorrow would be even worse.

CHAPTER 13

The early morning sun peeked through the partially closed drapes in the bedroom, rousing him from a fitful sleep. It was after three o'clock when he dozed off. The police hadn't left his home until midnight. Taking photos of the damage to his home and Jax having to fill out a victim's report for the officers all seemed to go on endlessly, especially when the lead detective asked the age-old question, "Mr. Berman, do you know anyone who would want to do this to you?"

Reminding the detective who he was and what he did for a living, the detective agreed it was, in this case, a rhetorical question. There were countless people who would have it in for Jax: old clients, victims of old clients for whom Jax had won an acquittal, and witnesses who felt Jax had brutally cross-examined them on the witness stand. Jax could go on and on. The detective put his pen back in his jacket pocket, gave Jax a copy of the report, and advised Jax to contact his insurance agent in the morning to report the damage. Jax, acting as if he hadn't already thought of it, thanked the detective for his time and advice. The two shook hands, both knowing this would likely go unsolved.

After the police left, he was too keyed up to think about going to bed. He spent the next hour cleaning up the mess and taping cardboard over the broken window. He was somewhat comforted by safeguarding his home as well as possible, because where would he have found a window-replacement business that made house calls in the middle of the night? He poured himself a short glass of red wine and took it to bed. Settled in with the blankets and pillows just as he liked them, he spent the rest of his wakefulness focusing on the real problem of the day. *Where in the hell was Olivia?*

The question popped into his mind within seconds of the morning sun awakening him. He showered and dressed hastily. He needed to take quick action to resolve the mystery of his daughter's whereabouts. Lying in bed was accomplishing nothing.

Somehow, despite his singular focus on finding his daughter, Jax arrived safely at his office without having committed any major traffic offenses. There were no sirens and flashing lights in hot pursuit; that was a good sign. He let himself into his office, chatted briefly with Marion as she filled him in on his schedule for the day, made a quick cup of coffee, and retreated to his office. Bailey woke from her early morning nap, which she had been enjoying in his chair. He picked up the yawning cat, held her to his chest, and stroked her on her neck. Purring and nuzzling Jax in appreciation, they enjoyed a few quiet minutes before the rush of the day.

Jax spent the morning dashing between courtrooms. He secured two new clients' release from jail, and he scheduled another client's case for jury trial. He met with two judges and their prosecutors in pretrial conferences in the hope of resolving their cases without trial and without Jax's clients seeing the inside of prison. All in all, it was a productive morning. None of this distracted him from his worry over Olivia. Walking back to his office, his cell phone rang. The caller ID showed it was Leonard.

"Leo, please tell me you have some good news," Jax breathed into the phone.

"I've got news. Can't say if it's good news or bad news yet. I've been watching your former home. Catherine pulled into the driveway a few minutes ago, parked the car in the garage. I don't know if Olivia was in the car with her or not. I didn't see her sitting, but she could have been reclined in her seat. She closed the garage door. I couldn't see anything after that."

"Stay put, Leo. I'm on my way."

Jax drove down the tree-lined street toward the house. He spotted Leonard parked a hundred feet beyond the house. Jax pulled into the driveway. He exited his vehicle and met him at the bottom of the driveway. They agreed Jax should go to the door alone. Leonard retreated to the sidewalk and watched while Jax rang the doorbell.

After ringing a third time, he heard the sound of the dead bolt lock being moved to an open position. The doorknob turned, and the door cracked open. Catherine's face appeared. She looked at Jax without saying a word, but her cold glare spoke volumes. There was indeed something terribly wrong.

"Catherine," Jax said in the calmest and quietest tone he could muster. "I've been trying to get in touch with you and Olivia for days. Is everything all right? Where is she?"

Jax could see she was wearing an old sweatshirt with mismatched sweatpants, certainly not the daily fashion she was accustomed to wearing. She had no makeup either. This was also out of the norm.

"Everything is fine, Jax. Olivia and I just needed some alone time, away from your intrusion, for a few days. You can leave now."

"Is Olivia in school today?"

"Of course she's in school, Jax. Where else would she be? You know how important her perfect-attendance awards are to her."

Jax paused, careful to find the right tone of voice when he said, "Olivia missed school yesterday. I was worried because on the rare occasion when she does miss school, you've always let me know. This time, I didn't hear from you."

Jax recognized the change in her facial expression because he had experienced it many times over the miserable final months of their marriage. "I don't know why you would think she missed school."

"I think so because the school secretary told me she missed school. I don't think it, Catherine. I know it. Where is Olivia?"

Catherine closed the door in his face. She secured the dead bolt.

The conversation left Jax bewildered. He knew Olivia missed school yesterday. The soccer coach and the school secretary confirmed it. Yet Catherine just stood here minutes ago and denied it. The school secretary told him Catherine said Olivia would be out of school for two days. Yet again, Catherine just looked him in the eye and told him that Olivia had been in school yesterday and that she was there today. *Who's losing their mind here? Catherine or me?* Jax agonized.

Leonard, too far away to hear the conversation, was able to watch the exchange between Jax and his estranged wife. He was familiar enough with Catherine to be able to assess the tone of the conversation without hearing the words. The two men met at the end of the driveway.

Jax ran his fingers through his hair and sighed, "Leo, something is terribly wrong. Everything is completely off here. Olivia's probably not in school, but I'm going there now to find out. If she's not there, I'll call Andrew for help. Don't you think it's best if you stay to watch the house in case Catherine leaves?"

"I do, buddy. Call me when you're leaving the school. If you have to call Andrew, let him know he can count on me for any assistance."

They shook hands a little longer than was customary, then they went to their cars.

Jax had his cell phone to his ear before even closing the door when he left the school office. Andrew answered the phone on the second ring.

"Jax, it's been weeks since I've seen or heard from you. What's up?"

Andrew Ferguson had been the county sheriff for more than twenty years. After winning his first election, he ran for reelection for four terms with no opposition. Sheriff Ferguson was a household name in the Cincinnati area. He began his career in law enforcement as a patrol officer in a small suburban police department. He transferred to the position of deputy in the Sheriff's Office, working night shift in the county jail. He moved through the ranks of road patrol and the detectives unit. Spending a few years as an undercover narcotics officer added to his experience. His name was in the papers dozens of times as the lead officer or detective on a newsworthy murder or drug bust. During his years of undercover work, he managed to find the time and the energy to attend evening classes at a local law school. His law degree made him the first sheriff in the county who was a licensed attorney. His tall stature, muscular physique, and ruggedly handsome face made him a local celebrity. It was no wonder he easily won his first election, and nobody challenged him for reelection.

Andrew counted Jax among a short list of close friends who practiced criminal defense. Conventional wisdom would question how there could be such a bond between two people on opposite sides of the system. Jax represented clients who had been investigated and charged with a crime. It was his job to undo the sheriff's hard work building a solid case against his client. Despite the professional rivalry, Andrew and Jax had a deep friendship. Whenever Andrew ran for reelection, Jax was honored to be his campaign chairman. Being the chairman of a campaign when the candidate is running unopposed is not exactly hard work.

"I need your help." Jax filled him in on the events of the past days.

"It definitely sounds strange, Jax. Let's try this for starters. I'll send a detective to Catherine's house for a wellness check. This would be reasonable since Olivia has missed two days of school, and Catherine has not provided the school with a doctor's note. I'll do it right away and report back to you."

"That's a good start, Andrew. You know where to find me. I owe you big time."

Jax returned to his office and moved Bailey out of his chair when his cell phone rang. Andrew's name appeared on the screen.

"Detective Audrey Simpson paid a visit to the home. We thought it would be a good tactic to send a female detective. Your wife answered the door. She let the detective into the home. She found your daughter in her pajamas under a blanket in the family room, watching cartoons. Catherine explained she was diagnosed with a bronchial virus. Audrey sat down near Olivia to strike up a conversation with her, but Olivia didn't respond to any of her questions. She would not make eye contact with her. Detective Simpson didn't notice any obvious signs of illness. No coughing, no signs of fever or chills. She reports that Olivia seemed shy, but not sick."

"That's bullshit, Andrew. You know Olivia. Is she a shy child?"

"Not at all. I told Audrey what I knew about Olivia. I told her, among other things, that she is the least shy child I've ever known. She can strike up a conversation with a perfect stranger. None of this feels right."

"Thanks to you, I've now got more information than I did an hour ago. It's just not the information I was hoping for. Rick

Meredith is representing me in my divorce. I'll get in touch with him and plan our next move."

Before Sheriff Ferguson ended the call, he said, "Let Rick know to call me if there is anything at all we can do for you. Please keep me posted."

Marion rescheduled his afternoon appointments. There was no way in hell he could focus on anything but Olivia. Driving home, he called Rick to give him the update. Rick arranged to meet him at his home within the hour. When Jax arrived, the glass company was replacing his broken window. *At least, something is being returned to normal,* he thought as he waved to the workers and let himself inside through the side door. Changing from his suit into jeans and a sweatshirt, he tried to put together in his own mind a plan of action to share with Rick. Jax preferred being the attorney plotting a strategy to being the client hoping his lawyer could come up with a plan. He went downstairs, poured himself a quick drink, and waited for his attorney to save the day.

CHAPTER 14

Another day, another drive to the office, fighting rush-hour traffic on the parkway rolling into the city along the river. Jax never tired of driving this route and watching the boat traffic making its way upriver to Pittsburgh or downriver toward Louisville. As a child, his boating experience consisted of taking the car ferry across the river from Ohio to Kentucky. He and his mother rode it occasionally as a treat, topping off the trip with a quick lunch at a hot-dog stand on the Kentucky side of the river. He hadn't been on the river since his day with Matthew Spencer. The memory of the day with a good but tragically misunderstood kid—coupled with the mental image of Matthew lying in the hospital bed, taking his last breath—sunk his already-somber mood to even lower depths. He must refocus. *Get it together. It's another beautiful autumn day. A great day to be alive. It's another day of court and needy clients.* Today, however, was not just another day.

Rick arrived at Jax's house in record time yesterday evening. Sharing a bottle of red wine, they tried to make some sense of the past few days. Olivia missed two days of school. Catherine looked him in the eye and denied it. Detective Simpson's observations of Olivia and her attempted conversation with the girl were frighteningly unlike the Olivia Berman Jax had raised. Olivia had never been shy in her life. Her first words likely were spoken to a stranger. She loved adults and children and always had something to talk about. She was comfortable in the adult world and in her circle of friends and peers. She had never gone one day without phoning Jax if they weren't going to spend time together. She hadn't called him for four days.

When Rick left, he realized he had gone an entire day without talking to Julia. This troubled him. A lot. There was no doubt he was falling in love, maybe for the first time in his life. These months with Julia were unlike his years with Catherine, even the early years. There was a peacefulness to this relationship. Shockingly he hadn't thought about her at all today. *Dammit*, he thought, *Catherine is really doing a number on my head.* Even though it was late and Julia was probably in bed, he dialed her number.

Her voice, when she answered the phone, was undeniably that of a person roused from sleep. She denied it, saying she was awake, reading. For the next hour, Jax told her about the events of the day, and he confided to her his darkest emotions. She listened with a kind and sympathetic ear, offering her insight and advice only when Jax asked for it. Sharing the depths of their feelings was another step toward a lifelong relationship.

Parking his car, Jax called Catherine again. No answer. He tried the landline. It went straight to voice mail. He sat in his car, listening to some blues on the radio in an attempt to decompress and get into his professional mode. *Time for your game face.* He switched off the radio.

Marion was feeding Bailey in the kitchen when Jax entered. He knew better than to interrupt breakfast.

"You don't look so good, Jax," observed Marion, putting the bowl on the floor.

"Long night, Marion. I'll rally after my first coffee. What fun awaits me today?"

Marion poured him a cup before answering, "You have a pretty light morning. Only two court appearances and they're both downtown. I've scheduled Officer Wilson this afternoon. I blocked out two hours. You're going to need it because the prosecutor sent over their discovery this morning. It's a thick pile of evidence they intend to use. I reviewed it quickly. It's not pretty. Not pretty at all."

Marion Anderson had never attended law school, but she was the smartest lawyer Jax had ever known. Her on-the-job training at Lamping and Jacobs as well as her decade with Jax gave her not only a real-world legal education but also a very pragmatic approach.

Her insights into Jax's clients and the information she obtained from them were invaluable. She was able to assist with trial preparation but, more importantly, with the best way to deal with each client's personality. Client control, Jax learned from Malcolm Lamping, was as valuable as sharp skills in the courtroom.

Taking his coffee into his office, he sat down and gazed out the window in a vain attempt to set aside his fears about Olivia. After several minutes of staring and wondering, he realized all he could muster was half of his mental energies. He opened the evidence file on Kevin Wilson, and he spent a few minutes reviewing the prosecution's evidence.

A copy of his personnel records from the police department established an exemplary record. *Almost too exemplary*, he thought as he scanned the pages of Officer Wilson's service with the department over the past five years. Assigned as a road patrol officer when he was hired, he earned three commendations during his rookie year. Last year, he had been recommended to take the exam for promotion to sergeant. Devoting several months of preparation for the test, he took the exam last month and was awaiting the results. Then he shot Henry Glover. Officer Wilson had been on administrative leave with pay, and his career and his life had been on hold since the bullet left the chamber of his service revolver.

Taking a quick look at the antique wall clock hanging in his office, he closed the file and headed to the courthouse.

He only had two court appearances, but it was more than two hours later when he was finally able to return to his office. Tossing his suit jacket onto the sofa, Jax sat at his desk, moved a napping Bailey from the top of the Kevin Wilson discovery file, and continued reading. Marion was right. It wasn't pretty.

His high school records were almost as perfect as his personnel records. Kevin excelled in his grades, and he played basketball and baseball. He was inducted into the National Honor Society. He enrolled at the University of Cincinnati School of Criminal Justice, earning his degree six months after being hired by the Cincinnati Police Department. Jax was certain Officer Wilson would be a sympathetic figure for a jury. This kid would be any parent's dream. How could any juror possibly believe he would intentionally shoot and kill someone?

With the turn of one more page in the file, his hopes were crushed. Jax cast his eyes on a series of color photographs of a young Kevin Wilson, probably age sixteen or seventeen, dressed in the uniform of a local underground organization named the Sentinels. The Sentinels, a dark chapter of local history for decades, is a notorious white-supremacist organization. It had been in existence since the end of the Second World War. Although none of its members had ever been convicted of hate crimes, there had always been a groundswell of rumors that the group's members had been involved in a number of arsons and assaults on members of the black community. Examining the photos, Jax knew by the ribbons and patches on Kevin's shirt that he had been more than just a rank-and-file member. He was one of the leaders when these photos were taken. Jax wondered if his client was still involved with the club. Not that it really made much difference. You might be able to take the man out of the Sentinels, but you probably would not be able to take the Sentinels out of the man.

Scratching the top of Bailey's head, Jax spent the next several minutes contemplating the ripple effect of this information. The impact extended far beyond the criminal case. The city was on edge since the shooting of Henry Glover. Social media was buzzing with posts and comments on both sides of the conflict. Leaders of the black community were filling the airwaves on local radio shows, demanding answers. They held town meetings screaming for justice. A group of more than fifty community activists stormed the most recent city-council meeting, dressed in T-shirts with Henry's school photo emblazoned on the front. Chanting and yelling, they demanded quick action by council. They wanted Henry's grieving mother to be paid a million dollars or else they were going to "tear this city apart." If and when they learned a Sentinel was hired as a police officer, the town would explode. Cincinnati is not a city immune to civil unrest. The Henry Glover case had the potential to be the latest episode of violent conflict.

Jax was considering the possible scenarios, none of them happy, when his thoughts were interrupted by his office door opening. Rick walked in and closed the door. Jax could tell the day was going to get worse. Rick wouldn't have come in person to deliver good news.

Rick sat down on the sofa, and he sank back into the cushions.

"For God's sake, what's going on?" asked Jax.

Rick said in a voice that was barely audible, "I just got off the phone with Barker. Jax, before I lay this on you, let me tell you Steve was stunned by Catherine's allegations."

Jax stood up and walked to the sofa. "Allegations? What the hell? Spit it out."

Rick sat up and bent over, looking at the floor. "Catherine alleges you have been sexually abusing Olivia since you and she separated."

Jax could not comprehend. It seemed like a windstorm, high-pitched noise whirring in his ears. *Maybe this is what it feels like to lose consciousness,* he thought. "What the fuck? I know she's hated me for a long, long time. But to say this about me? To say it about Olivia?"

"There's more," said Rick, still staring at the floor. "Catherine contacted Children's Protective Services and made a report. She claims Olivia recently disclosed the abuse to her. She claims Olivia told her the abuse has occurred on several occasions during your parenting time. A caseworker met with Catherine, and she interviewed Olivia at school without Catherine being present. Her initial conclusion is, while she does not have sufficient evidence to substantiate the claim, she cannot unsubstantiate it and close the case yet. The case is currently open, and the investigation will continue."

"Holy shit."

"Holy shit is right."

CHAPTER 15

J ax and Rick left the office in search of a quiet place to eat, drink, and reflect. Marion had already left for the day, so fortunately for Jax, there was no reason to put on a brave face. He would never have been able to pull it off. Marion could read his moods like a favorite book. He knew she would have to be made aware of Catherine's insane accusations eventually, but Jax was not ready to talk about it, not with Marion or with anyone else except Rick. What about Julia? Was their relationship too new to endure this crisis? Did she know him well enough to believe in him? Her entire career was devoted to caring for and protecting children. How would she react when she learned he was accused of harming his own child?

Jax shook off these thoughts as they entered a small diner. They slid into the booth to talk freely. Rick ordered two tall locally brewed beers from the bearded and tattooed server, took a legal pad from his briefcase, and started scribbling notes.

Jax took a long sip of beer and reflected, "Now I truly understand how it feels to be blindsided."

Rick stopped writing. "Can you think of any event, anything at all, that could have been misinterpreted by Olivia or by Catherine? Was there any sort of joking around or wrestling around that could have been twisted in their heads?"

"Absolutely not. I've already been combing through the past few years. Olivia is a good little athlete, and she handles herself really well on the soccer field. She plays basketball in a winter league. But my physical activity with her is nothing more than shooting hoops in the driveway and kicking the soccer ball in the backyard. We have—or I should say, Catherine has—a soccer goal set up in the backyard. I would be the goalie and Olivia would practice her kicks. Once she outgrew horsey rides on my back, our physical play has been limited to sports."

Rick sipped his beer. "Expect to be visited tomorrow by the Children's Services caseworker. He or she will call to make arrangements to meet. I recommend you meet at your house. It will give the caseworker an opportunity to see you at home and observe the type of environment you've created for Olivia."

"That seems logical."

"It is crucial," Rick continued, "to get out in front of this thing before it takes on a life of its own. I want to schedule a polygraph for you ASAP."

"For God's sake, I'm feeling like a criminal already."

"You're a person who has been accused of a criminal offense. You're not a criminal. Get a grip, Jax. Remember the advice you give to people seated across your desk accused of something they didn't do. It does happen occasionally, doesn't it? This is just a case of role reversal. You're now sitting on the other side of the desk."

"Good advice, but not terribly comforting. Schedule the polygraph. By the way, the view is much better from my customary side of the desk."

While Jax ordered another round of drinks and went through the motions of choosing an item off the menu, Rick made a few phone calls.

Rick picked up his menu after ending the last call. "Polygraph is the day after tomorrow morning at eight o'clock. You're a morning person, aren't you? Because you have got to be on your toes."

*****

The following morning, just as Rick predicted, Jax received a call from the Children's Services caseworker. They arranged to meet at his home at five o'clock. Jax was home an hour early to make sure the place was in spotless condition. He changed into casual clothes and waited. Promptly at five o'clock, the doorbell rang. He opened the door to a young woman who looked too young to have a driver's license. She extended her hand, introduced herself, and handed him her business card. Emily Cline entered the house for what Jax hoped would be her one and only visit.

The conversation started out very polite and superficial, then it quickly transitioned into an interrogation. For the second time in two days, Jax was experiencing role reversal. He was far more comfortable asking questions than he was answering them, especially questions of such a private nature.

After an hour of exhausting questions from Ms. Cline, she finished writing notes, stood up, shook Jax's hand again, and left. Closing the door, Jax had absolutely no idea how the interview went. Ms. Cline had as good a poker face as he had seen in quite a while.

He called Rick, gave him an update of the meeting, and went upstairs to take the hottest shower he could withstand. Dressing with the intention of staying home and wallowing in his misery, he quickly changed course. Deciding to confront this situation with Julia sooner than later, he dressed to go to her home and share with her the latest chapter in the drama that had become his life.

Julia was pleasantly surprised to see him. At least, thought Jax, her smile and warm kiss told him she was pleased to see him. *We'll see how long that lasts.*

Jax declined Julia's offer of a glass of wine, which signaled there was a clear purpose for the unexpected visit. She settled next to Jax on the sofa facing her fireplace, which was aglow with a warm blaze. Jax could spend the rest of his life in this room, with the woman of his dreams cozied up next to him.

"Julia," he began. "You and I have had the most incredible time together in the short time we've known each other. I still can't believe my luck; I was at the right place at the right time when we met."

Julia stiffened and sat up from her reclining position. "This sounds like an overture to a breakup, Jax."

He took her hands in his. "Not at all. In a way, that would be easier than what I have to tell you."

Still holding her hands, Jax confided everything to her. He started with Olivia's absences from school. He shared with her the findings of the deputy who conducted the wellness visit. He finished by recounting the phone call Rick received from Catherine's lawyer advising him of the sex-abuse accusation.

"Tomorrow morning, bright and early, I'm scheduled for a polygraph exam." He lowered his head. They watched the glow of the fire while struggling to find words. Jax broke the awkward silence. "I will truly understand if you want to distance yourself from my emotional baggage." He released her hands.

Julia remained quiet for what seemed, to him, to be a lifetime. He sat motionless, waiting for her to say something. "I sure wasn't expecting this conversation. I guess I should have known to expect the unexpected. It's what life is all about, right?" she asked with a semblance of a smile on her face. The tears welling in her eyes betrayed her attempt at humor. "This is a lot of information for me to process," she said in a whisper. "During medical school, I worked at the hospital's child-abuse center. I saw children who had endured unspeakable abuse, both physical and emotional. I treated children whose homes were filthy and without electricity, water, and food. Although the rotation there only lasted a few months, much of what I saw has left a permanent impression." The tears started falling down her cheeks.

"I also saw the other side there too. I saw mothers and fathers bringing their kids in time after time, alleging the other parent was harming the kids. But interviews with the children plus the medical evidence led to the conclusion there was no abuse. Instead, it was a bitter and vindictive parent trying to destroy the other parent. What they never understood was the only true victim was the child.

"Jax, I've never met your daughter. I've been with you for several months. Every time we're together, I know you better. In my heart, I can't imagine a scenario where these accusations against you are true. But your daughter would have had her interview and medical exam at Children's. Although I'm not directly affiliated with the child-abuse center, I am on staff at the hospital. This could make for an unnecessary complication for both you and me."

"What are you telling me?" asked Jax as he watched the fire. "Is this the end of us?"

Shaking her head, Julia answered, "Not the end. Let's call it a pause. You need to devote your energy to Olivia and to your current situation. It's your number one priority. I need to maintain professionalism. I need to take some time to think about everything you told me. Please don't think my feelings for you have changed. They haven't. The circumstances have changed."

She wiped her eyes before continuing. "We've spent our relationship in a cocoon, Jax. We've been wrapped up in each other. I still believe we were right not introducing Olivia to me yet. But maybe we got so comfortable in our cocoon that we've been blind to what's outside. Olivia will always be a vital part of our relationship. I haven't even met her yet, but I already think about her and what she would say or do at some moment."

Julia rose from the sofa and put another log on the fire. She remained standing at the fireplace. "Catherine will always be part of it too. While we probably won't be spending holidays together and she and I won't be girlfriends, she'll always be Olivia's mother. Regardless of whether you stay married or get divorced, the two of you have a permanent bond because of your daughter. For the next several years, you will co-parent her."

"We were doing that pretty well, at least, I thought so," Jax observed. "These accusations, however, definitely change things."

Julia returned to the sofa and sat next to Jax. "Then let's hit the 'pause' button on us. I said 'pause,' not 'stop.' Focus on you and Olivia. I'll sort through my feelings."

"Does this mean you want no communication with me?" he asked.

"It means," she replied, "we need to just step back. For now. Of course, I want to hear from you. I want to know what's happening with these accusations. I want to know how you're holding up. But we need to take a break from trips to Hilton Head and nights together."

"I'm worried that our pause may go from temporary to permanent."

A sad smile crossed her face. "I'm worried too. We will see what the future holds. I'm a firm believer that all things happen for a reason. There's a reason we met, Jax. Right now, though, we just don't know what it is."

*****

Jax arrived at the office of the polygraph examiner ten minutes early. When the examiner came to the waiting room, he greeted him. A retired police officer, Sam Davidson had known Jax when he was on active duty. He had sent numerous clients to Sam for a polygraph exam over the years.

"Jax, old boy, it's been a while. You don't usually come to my office with your clients. Where is he, or is it a she?"

Jax shook Sam's hand and said, "No client today, Sam. You're giving me the test."

Sam paused. "I looked at the file and saw it's a child-abuse case. I ran through the outline of questions. I saw your name on the file, but naturally I assumed your name was on the file as attorney for the examinee. Holy crap, Jax, I'm sorry."

"No need to apologize. It was a logical conclusion. I'm the one who should apologize for putting you in this position. My future ex-wife has decided to lodge sex-abuse allegations against me as part of the mirth and merriment of our divorce. I was just notified of the accusation two days ago, and I still can't breathe normally. My lawyer, Rick Meredith, scheduled the polygraph today so we can put this insanity to rest as quickly as possible."

"All right, Jax," sighed Sam. "Let's do this. It's showtime."

*****

Surviving the hour-long polygraph, Jax resumed his role as attorney for the accused. Six pretrials later, he returned to his office. Marion was more attentive than normal. He knew her intuitive instincts had been triggered by his mood and behavior. He couldn't slip past Marion without her sensing something was wrong.

After his final appointment, he called her into his office. She appeared in a flash; Bailey followed close behind.

He gave her a brief summary of the events he had endured over the past few days. She sat across from Jax, mulling over the information before speaking. "I never did like her very much, Jax. I could tell her kind right away. Only thinks of herself. Will step over anybody to get what she wants. The only good thing she did was give you Olivia. I love that girl as if she were my own. Just thinking about this latest trick up Catherine's sleeve and what it's doing to Olivia, well, it makes me absolutely sick. And my heart is breaking for you."

"Marion," Jax responded quietly, "I've never doubted your love for Olivia. I wanted to share this with you because, frankly, I knew you would figure out something was wrong, and I didn't want you thinking the worst."

"What could be worse than this? This is not only an outrageously false accusation, it's pure evil. When do you get your polygraph results? Not that we don't already know what the results will be."

Jax stood up, walked to the window, and stood next to Marion. "I'm supposed to be at Rick's office in a half hour. He'll have the results."

Turning to leave, she said, "Let me know the minute you hear. Then you can shove those test results right up Catherine's ass." She smiled and blew Jax a maternal kiss.

*****

Jax found Rick on a telephone call with a client. Jax made himself comfortable and read his emails on his phone.

Finished with his phone conference, Rick turned his chair toward Jax.

"You know you're going to have an interesting day when it begins with you being advised of your Miranda rights. Did you get my test results?"

Rick pushed a thin manila envelope across the desk. He said, "I'll save you the suspense. Congratulations. You're not a lying, deceitful child abuser. At least, that's what the polygraph results tell us."

Jax read the documents. He passed with flying colors. "Okay, that's over. Now what?"

"This afternoon, I filed a motion for visitation. You need a parenting-time schedule ordered by the court. No more informal arrangements with Catherine, not after this stunt. Let's not forget that you couldn't even find her or Olivia for days before she dropped the sex-abuse bombshell. If she disregards the court's visitation order, we'll file a contempt motion so fast her head will spin. Then she'll be the one facing jail time."

"That all makes perfect sense. Will the family court judge be able to consider my polygraph results? I know they can't be used in a criminal trial, but what about a divorce?"

Rick paused. "I'm confident Judge Westerfield will consider it."

"When do we go to court? It seems like years since I've seen or talked to Olivia."

"Monday morning at eight-thirty. Just five days from now."

Rick had just finished answering Jax's question when his assistant walked in to say there was a process server waiting at her desk. Rick excused himself, telling Jax he would return in a few minutes. Jax continued checking his emails on his phone. He had sent a reply to one email when Rick returned with a small stack of documents.

Rick returned to lawyer mode instead of friend mode. "I accepted service on your behalf. Catherine has filed a motion to suspend any visitation with Olivia, and she has filed with it a sworn affidavit laying out in detail her sex-abuse allegations against you. The court will hear this motion along with ours Monday morning."

"Detail!" shouted Jax as he jumped up and started pacing from one corner of the office to the other. "What detail? This is such complete and utter bullshit, Rick."

Rick handed Jax a copy of Catherine's affidavit. "Detail might have been too strong of a word. Read the affidavit. She alleges the abuse began after you moved out of the home, and it occurred while you were staying at the Manor Hotel. She also states it happened in your new home. She does not give specific dates or times, which is good for us. However, she does swear under oath in this affidavit that Olivia disclosed the abuse to her within the past two weeks. She goes on to say she and Olivia have been hiding from you until there's a hearing."

"What do we have to do to prepare for Monday's hearing?"

"Read through this affidavit several times over the next few days. Maybe something will jog your memory as to why she is hurling these accusations against you. The hearing is only scheduled for an hour, so your and Catherine's testimony will be brief. Our motion and Catherine's motion are both asking the court to issue a temporary order, which will only be in effect until the divorce is final. It will be a brief hearing, but it will be an extremely important first step in the divorce. My advice to you, my friend, is to follow the advice you give your clients before they take the stand. Tell the truth. Just answer the question without rambling on and on. If you don't understand the question, say so, and it will be repeated or rephrased. Do I have to tell you how to dress for court, or do you have that one puzzled out already?" Rick cracked a smile.

Jax returned the smile. "Yeah, I've got it covered."

*****

The weekend dragged by. He missed Julia. The pause in their relationship was a painful sign of the depths of his feelings. They exchanged text messages. He let her know about the hearing on Monday morning. She wished him good luck and asked him to let her know the outcome. Without Julia to fill his time and his mind, his thoughts were constantly drifting to the hearing. *The judge wouldn't keep him away from his daughter, would he?*

Jax spent Sunday night at home. He listened to blues records on his turntable, poured a glass of red wine, built a fire in the fireplace, and pulled out the photo albums he removed from Catherine's home, with her permission, a few months ago. Photos of Olivia when they brought her home from the hospital, just two days old. Her first birthday party. Preschool parties and concerts. School plays. Soccer tournaments. Every birthday party. Jax wondered if he would be invited to her upcoming eleventh birthday party. He would certainly get the bill for it, regardless of whether he was on the guest list.

Finishing his wine, he turned off the lights and went upstairs for what he anticipated would be another sleepless night.

CHAPTER 16

Jax fell asleep at dawn. He woke with a start when his alarm sounded. He rarely set it; he had always been an early riser. But today he could not afford to take a chance on oversleeping. For someone who spent thousands of hours of his life in a courtroom, Jax was as nervous as a cat about his upcoming hearing.

He met Rick in the hallway on the fifth floor of the courthouse. The fifth floor was dedicated to the family court. Jax never had any reason to be there until today. Rick ushered him into the courtroom. It had a completely different mood than the courtrooms where Jax spent his time. There were no jury trials in family court. The courtroom was only half the size of the courtrooms Jax frequented. It lacked a large gallery for spectators. The courtroom was comfortably appointed with pastel upholstered chairs at the tables. The witness stand was furnished with a matching chair. This was a change from the hard wooden seats in the trial courtrooms. It was locked to prevent the public from wandering in to watch families implode. Jax was taking his seat at counsel table next to Rick when the courtroom door opened. Catherine entered with Steve Barker.

Jax tried to hold her gaze, but she refused to make eye contact. Instead, she engaged in quiet conversation with her attorney.

The court bailiff entered from a door behind the judge's bench, and he beckoned Rick and Steve Barker into Judge Westerfield's chambers. This left Jax alone in the courtroom with Catherine. They both concentrated on their cell phones to avoid conversation. Jax was savvy enough to know anything he said to her would definitely be used against him. Catherine was quiet because she was a bitch.

Twenty minutes later, both lawyers reentered the courtroom. Rick signaled for Jax to follow him into the hallway.

They sat on a bench near the door. While lawyers and ordinary citizens walked past them, on the way to their own courtroom dramas, Rick told him about the conversation in the judge's chambers.

"There's no two ways about this. Judge Westerfield is going to do his best to avoid making a decision that will piss off you or Catherine. Which usually means he's going to make a decision that will piss off both of you. You've never appeared in his court, but he knows your reputation. He also knows if he even remotely appears to be ruling in your favor, Catherine will likely throw it in his face. Possibly in public too. He's up for reelection in two years, and he'll do everything he can to avoid any negative publicity."

"What do we do now?" asked Jax.

"We're going forward this morning with the emergency hearing. Our position is simple. You're entitled to a parenting-time schedule. Catherine's position is that your parenting time should be suspended until the final divorce hearing, if not permanently. She is basing this request solely on the abuse allegations."

Jax said, perhaps a little too loudly, "But we have the polygraph results. It will be admitted into evidence today, right?"

"Yes, it will," replied Rick as he thumbed through his file. "But hold on to your hat. Catherine also took a polygraph test, and she passed hers as well."

"We have a stalemate?"

"That's a good way of putting it. Let's get this show on the road."

*****

Judge Westerfield appeared to be paying very close attention to the testimony. Jax took the stand and, through Rick's questions, set the stage by describing his relationship with Olivia, both before and after he and Catherine separated. Steve Barker engaged in a contentious cross-examination of Jax, focusing on the allegations that Jax was a child molester. Being a master at cross-examination himself, he knew how to respond to Steve's questions, which were very caustic.

Catherine testified, and she portrayed herself as a dedicated wife and mother, only wanting what was best for her precious child. She held a tissue in her hand, occasionally bringing it to her face to dab at her eyes. Jax saw there were no tears to wipe away.

Catherine, in very dramatic fashion, answered Steve's questions about the sex-abuse allegations and how Catherine was so shocked and dismayed when Olivia disclosed this dark secret. When Rick had his turn at cross-examination, she was hazy about the details of the conversation. She was not even sure when or where the conversation occurred.

"All I know, Mr. Meredith, is Olivia came to me and told me what your client has been subjecting her to. I, her mother, was so devastated by this news that my mind has been doing its best to repress the conversation."

What complete and total bullshit, thought Jax while watching her performance.

After both attorneys presented closing arguments to the judge, he recessed court, promising a decision by the end of the day.

Jax made his way to his office, walking more slowly than usual while he reflected on the events of the morning. Was Catherine delusional or diabolical? Did she actually believe everything that came out of her mouth in the hearing? She did pass her polygraph. These thoughts gave Jax more cause for concern about Olivia's welfare than the accusations of child abuse. If Catherine had become so far removed from reality, what impact would this have on a girl approaching adolescence?

Jax checked in with Marion after he hung up his coat. She and Bailey let him know that his next client had arrived. Jax went to the waiting room, introduced himself, and led his new client into his office. John Ramsey settled himself in the chair across from Jax while Jax quickly reviewed the file Marion had prepared for him. He was the owner of Ramsey Landscaping Services, a large company serving hundreds of clients, both residential and commercial properties. The file held a copy of the indictment charging Mr. Ramsey with three counts of rape.

"Mr. Ramsey," Jax began as he closed the file, "the grand jury yesterday returned an indictment charging you with three counts of rape. Rape is a felony of the first degree. It carries a maximum sentence of life in prison and no parole eligibility until you have served twenty years. This is an extremely serious matter, and rape charges also have many emotional complications, especially if there is some relationship between the perpetrator and the victim. Let's begin with the victim, Melissa Ramsey. The last name tells me she is somehow related to you."

"The short answer is, she is my granddaughter. You also need the long answer."

Jax prepared for the complicated answer.

"First, Mr. Berman, I knew you when you were a kid in high school. My son, Michael Ramsey, graduated with you."

"I remember Michael," Jax remarked. "He's a great guy. He was really talented in every sport he played. He went to West Point, didn't he?"

"You have an excellent memory. He did indeed. After the academy, he joined the Army Rangers. Rose to the rank of captain. He served three tours in Iraq and one in Afghanistan. In between tours, he got married and had a little girl. Melissa is now fourteen years old."

"Where do Michael and his family live?"

John Ramsey paused before continuing his story. After looking out the window for several seconds, he looked at Jax and sighed. "Michael's last tour was truly his last tour. He was killed in Iraq five years ago. Melissa was nine years old. She and her mother were living in off-base housing in Seattle. Michael's widow, Jennifer, is a lovely woman, but the shock and grief were simply too much for her. She sank into a deep depression. She started abusing her prescription medication. She couldn't handle Melissa's own grief coupled with the growing pains of a young girl. My wife, Emma, and I have had custody of Melissa for about three years. It's a very amicable arrangement. We arrange for Jennifer to fly here twice a year to visit Melissa, during Melissa's spring break from school and Christmas. We fly Melissa to Seattle in the summer to spend a few weeks with her mother."

"My deepest condolences. I had no idea Michael had died serving his country. You must be proud of your son."

"We are, but we miss him every day. As do Jennifer and Melissa. We're trying to focus our energy on Melissa and provide a secure home for her. But we don't want to sever ties with her mother. I fear, though, this is where we made our mistake. It's why I'm in your office charged with a despicable crime. It makes me sick to think about what I'm accused of doing."

"Tell me how your kindness and concern for your granddaughter have been turned against you."

After another pause, John Ramsey picked up where he left off. "Over the past year, Melissa has become quite a handful. Emma and I raised Michael and his younger brother. We never had experience raising a girl. Let me tell you, Mr. Berman, raising an adolescent girl is a nightmare compared to boys."

Jax thought, in a few years, Olivia would be there. He wondered, especially in light of his relationship with Catherine, how rough a ride her teenage years would be. He quickly dismissed his fears and focused on his client's story.

"In addition to her grades slipping at school and her losing interest in soccer and Girl Scouts, she has really been pushing hard to move back to Seattle. I don't believe Jennifer is encouraging these thoughts, but she isn't discouraging them either. Melissa has complained to Emma and me, on more than one occasion, that we are too strict, too old-fashioned, and we just don't understand her. I may not have any experience raising a girl, but it doesn't take a genius to figure out Melissa thinks she will have fewer rules and more freedom if she lives with her mother."

Jax asked, "How is Jennifer's mental and physical health?"

"Pretty much the same. It's a double-edged sword for her. She is clinically depressed and needs medication to control her symptoms. But she is also an addict. She can't resist abusing her medication. She has never approached us to ask if Melissa can return to her home. Jennifer seems to understand her limitations, and she tells us how grateful she is for our support."

"You believe," said Jax, "Melissa has alleged sex abuse in the hope that someone, or the court, will remove her from your home and return her to her mother."

"Yes, Mr. Berman," John Ramsey replied. "You are absolutely correct."

"Well then, Mr. Ramsey, let's get to work. Please call me Jax."

"Thanks, Jax. I know you're the best. I also got to watch you grow up. I had the chance to hear you play the piano a few times. I hope you kept up with it because you're very talented."

"Thanks, Mr. Ramsey. Yes, I do. Playing the piano is a great stress reliever."

"I wonder if it's too late for me to start playing. I could use a good stress reliever." Putting on his coat, he added, "Please call me John."

CHAPTER 17

The conversation with John Ramsey left Jax shaken. Days after his polygraph to disprove the claims of child abuse, his client stood accused of sexually abusing his granddaughter. She was not just his granddaughter, but also a young girl whom he had been raising as if she were his daughter. What would Mr. Ramsey think if he knew his attorney was facing the same destructive accusation? Always trying to look on the bright side, Jax hoped this case would be cathartic for him. "Soldier on," he said to himself as he answered his ringing cell phone. The caller ID said "Rick."

"You'd better have good news," Jax said.

"It's not good news, but it's not necessarily bad news."

"I'm a big boy. Lay it on me."

"I just received the judge's temporary order by email. It confirms what I predicted. Judge Westerfield is a political animal, which means there are times when he's afraid of his own shadow. He doesn't want to offend you nor does he want to give Catherine cause to accuse him of being biased in your favor. He's giving you parenting time on alternating weekends."

"It's a start, but I can live with it."

"But wait, there's more, as they say on the television commercials," continued Rick. "He ordered your parenting time to take place at the marital residence."

"The marital residence? How in the hell will that work!" shouted Jax into the phone, causing Bailey to leave in search of a peaceful napping place elsewhere.

"Shut up and listen. This is the most complicated temporary order I've ever seen. He ordered Catherine to move out of the home while the divorce is ongoing. She has to rent an apartment or condo or something. I don't give a rat's ass where she goes, and it's not your problem either. She'll be at the house on the other weekends when you're not. The order calls for Olivia to live in the house, with the parents visiting regularly. He ordered Jenny Graham to move in and take care of Olivia. In addition to alternating weekends, Catherine will spend Monday and Wednesday evenings with Olivia from after school until eight p.m. You'll do the same on Tuesday and Thursday evening."

"Sounds crazy, Rick, but at least, I get to spend time with her. Jenny's a great choice."

Jenny Graham, a retired kindergarten teacher, had been Olivia's nanny during the early years of her life. She lived in the home and became a surrogate grandmother. When Olivia started school, Jenny moved into her own place, but she was always the first to be called when they needed a babysitter. Jenny continued to accompany the family to Hilton Head and other vacation destinations. Jenny was a member of the family. When she learned of Jax and Catherine's separation, she contacted each of them to tell them how much she loved them, how much she adored Olivia, and how she wished nothing but the best for everyone. She would never choose sides in the divorce. Jax and Catherine respected her position.

"You start your weekend rotation Friday. Catherine has to move out by then."

"No problem."

"Judge Westerfield also ordered you and Catherine to submit to a mental evaluation to be conducted by a psychologist appointed by the court. I predict he'll appoint Martin Harper. He has an office downtown and in the suburbs. He's been around a long time. He has earned a strong reputation. He's been involved in some of my cases. While he's not on my list of people I'd call for a few beers after work, he's very good."

"Let me know what I need to do."

"Will do. The judge also wants Dr. Harper to conduct an assessment of Olivia. He'll meet with her after he has finished with you and Catherine."

"Then what?" asked Jax, completely unfamiliar with the ins and outs of divorce procedure.

"We'll return to court, probably in about thirty days, and Dr. Harper will share his findings with us."

"Does this mean we could be back in court before Christmas?"

"I would think so. My guess is that's what the judge is shooting for. Except for Thanksgiving, there are no other holidays to deal with in this schedule. Thanksgiving is on a Thursday, so you get to spend it with Olivia and Jenny."

"Score one for the home team. I'll take it."

*****

Jax spent the rest of the week counting down the hours and minutes until Friday evening. He called Julia to update her on the visitation order. Their conversation lasted more than an hour. Jax was happy with the tone of the conversation but also unhappy he couldn't spend time with her other than on the phone. He respected Julia's request to put some time and distance between them until the storm passed.

Thoughts of Julia were overshadowed by his anticipation of the weekend. The days and weeks without seeing or talking to Olivia seemed endless. His overnight bag tossed into the passenger seat, he pulled into the driveway to hang out with his little princess. There was a groundswell of anxiety churning inside. How would Olivia respond to him? Would this be the first time in her short life when there was an awkward moment between them? Catherine had just spent the week with her. How did she go about preparing Olivia for the new schedule? How much blame did she lay on Jax? These new concerns were now overlaid atop the most pressing question: why would Olivia tell anyone her father had touched her inappropriately? With the exception of the hour or two each night when Jax fell into a restless sleep, the question burned in his consciousness every minute of the day.

He turned off the ignition, pocketed the key, and grabbed his bag. Walking tentatively toward the door, he was torn. Should he just walk into the house and announce his presence, or should he ring the doorbell? *You're overthinking this,* he scolded himself. His inner voice turned out to be right. Jax didn't have to make the choice. Jenny opened the door with her hands on her hips and a wide smile on her face. Without saying a word, she embraced him in one of her famous bear hugs. This one lasted longer than usual, which was Jenny's way of letting him know to relax. Jax didn't fight it. Jenny's welcoming arms were great medicine for his anxiety level.

When Jenny finally let go and he put his bag down, he saw Olivia standing behind Jenny, also wearing a huge smile. She rushed to him, wrapped her arms around his waist, and exclaimed, "Hi, Daddy! Boy oh boy, I've missed you. We've got the whole weekend to catch up. Jenny made fried chicken for dinner tonight because we know it's one of your favorites."

Still hugging his little girl, Jax replied, "You know it is, Princess. Jenny's fried chicken is the best in the world. Come upstairs and help me unpack."

Jenny's fried-chicken dinner was still the world's best. The chicken, mashed potatoes, green beans, and homemade biscuits were outmatched only by the free and easy conversation at the dinner table. Olivia seemed completely unaffected by the time spent apart from her father. Her conversations centered around school, soccer, and what she and her friends did for fun. Jax breathed an inner sigh of relief that boys did not seem to be a priority in her life. He knew it would be only a matter of time before she would enter the turbulent years of adolescent crushes and the occasional heartbreak. Jax was mentally preparing for life with a teenage girl, but he sure as hell wasn't looking forward to it. He vowed to enjoy every minute with Olivia before the dreaded transformation.

They were engrossed in a fierce game of Monopoly when Jax looked at his watch. It was almost midnight. Jenny said good night and settled into the first-floor bedroom, which was hers when she lived there. Jax took Olivia upstairs, tucked her in bed just like the good old days, and gave her a good-night kiss on the forehead. Closing her door, he made his way into the larger of the spare bedrooms. He was not going to get comfortable in the master bedroom. It had been Catherine's bedroom for the past year.

Saturday was unseasonably warm. Jax and Olivia enjoyed a long ride on the bike trail in the early afternoon then headed home to enjoy another scrumptious meal. After dinner, they finished the marathon Monopoly game from the night before. Olivia won handily. On Sunday morning, Jax and Olivia finished her homework, and later they went for a walk in the neighborhood. Jenny, in her role as supervisor, walked with them.

In the blink of an eye, the weekend came to an end. It passed so quickly yet so comfortably. It only made the nagging question burn even more strongly: why would Olivia say Jax had been abusing her?

*****

"I've never done this before, Doctor. Do I sit on this couch, or do I lie down on it?" asked Jax in Dr. Harper's inner sanctum.

"An age-old question, Mr. Berman. Sitting is fine. It's only in the movies that patients recline on the couch and have life-altering memories of their childhood."

"Fine, Doctor. Sitting is fine with me. I don't expect to have any epiphanies."

Jax endured fifty minutes of endless questions. Starting with his preschool years, his scant memories of his father, and his adolescence, he found comfort talking with a stranger about the highs and lows of his childhood. The questions became uncomfortable when they traveled through his relationship with Catherine, from happy beginning to bitter end. Whether by coincidence or by design, the line of questioning ended on a happy note—Jax's relationship with Olivia.

After Dr. Harper finished his notes, he escorted Jax into another office, where Jax was greeted by a doctoral student who was interning with the office. The aspiring psychologist administered the Minnesota Multiphasic Personality Inventory—known in the trade as the MMPI. The MMPI is a psychological test that assesses personality traits as well as symptoms of psychopathology. Its focus is on mental-health disorders or other psychological defects. Jax answered more than five hundred questions, all of which were in a true-false format. He exited the office two hours later and checked out at the reception desk. He was told Dr. Harper would complete his report "soon."

Arriving at his office, he realized he again had an interesting beginning to his day, but this time, he didn't have his rights read to him. Things were looking up.

*****

The weeknight visits were as easy as their first weekend. Jax picked up Olivia after school, and they stopped at her favorite ice-cream shop on the way home. The weeknight time went by too quickly.

Jax was leaving the house after his second weekend visit and was turning into his driveway when Rick called.

"Just had another great weekend with Olivia. I can't describe it. It's as if nothing has happened between us at all. Olivia seems totally oblivious to the period of time when I was kept away from her. There's not even a hint of awkwardness. It just doesn't jive with her accusations of child abuse."

"It's unlike anything I've ever seen in my career, I must admit. I've seen a thousand situations where one parent tries to alienate the children from the other parent. That game is as old as marriage and divorce itself. Unfortunately, in recent years, I've had cases where the mother plays the child-abuse card against the father. In the past, it has always been physical abuse—he beats the kids and calls them degrading names. But this game Catherine is playing is new to me too. It definitely has gotten Dr. Harper's attention."

"What do you mean?"

"The judge's bailiff just sent an email. On a Sunday evening. Dr. Harper needs more time to complete his assessment. He wants to conduct additional testing."

"Are you kidding me? Between my fireside chat with Dr. Harper and the MMPI, I spent more than three hours talking about my life. I'm done."

"Not you," Rick responded quickly. "He indicated he's completed his evaluation of you. It's Catherine he wants to see again. Something about an additional diagnostic tool. Next week's court hearing is off. We're rescheduled for January."

"Which takes us past Christmas. What do we do?"

"We'll stick to the same daily schedule. Christmas falls during the week. Catherine will be at the house on Christmas Eve, and you get Christmas Day. Same schedule the following week for New Year's Eve and Day. Thanksgiving is next week, so focus on that for now."

"Holidays this year are definitely going to be different. It underscores the reality of sharing a child with the other parent. It sounds simple on paper, but it's a major adjustment."

"Persevere, Jax. That's all you can do. Enjoy your holiday with your daughter. Don't overplay it or underplay it. Keep your family traditions alive as much as possible. Thanksgiving will be a great start."

"Good advice. I'll try not to buy the biggest turkey. Keep it simple, stupid. Isn't that how the saying goes?"

CHAPTER 18

Jax escorted John Ramsey from his office following his second appointment. His wife, Emma, had joined him for the meeting. Mr. Ramsey was the epitome of the American Dream. He grew up in a rural area near Cincinnati, the eldest in a family with many children and not enough money to provide for them. John dropped out of school and found a job working for a local landscaper. Being the newest and youngest employee of the company, John was assigned the menial and unappreciated tasks. He never complained. He kept twenty dollars from his weekly paycheck and gave the rest to help with the household expenses. Within a year, he was promoted to crew supervisor, which meant a significant pay raise. He used his extra income to complete high school, attending evening classes every weeknight. He enrolled in business courses at a community college. It took five years to earn a degree in business management, but he could proudly add a college education to his résumé.

He never prepared a résumé. When the owner of the landscape company announced he was retiring and moving to Florida, he offered to sell the business to John at a friendly price and friendlier payment terms. John Ramsey was the proud owner of the business, and he owned it debt-free in three years. He and Emma married and had children, and as his family grew, so did his business. Currently there were three locations and more than sixty employees working for Ramsey Landscaping Services Inc.

One of the sources of conflict with his granddaughter was John insisting she work ten hours a week in the business office. He wanted her to learn the business and develop a strong work ethic. Melissa had no interest in doing so. She wanted only to hang out with her friends, go shopping, and spend hours on Facebook and YouTube.

While John and his wife were encouraging Melissa to work in the family business, there seemed to be an increase in the amount of time Melissa spent communicating with her mother. Between the in-person visits, they spent more time on the phone or FaceTime. The Ramseys didn't know if Jennifer was promising a life with fewer rules and even fewer expectations. They did know the frequent phone calls coincided with a decided change in Melissa's attitude and behavior. Melissa told them she missed her mother and wanted to move back with her. While it was true that, during the past few years, the Ramseys maintained an open-door policy with Jennifer, allowing her quality time with her daughter, they knew in their hearts Melissa moving in with Jennifer would be a disaster. They feared Melissa would sink into the mire of her mother's daily life. If Melissa did move back to Seattle, the Ramseys would be thousands of miles away. They would essentially be out of her life completely.

As he said goodbye to the Ramseys and closed the waiting room door, Marion told him Jim Gaddis had called about the Kevin Wilson case.

Jax returned the call from his office, stroking Bailey, who was relaxing in Jax's lap.

"Thanks for calling back so quickly," said Chief Assistant Prosecutor Gaddis. "I've got to be candid with you. This case is scaring the life out of me. Have you reviewed the evidence I sent?"

"I have. I know why you're so concerned. It seems the police department somehow recruited a neo-Nazi. It's a key piece of evidence for you if you're still going for a murder conviction, but the fallout in the press and the city could be catastrophic."

"I couldn't say it better. We have to come to a plea deal to keep this evidence from coming to light."

"The only plea deal you could offer me is a dismissal of the charge. I have a solid self-defense argument to present to a jury."

Jim said in a very slow and deliberate manner, "I thought that would be your position. I could offer you a manslaughter, remove the gun specification, making the charge eligible for probation. I would even recommend probation at sentencing."

"Generous, Jim, but I doubt my client will accept it. I'll convey it to him. But your offer would mean he could never be a police officer again."

"I know, Jax, I know," sighed Jim. "I was just hoping against hope we wouldn't have to go to trial. On the other hand, would it be such a bad thing that a member of the Sentinels could never be a police officer?"

"I hear what you're saying, but as his attorney, I have to protect his career and his freedom. Let's look at other options. You could always present the case without the photos of Officer Wilson in a Sentinels uniform."

"I could, I suppose. But I've got a duty to pursue the case to the best of my ability. I can't remember the last time I was in such a quandary. This really sucks."

"It sucks out loud. I'll relay your offer to my client. We'll talk soon."

Jax leaned back in his chair, envious of the stress-free nap Bailey was enjoying on his lap. When was the last time he had a restful sleep? Had he ever been that lucky? *Don't dwell on misery,* he scolded his inner self. His thoughts returned to the Wilson case. His client had been charged with murder, with intentionally taking the life of a teenage boy named Travis Martin. The information on young Mr. Martin was impressive. He was an only child raised by a single mother working two jobs to support her family. Travis was a freshman at a small technology high school in the inner city. His grades were above average. No disciplinary problems were noted in his school transcript. He played football for the school. Jax couldn't find any explanation for being in a downtown alley in the middle of the night. Maybe, just as it was for his client, the initial information was too good to be true. He made a note to send the information to Leonard.

The following afternoon, Jax picked up the mail from Marion's desk. He planned to relax at his desk for a few minutes and go through the daily delivery of bills, correspondence from courts and attorneys, and the occasional payment from a client. He kicked off his shoes, assumed a reclining position on the sofa, his head resting on an end pillow, and opened the first envelope. Just as he was extricating the letter, his phone emitted the familiar ding. He had a text from Julia. Eager on one hand but apprehensive on the other, he swiped the screen to reveal her message: *Life without you would be miserable. I love you, no matter the baggage you bring. If you want to pick up where we left off, I'd love to share Thanksgiving Day with you after you celebrate with Olivia. How about 9:00 at my place?*

*****

Thanksgiving Day arrived at last. Jax was looking forward to spending the holiday with Olivia and Jenny. The day had always been special to Jax. It was a day to be together with friends and family and give thanks for everything that life had given. When Olivia was born, he always made a special effort to let her know how meaningful the day was to him and that she was at the top of the list of blessings in his life. This Thanksgiving Day would be no different, although the guest list would be smaller than it had been in years past. In happier times, Catherine always invited her parents from Chicago, and most years, one or both of her brothers came to celebrate the holiday.

Jax had gotten comfortable with his visitation schedule and the routine over the past weeks; he didn't hesitate to walk into the house through the side door without knocking. He was greeted by the heavenly smells of cooking. He entered the kitchen to find Jenny teaching Olivia the fine art of making gravy. Olivia was standing on a stepstool at the counter, wearing a bright red-and-blue plaid apron. Her sleeves were rolled up, and she was singularly focused on the cooking lesson. She broke her concentration long enough to give Jax a big hug and wish him a happy Thanksgiving.

With a football game playing on the television mounted on the kitchen wall, Jax took off his coat, rolled up his sleeves, and played the role of sous-chef until dinner was ready to be served. They carried the serving platters and bowls to the dining room.

Olivia offered a short blessing at the beautifully decorated table, complete with candles and pumpkins as the centerpiece. Great food and delightfully easy conversation overwhelmed Jax with joy. Despite the conflict with Catherine and the horrific allegations she had made against him, he found himself at peace in the moment.

After a generous serving of pumpkin pie and freshly made whipped cream, the trio cleared the table, stored the leftovers, and cleaned dishes and pots and pans. An hour later, Jax sat in front of the fire. Olivia and Jenny joined him, and the conversation continued until Olivia's drooping eyelids signaled it was time for her to go to bed. He walked upstairs with her and waited in her room while she went to her bathroom to change into her pajamas and brush her teeth. Tucking her snugly into bed, he kissed her on the forehead, thanked her for a most wonderful Thanksgiving Day, and said, "I love you more than you will ever know."

"I love you too. See you next Tuesday."

Minutes later, he was in Julia's living room and in her arms. The aroma coming from Julia's kitchen rivaled Jenny's feast. Jax had never eaten two Thanksgiving dinners, but he was going to give it his best effort. Jax followed her into her kitchen. She put the finishing touches on a sumptuous platter of oysters Rockefeller, their first course, accompanied by a bottle of fine champagne. Julia prepared a stuffed roast duckling instead of turkey, accompanied by sage dressing and grilled asparagus. Dessert would follow; it was a medley of fresh berries with orange liqueur and whipped cream. *Life is definitely great when you get two desserts with whipped cream in the same evening.*

Dinner was followed by the eagerly anticipated dessert in front of the fireplace. They snuggled together, sipping aperitifs and watching the dancing flames. Jax decided to seize the moment. If all went according to plan, this would be the best day in more than a year.

He put his hands on her shoulders and drew her into him for a lingering kiss. When they finally broke apart, he took a deep breath, his hands still resting on her shoulders. *Go for broke, Jax.*

"Julia, this is probably my favorite day of the year. A time to look back at the year and look back at life and all that has come my way. This year has been a mixed bag of happiness and misery. I'm learning the art of being a part-time dad. I'm trying to maintain civility with my estranged wife, who, quite frankly, is making it a daily challenge. I have been in the position of client, but fortunately my attorney also happens to be my best friend. It's pretty much an even split. Then you came into my life, and you really tipped the scale toward happiness. Despite all the turmoil, all the chaos in my life right now, I've never been so happy. And it's all because of you."

Tears welled in her eyes as she replied, "Jax, that may be the most beautiful thing anyone has ever said to me. I do love you. You are wonderful in every way. You show me every day, beginning with our first date at the hospital. Your concern and compassion for Matthew swept me off my feet. Even though our first date was in the cafeteria, it was more romantic than candlelight and champagne."

"You showed me early on that you were a cheap date," Jax laughed. Julia joined in the laughter, which led to another slow kiss.

"Julia," Jax continued after regaining his breath. "You're the best thing that's happened to me, with the exception of Olivia. I don't want this happiness to end."

"I'm honored to be second to your daughter. That's how it's supposed to be. While I think Bailey is an adorable cat, though, I do hope I'm a notch above her."

"Barely, Julia, but you're a notch above the cat."

Julia smiled and leaned back into the sofa.

"So," he whispered, "I want to spend the rest of my life with you. I want to be there for your happiness and sadness, your easy times and your challenging times, just as you've been there for me." He rose from the sofa, got down on one knee, and asked, "Will you marry me?"

Julia gasped. Jax didn't know if it was a good sign or a bad one. "I want to spend the rest of my life with you. But we still have some hurdles to get over before we can commit to marriage. The biggest hurdle is your daughter. I haven't met her yet. More importantly, she hasn't met me. My answer is a happy but qualified yes."

"A qualified yes?" asked Jax, confused. "You sound more like a lawyer than a doctor."

Julia chuckled. "I guess it comes with hanging around a lawyer."

"What are the qualifications?"

"Just one, Jax. My acceptance of your proposal is conditioned on Olivia's acceptance of me. If she doesn't like me or simply doesn't like you being in a relationship with someone other than her mother, I'll let you rescind your proposal."

"Rescind my proposal? You really have been hanging around a lawyer."

Julia laughed. "Okay, enough lawyer talk. I love you more than anything, Jax. This time we spent apart showed me that truth. I want to marry you and spend every day of the rest of our lives together. Just not at Olivia's expense."

Jax gave her a kiss before saying, "I can live with that. When the time is right, you and Olivia can meet and test the waters."

The newly yet qualifiedly engaged couple nestled together on the sofa, watching the fire in blissful silence.

CHAPTER 19

Jax and Julia flew to New York City for the holiday weekend. Jax didn't have parenting time with Olivia until the following Tuesday. The newly but qualifiedly engaged couple spent the weekend doing everything and anything they wanted. The trip was totally impulsive. They checked in to a boutique hotel in Midtown Manhattan. Bundled up in winter coats and boots, they embarked on a self-guided walking tour of the city. A trip to the Metropolitan Museum of Art was followed by window-shopping on Fifth Avenue. Julia admired the engagement rings on display in the windows of Cartier and Tiffany. The experience brought back memories of ring shopping with Catherine in Chicago. It seemed a lifetime ago. Jax reflected on all that had transpired since then. The obvious high point was Olivia entering his life and capturing his heart. Pushing aside the memories of a marriage that had devolved into vitriol and violence, he remembered the feelings when he was shopping with Catherine. He was a lot younger then. He had made a spontaneous decision to propose to Catherine when he was caught up in the emotional high of winning his first case.

He considered his relationship with Julia. He was older and more mature. Presumably. Compared to his earlier life with Catherine, this proposal was thoughtful and deliberate. He had not acted impulsively. He hadn't proposed while on an emotional high. To the contrary, he was currently at an emotionally chaotic low. Yet he and Julia weathered the storm together. Whether it was unknowing or by design, Julia had proven to Jax, from their first date in the hospital cafeteria, she was tough and tender. She truly was the finest person in his life—not counting his mom. Moms held a special place and a unique category.

He held Julia's gloved hand tightly as they strolled Fifth Avenue searching for the perfect Bloody Mary.

They scored afternoon matinee tickets to a Broadway show. They tapped their feet and hummed along to the score of "The Music Man." Jax felt the pangs of irony when Professor Harold Hill belted out, "*Ya got trouble, my friend, right here in River City.*" He sure as hell could relate to those words. They were a cruel reminder of the horrid allegations Catherine made against him. Since he received the news that he was an accused child molester, he found himself showering twice daily. He tried but couldn't wash away the filth that accompanied the label. Thankfully, the Children's Services investigation was confidential. The divorce proceedings were not open to public scrutiny. But what if this nightmare led to criminal charges against him? The world would know. He would be labeled a child rapist. Whenever he looked in a mirror, he would see it as clearly as if the words were tattooed on his forehead. *Get a grip, Jax. The truth will win out. It has to.*

He squeezed Julia's hand.

Following the performance, they went to the Rainbow Room for dinner and enjoyed the panoramic view of Manhattan at night. The holiday lights added to the sparkle of the cityscape.

Their last day was spent cruising the boutique shops in Soho. Jax found a bracelet for Olivia. Julia offered her input that helped him with the final selection. It seemed as if Julia had already met Olivia because she somehow knew his daughter's style.

*****

Driving to the office on Monday morning, still glowing with memories of the weekend, he arrived early to catch up with the mail and emails. He wasn't early enough to arrive ahead of Marion. She was hanging up her coat. Her first order of business was to comb through the mail, sorting the junk mail and tossing it into the trash. As she organized the mail worth opening, she came across a bright-red envelope addressed to Jax. There was no return address; her instincts told her it was personal. She handed it to him still sealed in the envelope; he opened it and found a Christmas card.

When he opened the card, he dropped it onto Marion's desk as if it were red-hot. Marion was motionless, waiting for Jax to say or do something. Anything. Cautiously, he picked up the card and finished reading it.

"What's on my schedule this morning?"

"Everyone is still in holiday mode, so you don't have any court appearances until this afternoon. I left the morning open for you to get caught up. You only have one client later this afternoon."

"Good to know."

He took the card and the envelope into his office and dialed the phone.

"How was the weekend?" asked Rick when he answered the call.

"I'll tell you all about it when I see you, which needs to be as soon as possible."

"I'm on the way to my office now. I'm free for the next hour."

"I'm on my way."

Jax pulled into the parking lot next to Rick's office building only seconds behind Rick. They walked to his office. Rick closed the door as Jax, still standing, held out the red envelope for him to read.

Rick removed the card from the envelope. He carefully perused the front of the card, which was adorned with an old-fashioned Christmas scene and warmest greetings for the holiday. Opening the card, having read the rhyming holiday wishes, he turned his attention to the handwritten words on the left side of the card.

"What do you want me to do with this?"

Jax was stunned by the nonchalant tone of his question. "I think it's important to show Catherine's state of mind or maybe the absence of a rational state of mind."

Rick was confused. "What do you want me to do with an old, mushy holiday card from your wife? I'm surprised you held onto something like this after all these years."

"Rick, you're missing the point. This is not some sappy Christmas card from Christmas past. I received it in the mail today! Catherine sent it directly to my office."

Rick was shocked. He picked up the card again and read Catherine's words aloud. "Dearest Jax, this is the time of year to reflect. I just want to thank you for your devotion to our daughter. You have always been her hero since the day she was born. You will always be her shining star. Even though we have had our differences, you always put Olivia above all else. I will always love you for that. Love and Merry Christmas, Catherine."

Listening to those words being read out loud sent a shiver up Jax's spine.

Rick sighed, "This is not exactly in line with Catherine's accusations of child abuse. Maybe this type of behavior is why Dr. Harper insisted on conducting more diagnostic testing. The first order of business is for me to forward a copy of this to Steve Barker. Then he and I will see Judge Westerfield as soon as possible. This will be the pathway to getting a copy of this card to Dr. Harper. I'm confident he'll find this information very useful in his evaluation."

"Makes sense. I've got to tell you this has rocked me to the core. The frightening probability is, she has some sort of split personality developing. It's the only possible explanation. How can she make these sex-abuse claims against me, knowing, at the very least, I would be deprived of any contact with Olivia and, at the very worst, I could spend the rest of my life in prison? Now I'm faced with the same person, the one who is hell-bent on ruining me, praising me and thanking me for everything I've done for our daughter, the daughter who is allegedly my victim. I've seen my share of mentally ill people in my business, but I've never been faced with this."

"You're describing a divided self, Jax. I had a case years ago where my client suffered from the disorder. Essentially there were two people living inside her. In fact, each of them had a different name. I actually met and talked with both of them. One was Sheila, and the other was Samantha. I could tell by the voice inflection which one was sitting in my office. It was a fascinating and creepy experience. Sheila wanted to reconcile with her husband, but Samantha wanted to kill him. I mean literally she wanted to kill him. She wanted to end his life in a very brutal manner. On the day of the final divorce hearing, there was extra court security in case Samantha showed up for the hearing instead of Sheila."

"Fascinating story, but it's not offering me much comfort right now."

"I told you to let you know you may be right about Catherine. But I'm not a professional. I just want you to know there's a possibility Catherine could be experiencing the same condition. I also told you because you need to know this type of situation exists beyond Catherine. We definitely need to relay this information to Dr. Harper. I'm sure his final report will not only make recommendations concerning custody and visitation but also recommendations for treatment or counseling going forward."

"Thanks for seeing me so quickly. I'm not sure I feel any better than I did when I walked in, but at least, the information will get into the right hands. Since it's way too early for a cocktail, I'll immerse myself in my clients' misery for the rest of the day."

"Good plan. I'll meet you after work at the Manor. Then it won't be too early for that cocktail. Or two."

"I'll be there." Jax shook his best friend's hand, and as he opened the door, he turned back to Rick and asked, "I need to know the final chapter. Who showed up for the divorce hearing? Sheila or Samantha?"

He replied, "Unfortunately Samantha came to the show. It was a real show all right. Before we went into the courtroom, Samantha spotted her husband walking down the hallway with his lawyer. She let out the most terrifying guttural scream. It wasn't human. It's still ringing in my ears. She took a flying leap at her husband, knocking both him and his attorney flat on their backs. She delivered four or five good punches to her husband's face before court security officers were able to pry her off. I attended the hearing without her. While the judge was granting the divorce and awarding custody of the kids to the husband, she was in lockup being booked on assault charges. She was released from jail the next day. Samantha's, or Sheila's, mother filed the necessary papers in court to have her involuntarily hospitalized in a psychiatric ward for seventy-two hours. From there, she went to the Langley Care Center for inpatient psychiatric treatment.

She was hospitalized for six months. After her release, she moved in with her mother." Rick paused and shook his head. "It's a sad tale. Although it's been years ago, Sheila and Samantha often cross my mind. The whole situation was doubly tragic because she and her husband had two young kids. They must be in high school now. They've grown up without a mother. Sheila, or Samantha, was only allowed parenting time under the supervision of her mother."

"Let's hope Olivia doesn't have to go through that experience. If Catherine does need help, even though our marriage is over, she's still the mother of my child. I'll take care of anything she needs."

"We've traveled a long road together. You didn't have to tell me."

*****

Although court hearings traditionally begin at nine o'clock, Judge Westerfield scheduled an emergency pretrial hearing in the case of Berman vs. Berman. Jax and Catherine, with their attorneys, were in the courtroom at eight o'clock two days after Jax delivered the Christmas card to Rick. Dr. Harper was present. He had a copy of the card for his review.

Judge Westerfield entered the courtroom and gestured for everyone to be seated.

"This matter has been set on an expedited docket, primarily at the urging of Dr. Harper," the judge remarked. "I appreciate everyone coming in at this unusually early hour. There have been some developments in need of immediate attention. Am I correct?"

Rick rose from his seat. "Correct, Your Honor. Dr. Harper has some information essential to this case. Furthermore, he apparently wishes to make recommendations for temporary orders."

Rick sat down. Steve Barker stood and stated, "Your Honor, I had the opportunity to talk with Dr. Harper. We have no objection to him testifying today and making recommendations. Quite frankly, my client wants to move this case forward as quickly as possible and bring this divorce to its final conclusion."

Dr. Harper, after being sworn, settled in the witness stand. He answered preliminary questions asked by Judge Westerfield. In his most professional tone, he explained the latest developments.

"Since the court's order requiring psychological evaluations of the parties as well as their daughter, I have made substantial progress in my assessment of Mr. Berman and Olivia. Mr. Berman promptly scheduled his appointment. I found him to be forthright in his answers. He completed the standard personality testing I administer in these evaluations. I met with Olivia on two occasions. Jenny Graham brought her to both interviews. While Mrs. Berman was cooperative in her clinical interview as well as the standardized test, I explained to her that, based on her results, I wanted to conduct supplemental diagnostic testing. This is where I have run into a brick wall. Mrs. Berman has not scheduled an appointment for the additional testing. She has not returned my phone calls. I left several voice mail messages to no avail."

Judge Westerfield looked at Catherine before asking Steve Barker, "Counselor, does your client confirm or refute this testimony?"

Steve rose from his chair and answered, "My client has not scheduled the appointment. She believes the testing is unnecessary. She completed the same evaluation as Mr. Berman. It should be sufficient for Dr. Harper to complete his assessment." Steve sat down. He cast a sideways glance at Catherine, who was nodding in assent.

Before Rick could make any counter argument, Judge Westerfield interjected. "I understand your client's position. However, Dr. Harper, in his professional opinion, is recommending further diagnostics. He's the psychologist involved in this matter, unless your client has the necessary education in psychological testing and treatment. Does she, counselor?"

"No, your Honor, she does not."

"I didn't think so," sighed the judge, casting an annoyed glance at Catherine. "Dr. Harper, when is your next available appointment?"

"The day after tomorrow, I could meet with Mrs. Berman at five o'clock. The testing should take less than two hours."

"Excellent. Mr. Barker, your client is ordered to appear on that date and time. She is further ordered to cooperate fully with Dr. Harper. Does she understand?"

Catherine nodded slowly while Steve stated for the record that she understood and would cooperate. Jax didn't know whether Catherine's nod indicated quiet acquiescence or a slow burning anger.

Dr. Harper said, "Your Honor, I am also recommending a modification to the current parenting-time schedule. I understand from speaking with the parties and Olivia the current schedule has been going smoothly. Jenny Graham has been a tremendous asset. However, for the well-being of the child, my recommendation is as follows: Although the same schedule should remain, Mr. Berman's parenting time should now be unsupervised, and he should be able to take Olivia from the home for his visits. This means Olivia would spend alternating weekends at his home. The weeknight visits would also be spent either at Mr. Berman's home or any other location such as a park or restaurant. Mr. Berman should be free to engage in parenting time with his daughter at any location and without any supervision."

The judge paused, considering the testimony, then inquired, "What are your recommendations for Mrs. Berman?"

"Judge, until I can complete my evaluation, there should be no changes made to her parenting time. It should remain under the supervision of Jenny Graham and continue to take place in the home."

The judge allowed both attorneys to ask questions of Dr. Harper before he left the witness stand. He recessed court for thirty minutes to consider the evidence and issue an order.

When he returned to the bench, he announced his decision. "The court adopts Dr. Harper's recommendations, effective immediately. Mr. Berman, the upcoming weekend is your weekend in the rotating schedule, which means you shall pick up your daughter Friday evening and return her to the home on Sunday evening. My order also removes the requirement that your parenting time be supervised. There shall be no other changes to the current schedule.

Mrs. Berman shall continue to exercise her visits at the home under Ms. Graham's supervision."

He paused and scanned his notes before continuing. "The court orders the appointment of a guardian ad litem in this action. I can see by the look on Mrs. Berman's face this is unfamiliar to her. Mrs. Berman, a guardian ad litem or GAL, is an attorney appointed by the court to advocate for the best interest of your daughter. The GAL will interview you as well as Mr. Berman. She will visit your homes. She will observe your daughter's interaction with you. She'll do the same with Mr. Berman. She will meet with Olivia and get to know her as well as her feelings and concerns. She will have access to Dr. Harper's records. She will visit your daughter's school to talk with her teachers. After the GAL has completed this, he or she will file a written report and recommendation. You and your attorney will be able to review the report."

Catherine, in a subdued tone, thanked him for the explanation.

"The court appoints Allison Wells as the guardian ad litem. She will contact the attorneys to schedule the visits. This will be included in my order. Court is adjourned."

Jax was scheduled in two courtrooms at nine o'clock. He gave Rick a very grateful handshake and friendly squeeze on his shoulder, then he exited the courtroom to switch roles from client to attorney.

Court was followed by a quick-lunch stop at Harold's Deli. When Jax returned to the office, Marion was on the phone. She gestured for him to stay until the call was complete. He read her notes. He saw the name "Miles Kaplan." It was followed by "wife murdered." Marion hung up as Jax was still trying to decipher the rest of her notes.

"Miles Kaplan? The CEO of First Citizens Bank?"

"That's the one," she answered while writing more notes. "He was calling from his home, which is now a crime scene. He came home late from a dinner meeting last night to find his wife dead on the kitchen floor in a massive pool of blood. Her body is at the morgue. Coroner is performing the autopsy and should have an official cause of death later today. The police want to interview Mr. Kaplan, but as he explained to me, he's watched enough true crime shows to know the spouse is always at the top of the suspect list. He wants to retain you. He hopes you can meet him today." Marion took a sip of her afternoon coffee. "Poor man. He sounded absolutely devastated. I told him you would be there at four-thirty."

"I've met him at fundraisers. I've only chatted with him briefly. He's done a lot of good things for this city, both with the bank's philanthropic fund and his private foundation."

"The new parks and green space popping up in the city are thanks to him. He has pumped a lot of money into vocational programs in the inner-city schools. If you recall, last summer, he launched a day-camp program to give underprivileged kids the chance to try camping, hiking, and horseback riding."

"Looks like I'm going to get to know Miles Kaplan up close and personal. Nothing like a bloody crime scene to lay the groundwork for a new friendship."

CHAPTER 20

When Jax arrived at the bronze gate at the entrance to Miles Kaplan's estate, he noticed an unmarked police cruiser parked on the street. He waved to the two detectives inside and pressed the intercom button. Upon identifying himself, the gate swung open slowly and majestically. Jax drove a thousand feet on a winding driveway to a grand stone mansion. Bevelled floor to ceiling windows, six fireplace chimneys, turrets, and a slate roof enhanced its grandeur.

Following the directions Marion had written for him, Jax walked to the far side of the home, which had a commanding view of lush-green hills and valleys. He made his way to what appeared to be a separate cottage. Miles opened the bevelled glass front door before Jax could ring the bell. Jax entered a spacious gathering room. The rear wall was nothing but glass. The view revealed a slate terrace furnished with chaises and a dining table with six chairs crafted from teak that was well-oiled. The gathering room was outfitted with blue-and-yellow floral sofas facing each other in front of a stone fireplace.

"I've never had the opportunity to stay in the cottage," Miles said as he sat down on the sofa. Jax took the opposite sofa. "I guess there's a first time for everything." He tried to manage a smile.

Jax replied, "I'm sure, Mr. Kaplan, the last place you wanted to spend last night was in your house. It's also still"—Jax searched for a euphemism for crime scene—"an investigation scene."

"The officers were very understanding last night. They danced around the notion that my kitchen was an active crime scene. They made it sound as if it were for my own good that I vacate the premises. I appreciate their valiant attempt to convince me I was not a suspect. But I'm not an idiot. The husband is always the first person of interest." He hesitated before continuing, "There it is. *Person of interest.* Just another kinder, gentler way of saying *suspect.*"

"Mr. Kaplan, when I pulled up to the house a few minutes ago, I saw two police cruisers and a crime-lab van still here. I wouldn't think of asking you to return to your kitchen so soon. However, I need to examine the scene to get the best sense of what took place. I'll return shortly, and we'll talk about last night."

"I will wait here. By the way, please call me Miles. May I call you Jax?"

When Jax approached the front door of the main house, a uniformed officer was stationed outside. The officer radioed the detective leading the investigation. When he was cleared to enter, he shook hands with the officer and pushed open the door. He was familiar with the protocol. Defense counsel can view a crime scene but only when escorted by the officer in charge.

The officer led him to the kitchen door, where the detective was waiting. Following the detective into the kitchen, he was awestruck by the enormity of the crime scene. The floor was lined with plastic tarps affixed with blue masking tape, remnants of the crime-lab technicians who worked through the night processing the area. The kitchen was off-limits, not that anyone would want to cook a meal there.

The pale oak floor near the island was saturated with blood. It oozed over a five-foot radius, coming to a stop at the base of the island. The tavern stools were knocked on their side. One of the stools was broken in half. Shards of broken glass surrounded the area where Judy Kaplan's body had come to its final resting place. Jax wasn't sure where the glass had come from; it was probably glassware on the island. It shattered during the struggle between Judy and her killer. A familiar odor permeated the air. It was the smell of blood, indescribable to someone who had not experienced it. It had an acidic scent combined with human decay. It was undeniably the smell of death. Jax took his handkerchief out of his pocket and covered his nose and mouth to quell the nausea.

The lead detective shook his head back and forth, letting out a long breath. "This is one of the worst ones I've seen, Jax. We've been here all night just trying to make sense of what the hell happened."

"I can't imagine the horror this poor woman experienced. What's your gut instinct telling you? One assailant? Or more?"

"Too soon to tell. We should have the autopsy results today. The techies are processing the blood to determine if it's all from the victim or if it's from others too."

"Keep me informed, Detective. Thanks for allowing me a first-hand look. I've seen all I need or want to see at this point." He shook the detective's hand and returned to the guest cottage.

Jax found Miles still seated on the sofa. He hadn't moved while Jax visited the main house. Jax returned to his wingback chair. After some preliminary conversation—age, no prior criminal record, his years with the bank, his private foundation, and his prior military service—the conversation turned to his marriage and its gruesome end.

He and Judy met thirty years ago in college. Miles was a finance major, and Judy studied business and marketing. Miles was an officer in the Army ROTC. Judy was elected vice president of the student body. After graduation, the two were engaged, but they postponed the wedding until Miles completed his three years with the Army. He left with the rank of captain, and he earned his master's degree in economics during his service. He returned to Cincinnati and worked as a loan officer for First Citizens Bank. Six months later, Judy moved to Cincinnati and became Mrs. Miles Kaplan.

Miles quickly rose through the rank-and-file positions at the bank. When he was forty years old, he assumed the title of CEO. The bank had grown as quickly as he had. Its roots in Cincinnati, the bank had hundreds of offices in a dozen states east of the Mississippi. Miles Kaplan was one of the wealthiest men in the city.

The couple added two daughters to their family. Jenna was a law student at the University of Cincinnati and rented an apartment near the school. Madison, the younger daughter, attended college in Arizona. Miles and Judy had been planning a twenty-fifth anniversary party.

Miles, his head in his hands, talked about last night. "I worked late after the board meeting broke up at seven o'clock. I had a quick burger and a martini at the restaurant in the lobby. I sat at the bar, alone, and stayed for an hour or so. I came home a little after nine o'clock."

"What about the security gate at the end of your driveway?"

"Nothing unusual," answered Miles. "The gate was closed. I entered the code to open it."

"What door did you enter?"

"I parked my car in the garage, like I always do. Wait, now that I think about it, there was something out of the ordinary, but at the time, I didn't pay much attention to it. After I went into the house and found Nancy, it totally escaped my mind until now."

"What's that, Miles?"

"When I got out of my car and walked to the door leading from the garage into my home office, I prepared to enter the code to the home security system. It was late, and Judy always sets the alarm system before she goes upstairs to bed. It wasn't engaged last night. I just walked into the house."

Jax wrote this on his notepad. "We'll make sure to share this with the detectives when we meet with them. It could, at the very least, help establish time of death. It could also mean whoever did this had access to your security code."

Miles nodded before continuing his story. "I walked down the hall leading to the kitchen. Judy's office is off the hallway to the right. The laundry room is on the left. There were no lights on in those rooms, and the hallway light was off. When I entered the kitchen, the only light was the one over the stove. At first, I didn't notice anything at all. Then I noticed a strange odor. I never smelled anything like it before. Now I know it was the smell of blood." Miles took a deep breath and let it out slowly. "I walked past the stove to check the mail. Judy always has it waiting on the island. As I was reaching for the stack of mail, I saw, on the other side of the island, Nancy's hand on the floor. I thought maybe she had passed out, which was a scary thought in itself. In all of our years together, Judy never had any fainting spells. But you can see it would be a logical conclusion, right?"

"Of course," Jax responded.

"I dropped the mail on the counter and rushed over to her." Miles paused. His eyes shut tightly to stem the flow of tears. "There she was. The blood. There was just so much blood. It's all I can see when I close my eyes. I lost all sense of time, but I believe it was just a minute or so before I was able to take my cell phone out of my pocket and call 911."

"Miles, let's take a break from this conversation for a few minutes. Take some deep breaths and collect your thoughts." Jax rose from his chair and left through a set of French doors opening onto a slate terrace. He, too, needed some deep breaths and a few minutes to collect his thoughts.

Returning to the gathering room, he found Miles standing near the window, looking out on his manicured landscaping. He had been crying. Blowing his nose into a tissue, he resumed his place on the sofa.

"Do you have any idea who would do this to your wife?"

Miles sighed. "Judy didn't have an enemy in the world. She had a huge circle of friends. She even kept in touch with childhood friends from her hometown, and they would get together twice a year for a girls' weekend at our home in northern Michigan."

"Do you know anyone who would have done this to get back at you for something, Miles? You actually could have been the target, but he or she decided this would make you suffer even worse than if they killed you."

Miles thought for a moment. "I'm sure I have people who resent me for one reason or another. But I can't think of anyone who has threatened me recently or has any real motive to do this."

"This has been an exhausting day for you. I'll contact the police and the prosecutor to make arrangements for us to meet with them tomorrow. The sooner they can eliminate you, the better the chances are of finding the perpetrator."

"Thanks for coming to meet with me, Jax. I know your reputation. I can't believe I would ever have needed to retain your services. Another one of life's cruel ironies, I suppose. I know you're the best. I want the best on my side. I'll wait to hear from you."

It was early evening when Jax left the Kaplan estate. Dusk was settling on the city as he drove to the office. He wanted to check his messages from the afternoon, and he wanted to be sure Bailey had fresh food and water. He knew Marion always did this at the end of the day. It was just an excuse for him to spend a few minutes with his cat. Time spent with Bailey always had a calming effect.

Instead of parking in his lot at the rear of his office building, he pulled up to the front and stopped the car in a parking space on the street. As he exited his car, even though it was dark, he could see broken glass littering the sidewalk. His office window had been shattered. "Bastards," muttered Jax as he pulled out his phone to contact the emergency glass-repair company. *I wonder if they give discounts for regular customers.*

CHAPTER 21

While Jax awaited the arrival of the emergency window-repair company, he phoned John Harrison, the county prosecutor. He could have contacted the chief assistant, but Jax knew John himself would head the investigation into Judy Kaplan's murder. This was going to be headline news, both locally and nationally. John Harrison was up for reelection next year. Being the lead story on the news beats the hell out of traditional campaigning. Headline news is free publicity; campaign signs, billboards, and television commercials cost tens of thousands of dollars.

After engaging in small talk about their golf handicaps, Jax and John made arrangements to bring Miles Kaplan to the Prosecutor's Office the following afternoon for an interview with the lead detective. Harrison promised he would attend.

After the call, Jax gave his undivided attention to the most important part of his day. He drove to his former home to pick up Olivia for her first overnight visit since Judge Westerfield issued the new visitation schedule. Olivia opened the door, and Jenny appeared with a suitcase and backpack. Jenny and Jax hugged quickly, and Jenny planted a big kiss on Olivia's cheek. Father and daughter hopped in the car to travel back to Jax's house and hopefully back to normalcy.

She brought and packed her largest suitcase with items to leave in her room permanently. She announced, "I want to make the bedroom *my* bedroom."

Jax, feeling emotions welling up inside, lovingly ruffled her hair and replied, "It is *your* bedroom, Princess. Do whatever you want. This is your home too."

Olivia thought Jax's car was her car too. She tuned the radio to her favorite station. Jax tried to drown out the noise that was the number one pop song from the latest boy band. He longed for his blues station. Hell, he even missed Julia's rock and roll. In spite of the music, he was getting a kick out of his little girl singing the lyrics.

Arriving home, Olivia ran upstairs to her room to unpack. When she walked into the kitchen a half hour later, Jax had a fire roaring in the fireplace and a cheese tray waiting.

"How does a steak and french fries sound? It's too cold for out-door grilling, but we can do them inside just as well."

"Perfect, Daddy! Let's dig into the cheese and watch something fun on Netflix."

Olivia sipped on a Shirley Temple, and Jax indulged in a small glass of red wine. Together they watched a corny adolescent show, its dialogue replete with one cliché after another. Not needing to devote his intellectual resources to the show, he was able to watch and assess the current situation. Any concerns about Olivia needing a period of adjustment to the new schedule were laid to rest. It was as if the period of separation, followed by weeks of Jax visiting Olivia at her home, hadn't occurred at all.

The father-daughter cooking duo prepared their steak dinner together, chatting about school and friends. The conversation continued at the kitchen table.

Olivia steered the conversation in a different direction. She casually mentioned Catherine. "I'm really glad I get to come to your house again. It just makes me feel happy." She paused. "And safe too."

Jax was surprised by the comment. "You know you're safe here with me. You're also safe with your mother. You're lucky to have two parents who love you to the moon and back."

Olivia was silent for a little too long before saying softly, "I feel safer here with you, Daddy."

"What do you mean?"

The floodgates opened. She told him how uncomfortable and unsafe she recently began to feel when she was with her mother. She confided that Catherine had found religion and started attending some small church in the suburbs a few times a week. Catherine grew up with a Jewish father and a Catholic mother. Neither of her parents had any interest in organized religion. Jax was not even sure if she had ever been baptized. Now she was a churchgoer?

Jax eased into the conversation. "Do you go to church with her?"

Olivia munched on a french fry before answering. "I went a couple times. It's not a very big church. While the grown-ups are in the church service, the children spend the time in a meeting room in the basement. The other kids aren't very talkative. They're all home-schooled because the church doesn't believe in public education. I was pretty much treated like an outsider because I go to a real school. It took a lot to convince Mommy how uncomfortable it was for me, but she finally understood. She doesn't make me go anymore."

Jax absorbed this information. He was still reeling from the drastic turn in the conversation. "Olivia, if your mom wants to attend church, it's her choice. Keep in mind she has respected your wishes not to go. Give her the same respect in return. She doesn't make you go, and you shouldn't make her *not* go. Don't criticize her or stand in the way if it's something she really wants to do."

"I understand what you're saying. But it's not as simple as her going to church a few times a week. This whole church thing has taken over her life. Everything she does revolves around the church and the sermons. Even though I don't go to church anymore, when she comes home, she tells me about the sermon. She practically tells me word for word what the minister preached. Instead of listening to music when we're in the car, Mommy listens to church sermons on podcasts. Before she moved out of the house, she built some weird wooden altar with a cross on it, and she would pray before it. Sometimes, when I came home from school, I found her curled up asleep underneath it. It gave me the creeps."

Jax thought this through before saying, "I don't recall seeing anything like an altar when I was visiting you at the house."

"That's because she took it apart and stored the pieces in the basement when she moved out."

Jax chewed on a piece of steak as he tried to make sense of what Olivia was telling him. Was he really dealing with two Catherines? Was she a divided self? If so, how long had this been going on?

"Here's what really bugs me," she continued. "Mommy is supposed to be all religious and into obeying God's laws, but the things she says about you aren't very religious, if you know what I mean."

Jax laughed. "Mommy and I are not together anymore, but we stand together when it comes to loving you and raising you. Mommy might still be angry with me, but she loves you with all her heart. She would never do anything to make you unhappy."

Olivia cut Jax off. "But she says such awful things about you. It hurts my feelings. She talks about how evil you are and how you work with criminals and dangerous people to make sure they stay out of jail so they can still do bad things to other people. She even told me last week that you're Satan."

Well, that is a bit extreme. Jax sipped his wine. *If this conversation goes much longer, I'm going to need a bigger glass of wine. Hell, I'll just get a straw for the bottle.* "Olivia I'm sorry you've been put in this position. But I'm glad you told me about it. I don't know if you have met her yet, but the judge has arranged for you to meet a nice lady who will help sort through the details of how you'll spend a lot of time with Mommy and with me."

"Her name is Allison Wells. She's coming to the house in a few days to see me. Jenny talked with her on the phone to schedule the visit. Jenny said she sounded nice."

"I'm sure she is. She'll get to know you. Then she'll be able to share your feelings with the judge. Think of her as a good friend you can talk to about anything."

"I wish we could all go back to the way it was before. You know, Mommy and you and I living together and going to Hilton Head together and doing all the fun things we used to do." She paused, taking a sip of her water. "I know that's probably not going to happen. The next best thing is, I get to see both of you and still get to do fun things."

He squeezed her hand. They finished their dinner engaged in lighter conversation.

They were loading the dishwasher when his cell phone rang. He knew from the caller ID it was Miles Kaplan. He dried his hands on the kitchen towel and answered the phone. "Good evening, Miles. I was going to call you later to brief you on my conversation with the prosecutor. We have a meeting in his office tomorrow. You'll give a formal statement to him and the lead detective."

"I think there's been a change in plans."

Jax sat on a tavern stool. "What are you talking about?"

"What I'm talking about is, the lead detective is here right now with several other detectives. They just served me with an arrest warrant. They charged me with murdering my wife. They allowed me to call you before they put the handcuffs on."

Jax was dumbfounded. "I talked to John Harrison just a couple hours ago. We have the meeting arranged. Put the lead detective on the phone."

After several seconds, another voice came on the phone. "This is Detective Mike Richardson. What can I do for you?"

Jax took a deep breath in an effort to keep his anger from getting the best of him. He exhaled slowly before answering. "Well, Mike, what you can do for me is tell me what the hell is going on. Mr. Kaplan and I have a meeting tomorrow afternoon in John Harrison's office to give a statement. He and I also agreed you should be there. Didn't he contact you?"

"He did, sir, but let's face it. This so-called meeting would just be the typical dance between the prosecution and the defense about what questions your client could or would answer. You'd probably shut him down on almost every question, with the possible exception of what he had for breakfast that morning, which would amount to absolutely nothing productive coming from the meeting. Our investigation, without your client's statement, has established sufficient probable cause to file murder charges against him."

"Mike, you and I have had so many cases together I can't begin to count. You know me. If I said I would have my client at Harrison's office tomorrow morning, you know from personal experience my promise is solid."

"No disagreement there, Mr. Berman. It's nothing personal. It's simply the nature of the beast. Prosecutors want answers, and defense attorneys do their best to avoid giving the answers. I already told you we have enough probable cause to make an arrest."

"You'd better plan on attending the bond hearing in the morning, Mike. I'm going to have a lot to say on the record about what just went down. I don't want to talk behind your back. You don't want to miss the chance to defend yourself. What were the words you just said to me? 'It's nothing personal.' Put my client back on the phone."

Jax could hear muffled voices before Miles was back on the phone. "Miles, this whole situation is seriously fucked up. They filed charges against you without waiting for your official statement. I'll find John Harrison as soon as we hang up. You have to go with the officers to be processed. I'll do everything in my power to get you out of jail in a few hours but prepare to be there until your bond hearing tomorrow morning. The court conducts bond hearings on Saturday mornings, so there will be zero chance of you staying in jail for the entire weekend."

"Jax, twenty-four hours ago, I was a married man who spent a normal day at the office. Now I'm a widower, having found my wife slaughtered. Now I'm a murder suspect. I feel like I am spiraling down the proverbial rabbit hole."

"Miles, I need you to stay strong, okay? I'll see you as soon as I can. At the very latest, I will see you in court in the morning. Cooperate with the police but keep your mouth shut. Answer no questions. Tell them right now that you will not answer any questions unless I am present. I'll try to track down John Harrison."

With a crack in his voice, Miles replied, "I understand, Jax. I'll do everything you said. I'll hope for the best but prepare for the worst. At the worst, I'll see you tomorrow morning."

*****

Saturday morning in the courthouse had an eerie, almost haunted, atmosphere. The arraignment courtroom was the only one open for business. The clerk's office had a skeleton crew to process the cases coming out of the courtroom. Jax still felt the hairs on the back of his neck prickle every Saturday. He walked the long hallway to the courtroom with Olivia by his side. She would soon be celebrating her eleventh birthday, but Jax was uncomfortable leaving her home alone. Although it was daylight and he would be gone for only a couple of hours, he didn't want anything about his first weekend with her to fail under scrutiny by the guardian ad litem. Olivia was no stranger to the Saturday arraignment docket. She had been tagging along with him for years.

His worst fears were confirmed. Every local news channel had a camera crew and reporter waiting for the case of State of Ohio vs. Miles Kaplan. Jax's anger had been on a slow simmer all night after speaking with Detective Richardson. His efforts to bring Miles in quietly and discretely for an interview were all meant to eliminate him as a person of interest in his wife's murder. It was also intended to accomplish it without the media turning it into headline news. Those goals were now flushed right down the proverbial toilet due to this underhanded stunt. His simmering anger was growing into a boiling rage as the judge took the bench and the bailiff called the first case.

"State of Ohio vs. Miles Kaplan," she announced from her desk next to the judge's bench.

Court security officers escorted Miles from the holding room behind the courtroom. The cameras started rolling. A hush fell over the room.

Jax was grateful they did not parade his client out in a bright-orange jail uniform. Miles was dressed neatly in the polo shirt and khaki slacks he was wearing when he was arrested.

The deputy removed the handcuffs as Jax approached the bench and stood next to his client. They shook hands as the judge addressed the courtroom spectators.

"This case is being called out of order to accommodate the members of the media here today," announced Judge Marsha Ratcliffe. *Despite their judicial demeanor, judges always have one eye on their next election,* thought Jax as he mentally rehearsed his remarks.

Judge Ratcliffe signaled for the assistant prosecutor to open. Nothing he said was unexpected. Murder in the first degree. Possibility of life in prison. Serious charges such as murder always carry a risk that the defendant will abscond from the jurisdiction of the court—

in layman's terms, to disappear without a trace. With his considerable wealth, the defendant had the means to flee the State of Ohio and to leave the country. He closed by asking for a million-dollars "cash only" bond. This meant the only way Miles could be released from jail was to post the entire one million dollars. He returned to his table and sat down, awaiting Jax's response. Jax didn't know this assistant prosecutor. He had never seen him in a courtroom before. He was probably a new lawyer on staff; the rookies usually got stuck with Saturday-morning arraignments.

The judge thanked the prosecutor for his recommendation and turned toward Jax. "Mr. Berman, what do you wish to offer on behalf of the defendant?"

"Actually, Judge," began Jax, "I have a lot to offer. I hoped the lead detective, Mike Richardson, would attend this hearing. I invited him by phone last night when he and I discussed the police department's blatant disrespect and disregard for the process initiated by the Prosecutor's Office yesterday."

"I don't know what you mean, Mr. Berman," replied the judge with a sincerely perplexed look on her face.

"Your Honor, I assure you by the time I finish with my remarks you will know *exactly* what I mean."

Ten minutes later, Judge Ratcliffe as well as every other person in the courtroom knew exactly what he meant.

"Your Honor, standing before you is one of the most prominent and philanthropic members of our business community. Of our entire community. Miles Kaplan has no prior criminal record. He doesn't even have a speeding ticket. His accomplishments in the banking community extend far beyond our city. He and his family have always served the charitable community. They are iconic examples of paying it forward. Less than forty-eight hours ago, Mr. Kaplan arrived at his home and witnessed a scene no human being should suffer. He found his wife of twenty-five years, the mother of his children, brutally murdered in their own home. He immediately dialed 911, and the recording of the call unmistakably captures the raw emotions Mr. Kaplan was experiencing. Your Honor, I have it captured on this flash drive, and I ask permission to play it for the court."

The judge, the media, and the spectators sat in stunned silence as the three-minute call echoed through the courtroom. As Jax got ready for his verbal attack on Detective Richardson, he noticed several people in the room, including the news reporters, wiping away tears. He turned toward Miles, who was silently weeping, his head bowed.

"Your Honor, it is against this backdrop that I, after consulting with my client at his home, contacted our county prosecutor, John Harrison. Yesterday afternoon, by phone, he and I agreed Mr. Kaplan and I would appear at his office this afternoon for the purpose of Mr. Kaplan participating in an official interview. We agreed Detective Richardson would be included in the interview."

Judge Ratcliffe interjected, "Then why was your client arrested last night?" *The judge has gone from calling Miles "the defendant" to "your client." A good sign*, thought Jax as he responded to her question. "As I stand before you, Judge, I don't have an answer to your question. I can only tell you Detective Richardson told me last night he wasn't interested in an interview because I, as his lawyer, could and would stop Mr. Kaplan from answering any questions."

The judge considered this answer before asking the assistant prosecutor, "Do you have any helpful information on this issue?"

The young lawyer, having expected a low-key arraignment docket typical of Saturday morning, rose from his chair, his cheeks flushed red. Jax felt sorry for the kid. "Your Honor, I have nothing in this file except the charging documents and a note from my supervisor directing me to ask for the million-dollar cash bond. I apologize."

"No need to apologize," replied the judge, with a hint of a smile on her face. She obviously felt sorry for the kid too.

"Do you wish to offer anything further on behalf of your client, Mr. Berman?"

Stifling the desire to chuckle, Jax simply said, "Your Honor, there is a lot more I could offer on behalf of my client, but I believe I have sufficiently responded to the sole issue of bond this morning."

Judge Ratcliffe reviewed the charging documents, including an affidavit from Detective Richardson with his summary of the investigation. "Based upon a review of the court filings, while I do make a finding that the complaint contains sufficient evidence to establish probable cause, the court does find the State's bond recommendation to be unreasonable in these circumstances. Bond is set at five hundred thousand dollars, and the defendant may post ten percent of that amount in order to secure his release. Bailiff may call the next case."

Jax walked with Miles back into the holding room to make the necessary arrangements for posting fifty thousand dollars to set him free. Before he left the courtroom, he looked over into the front row of the gallery and gave a quick wink to Olivia. She had been to enough court hearings to know his wink meant she was to sit there until he returned.

Jax always knew that owning a bank would have some benefits. He never saw fifty thousand dollars transferred so quickly from one account to another. Miles, with one phone call lasting fewer than sixty seconds, had the money available to post with the clerk. He was already wearing his street clothes; there was no added delay in releasing him.

Jax and Miles made an appointment for Monday afternoon. Miles was going straight home to catch up on the sleep he missed the night before. Jail cells are not conducive to a restful night.

Jax went to the courtroom to retrieve Olivia. He had promised her breakfast at a charming downtown diner known for the best pancakes in the area. They were walking toward the rear doors of the courtroom opening into the public hallway when Jax felt a tap on his shoulder. He turned around to find the young assistant prosecutor who had handled the bond hearing.

"Mr. Berman, my name is Stephen Norman. I've never met you, but I've heard a lot about you. I just passed the bar exam and joined the Prosecutor's Office. So far, it's been an easy and maybe even a little boring experience. But you sure livened up the morning for me. I want to thank you for the educational experience."

Jax laughingly responded, "Glad to help, Stephen. I'll look forward to seeing you in the future."

With his arm on Olivia's shoulder, they left the courthouse to enjoy the rest of their weekend.

CHAPTER 22

"What do you mean he fell off the face of the earth?" Jax asked in a louder-than-normal voice.

Leonard dropped into the chair next to Marion's desk. Officer Kevin Wilson was missing. "I can't find him. Anywhere. I've been on his trail for the past few days. I didn't trouble you with a blow-by-blow account because I know you've been otherwise occupied." Jax had confided to Leonard the details of his divorce proceedings. Leonard continued, "I've tried his cell phone, his landline, his email, his Facebook page, and his Instagram account. No activity on any of them. I've staked out his house in the evenings, hoping to catch him. No luck. I contacted his parents, primarily because they're his parents but secondarily because they're paying your fee. They haven't heard from him since Thanksgiving. They told me it was a quiet family celebration in light of their son's current situation. Kevin seemed quieter than usual, but they didn't give it much thought. They understood he was under a lot of stress. The Wilsons gave me the names of Kevin's closest friends. Some are police officers, but most of them are not. I ran down every one of them, and nobody has heard from him."

Marion interjected, "Kevin Wilson is on the calendar tomorrow afternoon at three o'clock for an appointment. Let's see if he shows up."

Jax nodded to her. "Good idea. I think he and I have a good relationship. In our conversations, he seems to trust me. If he doesn't come tomorrow, let's decide our next move. There are no upcoming hearings requiring his appearance, so we don't have to worry about his bond being revoked. But this case is still heavy on the minds of the community, and the last thing we need is more fuel on the fire by having our client skip bail."

Leonard put on his overcoat. "I'll keep looking till then. Marion, please let me know if Kevin keeps his appointment tomorrow." He exited the office, taking great care not to step on Bailey, who had come into Marion's office in search of a good napping spot, which is defined by a cat as a warm rug and sunshine pouring through the window.

*****

Julia agreed to cover an evening rotation at the hospital for a colleague; Jax met her for a quick dinner. They settled in a booth near the back of the bistro-style restaurant. Most of the customers were medical staff. Julia stopped at a couple of tables to exchange greetings. During dinner, Jax and Julia spent most of the time making plans for the upcoming weekend together. After a quick embrace outside the restaurant, Julia returned to the hospital, and Jax drove home.

Navigating through the business district, he saw in the distance the pulsating lights of emergency vehicles. They seemed to be stopped somewhere near his office. A chilling and nauseating feeling overcame him when he realized the emergency crews were in front of his building. He pulled his car over to the curb and ran toward his office, which had thick dark smoke billowing from the rear.

A firefighter stopped Jax, yelling, "Sorry, sir, emergency personnel only! Spectators need to keep a safe distance!"

"I'm not a spectator!" Jax yelled, out of breath from a combination of the run and fear. "I own the building!"

"That's different, sir. Let me escort you to the officer in charge." The firefighter led the way. Jax followed close behind.

He could see the fire had been brought well under control, and there was only a relatively small stream of smoke. As the officer in charge was walking toward him, Jax suddenly thought of Bailey. He ran toward the side door of his building, but he was stopped by the same firefighter who escorted him.

"Sir, you can't enter the building while it's an active fire scene."

"My cat is in there!" Jax pushed his way past and opened the door.

"Your *what* is in there?" the firefighter shouted, but not loudly enough for Jax to hear the question.

Entering the office, he was met by the overwhelming stench of burned wood and insulation. Activating the flashlight on his cell phone as he made his way through the first floor, the light magnified the hazy smoke in the air. He took off his wool scarf and wrapped it around his nose and mouth. The damage was confined to only a small part of the office, but he dismissed the thought for the moment. He had to find Bailey.

Going from room to room, calling Bailey's name, he heard nothing. When he entered his office, he crawled on his hands and knees to escape the smoke. Moving his flashlight in a sweeping motion as he searched for the cat, he found his desk. And Bailey. She was curled up under the desk. Looking as if she were asleep, he knew in his heart she wasn't sleeping. She didn't respond to his voice. She didn't respond to his touch.

Jax put his ear down to Bailey's face. He held his own breath as he listened, hoping for a heartbeat or the sound of her breathing. When he was about to abandon all hope, a sound emanated from her. Not so much a typical feline meow but more of a wheezing gasp.

Jax picked her up, wrapped her in his scarf, and found his way out the front door of the building. He assumed there would be, at least, one pissed off firefighter waiting for him at the side door, and he needed to avoid any confrontation. His top priority was getting help for Bailey.

He ran with his unconscious cat back to his car. Hurriedly settling her on his lap, he drove straight to the nearest emergency veterinary hospital. He stopped the car at the entrance, not taking the time to find a designated parking place, and he rushed through the lobby toward the intake desk.

Bailey was still unconscious and wrapped in his scarf as the technician behind the counter stood up, approaching him with outstretched arms. Jax handed Bailey to her while he gave an abridged version of why he was there. With a warm and sympathetic smile, she directed Jax to the waiting room, then she whisked Bailey through the double doors leading to the treatment rooms.

Jax was mindlessly watching whatever home-decorating show was playing on the waiting room television for, at least, an hour. A petite blonde wearing horn-rimmed glasses and a set of pale-blue scrubs came into the waiting room. She introduced herself as Dr. Danielle Acomb and explained she was a veterinarian with specialized training in animal pulmonology.

"You did the right thing getting Bailey to us so quickly, Mr. Berman. We have her comfortable in an oxygen cage where she can receive therapy for her lungs without having to be hooked up to tubes or machines."

"It looks like she's in good hands. This is my first time in an emergency vet clinic, and I must say it's impressive." *And quite expensive too, I'm sure. I wonder how much I'll be billed for this conversation.*

Jax cast aside his cynical thoughts about the cost and instead focused on the doctor's information. "Is she awake yet, Doctor?"

"Yes, she is. Our examination reveals she has no burns on her skin. We have taken an x-ray and have drawn some blood to assess the extent of damage to her lungs. We have also examined her eyes and happily found no ulcerations there, which is another potential injury to cats caught in a fire."

"So mostly good news then, right?" Jax asked cautiously.

"Yes, mostly good news. We'll have the x-ray and blood-test results within the hour. If you wish, I can phone you with the results if you don't want to wait."

"When would I be able to see her?"

"Mr. Berman, you should be able to go back to see her in a couple hours."

"I'll wait. Let me know when you get the results."

Dr. Acomb smiled and gave him a gentle squeeze on his shoulder. She returned to the emergency room, and Jax returned to the home-decorating show.

It was two o'clock in the morning when Jax arrived home. The test results on Bailey were encouraging. There was no indication of severe lung damage, but she would need to remain in the oxygen cage for seventy-two hours. Jax was allowed to visit her, and Bailey recognized him. He sat next to her oxygen cage for almost an hour. He planned to visit, at least, twice a day until he could take her home. He knew Olivia would want to visit her too.

Instead of driving directly home from the veterinary hospital, he went to his office. The emergency vehicles were long gone, and the pavement was drying out from the water used to extinguish the fire. Although it was the dead of night, Jax could see the damage was not very extensive. The major task was going to be cleaning and fumigating the inside to get rid of the smoke. When he called Marion from the waiting room at the animal hospital to tell her about the fire, she swung into action. While he learned how to decorate a kitchen with antique cans and bottles, she texted him to let him know a cleanup crew would arrive in the morning.

Despite being exhausted from the events of the day and the emotions that went with them, he checked his office voice mail for messages. The only message was from Lieutenant Roberts of the fire department, advising him the fire marshal will visit the fire scene in the morning to confirm the initial assessment of the origin of the fire. It started in or near the rear door of the office building leading to Jax's private parking lot. The more disturbing part of the message was the report of evidence of an accelerant, which indicated the fire had been intentionally set.

Broken flowerpots and windows are one thing, but arson? Who in the hell is behind this?

When Jax arrived the next morning, Marion was already there—of course, she was—engaged in deep conversation with the fire restoration crew she contacted the night before. Jax caught up with the conversation. While the actual fire damage to the back of the building was confined to a back room, which served as a combination of kitchenette and storage room, the entire office would require deep cleaning to eliminate the smoke damage to the walls, floors, and furniture. Giving a quick approval of the estimate for the job and securing a guarantee from them that their work would be complete in three days, Jax gathered the files Marion had already packed for him and set out for his temporary location at Rick's law firm. When Jax phoned Rick to tell him about the fire, Rick did not hesitate to offer him refuge in an empty office at his firm. Marion planned to remain at the office to oversee the cleanup crew and to field incoming phone calls. She would also phone all clients who had appointments scheduled and give them the address of Jax's temporary office.

Marion contacted one of the premier homebuilders in the city, and he immediately offered to have a crew available for the reconstruction job. They would begin when the fire marshal completed his investigation. Jax had, a year earlier, cleared the homebuilder's teenage son of marijuana-possession charges, which saved his college football scholarship with a Big Ten program. While Jax had amassed an untold number of people who would want something bad to happen to him, he probably had an equal number of grateful clients and family members who would be willing to offer help if he needed it.

Thankfully Jax had no court appearances scheduled for the morning, which gave him the opportunity to organize his temporary quarters. His only appointment for the afternoon was with Miles Kaplan, and it wasn't until one o'clock. This gave him time to visit Bailey. He picked up a corned beef sandwich from Harold's Deli and went to the veterinary hospital to have lunch with her. He planned to share his sandwich if the doctor permitted.

*****

Miles Kaplan was waiting for Jax when he returned after lunch with Bailey. Jax explained the events of the previous evening that necessitated the temporary relocation. Miles was sympathetic to Jax's plight. His genuine display of concern and compassion was just what Jax needed to regain his equilibrium. *This guy recently lost his wife, and he's charged with her murder. In contrast, I've got some minor damage to my office, and my cat is recovering in an outrageously expensive animal hospital. All in all, Jax, life could be a whole lot worse.*

"Miles," Jax began, "the past few days have been a blur for you, I know. We've had very little chance to sit down and go over the facts. We've not been able to review together the circumstances leading up to the death of your wife. We have plenty of time this afternoon to go through the details of the tragedy as well as events and activities leading up to the crime. Share as much information as possible, no matter how insignificant it may seem to you. One never knows what may be hidden in facts which, on their face, seem trivial."

"Fire away with your questions."

"Let's begin at the beginning. You already told me how you and Judy met in college, your military service, your move to Cincinnati, and your career with the bank. Your daughters are still in school, one in Arizona and one here in law school. Is all of that accurate?"

"Yes, it is."

"Okay, let's go from there."

The door to the office opened, and in walked Leonard. Jax made the introductions and explained Leonard's involvement in the case.

For the next hour, Miles answered Jax's and Leonard's questions. While Miles Kaplan was the embodiment of the American Dream— college education, serving his country, married to his college sweetheart, two overachieving children—there was swirling underneath the not-so-unique dark side to his story.

Miles explained while he had always loved his wife, he was *in love* with another woman. If that wasn't enough of a precarious situation, Miles made it doubly so because the other woman was a vice president of his bank. To make it even more complicated, she was only a few years older than Miles's eldest daughter. Miles and Hannah Gilbert had worked together for five years, and they had been having an affair for the past two. Hannah had been hired away from another local bank and assigned as a branch manager. She was promoted to vice president in charge of wealth and asset management after three years with the bank. This promotion meant she would be working closely with the president of the bank. The close working relationship developed into a close social and personal relationship. It became a true love affair two years ago.

In answer to Jax's question, Miles said Judy knew nothing about the relationship. She never showed signs of being suspicious.

Hannah had been married but was now divorced. She and Harrison Gilbert had been married for five years and had no children. Hannah left her husband, and their divorce was amicably negotiated and became final about six months ago.

Her ex-husband was employed as a project manager for a national construction company headquartered in the city. Miles knew nothing else about Harrison Gilbert. He was unsure if he knew about his wife's affair. Leonard made a few notes with the intention of finding out much more about Mr. Gilbert.

Miles explained, since her divorce, Hannah was pressuring him to leave his wife and marry her. She even mentioned the notion of having children together, a prospect not especially appealing to a man who had already raised two children. He last saw Hannah two days before the murder. After a quiet dinner at her home, he and Hannah argued about their future. Miles reminded her he had never, in their entire relationship, made any promises about marriage. Hannah became extremely emotional during the argument and threatened to call Judy to expose the affair. Almost immediately after those words left her mouth, she apologized for having made the threat. She assured him it was said in the heat of the moment, and she really would never do such a thing. The evening ended quickly.

"It was a side to her I had never seen before. It was quite startling. Since that evening, I had been really wrestling with the idea of ending it with Hannah. But then, with everything that's happened since then, I've had far more important matters to deal with besides her outburst." Miles turned his attention to the window behind Jax, and his eyes glazed over with tears. Jax could see the toll this conversation was taking on his client.

"Miles, thanks so much for your candor and honesty. I'm sure it was difficult."

Miles blew his nose into his handkerchief and returned it to his pocket. "Jax, I haven't told a living soul about my relationship with Hannah. In a way, it feels like a huge weight has been lifted from my chest. My Catholic upbringing gave this conversation the feeling of a confession. I hope it was as helpful for you."

Jax rose from his chair and said, "You've given us some good information. Leonard will take the investigation from here. I'll keep you advised. Please don't leave town. It's one of the conditions of your release from jail. I'll let you know when our next court appearance is scheduled."

Miles shook hands with Jax and Leonard, picked up his coat, and exited. Looking at his slumped shoulders and the slow shuffling of his feet, it seemed his client had aged ten years in the few days since they first met.

While Jax and Leonard together sifted through the information Miles provided and plotted their initial strategies, Jax's cell phone rang. The caller ID showed the caller was Marion.

"Is Leonard still there with you?" she asked.

"He is. Do you need to talk to him?"

"Not really. I'm calling to let you know I could never get Kevin Wilson to answer his phone, which means he wouldn't know the appointment with you has been moved to Rick's office, which means he would have shown up here. His appointment was scheduled to start fifteen minutes ago. There's no sign of him."

"Thanks, Marion, I'll let him know." He ended the call and looked at Leonard.

"Looks like our officer Wilson has indeed fallen off the face of the earth. I'll step up the search immediately."

CHAPTER 23

The next few weeks passed by uneventfully. If Jax had to endure any more eventful weeks, it probably would be the death of him. The office was restored to its former self, with a few improvements to the layout of the kitchenette and storage space. New flooring, new appliances, a fresh colorful paint on the walls, and wood-crafted shelves for storage made the space more efficient and appealing. It was all the product of Marion's inspiration. The other improvement was the installation of security cameras on all four corners of his building. This was Jax's inspiration. It brought some calm and order to his professional life. However, there was one not-so-insignificant matter exerting an uncertain and anxious mood in the office.

Officer Kevin Wilson was still missing.

Bailey was released from the veterinary hospital after receiving oxygen therapy for two days. Happy to return home, she dashed from room to room, ensuring her toys and her food bowls were exactly where they were supposed to be. Jax and Olivia visited her in the hospital twice. Olivia brought Bailey a new toy to amuse herself while she was sequestered in the oxygen cage.

Olivia adjusted to the expanded visitation schedule with her father. On weekdays when she spent the night, she and Jax enjoyed an early breakfast at a diner near school.

Olivia was still visiting with Catherine as she always had. The court hadn't changed her schedule. She seemed, to Jax, to be unusually quiet and reserved when talking about her mother. While she mentioned Catherine in passing, she seemed to be purposely avoiding any direct discussion about her. He surmised Olivia harbored feelings of disloyalty to her mother by having revealed to him the sudden changes in Catherine's activities. Jax kept his observations to himself. Olivia appeared to be doing very well in all other aspects of her life—school, friends, and preparing for the upcoming spring soccer season.

It was against this backdrop of calm and a return to normal—or a return to the new normal—that Jax decided the time was right for Olivia and Julia to meet.

"Let's talk about our plans for this weekend," he said as they were driving to school. "I thought it might be nice if you met a friend of mine. We could get together for dinner Saturday night. You can pick the restaurant."

"Sure. Who's your friend?"

Taking a deep breath, Jax replied, "My friend is a doctor at Children's Hospital. She has a very important job there treating seriously ill children who come from all over the world."

"She sounds important. What's her name? How long has she been your friend?"

"Her name is Julia. Dr. Julia Winston. I met her a few months ago."

Olivia, reaching for her backpack as Jax turned into her school parking lot, gave him a quick kiss on the cheek and said, "I'd like to meet her. Let's go to Antonio's for some lasagna Saturday. Does Julia like lasagna?"

Jax smiled. "I'm sure she does. Have a good day at school. I love you."

Exiting the car, Olivia turned and waved, blowing him a kiss as she ran up the steps.

Letting out a huge breath he was unaware he had been holding, Jax blew Olivia a return kiss and drove to the office. Savoring the moment and relieved Olivia wanted to meet Julia, his thoughts turned to the missing Kevin Wilson. Hopefully Leonard would have some positive news for him.

Leonard did not.

*****

Julia was seated at a corner table at Antonio's when Jax and Olivia arrived. They discussed the logistics of this very important evening, and both agreed it would be best if Julia met them at the restaurant. After making the preliminary introductions, they took their seats across the table.

Julia and Olivia talked about anything and everything. The conversation began with Julia asking Olivia about school, soccer, and topics of interest to a preadolescent girl. Julia had been one herself, whereas Jax had never had the experience. Olivia seemed fascinated when the conversation turned to Julia's work at the hospital. He was amazed at the insightful questions she asked about pediatric cancer, the kids' families, and the details of Julia's typical day of work. By the time their lasagna was served, it was as if Olivia and Julia were lifelong friends.

Sharing a generous portion of tiramisu, Olivia said, while still chewing her dessert, "This has been such a fun evening. Julia, I really like talking with you. You have so many interesting stories. I know you're my Dad's friend, but maybe we could be friends too."

After exchanging a quick glance and smile with Jax, Julia replied, "Olivia, I see a great friendship in our future. As I told you, I don't have any children of my own, and the only children in my life are my patients. They're focusing on getting well, and they don't have time for the fun things like school and friends and soccer. Hearing about your activities reminds me there are healthy and happy kids like you who are enjoying life. Having you as a friend will be very good for me."

Olivia smiled. "I would never have thought of it that way. I guess that's because I'm still a kid. But I'll be glad to help you, Julia."

Jax, who had been not much more than a silent spectator throughout the evening, offered an observation. "Ladies, this has been one of the best evenings I can remember. My favorite daughter and my friend have struck up a friendship of their own." He raised his glass of wine to toast the occasion.

Olivia raised her Shirley Temple to toast Jax and Julia. "I'm your only daughter, so of course, I'm your favorite daughter. You've been saying that since I was a baby. But I guess it's still funny in a way."

Jax laughed out loud and responded, "It's nice to know you think I'm somewhat amusing."

"You're somewhat amusing. But it wouldn't hurt to come up with some new material. I'm not a baby anymore."

"Noted, Princess. I mean, noted, Olivia."

Olivia finished her final bite of dessert. "I'm glad you're my dad's friend, Julia. I worry about him being alone when I'm not there."

Jax replied, "You're sweet, but please don't waste your time worrying about me or about your mother either. We'll always be there for you. You don't have to take care of us, understand?"

"I do. But I'm still happy that you have Julia as your friend. Mommy has Charlie as her friend, so I don't ever worry about her being lonely when I'm not there with her."

Charlie? Who the hell is Charlie? Jax paused before asking the obvious question, being careful to use the right tone of voice. "I'm glad your mother has a friend too. I don't think I know Charlie."

Olivia answered, "Probably not. I didn't meet him till after you moved out. He's pretty nice. When Mommy was still living at the house with me, Charlie would come over a couple times a week. He's really good at playing Monopoly, but I've actually beaten him once or twice."

"Have you done any other fun things with Charlie and your mother?"

"Nothing really exciting. Out to dinner, to the movies, just little things like that. I haven't seen him since Mommy moved out of the house, but I'm sure they still do things together."

"Do you know Charlie's last name?"

Olivia thought for a moment before shaking her head and telling Jax she didn't remember.

Another item on Leonard's to-do list.

When they left the restaurant, a light snow was falling. It accumulated on the cars and the parking lot. Olivia ran ahead, trying to catch snowflakes on her tongue. Jax was careful not to reach for Julia's hand or put his arm around her shoulder. This first meeting of his two favorite girls had gone so smoothly; he didn't want to take a chance of tarnishing the evening. Olivia ran back to them as they approached

Jax's car; Julia's was parked nearby. Olivia gave Julia a quick hug. Jax was enjoying the moment when a loud cracking sound rang out. It was a sound he had never heard yet recognized immediately. Almost simultaneously the rear window of his car exploded. Julia grabbed Olivia and pulled her to the ground. Jax crouched down and crawled to them. He shepherded them toward the front of his car, away from the direction of the gunshot. While he was doing this, making sure they stayed low to the ground, he heard the squeal of tires. They stayed low and close to the front of the car, listening to the fast-moving car roar through the parking lot onto the street.

Still in position by the front of his car, Jax dialed 9-1-1. His second call was to Leonard, who arrived only minutes after the first responders. Olivia was crying and on the verge of hyperventilating. Julia had her arms around her in an attempt to console her. She was oddly grateful for the opportunity to comfort Olivia, for it distracted her from the abject terror pulsing through her body. They remained in position as Jax rose and approached the police officers. Three cruisers, with two officers in each, responded to the dispatch. A small crowd of onlookers, mostly customers leaving the restaurant, gathered.

One bystander was not a customer. A young man who was walking his dog approached the officers. He told them he might have some helpful information.

"Sir, anything you saw or heard, I'm sure, will be helpful," answered the officer in charge. Leonard joined the conversation.

The dogwalker responded, "I was taking Millie for her nightly walk, like I do every night. I take the same route every night. I've never had a problem, ever. Naturally it was quite a shock when I heard a gunshot and then the sound of glass breaking. I looked over and saw those people,"—he pointed to Jax and Julia and Olivia—"hitting the pavement. Then I heard a car going really fast, and I got a glimpse of it as it left the parking lot."

Leonard felt comfortable asking the questions, even though this was an official police investigation. He knew all but one of the officers who were on the scene. And they knew him. "Did you get a description of the car or the driver? Did you see which way it turned when it left the parking lot?"

"It was really dark, and snow was falling. It happened all in an instant. The car turned left when it came out of the parking lot. Millie and I came to a dead stop to make sure we didn't get hit. There was just one person in the car. The driver was a man, but that's all I can tell you about him. His car was a black German luxury car, either a Mercedes or a BMW. Maybe an Audi, I can't say which one for sure. I'm sorry."

The police officer said, "No need to be sorry, sir. Your information is extremely helpful. If you and Millie don't mind, I would appreciate you preparing a written statement. We can make you and your dog comfortable in the back of my cruiser."

The eyewitness with Millie prepared his statement. Leonard and the officers turned their attention to Jax. By this time, Julia and Olivia felt safe enough to emerge from their hiding place.

The officer in charge began with preliminary questions of Jax. The officer recognized Jackson Berman from his many hours spent in courtrooms, but as a precautionary measure, he asked vital statistic questions—name, address, phone number, and occupation. His next question was a standard question, but for the second time in the past few weeks, Jax gave an answer that was not so standard.

"Mr. Berman, this could be totally random, or it could be a targeted attack on you. Do you know of anyone who would have motive or reason to cause you harm?"

Jax, just as he did with the officer who had come to his home to take the report on the damage to his landscaping, rattled off a list of categories of people who might want to cause him harm: victims who thought they were denied justice because Jax had won their offender's case, victims who felt they had been victimized again after enduring cross-examination by Jax, and people who generally were offended by the nature of Jax's work. He was getting ready to add more when the officer nodded, indicating he understood there could be an infinite number of people on the list.

Two other officers were talking with Julia and Olivia to determine whether they needed medical treatment. Although they were both visibly shaken from the ordeal, neither had any physical injuries.

After preparing his written statement, Jax rushed to them. Olivia wrapped her arms so tightly around his waist he could barely breathe, but he was not about to let her go.

Leonard approached them. Putting his large hand on Jax's shoulder, he shook his head in stunned disbelief. "I read your statement. Did you leave anything out? Any little detail?"

With Olivia still clinging to him, Jax shook his head. "At this moment, I'm still trying to wrap my head around the whole scene. It seems like something right out of a bad movie, Leo. A few inches one way or the other, and one of us might have been hit. The shock is wearing off, and I'm descending into all of the possible scenarios. What do your basic instincts tell you? Random shooting or was I the target?"

Leonard pulled his notepad out of his jacket pocket, reviewing the notes he had taken while talking to the eyewitness and the officers. "Too soon to tell. I heard your answer when the officer asked you about anyone who may have motive. Hell, if you recall, I wanted to kill you once myself. Remember our elevator ride? And I was a client. You might even have an angry client out there. That's a whole other list of potential suspects if, in fact, this incident was directed at you."

"Right now, I don't think we need to create new lists of people who want to hurt me."

"True that," replied Leonard in a feeble attempt to inject a little levity into the dialogue. He put his notepad back in his pocket and said, "I'm not going to make a determination on whether it was a random or targeted attack until I get more information." He pointed to the corner of the restaurant. "Not until I see what the security camera can tell us. I'll visit the restaurant with the officer in charge to arrange for the release of the camera footage. We should know something tomorrow."

Olivia and Jax got into Leonard's car after Leonard made arrangements for his car to be towed. They rode together in silence as they followed Julia to her home. Once Jax got Julia into her house and made sure she was safe, Leonard drove him and Olivia home. Leonard had them wait in the car until he entered the home and searched it to make sure it was secure. Finding nothing out of the ordinary, Leonard escorted them into the house. Before he closed the door, he gave Jax a quick hug and a slap on the back. It was his way of letting Jax know he would not rest until he had answers.

Olivia had a very fitful sleep in Jax's bed. Jax knew this because he didn't close his eyes all night. He lay awake, staring at the ceiling. His thoughts bounced from fear and concern about his daughter to whether or not someone was after him and who that someone might be.

CHAPTER 24

Watching dawn break over the horizon, he replayed the shooting in his mind. The sound of the gunshot echoed every time he closed his eyes. His thoughts raced as he considered all possible scenarios, including actually having been shot. His brain was on overdrive as he tried to determine if it was a random act or if he had been targeted. If he had been targeted, then he puzzled over the who and why.

Sunday was uneventful. Jax and Olivia never left the house. They made pizza from scratch, and they watched happy, nonviolent movies all day until it was time for Olivia to return home. When he delivered her to Jenny, he told her about the shooting. Jenny was speechless, but once she recovered, she assured him she would let him know if there were any changes in Olivia.

Based on how he felt when he climbed out of bed on Monday morning, he was certain that Sunday had been another sleepless night.

Leonard startled him when he blew into his office. He was stretched out on the sofa, trying to sleep. Leonard took a seat at Jax's desk, and he waited for Jax to sit up and put on his shoes.

"I have two reports for you. One on the Kaplan case and the other on what I've found out since Saturday night. But first, Jax, how is everyone?"

"Olivia seems okay. We laid low together yesterday, just hanging around the house and watching movies. She never mentioned what happened in the parking lot. I'll keep a close eye on her, as will Jenny. It could be as simple as the resiliency of youth that will get her through this. I hope so. I want to be sure she's not repressing her emotions only to have them emerge later."

"Olivia's a great kid. My hunch is she'll soar through this with flying colors. With you and Jenny on guard, she's got a good support system. I hate to bring this up, but what did Catherine have to say about it?"

Jax straightened up in his chair. "I never even gave her a thought." Jax turned to gaze outside and collect his thoughts. Turning back to face Leo, he exclaimed, "That's inexcusable. I would definitely want to know if something traumatic had taken place while Olivia was with Catherine. I owe it to her. I could kick myself for not having thought of it myself."

"Don't beat yourself up over it. You first obligation is to Olivia, and you've done a fantastic job. Let's get our business over quickly so you can call Catherine. You definitely need to let her know before she hears it from Olivia." Jax nodded in agreement.

Leonard had obtained a copy of the security-camera footage from the restaurant, and he would complete his review by the end of the day. He was confident he would find the black German luxury car on the film, and he was hopeful he would be able to narrow down the type of car and possibly the license plate number. Then he turned his attention to the latest developments in the Kaplan murder case.

"Miles Kaplan is squeaky clean, except for the affair with his employee. Not an insignificant exception, but so far, I have found no other skeletons in his closet. No prior criminal record, not even a speeding ticket. Miles gave me a list of his close friends as well as a list of bank employees who worked for him over the years. He belongs to the country club near his home and plays golf there a few times a week. His wife played in a ladies' golf league. He provided me with the names of members he socializes with. I tracked down several of his friends, employees, and golfing buddies. None of them could believe he was involved in his wife's murder. Most of them knew Judy too, and they had nothing but positive comments about her. Miles Kaplan sounds like a great guy in all walks of his life. I plan to talk to his daughters. They might have a different perspective of their dad as well as their parents' marriage. I'll keep you posted."

"Did any of them know about the affair with Hannah Gilbert?"

Leonard shook his head. "None of them even hinted at such a thing. Of course, I didn't bring it up. It's possible they don't want to speak ill of the dead and the person accused of making her dead, if you catch my drift. Or it could simply be that Miles is correct and nobody, not even Judy, knew anything about the affair. I've got some more interviews to do. Then I'll devote the rest of the day to watching your security-camera footage."

Leonard and Jax shook hands, and Leonard left the office. Jax returned to the sofa in the hope of getting an hour's sleep.

*****

On Tuesday afternoon, Jax was on his way to pick up Olivia after school. They were meeting Julia for dinner at a gourmet hamburger joint near the hospital. Julia was coming after her shift ended. When Olivia hopped into Jax's rental car, she was her usual happy, talkative self. Perhaps being over-vigilant, he watched and listened for any signs of trauma from the events of the previous weekend. He was confident Olivia was handling it as well as could be expected. He would be happy to listen to anything she had to say about it, but he felt it was better not to bring up the subject himself. They talked about school and their plans for the evening.

"I'm excited to see Julia again. I have some more questions about the kids she takes care of at the hospital. Do you think she'll mind?"

"Of course not, honey," answered Jax as he drove toward home. The rental car definitely did not handle curves as well as his Porsche. "She'll be flattered."

Pulling into the driveway and seeing no evidence of any further vandalism, they entered the house. Olivia finished her homework while Jax returned client calls from his first-floor study. They changed into clothes fit for burgers and fries.

*****

Jax and Olivia were waiting at the table when Julia arrived. Olivia saved a seat next to her, and she gestured for Julia to sit there. *Another encouraging sign,* Jax observed with a smile.

The conversation never lulled, not during the appetizer basket of onion rings nor the cheeseburger sliders and truffle fries. They shared their day with each other, talking about the high points and the "super boring" points of the day, to use Olivia's vernacular. Sharing a warm brownie topped with ice cream and chocolate sauce, Olivia changed the conversation to Julia's work.

"Olivia," Julia said as she took a bite of the brownie, "would you like to come to the hospital and see what goes on there? This is a good time of day for you to visit, because most of the children's families have gone home for the night. The doctors and nurses will be busy, but not as busy as it is when there are visitors."

"Do you mean it? That would be awesome. Can we go, Daddy? I finished my homework, so there's nothing we need to do when we get home. Please?"

How could Jax refuse? Besides, he was equally intrigued by Julia's work. "I'll get the check, ladies. Let's go to the hospital."

Jax lingered behind while Julia and Olivia, walking side by side, toured the pediatric-oncology floor. Most of the children were already in their rooms for the night, but there were a few older kids hanging out in the recreation room. All of them had IV bottles hanging from a mobile apparatus to give them some freedom of movement. *My God, they are all around Olivia's age,* Jax observed in disbelief. *Can there be any worse nightmare for a parent than to have a sick child and to be powerless to fix them or ease their pain?* One of the greatest joys for a parent is tucking their children in at bedtime, reading them a book, and giving them one last kiss on the head before turning off the light. The parents of these kids and these kids themselves were robbed of that pleasure night after night and sometimes forever.

Olivia was seeing the hospital through the innocent eyes of a child, not weighed down by the emotional devastation accompanying a child's terminal illness. She hung on every word Julia said. She was fascinated with the technology and the equipment available to help these young patients. Jax was likewise fascinated. He was also overwhelmed with feelings of love and respect for this amazing woman who had entered his life by sheer luck and good timing.

An hour later, they said good night in the hospital parking lot. Julia returned to her office to check her messages, and Jax and Olivia drove home.

Jax spent extra time tucking his daughter into bed. His experience at the hospital led to the realization that, while thankfully Olivia was a happy and healthy child, his days indulging in the bedtime ritual were probably numbered. When she would be a teen, Olivia wouldn't put up with bedtime stories and good-night kisses.

As he reached to turn out the light, Olivia sat up in her bed and whispered, "I think you should know you have my permission to marry Julia."

Jax turned toward her daughter. "Why would you think I want to marry Julia?"

Lying back down on her pillow, she replied, "Why wouldn't you? She's smart and she's funny and she knows about lots of cool stuff. She's fascinating, and I'm sure you think so too. Anyway, Mommy's got Charlie, and you have Julia. I'm okay with all of it."

Jax leaned down for one more good-night kiss. "Princess, you never cease to amaze me. I'll keep it in mind. If I decide to marry Julia, trust me, you'll be the first to know."

Olivia rolled her eyes. "Daddy, I'll be the second to know. You should let Julia know first," she giggled.

He turned off her light, closed her door, and went straight to bed. He hoped the conversation would be a prelude to a good night's sleep.

The following day, after a full morning of court hearings and an afternoon filled with client appointments, Jax and Leonard sat in his office, enjoying the quiet. Leonard had been involved in every appointment, either giving a report on the findings of his investigation or getting information to begin one.

"I'd like to talk about the John Ramsey case," Leonard suggested.

Jax rose from his chair and moved to the sofa. "Go ahead, Leo. It's time to start taking a serious look at potential witnesses who can help our case. Rape cases are so tricky. This one is complicated because the alleged victim is a child, and she's related to our client. Cross-examining a sexual-assault victim is always one of the biggest challenges for the defense."

"That goes without saying," sighed Leo. "I've been through dozens of them with you." He continued, "This one has a totally different feeling though. I'm just going off my pure, unadulterated intuition or maybe cynicism, but this *alleged* victim just seems totally wrong in many ways. I've read her statement she gave the police, and I've reviewed the transcripts of the interviews with Children's Services. I haven't put my finger on it yet, but her story just doesn't ring true."

"John Ramsey could be dead right when he offered us a possible motive for Melissa fabricating this whole crime. In her mind, it's her only pathway back to her mother and away from the rules of the Ramsey home."

"I agree, which is why I'm going to make a suggestion I have never made in our years together."

"Fire away."

"I've never even thought about investigating a kid before, but I have a hunch her motivation to lie has even deeper roots than just wanting to run back to the easy life with Mom. I want to do some surveillance on Melissa in addition to the customary background investigation."

Jax considered this unorthodox proposal for a full minute before responding. "You're right. This has never come up before. It borders on the creepy side of life to run surveillance on a minor, but your hunches have never failed us. Do what you think is best but don't intrude any more than is absolutely necessary."

Leo rose from his chair, gave a silent salute, and left the office for the day.

Jax rose from the sofa, put fresh food in Bailey's bowl, and left to spend a quiet evening at home with Julia.

CHAPTER 25

The past month was a complete blur. Jax and Rick made their way to Harold's Deli, having not uttered a word since leaving Judge Westerfield's courtroom. Berman vs. Berman had taken an astonishing turn.

Jax's thoughts took him back to the Christmas holiday.

Jax and Olivia embarked on one of her favorite weekend sojourns—the dreaded shopping mall. A mecca for preteen girls and those who rely on retail therapy to find balance in their lives, it was a nightmare for others who were not slave to fashion trends or the biggest sale of the season. Jax couldn't think of a more miserable experience. To add to his misery, they were trudging through the mall at the height of the Christmas season. Classic holiday music radiated from every corner of every shop as people rushed and bumped into one another without so much as an apology, much less a holiday greeting. Olivia insisted on finding the perfect gift for her mother, and Jax was not about to be accused of throwing any obstacles in the mother-daughter relationship. However, the last thing he wanted to do was bestow gifts on the woman who was hell-bent on ruining him.

After more than an hour scurrying from store to store, she selected a pair of leather gloves and a cashmere scarf. While it was being gift wrapped, the two weary shoppers went to the food court for a dish of chocolate gelato. They listened to a choir of grade schoolers singing Christmas carols in a futile attempt to infuse holiday spirit into the throngs of hostile shoppers.

After dinner on Saturday night at a downtown restaurant, they walked the streets around historic Fountain Square, admiring the lights and enjoying an *a cappella* ensemble. The traditional music provided the perfect backdrop for the fifty-foot Christmas tree and its thousands of lights twinkling in the clear, brisk night.

After a holiday cocktail with Rick, he and Julia spent Christmas Eve at her place. Jax couldn't remember a more wonderful Christmas Eve, with the exception of those spent with Olivia. This year, Olivia was spending Christmas Eve with her mother.

He and Julia sipped champagne and dined on chilled lobster and marinated roasted vegetables, all prepared expertly by Julia with Jax assisting. They lounged together in front of a roaring fire, talking about everything and nothing while classic Christmas movies played in the background.

On Christmas morning, Jax picked up Olivia at the house. After gift exchanges with Jenny, they returned to his home. Jenny locked up the house and went to her family's Christmas celebration. Jax and Olivia opened gifts together as soon as they took off their coats. Olivia bought Jax a key chain with her photo inlaid in the key fob. Clearly Catherine had been helpful with this, which made Jax happy he made the effort to help Olivia find the perfect gift for her mother. They enjoyed a Christmas breakfast of pancakes and bacon. They went to Jax's office to celebrate Christmas with Bailey. While Bailey enjoyed her collection of new cat toys and gourmet cat food, Jax and Olivia watched a Christmas movie on the flat-screen television in his office. He wasn't sure how gremlins and UFOs fit into the plot of a holiday movie, but it was Olivia's favorite. At least, it was better than the shopping mall.

Following Christmas dinner at home, he delivered Olivia to Jenny. After a happy and grateful hug and kiss, he drove to Julia's home to top off the holiday celebration. All in all, he mused, it was a very happy holiday despite the bizarre circumstances in his life.

The New Year having been rung in with a quiet dinner with Julia at a small but elegant Italian restaurant, the holidays were a thing of the past, and the world returned to normal. The same could be said for Jax until the hearing before Judge Westerfield.

It seemed that Dr. Harper had been on the witness stand for days when, in actuality, his testimony lasted two hours. Every word he uttered was still reverberating.

"I have completed my evaluation of Mr. Berman and Mrs. Berman as well as their daughter, Olivia," Dr. Harper began. He explained his evaluation and conclusions concerning Olivia. No surprises there. He was concerned about the risk of anxiety and depression in Olivia in response to her parents' separation and the resulting disruption of her family and homelife. He went on at some length about the need for ongoing counseling as an outlet to vent her concerns and emotions. He believed the current visitation schedule was appropriate. Allowing Olivia to visit her father at his home was key to restoring stability to her daily routine.

Dr. Harper shared his findings following his evaluation of Jax. He made a point of telling the judge about Jax's high level of cooperation with the process as well as his candor answering his questions. He concluded Jax was at a heightened anxiety level, and it was explained by his current marital situation and, perhaps more significantly, by the allegations of sex abuse pending against him. He found no symptoms of any neurosis or psychosis. Jax recalled breathing a huge sigh of relief. *At least, I'm not insane,* his inner voice said to him, *although it would be a very short trip to Crazyland.*

Dr. Harper turned to his assessment of Catherine. "As you know, Your Honor, I was in your court recently because I needed additional time to complete my work on this case. If you recall, it was due to Mrs. Berman's lack of cooperation with the additional diagnostics I recommended. I believed they were necessary for a thorough evaluation. Having now completed those additional tests, I can confirm they were indeed crucial to an accurate assessment of Mrs. Berman."

Dr. Harper launched into his opinion about Catherine's mental state. Jax had heard the psychological terminologies before but never in regard to someone he knew, certainly not in regard to someone in his family, someone whom he had once loved. "Mrs. Berman participated in the same diagnostic testing as did her husband. At that point, I found her to be sufficiently cooperative and honest in her answers. I was able to make some initial observations but not a complete and accurate assessment. However, some of her answers as well as other indicators of her thought processes were disturbing enough to compel me to request additional personality inventory tools. This is why I asked the court to compel her cooperation."

Jax recalled holding his breath when Dr. Harper paused to review his notes.

"I employed the narcissistic personality inventory. Mrs. Berman did participate in what I found to be an open and cooperative spirit. The additional testing has led me to conclude, to a reasonable scientific certainty, that Mrs. Berman has a dual diagnosis, which is highly relevant to the issues before this court."

Judge Westerfield looked up from his notepad where he had been writing and said, "Dual diagnosis?"

"It is my considered opinion that Catherine Berman suffers from both an obsessive-compulsive disorder, OCD as it is commonly called, as well as a narcissistic personality disorder. I must hasten to note that both diagnoses are personality disorders and are not a mental illness or defect."

"Dr. Harper, I am aware of obsessive-compulsive disorder, but please explain for my benefit as well as the parties and counsel this diagnosis of a narcissistic personality disorder," said the judge.

"I'm not concluding that Mrs. Berman suffers from mental illness or defect. However, it is an extreme personality disorder. It encompasses demeaning, bullying, and belittling behavior toward others. This personality demonstrates an alarming lack of empathy for the negative impact she has on the rights, the needs, the feelings of others. She demonstrates an extreme need for constant praise and admiration. She displays an alarming sense of entitlement to special treatment, both from her family and friends as well as acquaintances in her life. She suffers from intense jealousy and envy of other people, including people she knows as well as others she doesn't know personally. She is totally incapable of accepting blame or personal responsibility for her actions. She has an amazing ability to project blame onto others."

Yes, sir, that's my wife.

The judge signaled to Rick that he could question the witness.

"Doctor," he began, "you have described some very negative personality characteristics. Would this personality be adept at manipulation and exploitation of others?"

"Without question. This personality is essentially narcissism on steroids, if you'll excuse the phrase. But it's a good way to put it in perspective."

"Would this personality be capable of lying, of fabricating events to serve his or her needs?"

"Certainly. This personality will make up events and situations out of thin air, if it serves his or her purpose. This personality can get so immersed in the false scenario that he or she can easily forget that it is all based on lies."

Rick pursued the issue. "Would it be possible for this person to pass a polygraph even though the answers are false?"

"That is a common occurrence. This personality embraces the lies as if they were absolute truths." Dr. Harper paused, presumably to give everyone in the courtroom a minute to absorb this information. "Narcissistic personality disorder is probably genetically based as well as environmentally based," he continued. "There may be some biological or brain chemistry imbalance that has been present for all of Mrs. Berman's life. Then there likely occurred some social or environmental factor which caused these symptoms to fully manifest themselves, and these symptoms probably emerged sometime in late adolescence or early adulthood."

The judge was intrigued. He inquired, "What sort of emotional or environmental factors, Doctor?"

"That's not something I can easily answer. It could stem from physical or emotional abuse as a child, or it could be the other end of the spectrum. It could result from being extremely overindulged as a child or from receiving excessive praise or reward for every menial accomplishment. Don't forget the genetic or biological component. Not every overindulged 'spoiled child' develops this personality disorder. Nor does every child who suffers some form of physical or emotional abuse."

"What can be done for someone with this condition?" asked the judge.

Dr. Harper took off his reading glasses and answered, "There is no magic pill. No medication is effective with this type of condition. Cognitive behavioral therapy is the only recommended course of action. While there is a possibility Mrs. Berman would respond well to this treatment, her chances would have been better if she had been properly diagnosed earlier in life."

"What is your recommendation, Doctor?"

"Your Honor, I recommend, while this divorce is pending, the current visitation schedule remain in place. Perhaps modify it so Mr. Berman's weekday visitation be expanded to include overnights. He can take Olivia to school the following morning instead of returning her to the marital residence late in the evening. As for Mrs. Berman, I recommend her visits with the child remain as they are, and they continue to be supervised, at least, until she has completed six months of the recommended therapy. The therapy should occur twice a week during this time."

Both Rick and Steve Barker had the opportunity to ask Dr. Harper additional questions, and Allison Wells asked a few questions. But Jax's brain was on complete overload. *It's almost a certainty that Catherine fabricated the sex-abuse charge. But what about Olivia? Why would Olivia say such things?*

The next clear recollection Jax had was Dr. Harper exiting the courtroom and Catherine screaming at her attorney, "He called me fucking crazy!" and "This whole hearing has been a fucking setup by my fucking husband!" followed by "I'll see you in hell for this, Jackson Berman. You have no idea what you've done." She charged out of the courtroom with her attorney following. Jax couldn't remember if Judge Westerfield was still in the courtroom when Catherine flew into her rage, but he was confident he could hear it from his chambers.

Without a word spoken between them, Jax and Rick left the courtroom and headed directly to Harold's Deli.

Both finally spoke after placing their lunch order. They handed their menus to the server and looked across the table at each other. Both men slowly shook their heads in stunned disbelief.

185

Rick started the conversation, but only after letting out a long and considered exhale. "I must tell you this has been the wildest ride of my career. It's probably got a lot to do with the fact that you're my best friend. It makes this case personal for me. But man oh man, Jax, I never thought Dr. Harper would diagnose Catherine the way he did."

Jax took a long drink of water. "Ever since his testimony, I've been mulling over the symptoms he described for narcissistic personality disorder. They fit Catherine, no question about it."

"I suppose you're right. All these years, though, I just thought she was a bitch. I didn't know they had a fancy diagnosis for 'bitch.'"

That witticism was just what Jax needed at the moment. He laughed so loud and so long he had to wipe the tears from his eyes when the server brought their lunch to the table. He could not remember the last time he had laughed like that. He didn't know it would be a very long while before he would do so again.

CHAPTER 26

Olivia was spending the weekend with Catherine and Jenny. Jax and Julia flew to Hilton Head for a long weekend. They took a side trip to Charleston to buy furniture for Jax's new home.

In his recent meetings with Rick, Jax was preparing to be named Olivia's legal custodian. The handwriting was on the wall; the judge expanded Jax's visitation schedule while keeping the restrictions on Catherine's visits. Catherine still was not permitted to be alone with Olivia. She had months of intensive psychological counseling to complete before the court would consider giving her more time. The property settlement would be finalized in a few weeks. Steve Barker abandoned his seek-and-destroy mission against Jax. He would no longer be married to Catherine, and he would be the primary parent, the one responsible for the day-to-day decisions that come with parenting.

Jax was astonished by Catherine's reaction to the shooting. Completely devoid of emotion, she asked if Olivia was okay; she asked if Jax was okay. That alone was noteworthy. It had been almost a year since Catherine had given a damn about how he was. She never asked who was responsible for the shooting or whether the shooter had been arrested. She simply thanked Jax for letting her know and ended the call. The call lasted less than three minutes, not long enough for Jax to discern if Catherine was sober.

Olivia still had not talked about the shooting. She seemed to have put it out of her mind. She went to bed at her usual time, and she awoke in the morning rested and refreshed. Jax, in contrast, had yet to have a full night's sleep. When he turned off the light, after trying to lull himself to sleep by reading a book, his mind began to race through the mental images of that night. He envied Olivia's ability to store the memory somewhere in the recesses of her mind. He was still keeping a very watchful eye over her, and he continued to ask Jenny if she had noticed any changes in Olivia. So far, she told him, Olivia seemed to be her usual happy self.

The shopping trip to Charleston was a success. Jax and Julia found English antique pieces for the gathering room and master bedroom. They found new furniture items as well. The greatest discovery was a distressed white armoire accentuated with hand-stenciled flowers. It would be a wonderful addition to Olivia's room. They sent her a photo; they wouldn't buy it without her approval. She made it abundantly clear she wanted to decorate her room exactly the way she wanted it. Immediately Olivia sent a response with a happy face and a thumbs-up meme. They interpreted it to mean she approved of the armoire.

While in Charleston, they ate lunch at Husk on Queen Street. They lingered over salads, homemade buttermilk biscuits, and the chef's signature dish of shrimp and grits. A bottle of white wine topped off the experience.

Returning to the house later in the afternoon, both agreed lunch was so fabulous and filling that cocktails and a small cheese tray were all they needed for a late dinner.

Sipping more wine and nibbling the cheeses, they relaxed on the patio and watched the sky move from daylight to dusk. Jax set his wineglass on the table and turned to Julia.

Taking a sip from her glass, she returned the look with a sly smile.

"You definitely have something on your mind, Mr. Berman."

Jax returned her smile before he replied, "Yes, Dr. Winston, as a matter of fact, I do."

Her smile faded, and her brow furrowed. She asked, "Are you okay? Is something wrong?"

Jax stood up and took a few steps toward the edge of the patio. He turned to face her. "I am so okay it's almost frightening, and it's all because of you." He walked back to his chair and sat beside her. "Julia, on Thanksgiving, you qualifiedly accepted my marriage proposal. It was conditioned on Olivia's reaction to you and to us. I know you'll agree with me when I say, so far at least, things couldn't have gone any better. Olivia clearly likes and admires you. I had a conversation with her a few days ago. She gave me her blessing to marry you."

Julia set her glass on the table before she exclaimed, "She did what?"

"You heard me. I was tucking her into bed, and out of nowhere, she told me she thinks it would be just fine if you and I got married. She implied I would be a fool if I didn't."

Julia smiled. "Olivia is a very wise little girl. I'm quite a catch." She laughed at her own joke.

"Yes, Dr. Winston, you are quite a catch. As a couple, we get better and better together, in my humble opinion. Throughout the drama known as my divorce, you've been a rock. I don't know how I would have maintained my sanity without you. But beyond that, what is amazing to me is, with everything that's happened lately, most of which has been chaotic beyond belief, I've never been happier in my life." Jax rose from his chair and got down on one knee. He held her hand. "Julia Winston, will you unqualifiedly say yes? I love you with all my heart and soul and can't imagine my life without you."

With tears forming in her eyes, she said in a breathless whisper, "Yes, Jackson Berman, I unqualifiedly accept. I love you so much it scares me. So yes, yes, yes, this is an unqualified yes!"

Jax rose from his kneeling position, and Julia stood up from her chair. As the last light of the day gave way to a starry night, the newly engaged couple embraced and enjoyed a lingering kiss before hurrying to the bedroom.

*****

The following week, Rick called Jax to make an appointment. They spent an hour reviewing the settlement agreement prepared by Steve Barker. Catherine had already signed the original.

"The bottom line is this," Rick explained. "You will have sole custody of Olivia. Catherine keeps the house here, and you hold on to the Hilton Head property. Catherine pays no child support, and in return, she will accept a reduced alimony payment. You split the liquid assets accumulated during the marriage. Because you have acquired no new apartment buildings since the marriage, they are all premarital assets and will be set off to you."

Jax paused before answering. "I'm good with all of it. Hell, it's a lot less than we offered originally. How is Olivia going to spend time with her mother?"

Pushing another document across the desk, Rick replied, "It's in this addendum to the settlement agreement. It basically keeps the arrangement as it is currently. Catherine will move back into the house. When Olivia has her weekend visits there, Jenny will continue to stay and supervise the visit. Once Catherine has completed the counseling ordered by Judge Westerfield, she'll undergo a follow-up evaluation with Dr. Harper. He'll make a recommendation on whether or not to remove the supervision requirement."

"Catherine agreed to this?"

"Her signature is on the dotted line."

Jax signed the documents in silent contemplation. The simple act of filing these papers with the court would end a relationship that lasted almost fifteen years, although it began with promise and hope of lasting a lifetime. The stroke of a pen would sever years of emotional highs and lows that accompany any marriage. He and Catherine could not weather the tidal waves of emotions together. He hoped they could travel through the journey of parenting in some new form of togetherness.

Handing the signed documents back to Rick, he asked, "Now what?"

Placing them in his file labeled "Berman vs. Berman," he answered, "It's downhill from here. I'll deliver them tomorrow morning for Judge Westerfield's signature. Then it goes to the clerk's office for filing. You will have a certified copy in your hands by the end of the day tomorrow. You'll be a free man."

Absorbing this information, Jax asked, "I need a certified copy of the divorce decree when I get a marriage license, right?"

Rick was speechless, but only for a moment. "Are you serious? You're thinking about diving into another marriage?"

Jax stood up, smiling, and replied, "I proposed to Julia, and she accepted. Olivia has met her and really enjoys her. Rick, you know how the stars lined up for me to even meet this incredible woman. There was a reason for it. That reason is clear to me now. She is meant to be a part of my life and Olivia's life too.

"Listen, man, I've had so many clients who jumped right back into the marriage pool after I rescued them from drowning. Most of the time, they come back to me to get them out of the pool again. I don't want you to be one of my drowning victims."

Jax smiled at his friend and replied, "Great advice. But this is the right thing for me. I loved being married. I need the comfort that it brings, knowing I have someone in my life who I can count on through good times and bad."

"Hell, you've got me for that!"

Jax broke out in laughter before continuing. "You're right, Rick, I can always count on you. But you know what I'm talking about. Or maybe you don't. Haven't you ever thought about getting married? Wasn't there any woman who tempted you?"

Rick thought for a moment. "Maybe there were one or two, but off the top of my head, I can't think of anyone."

"Olivia really likes Julia. She even let me know, from her child's view of the world, that I should marry her. That's a ringing endorsement."

Rick paused. "That is, I agree. But you'll be a single man tomorrow. How quickly are you and Julia planning to get married?"

"Not the day after tomorrow, don't worry. Maybe in a month or so. It really depends on how we do it. Julia has never been married before. She might want a traditional wedding. It's up to her."

"If you're happy, then I'm happy. Julia is a wonderful person. But..." Rick stopped in midsentence.

"But what?"

"If you stayed a single, unattached guy, do you have any idea how much fun we could have?"

"Probably so much fun it would kill me!"

*****

Leonard was waiting in Jax's office, talking on his cell phone. He ended the call quickly and sat on the sofa next to Bailey.

"I've got some information on the mysterious car that shot at you. It's definitely a BMW. The security camera is not the highest quality, but I can tell it is either dark gray or black in color. It's got an Ohio license plate, but I wasn't able to make out the number. It's too blurry. The lead detective and I watched it together. Our next task is combing the state motor-vehicle records to narrow down a list of black or gray BMWs. It's sure as hell going to be a long list but nothing insurmountable. I'll keep you posted."

"At least, it's something to go on. Let me know if you need anything from me."

"Sure thing," Leonard replied. "Now let's get down to the Kaplan case. I've got some good preliminary stuff."

During the next half hour, he briefed Jax on everything he uncovered. Running a criminal-record check on Hannah Gilbert and her husband, he found nothing on Hannah. Her husband was a different story.

Harrison Gilbert was a self-employed building contractor. He began his career with a national home-building conglomerate. He opened his own company five years ago. Business seemed to be good; he had more than a dozen full-time employees and was building twenty custom homes a year. He and Hannah had no children, but he had a daughter from a prior relationship, who lived in Nashville. He was current in his child-support payments.

"Mr. Gilbert grew up here. He has a juvenile record for assault. As an adult, he has a couple of drunken disorderly convictions, but nothing on his record for seven years."

"This is a good start. Keep digging though. I can't shake the feeling that the affair and Hannah and her husband will somehow be the connection to who killed Judy Smith. I have an appointment later today at Miles's home. I'll share this with him."

*****

Seated in a spacious sunroom, Jax admired the perfectly manicured lawn at the Kaplan estate. The part of the home that was the crime scene had been professionally cleaned and sanitized weeks ago. Miles moved from the guesthouse back into the main house yesterday.

Miles listened without interruption to Jax's update on Leonard's findings.

"Miles, have you ever met Harrison Gilbert?"

"Just twice. The first meeting was in passing. The second time was much more memorable."

Jax asked him to elaborate.

"The first time," Miles began, "was a few years ago at the office Christmas party. Judy and I always hosted a holiday gathering here at the house for the employees, from the bank tellers to the vice presidents. We usually had a couple hundred employees and their guests, so there was never time for deep conversation. This was before Hannah and I became involved. She introduced us, we shook hands, I asked some obligatory question about whether they were enjoying the party, wished them a merry Christmas, and that was the end of it."

"What about the second time?"

Miles looked out the window for several seconds before responding. "It happened about six months ago. It was after dark, and I was driving home from the office. I was a few miles from the house when I noticed headlights coming up behind me out of nowhere. The car tapped my rear bumper. It was enough to jolt me, so I pulled into a driveway. When I got out to inspect the damage, the car that hit me pulled over. It took me a few seconds to realize it was Harrison Gilbert. I hadn't seen him since the Christmas party, but there were enough pictures of him in Hannah's office for me to recognize him."

Jax continued making notes as he asked, "Obviously not a coincidence, right?"

"No, not a coincidence." Miles continued his story. "As I said, it was dark. The only light was coming from our cars' headlights. Harrison walked right over to me, identified himself in case I didn't remember him. He told me Hannah was divorcing him and that I was responsible for destroying his marriage. He started yelling at me about sleeping with his wife. He finished by threatening to ruin my life just as I had ruined his. He's a big guy too. He towered over me, and I think it was the first time in my life I was in fear for my safety. But he didn't attack me. He went back to his car and drove off."

"Does Hannah know about this?"

"I didn't tell her about it until recently, maybe a week or so before Judy...passed away." Tears welled in his eyes.

"Do you know the name of his construction company?"

"Park Ridge Custom Homes," Miles offered. "He seems to do very well for himself. He and Hannah have a beautiful home, which obviously he built. They're planning to sell it and divide the profit as part of their divorce settlement."

"Thanks, Miles. That's all I have for today. I'll pass your information on to Leonard. He still has much to do on this investigation."

CHAPTER 27

The gray slush of winter was giving way to warmer weather and sunny skies. Sitting in the bleachers at the soccer field, Jax admired the blooming trees and the tulips and daffodils. Olivia's soccer team was into their twice weekly practice schedule. Almost as competitive as the soccer league she enjoyed during the autumn season, the spring league was a chance to compete with teams from the other side of the city.

Jax took her to the practices. Occasionally Catherine showed up. She made it a point not to engage in conversation. She usually found a seat on the opposite side of the field. Sometimes she sat with other soccer parents. When practice was over and he and Olivia walked to his car, they usually ran into her in the parking lot. Olivia always greeted her with a hug. Mother and daughter chatted together for a few minutes. He was careful not to overhear their conversation. Despite the malicious lies she fabricated, he vowed never to forget she was Olivia's mother. Olivia deserved a healthy relationship with her. Catherine's time with her daughter was not only very limited but also still under the watchful eyes of Jenny. Jax, having had his parenting time with Olivia restricted for what seemed to be an eternity, could empathize with Catherine. But still looming was the great unanswered question: why had Olivia told the authorities her own father was abusing her? There was nothing in their conversations, nothing in the time they spent together, and nothing in their phone calls that even hinted at Olivia being scared or uncomfortable. Catherine never said anything directly to Jax about the accusations. Although the divorce was final, he was committed to finding the truth.

Olivia gave her mother a goodbye kiss and bounded over to Jax, who was leaning against his car. He pushed the nagging questions from his mind.

"Great practice, kiddo," smiled Jax. "Your penalty kicks have gotten much more accurate. You've really improved your strength over the winter."

"Thanks. I've tried to run, at least, two miles three times a week. I think it's helped."

"Yes, it has," Jax replied. "I've always been proud of your dedication to training and keeping in shape. But I hope this doesn't mean we can't take home a veggie pizza for dinner."

"A veggie pizza almost sounds like it's good for us. I think it's our duty to eat it."

Jax phoned in the pizza order, and they picked it up on the way home. They listened to rock and roll. Jax noticed happily that Olivia tuned in to Julia's favorite music channel. *Just another way Julia has been influencing my daughter,* he mused.

Julia had been spending more and more time at the house with them. The two ladies in his life were forming a true friendship, built on baking cookies and doing crafts projects together at the kitchen table. They recruited Jax to play Monopoly and other board games. Olivia returned to the hospital with Julia. She was interested in volunteering when she would be old enough. She had two years before she qualified, but the casual visits with Julia allowed her to observe the volunteer teens in action. They worked in the large recreation area, playing games with the older patients and reading books to the younger ones. It was a wonderful opportunity for these children, who were spending all their time and energy just trying to survive, to have normal conversation with other kids. They talked with somebody close to their own age, and they discussed anything and everything besides their fight to live to adulthood. It was their only real chance to just be a kid, talking about kid stuff with other kids.

*****

The next day, Leonard Kurtzman—retired police officer, now private investigator—found himself parked in his car, staking out a high school parking lot. Focusing on the task at hand, he ignored the creepy feeling consuming him. He really was running surveillance on a teenage girl. He downed a sandwich and lemonade while he awaited the end of the school day.

"Some things never change," he chuckled to himself. At exactly three o'clock, the front doors and the side doors of the school banged open. A tidal wave of students rushed outside as if the school were on fire. Leonard observed girls and boys walking hand in hand and groups of girls giggling together. There was the occasional bevy of boys huddled together trying to look extremely cool and nonchalant. *No doubt about it*, thought Leonard, *some things will never change*.

Five minutes passed before he caught his first glimpse of his subject. Melissa Ramsey exited the side door with her best friend, Sadie Parker. As a condition of his release from jail, John Ramsey was not allowed to have any contact with her. She was staying with Sadie's family; it was not surprising to see the two friends leaving school together. What happened next was unforeseen.

With near-perfect timing, as Melissa and Sadie approached the sidewalk in front of the school, a dark-gray Dodge Charger roared up and screeched to a stop. Both girls waved to the driver. Melissa gave Sadie a quick hug, handed her backpack to her, and hopped into the front seat of the waiting car. Sadie walked to the student parking lot, and Melissa rode away in the car with the unidentified driver.

Leonard followed the Charger from a safe distance. He had been in this game long enough to know not to tip off the driver. He was close enough to read the license plate, which he captured with his cell phone camera. Melissa was the only passenger, and the driver was a male wearing a baseball cap.

The car wound its way toward the west side of the city, traveling in the opposite direction of the Ramsey home and Sadie's house. Leo stayed back as he followed the car into a warehouse district, which had seen its better day. Most of the businesses were boarded up to keep the homeless from encamping there. This was rarely a foolproof plan. This part of town, over the years, acquired a reputation for drug trafficking and violent crime. It was not a place where a teenage girl like Melissa Ramsey would visit. Yet here she was, heading straight into the lion's den.

Beyond the last abandoned factory was a residential neighborhood, which had also seen its better day. Some homes had boarded up windows, probably due to bullets. Residents congregated on the front steps of the homes or on the sidewalks, drinking beer and listening to loud music on their car sound systems. The Charger turned abruptly into a driveway on the left side of the street. Leonard parked his car a half block away and adjusted himself to get a good view of the driver.

Melissa exited the passenger's side of the car and ran to the driver's side. As soon as the driver emerged, she threw her arms around his neck and planted a long, slow kiss on his lips. Leonard captured the moment on his camera. The driver appeared to be in his twenties, definitely older than Melissa. His long blond hair was pulled back in a ponytail, and he had a short beard. Leonard saw tattoos on both arms. After a few more kisses, Melissa and the mystery man entered the house.

Leonard took more photos of the house and the Dodge Charger. He photographed the other cars on the property. Parked in the driveway was a late-model red pickup truck with a Kentucky license plate. Sitting in the grass next to the driveway was a black BMW with an Ohio license plate.

Before he pulled out of his parking space, he accessed the website available only to law enforcement and submitted both license plate numbers. He would have the names and addresses of the registered owners by the time he reached Jax's office.

CHAPTER 28

Julia was included in all the weekend fun. Olivia insisted on spending as much time as possible with her. The time seemed right to announce he and Julia were engaged.

The threesome spent the morning at Olivia's soccer practice, followed by a round of miniature golf. Olivia won handily. Julia bested Jax by one stroke. He was so caught up in the moment he ignored the blow to his male ego.

They took a long walk along the city's Riverwalk before dinner at an outdoor restaurant. Jax delivered the big news. Olivia almost knocked over her drink when she hugged and kissed him and Julia.

"This is amazing," Olivia declared breathlessly. "Julia, we'll be friends *and* family!"

"I'm excited to be part of your family, Olivia," smiled Julia. "Being your friend has been wonderful."

They discussed wedding plans. They wanted a private ceremony attended by Olivia as maid of honor and Rick as best man. After the wedding, the newlyweds planned a weeklong honeymoon in Paris. A reception would take place a month later to celebrate with family and friends.

Olivia was still talking nonstop about the wedding when they went home. The conversation continued in front of the outdoor fireplace. The soon-to-be new family laughed and talked and roasted marshmallows.

Olivia sighed, "I hope you can tell I'm super thrilled about this. I told you I was worried about you being alone, especially because Mommy has Charlie."

Jax refrained from asking prying questions, but he still had no information about Charlie other than his first name. Charlie was in

Catherine's life, which meant he was part of Olivia's world. Whenever she mentioned him, her tone of voice assured him she liked the man. But as her father, Jax felt compelled to find out more about him.

Watching the flames dance in the fireplace, Jax asked, "Do you get to see Charlie very often?"

"Yeah, he's there pretty much the whole time I'm home with Mommy."

Jax was careful not to turn this conversation into an interrogation. "Do you like him? Do you and he do things together?"

"He's nice. He can be really funny at times. If he's there when it's my bedtime, he comes in and tells me a story he makes up all on his own, just for me. He's really good at doing funny voices. He can imitate humans and lots of different animals. I'm probably too old for bedtime stories, but he's very entertaining."

"He sounds like a nice guy. I'm glad you like him." *I have got to know more than he's a nice guy.*

"I do. I'm happy Mommy isn't alone, just like I'm happy you're not alone. Besides, I have two new friends—Julia and Charlie!"

*****

After two long days in a courtroom adorned with velvet drapes and oversize paintings of judges from decades earlier, twelve men and women were selected to determine the fate of John Ramsey—successful businessman, devoted family man, and accused sex abuser. Dozens of prospective jurors were questioned by Jax and the lead assistant prosecutor, Casey Osbourne. Sitting second chair with Casey was Connor Gleason, another seasoned veteran of the Prosecutor's Office specializing in sex crimes. Jax had several cases with both of them over the years, and he had as much genuine respect for their ethics and professionalism as they did for his. During the months of trial preparation, they congenially exchanged evidence in accordance with the time-honored rules of court. Trial was the unavoidable outcome despite the many pretrial conferences and plea-bargain discussions.

Jax, with Leonard's assistance, scoured the statement Melissa Ramsey prepared for the police. He read her written statement so many times he could recite every word and punctuation mark. He lost count of the number of times he reviewed the video recording of her interview.

Leonard ran surveillance on Melissa Ramsey and her boyfriend, Ronald Carter, five times after his first encounter with them. He followed them to the Franklin home again, and he trailed them to two other filthy, dilapidated apartments occupied by an untold number of people. He was able to identify several of them. There was no doubt they were all gangsters. Photos taken at long range revealed tattoos that signified an affiliation with a drug gang known as the Fulton Street Family.

The Fulton Street Family, also known as the FSF, planted its roots in Cleveland a decade earlier and was reputed to be a deadly drug gang with tentacles spreading westward across the country. Ronald Carter, Melissa's love of her young life, moved from Cleveland two years earlier, seemingly for the purpose of establishing the gang's drug territory in Cincinnati. They quickly and violently infiltrated the local heroin and meth markets. Gary Franklin, a homegrown FSF member and a friend of Ronald, was born and raised in the area. He lived in the home where he grew up. The house was owned by his father, Curtis Franklin, a terminal-lung-cancer patient at the Veterans Administration Hospital. It was unlikely Mr. Franklin would ever leave the hospital.

What was not clear was whether Melissa was involved with drugs, either as a user or a trafficker. When Jax shared Leonard's findings with his client and his wife, they were appalled. The Ramseys assured Jax they had never found any drugs in their home nor had they ever discovered anything that would cause them to suspect Melissa was using. They were also quick to add, having never done any drugs themselves, they might not be savvy enough to detect telltale signs.

Connor Gleason concluded his opening statement to the jurors, having given them a preview of the State's evidence. Jax spoke to the jury about his case, careful not to give away the bombshell he was about to drop. Then it was showtime.

The lead detective was the first witness called to the stand. Casey led him through the usual questions designed to educate the jury on the process of investigating a sex-abuse case, a delicate and emotional situation compounded by the victim and the perpetrator, in this case, being family members.

After the detective was cross-examined by Jax, the jurors knew there had been interviews of Melissa Ramsey at the hospital where she had been taken upon making the allegations against her grandfather. She gave a follow-up interview at the police station. The jurors watched the video recording of her interview. The jurors learned the medical examination of Melissa did not reveal any physical trauma. The medical exam did not verify sex abuse nor did it refute the accusation of sex abuse. Jax considered this evidence to be a draw; neither side scored any points with the jury.

Following the lunch recess and brief testimony of the hospital physician who examined Melissa, the prosecution called their most important witness.

The star of the show, Melissa Ramsey, was ushered into the courtroom by the bailiff. She was dressed in a charcoal-gray pantsuit and a pink blouse. Her hair was pulled back into a sleek ponytail. Her multiple ear piercings were removed. She looked nothing like the girl who hopped into a car with a known gangster and partied with his associates on a regular basis. *Oh, how looks can be deceiving,* thought Jax.

Melissa's performance on the witness stand matched her demure outfit. She painted a very sympathetic picture for the jury. Jax acknowledged she had been dealt a cruel hand in her short life. She lost her father when she was a child, and while she loved and revered him for his heroism, she missed him every day. Her mother's struggles with mental illness and addiction left deep emotional wounds compounded by her emotional highs and lows of adolescence. She was uprooted from everything and everyone she had known in Seattle and began a new life in Cincinnati. She faced a new school and new friends. She transitioned into a new home. Melissa missed her mother; she missed her mother's rules and expectations or perhaps the lack of them. She had to adjust to her grandparents' home and their rules. Theirs were the polar opposite of her mother's. In typical adolescent fashion, she resented the structure, and she rebelled. However, her rebellion transcended typical adolescent behavior. Accusing her grandfather of a crime that could send him to prison for the remainder of his days was inexcusable. It was Jax's task to persuade the jury toward this view.

Jax observed Melissa answered the prosecutor's questions exactly as she rehearsed. She dabbed at her eyes with a tissue, exactly as she practiced. It was her mission to convince the jury she was telling the truth. Jax examined the evidence, including the information uncovered by Leonard, and he created an image of Melissa Ramsey's thoughts and motivations. It was her only pathway back to Seattle and freedom. Freedom, from her perspective, would be doing what she wanted, when she wanted, and with whom she wanted. She would have no problem overstepping her mother's feeble attempts to control her.

This only strengthened his resolve to save the life and reputation of his client.

Don't get emotionally involved with the clients, Jax, he could hear Malcolm Lamping whispering in his ear. *Dammit, Malcolm, sometimes it just isn't so simple. This could be in my future, on trial for my life.*

After almost three hours of direct examination by Casey, the court recessed for the day. The jury had listened attentively to her life story. They sat in silent disbelief as she described in detail the first time her grandfather abused her. She testified about incidents in the dead of night while she slept in her bed. She described occasions where her grandfather would pull her into the basement while his wife, Melissa's grandmother, watched television in the family room. She tearfully identified the clothes she was wearing when she went to the hospital for the sex-abuse examination. After hours of emotional and shocking evidence, the jury needed the recess more than anyone in the courtroom.

After cautioning them not to discuss the case, the judge instructed the jury to return the following morning for the defense questioning of Melissa. When the jurors filed out of the courtroom, none of them attempted to make eye contact with John Ramsey. Jax always watched the jurors when they left the courtroom, whether it was for a recess or to deliberate on a verdict. He developed his own divining rod to predict their decision. The more eye contact with his client, the better the chances of a not-guilty verdict. No eye contact spelled trouble for the defense. It didn't mean the case was lost; it only meant Jax had an uphill fight to win their sympathies.

The following morning was an unseasonably cool day. Jax enjoyed the fresh air and breezy sunshine as he walked to the courthouse. He would have preferred a day on the river to a day in the courtroom, but it was not to be. Entering the courthouse and passing through the security checkpoint, he geared up for his cross-examination of Melissa. Subjecting a child victim to cross-examination was a challenge. Jax had questioned young witnesses before; he was keenly aware of the tightrope act. He must discredit her testimony without going so far as to evoke sympathy from the jurors. Nobody likes a bully.

Melissa entered the courtroom, her hair again pulled back in a ponytail. She was dressed in a sweater and skirt. Her earrings were still absent. She took her seat in the witness stand, swore to tell the truth, and kept her eyes on Jax as he gathered his notes and walked to the podium.

"Good morning, Melissa. My name is Jackson Berman. We've never met before. Just like Mr. Gleason and Ms. Osbourne, I am an attorney. I represent your grandfather, John Ramsey."

Careful to avoid eye contact with her grandfather, she nodded. Her facial expression displayed no emotion.

Jax left his notes on the podium and approached Melissa, coming within an arm's reach of the witness stand. "Melissa, let's go back in time to when you were still living in Seattle with your mother. Let me first begin by letting you know I went to school with your father. He and I played sports together. I'm sorry he gave his life for his country. You must be proud of him."

"I am. But it was really hard on my mom and me when he died."

"I'm sure it was. You were so young. You were only eight or nine years old, weren't you?"

Genuine tears welled in her eyes as she replied, "Yes."

"You lived with your mom for almost a year, correct?"

"Yes. Then things just got too hard for her. My grandparents offered to help out. The next thing I knew I was moving to Cincinnati to live with them."

"You were in the fifth grade when you moved to a new school?"

"Yes. It was hard for about a week. Then I started making friends, and it turned out to be okay."

"You were able to visit with your mother, right?"

"Sure. I go to Seattle and stay with her during spring break and Christmas. Mom comes here a couple times a year, and she stays with us."

"Melissa, do you know how you and your mother are able to be together for visits?"

"Sure. Grandma and Grandpa make the arrangements."

"Are you aware they also pay for the plane tickets?"

Melissa nodded without saying anything. Jax continued his line of questioning.

"Are you grateful to them?"

Glancing quickly at Emma Ramsey, seated in the front row, Melissa answered softly, "Of course. Thanks to them I get to see Mom pretty often." She continued to avoid looking at her grandfather.

It was time for Jax to fire his first volley. "But it's not the same as living with your mother, is it?"

Wiping her eyes with a tissue and looking straight at Jax, she answered, "No. Grandma and Grandpa have been good to me, but I miss my mom every day. I worry about her being alone."

When Jax asked her about the differences between her home with the Ramseys and her life with her mother, Melissa rushed through a list of comparisons. Bedtimes were different. Melissa had more time alone at her mother's house, and the older she got, the more she enjoyed the freedom. Mom never lectured her about the importance of good grades in school. When Melissa went out, her mother never asked where Melissa was going or who she was going with. The Ramseys, in contrast, constantly asked her about her school assignments and her grades. They always lectured her on the importance of a good education. They hovered and smothered her constantly. They demanded a detailed plan for the evening when she went out with friends—who, what, where, when, and why she was doing whatever she planned. No, she replied, she did not acknowledge and appreciate her grandparents' love and concern for her safety. They were too strict and were always nagging her.

"If you had your choice, Melissa, you would be back in Seattle with your mother, living under her rules. Am I correct?"

"Absolutely. Then I wouldn't have to answer so many questions and explain what I had been doing."

"You're fifteen years old, Melissa. Are you allowed to go out on dates?"

Straightening up in her chair, she said, "Not in my grandparents' home. No dating until I'm sixteen. My mom would be okay with it though."

"Would she be okay with you dating an adult like Ronald Carter?"

Melissa's eyes almost popped out of her head. She gripped the upholstered arms of the chair so tightly her knuckles turned white. "What do you mean? I don't know anyone by that name." She started twisting the tissue in her hand until it was a tiny ball.

Jax walked back to the podium and retrieved photographs already marked as exhibits. He handed her a dozen colored pictures of her jumping into the Dodge Charger, hanging out at the Franklin home, and leaning against the cars in the front yard. The last photos in the collection showed her kissing Ronald Carter.

"Look through the photos. You'll see what I mean and who I'm referring to."

He gave her a minute or two to review the photos before resuming his questions.

"That is you in those photos, is it not?"

Wiping her eyes, Melissa nodded.

Jax persisted. "You need to answer my question out loud. You need to use words. Yes or no, Melissa, is that you in these photos?"

Giving Jax the coldest stare she could muster, she answered, "Yes."

"Who's in the photos with you?"

She looked toward the prosecutor, hoping he would say or do something to keep her from answering the question. He remained silent. "Ronnie Carter."

"If your grandfather is found guilty of abusing you and you move back with your mother, are you going to break up with Mr. Carter? Or do the two of you plan to move to Seattle together?"

After a very pregnant pause, Melissa responded. "I don't know what you're talking about."

"Oh, Melissa," Jax sighed as he walked back to the podium. "I'm confident you know exactly what I mean."

She glared at him as he continued.

"Do you know what your boyfriend does for a living? Do you know how he earns money?"

"He says he works construction." An interesting answer considering she initially denied knowing him. Jax paused for a moment to let it sink in with the jurors. Glancing quickly toward the jury box, it was obvious it had.

"What about his friends? What about Gary Franklin? Does he also work construction?"

"I think so, but I'm not real sure."

"Have you ever asked your boyfriend about his tattoos? About their meaning?"

"Maybe."

"Maybe you know he and Mr. Franklin are members of a gang known as the Fulton Street Family? Nicknamed the FSF?"

"Maybe."

"Is Ronald Carter your boyfriend?"

After a long contemplative silence, Melissa muttered, "Yes. We've been together for about six months."

"Six months is a pretty long time for a relationship at your age. Have there been talks about a future together?"

"He tells me he loves me. He's really good to me. We want to be together. And that's not going to happen so long as I have to live with my grandparents."

"You and Mr. Carter talked about how to get you away from Grandma and Grandpa and to get out from under their strict rules?"

"It's the only way for us to have a life together."

"The plan is to somehow get back to Seattle, right?"

"We've talked about it."

Jax kept up the attack. "Do you think your mother would approve of your relationship with a twenty-two-year-old man? Who supposedly works in construction?"

Melissa could not conceal her rising anger. "Mom wouldn't care. She probably wouldn't even pay attention."

"Does your boyfriend have a job lined up in Seattle?"

"He told me he's got connections there and money won't be a problem."

A few of the jurors smirked despite their best efforts to show no facial expression. They could not hide their dismay at this teenage girl's plans for her future and what she was willing to do. "That's fine. I'm happy you and Mr. Carter are planning for your financial future together. You do plan to finish high school, don't you?"

"Of course. But I can get a part-time job to help out with our living expenses."

"Why do you have to help your mother with living expenses?"

With an exasperated sigh and a teenage roll of the eyes, Melissa snorted, "Not Mom. I'm going to be staying with Ronnie when he gets his own place, and I'll need to help out."

"That makes perfect sense," Jax said, shaking his head. "Now that we know each other better, let's take a look at the accusations you made against your grandfather."

For the next hour, Jax engaged Melissa Ramsey, alleged victim of sex abuse, in a grueling series of questions about the disparities in her statements she gave during the investigation. Jax emphasized that, in her written statement, she said the first time John Ramsey sexually assaulted her was in the middle of the night. Yet in her videotaped interrogation, she claimed the first time occurred after school while her grandmother was shopping. More discrepancies snowballed from there. She was wearing pajamas the first time; she was wearing a tank top and a skirt the first time. Grandpa threatened to kick her out of the house if she told anyone. Grandpa apologized and promised it would never happen again. It happened only one other time. It happened a dozen more times. Where it happened was also vague and confusing. Her statements alleged it occurred in the bedroom, in the kitchen, and on vacation in a hotel room. She never mentioned the basement until she was on the witness stand yesterday. When she was questioned about the hotel-room incident, Melissa suddenly remembered they had never stayed in a hotel room on vacation. They always rented cottages or condos for their trips. With every question asked and every faltering response, the jurors had a difficult time concealing their opinion of Melissa.

Melissa was weeping openly when Jax completed his cross-examination. She was mourning the death of her dreams of unfettered freedom in Seattle. The judge recessed the trial for fifteen minutes to allow her to regain her composure.

Casey asked Melissa questions on redirect examination in an effort to rehabilitate her testimony. It was beyond repair, but it was the prosecutor's duty to make every effort to resurrect her credibility as both a witness and a victim.

The prosecution announced they had completed their presentation of evidence and rested their case. Jax rose and advised the court that the defense would not present any witnesses and his client would not testify.

Court adjourned for the day. The judge explained to the jury they would return the following morning to hear the closing arguments of the prosecution and the defense.

When the jurors left the courtroom, a few made eye contact with John. *Score one for the home team,* Jax thought to himself.

*****

Another glorious sunny day wasted in the courtroom, Jax thought, listening to Casey Osbourne deliver her closing argument. She slowly and methodically reviewed the highlights of the State's evidence, and she did her best to minimize the glaring problems with her victim's performance on the witness stand. After an hour, she thanked the ladies and gentlemen of the jury for their service. She picked up her notes from the podium, nodded to Jax, and took her seat next to Connor Gleason.

While closing arguments are not evidence and the court always explains this to the jury, Jackson Berman had earned a reputation for his masterful and theatrical closing arguments. Attorneys and court employees always packed the courtroom to watch his performance. Jax was good at closing arguments. In fact, he was brilliant. It was his favorite part of the trial. He always had a restless sleep the night before closing argument because he experienced the same anticipation he felt when he was a child on Christmas Eve.

Jax walked to the podium. He gathered his notes and carefully arranged them to refer to them if needed. He rarely needed them. Over the years, his notes had become more of a prop than a necessity. From the process of selecting a jury through the testimony and exhibits, Jax craftily extracted bits and pieces, words and phrases, to weave into his remarks.

The trial of John Ramsey was no exception. He opened with thanks to the jurors for their time and attention. He, like the prosecutor, reviewed the highlights of the State's witnesses. However, when he concluded his critical analysis of their testimony, the luster of the State's highlights began to fade.

Jax reviewed, in minute detail, the testimony of Melissa Ramsey. For the next half hour, he painstakingly reminded the jury of the many discrepancies in her statements during the investigation. He paralleled her statements with her testimony in the courtroom. He reminded the jury of Melissa's appearance during her videotaped statement. He waved the photos of her and Ronald Carter, pointing out her choice of clothing when she was hanging out with her much-older boyfriend. It was a hot-pink tank top so short and tight it exposed her midriff and cutoff denim shorts so skimpy they revealed the color of her underwear. Jax pointed out the multiple ear piercings. He knew the jurors would agree this was in sharp contrast to the demurely outfitted Melissa on the witness stand.

Pausing momentarily, Jax left the podium and moved to the front of the jury box. He placed both hands on the wooden railing separating him from the jury. He looked each juror squarely in the eye as he delivered his knockout punch.

"Ladies and gentlemen, there is no question in my mind. When you retire to the jury room to deliberate on a verdict, you will conclude the State has failed to meet its burden of proof beyond a reasonable doubt. I will thank you in advance for your careful consideration of the evidence. But I will ask you for something in addition to a verdict of not guilty. Something I have never asked another jury in my years of practice."

Jax straightened up but remained in front of the jury box.

"The judge will instruct you on the definition of *reasonable doubt*. You can return a verdict of guilty or not guilty. Listen carefully to the court's instructions. You do not have the option of returning a verdict of innocent. A not-guilty verdict means the State has not proven its case beyond a reasonable doubt. As you already know from the judge's comments at the beginning of this trial, John Ramsey is under no obligation to prove his innocence.

"But think about everything that has been said in this courtroom. Unquestionably there is not sufficient proof of Mr. Ramsey's guilt. But I submit to you there is, in fact, sufficient proof of his innocence.

"Being charged with a sexual offense carries with it an indelible mark on the life and reputation of a person." *I know this from personal experience,* a voice echoed in Jax's mind. "Mr. Ramsey is no exception. You know he's a successful businessman, starting with nothing and building a company employing dozens of people. You know he's a kind and generous contributor to local charitable causes, from Little League sports to food pantries. He's a devoted family man. Tragically, his son gave his life for our country, and he mourns his death every day. When he and his wife were at that point in their lives where they could enjoy the good life, they selflessly took on the task of raising another child. Yes, they raised Melissa as if she were their own child. They also took care of Melissa's mother, going to extraordinary lengths to ensure that she and Melissa saw each other regularly and maintained a close mother-daughter relationship. What thanks did John get for his kindness? A false and malicious charge by his granddaughter alleging unspeakable horrors.

"Ladies and gentlemen, a not-guilty verdict is not enough in this case. After you return to the courtroom and deliver your verdict, I ask, when you leave this courtroom for the final time, please come to Mr. Ramsey, shake his hand, and let him know everything will be all right. Your gesture will remove the taint of these accusations forever, and John Ramsey can continue to do all that has been beneficial to his family, his employees and their families, and our community."

Thanking the jurors again, Jax retrieved his notes from the podium and took his seat next to his client, who was wiping away tears.

The jury deliberated for less than an hour before they returned to the courtroom to deliver their verdict of not guilty. Standing next to Jax, John Ramsey remained stoic and suppressed his elation at his acquittal. Melissa, however, was not silent. She jumped up from the front row of the courtroom and screamed, "You ruined everything! All of you have ruined my life!" She ran from the courtroom before court security officers could reach her.

The judge issued his own thanks for their jury service. He told them they were discharged and free to leave the courtroom.

The foreman of the jury was seated in the front row of the jury box. Whether the jurors had discussed it in the jury room or whether it was a spontaneous act, the foreman led the procession of jurors toward the table where Jax and John were still standing. The foreman and each of the jurors took a moment to stop and shake the hand of John Ramsey. Each of them offered words of encouragement to the man whom, judging by this gesture, they had determined to be innocent. John was so overwhelmed by this act of kindness he could only bow his head in response. Emma, who sat steadfastly behind her husband during the trial, was on her feet, weeping tears of joy and gratitude. Several gave her a knowing nod and smile.

After the judge left the bench, Jax was in a warm embrace with his grateful client, followed by a hug and kiss from Emma. John and Emma sobbed. They were tears of joy for the verdict and the support of the jurors. But they wept for the fractured relationship with their granddaughter and their fears for her future. Jax gave them their privacy. He gathered his files and waited for them in the hallway.

CHAPTER 29

The marble floors and soaring ceilings in the hallway ampli-
fied every footstep and voice of souls seeking justice. It was
eerily quiet when Jax and the Ramseys left the inner sanctum of the
courtroom. John and Emma held hands and trailed behind Jax and
Leonard. Leonard witnessed Melissa's melodramatic exit. Uncertain
of her whereabouts, Leonard led the group through a maze of private
hallways that served as a conduit for judges, bailiffs, and attorneys
to move from courtroom to courtroom out of the public eye. The
silence seemed to indicate the coast was clear; Melissa had left the
building. Leonard did not want to take any chances. At the risk of
being overcautious, he opted for the secret passageway.

The group descended several flights of hidden stairs to a private
exit on the side of the courthouse. It had served many others in the
past who wanted to leave without having to forge through large gath-
erings at the main entrance.

Leonard opened the door and held it as Jax and the Ramseys
stepped into the sunlight. Jax looked up at the blue sky and inhaled
the fresh air. It always rejuvenated him after being trapped in the
stagnant air of the courtrooms. The building was almost two hundred years old and was not built with the comforts of modern air
conditioning. All offices and courtrooms were outfitted with the best
portable air conditioning units available, but on warm days, they
were no match for the heat and humidity.

Jax was still directing his gaze skyward when he heard a car
accelerating rapidly. He turned in the direction of the roaring engine
running through its gears. The high-pitched scream of tires, spinning
to gain traction on the street, pierced his ears.

In a split second, the source of the all-too-familiar sounds careened around the corner, coming parallel to the door Jax and his group exited. Leonard's response time was a split-second quicker than his. He hustled them to the pavement, yelling, "Get down and stay down! Cover your heads with your arms!" Leonard followed suit when they were safely in place.

A hail of bullets flew over their heads. They ricocheted off the walls. One bullet hit the window in the door, and the glass fragments pelted them.

The shooting seemed to last for hours, but it was over in seconds. Leonard was the first to get on his feet. Rising from his crouching position, he drew his gun from his jacket pocket and fired two shots in the direction of the speeding vehicle. Taking aim at the rear tires of the car, he first made certain nobody was in his line of fire. His first and only shot struck the rear tire on the passenger's side. The tire exploded, sending the Dodge Charger into a tailspin. The vehicle came to rest after striking a telephone pole head-on.

Court security officers ran toward the mangled car, but Leonard was the first to reach it. He yanked the damaged driver's door open and pulled out the driver. He held him with his hands behind his back until the officers arrived with handcuffs. He kept his gun trained on the driver until he was properly secured.

Leonard knew, without asking for identification, he pulled Ronald Carter from the vehicle. He had seen his face many times during his surveillance of Melissa. The officers removed Gary Franklin from the passenger's seat. When he slid from the seat, his gun, tucked under his left leg, was exposed. Ballistics testing would undeniably prove it to be the gun used to fire in the direction of Jax and the Ramseys.

While Ronald and Gary were escorted to the holding cell in the basement of the courthouse, Leonard checked the back seat of the Charger. Huddled on the floor behind the driver's seat was Melissa Ramsey. She had a sizeable cut on her forehead from the impact, and a trickle of blood was creeping down her cheek. Her crying had nothing to do with her injuries. Leonard signaled for the officers to return to the car. They wrestled the hysterical teen into handcuffs for transport to the juvenile detention center.

Jax helped John and Emma to their feet. With the exception of some scrapes on their arms, both were uninjured. Although they had no physical injuries, they were overwhelmed with horror and sadness watching their granddaughter being handcuffed. Jax assured them the nursing staff at the detention center would tend to the cut on her face.

John looked at Jax, tears flowing uncontrollably. "My God, Jax, what will happen? What do we need to do?"

Jax was still trying to regain his composure. This was his second encounter with flying bullets, but it was not something a person would get used to. Brushing debris and glass fragments from his pants, he took a deep breath before responding. "Your granddaughter is fifteen years old. She could be charged with being an accessory to the shooting, which would make her eligible for transfer to adult court for prosecution. She has no prior criminal record, which means she'll probably face charges in juvenile court. She'll stay in their detention center until her initial hearing."

John was trying to absorb the information, but his emotions were a hinderance. Emma continued with the questions. "What will happen next?"

"Juvenile court is designed to deal with these situations. They have a different approach than adult courts. My guess is, she'll be committed to a residential facility to help her deal with something known as criminal thinking errors. There are wonderful programs available to help girls like Melissa who have gotten themselves caught up in crime, even violent crime, because they fell under the control of a dominant older male companion. This describes Melissa perfectly."

Emma considered this as Jax continued.

"Melissa seems to have been a sweet and rule-following young lady until Ronald Carter came into the picture. She definitely has the ability to return to her former self. That's the purpose of these programs."

John asked, "Can you be her attorney, Jax? Can you make sure she gets the help she needs?"

Jax answered, "When her companions started shooting a gun in your direction, I, too, was in the line of fire. It makes me a victim, just like you. I would have a huge conflict of interest. If it goes to trial, I would be called by the prosecution to testify. I'll refer you to an outstanding attorney who specializes in juvenile criminal defense work. Melissa will be in good hands."

"Thanks for everything, Jax. You saved my life. Now we'll focus on saving Melissa's."

"I'm just happy the verdict was what we hoped for. I must say, John, I've never experienced a response to a verdict like this one." He and his client enjoyed a brief ironic laugh together.

"Let's hope it never happens again to you or to anyone else," John rejoined as he clasped Emma's hand.

Leonard and Jax escorted the Ramseys to their car to make sure they were safe. John Ramsey was a free and vindicated man. His next goal was to restore his granddaughter to the young lady he and Emma had raised and loved for years. Jax had no doubt, just as the jurors had removed the taint of sex-abuse charges from John, he and his wife would erase the shadow of recent events from their relationship with Melissa. The love of a parent or a grandparent for a child is unconditional. When a child falters, the parents renew and embolden the devotion created by the child's first breath. John and Emma Ramsey were the embodiment of such love. Despite the harsh reality that Melissa was willing to kill them in order to attain her dream of a new life in Seattle, they would persevere to help her and welcome her into their lives.

Jax walked back to his office with Leonard. Together they organized the Ramsey file and stored it with hundreds of other closed files. They shared a quick Scotch on the rocks before calling it a day. What a day it had been.

Jax took a longer route home. Julia had picked up Olivia after school, and they were spending the evening looking for the perfect dress for Olivia to wear for the wedding. They planned to have dinner before coming home. Jax loosened his tie and turned the radio to Julia's favorite rock station. "For better or for worse" included occasionally having to listen to rock and roll.

He actually knew the lyrics to a couple of the oldies. He cranked up the volume and sang along as he drove through the tree-lined side streets and charming east-side neighborhoods.

Any kind of music is good for the soul. Jax was decompressing from the tumult of the trial and the shootout. He cast aside the thought that twice he found himself in the path of gunfire. He wasn't sure if he was the target or collateral damage. Instead, he looked forward to grabbing leftovers from the refrigerator and watching something humorous and mindless on television before the girls in his life came home.

He was humming along to a song, because he didn't know the lyrics, when he turned onto his street. It was dinnertime for the neighbors; no need to slow down or swerve around kids on bicycles and skateboards. Approaching his house, he spotted an unfamiliar car parked in his driveway. It wasn't Julia's. His housekeeper was not scheduled to work. The car didn't have any signs indicating it was a commercial vehicle. He hadn't scheduled any repairs. There was no explanation for the strange car parked on his property.

Could it somehow be associated with the shooting? Had another gangster come to finish the job? Were the Ramseys safe, or was someone lurking around their home waiting for them to return?

Jax was less than a hundred feet from his driveway when he dialed Leonard's number. He ended the call before Leonard could answer. The mystery was solved.

A familiar figure opened the driver's door and slowly exited. He closed the door and leaned against the car, looking in Jax's direction.

A perfect fucking end to an unbelievable fucking day.

He turned off the ignition and greeted Kevin Wilson.

CHAPTER 30

Officer Kevin Wilson, still leaning against the driver's side of his pearl-white Cadillac Escalade, took his hands out of his pockets to offer a handshake to Jax.

Jax waited for him to initiate the conversation. It seemed logical. He sure as hell had a lot of explaining to do. But he said nothing.

"Nice car, Kevin," he remarked, hoping it would serve as an icebreaker.

"I only drive this on my off days. I have an old Toyota SUV to drive to work. I get enough teasing about being a 'trust-fund baby,' and the Toyota helps me fit in."

"That makes sense. It's not your fault your family has money. You shouldn't have to apologize. You just want to be one of the guys, right?"

"One of the guys *and girls*. It's the age of political correctness."

"Kevin, this is a wonderful chat, and I'm relieved to see you. But let's get down to it. Where in the hell have you been for the past few weeks?"

Running his fingers through his closely cropped hair, Kevin began pacing nervously. Gone was the cool and calm demeanor he displayed minutes ago. Jax observed Kevin moving back and forth, his fists clenched at his side. He looked for signs of intoxication but couldn't detect any. Not ready to rule it out, he continued to pay close attention. "I've been everywhere and nowhere, Mr. Berman. I had trouble sleeping the night after my last visit to your office. I decided to get in the car and go for a drive to calm down, to try to get my head on straight. The next thing I knew I was in Tennessee coming up on the Alabama border. I pulled into some little town to fill up the car. While the gas was pumping, I figured I had two choices.

Either I could turn around and head home or I could keep going wherever the road took me. When the tank was full, I kept going."

"You've been on the road this whole time?" asked Jax, discretely monitoring Kevin's body language.

"Yes, sir," he answered without interrupting his edgy pacing. "From Alabama, I drove through Texas. When I hit El Paso, I gave serious thought to fleeing to Mexico and living life tending bar in some resort town. I was thinking about Cabo or maybe Acapulco. But I abandoned the plan pretty quickly. I didn't want to spend every waking minute looking over my shoulder, waiting for my past to catch up with me."

Jax, in an attempt to restore Kevin's composure, said in an assuring voice, "You made a wise decision. I'm glad you thought better of that plan."

"I may have made a good decision then, but my thoughts got much darker afterwards." He reached into the back pocket of his jeans and pulled out a .25 caliber revolver.

Holy shit, another gun being waved in my direction. What the hell? Twice in one day! screamed Jax's inner voice. *At least, this time, I know who's at the other end of the gun. Thank goodness for small favors. But this shit is getting old.* "Kevin, I thought your service revolver was confiscated when you were put on administrative leave."

"It was. This is from my private collection. When I hit the road, I thought it would come in handy in case I needed protection. I have to confess something to you. After I trashed the idea of Mexico, I thought about using it to bring it all to an end."

"I hope to God those thoughts have left your mind. We're only in the early stages of your case. You can't give up hope."

Still holding the gun at his hip, pointed toward the ground, Kevin smiled. "I've pretty much put suicide out of my head. Don't worry. But I'm not stupid. I know the reality of the situation. Even if the trial does go in my favor, I'll always be branded a killer."

"We had this conversation during your first appointment with me. Yes, you took another person's life. But remember there is moral guilt, and there is legal guilt. As your lawyer, I'm here to help resolve the issue of legal guilt. Under what circumstances did you take another man's life? Was it intentional, without any provocation on his part? Or was it justified under the law? Was this a case of self-defense? Was it justified in light of the actions of the deceased? Did he threaten you? Did he cause you to be in fear for your own life?"

"I know. I remember everything you told me. While I was driving through the country, I had plenty of time to reflect. Maybe I did intentionally take his life. Maybe I, for once, was subconsciously looking to make a mistake in judgment, and Henry Glover was a target of opportunity."

Stunned by this epiphany, Jax was at a loss for words. Then Olivia popped into his head. He had to contact Julia and let her know not to come home yet. "Kevin, I want to keep exploring this with you." Without making any sudden moves, he said, "But I'd be more comfortable if you put away the damn gun."

While Kevin secured the gun in the console of his car, Jax sent a quick text message to Julia, letting her know what was happening. He asked her to take Olivia to her house and promised to keep in touch. He received an immediate reply: *Understood. I'm worried about you. Olivia can spend the night with me. We will make it a girls' sleepover. I can take her to school in the morning. Text me ASAP so I know you're OK.*

Free of worry about the gun, Jax took Kevin into the house to continue their conversation. Settling into the sofa in the gathering room, Kevin immediately decompressed.

"Let's pick up where we left off," Jax began, bringing a glass of ice water to him. "Why would you be looking to make a mistake?"

Gulping down the glass of water, Kevin searched for the right words. "Mistakes weren't tolerated when I was growing up. My father was, to say the least, a perfectionist, whether it was building his company or engaging in sports or hobbies. Everything I wanted to try as a child—soccer, baseball, basketball, Boy Scouts—my father insisted I be the best. If I wasn't, it was a complete waste of time. My time as well as his. More his time than mine.

"The lesson was ingrained in me. I became the youngest Eagle Scout in the state, and I still hold that distinction today. I was the valedictorian of my class. I received one B in my entire high school career, and you would have thought I'd robbed a bank. He made no effort to conceal his frustration. I made select teams in every sport. But if I had one bad game, I endured hours of lecturing from dear old Dad. The lectures always began with his 'helpful' tips on how to improve my game, but he never missed a chance to let me know I was a disappointment to him."

"How did joining the Sentinels fit into this?"

"I'm not sure. I know that part of my life is a huge problem in my case. If it makes any difference, I quit after a year. At first, it was just something different. It seemed most of the other members lived under the same high standards at home. I guess it was my way of rebelling. My parents never knew I was a member. In a sense, it was probably the first independent decision of my life. But when I figured out the group was bordering on fascism, I got out."

This is the personification of the poor little rich kid. Watch out, Jax, don't get emotionally involved. "How did your father react to your career in law enforcement?" asked Jax as he refilled his water glass.

Kevin smiled wryly and replied, "How do you think? He was disappointed on two levels. First, I wasn't going to join the family business and perpetuate the dynasty. Second, he saw the policing profession as something beneath me in terms of challenge and financial compensation. It certainly was beneath him. He didn't use those words, but he didn't have to.

"Mr. Berman, with all of this being said, hopefully I've painted a picture of my father as someone with no tolerance for underachieving people. Driving across the country, I examined my own personality and wondered if I shared his point of view. After all, the world is full of underachieving people, and as a police officer, I come into contact with them on a daily basis. I asked myself if my father's example was instilled in me to the point where I'm too judgmental of others. I still don't have an answer to the question. It scares me."

"Kevin, we need to get you to the right people to help you through this. As I've already said, my job is to resolve the issue of legal guilt. I am not built to deal with the moral guilt question. We'll make an appointment with a therapist who can guide you through the trauma of the shooting. Once you've taken the steps to reconcile yourself to it, you can begin self-reflection. Regardless of whether or not you choose to stay in law enforcement, these questions need answers. Then you can have peace of mind and fulfillment on any path your life takes you."

"Well said. You've definitely given me a lot to think about. I guess the first order of business is to get through this trial to make sure I have the freedom to make choices other than which prison will be my home away from home."

"You have to promise to stick around and prepare for trial. I can't do it without you, Kevin. You need to call your parents right now and let them know you're here with me and you're safe. They've been worried sick about you."

Taking out his cell phone and dialing his parents' number, he nodded. Jax left the room to give him privacy. Jax texted Julia to let her know everything was fine and he was safe. He made arrangements to meet her and Olivia for breakfast the following morning.

Jax entered the room when Kevin ended his call. He told him to spend the night. He gratefully accepted. While they awaited delivery of a pizza, Officer Kevin Wilson fell fast asleep on the sofa.

Don't get emotionally involved, Jax, Malcolm Lamping's words echoed. Jax reflected on his time with Kevin over the past few hours. He never explored the depths of a client's life experiences and emotions before, with the possible exception of Matthew Spencer. Flashes of Matthew's last breath in the hospital infiltrated his thoughts. Here he was, again, dealing with a young client who had everything he could ask out of life. Yet he was fraught with inner conflict and turmoil. Jax vowed Kevin's story would have a happier ending than Matthew's.

Placing a blanket gently over his sleeping client, he settled down to read a book before the pizza was delivered.

*****

Leonard made himself comfortable in the conference room, enjoying a pulled pork sandwich and fries, the specialty of a Southern barbecue restaurant around the corner. In between bites, he checked his emails and returned phone calls. He heard Jax's door open and saw him escorting a new client toward the waiting room. Leonard finished his lunch, cleaned up his mess, and went to Jax's office to wait for him.

"What was her story?" Leonard inquired about the attractive and stylishly dressed brunette.

Jax sat down at his desk and replied, "Nothing that will need your services, Leo. She's charged with embezzling money from her employer."

"That should be simple enough. Return the money to the employer and plead to a misdemeanor theft," Leonard offered.

"Under ordinary circumstances, you would be correct. However, it appears her employer is probably a front for a money-laundering scheme run by a Mexican drug syndicate, and she can't pay back the half-million dollars she pilfered over the past five years."

Leonard whistled softly. "She's been ripping off a drug cartel? Hopefully she saved enough of her bounty to pay you and hire private security."

"Embezzlers usually do. There's something about that breed of criminal that fascinates me. Unlike most criminals, they always have contingency plans if they get caught. Other criminals rarely give it more than a passing thought. Your typical criminal believes he is so damn clever he can get away with whatever crime he chooses to commit. In answer to your thought, she does indeed have enough money to retain me. If she lives long enough. Your suggestion of security is a good one in her situation."

"I don't understand. Her employer, who may be a front for a drug cartel, contacted the police to report the theft?"

Bailey jumped up onto Jax's lap as he explained, "Sure he did. It's an extraordinary effort to perpetuate the myth that he's running a legitimate business. The business owner has been victimized by an employee. It's not exactly a unique situation. The employer makes the report to the police to bolster his credibility as a law-abiding business owner. He becomes somewhat of a sympathetic figure too. He's smart enough to know the employee is not going to tell the cops she stole drug money funneled out of Mexico. She'd be dead before she finished signing her statement."

"Let's see if I can finish this story. The employer gets rid of the employee, he might get some of the money returned to him, and he gets on the good side of the local police. Clever," offered Leonard.

"It's clever all right," Jax sighed. "But I've got to be clever enough to keep her from a long stint in prison, where she could end up dead at the direction of the syndicate. You know as well as I do, Leo, professional hits on prison inmates happen all the time."

Leonard reached for one of his files. "Good luck with that one. You know to call if you need anything from me."

"I do. Enough about her. You've got some new information for me?"

They spent the next hour discussing Leonard's updates on the Kaplan case.

"Let's start with Miles Kaplan," Leonard began. "I interviewed the daughters as well as the friends and employees. Their daughters are devastated, as you can imagine. They had only a matter of hours to absorb the news that their mother had been brutally murdered before they had to deal with their father's arrest. They are amazing young women, Jax. Jenna is in her second year of law school at the University of Cincinnati. Madison is in her third year at Arizona State University. She was finishing the semester when her mother was killed. Her professors are accommodating her so she can complete her classes online and stay home to deal with the tragedy. Both girls describe a very normal homelife. Naturally money was never an issue. The family vacationed together a couple times a year, and they describe both of their parents as being very involved in their sports and other activities. They don't recall any bitter arguments, and they denied ever being abused by their parents or seeing them get violent with each other."

"I'll take that as good news. What about the friends and employees? Any bombshells?"

Leonard shook his head. "Nothing at all, Jax."

Jax finished writing some notes and said, "We have nothing in his personal life which would provide a motive for eliminating his wife. We can work with that."

"I'm not finished," Leonard went on. "I started digging into Hannah Gilbert and her ex-husband. I uncovered some intriguing bank-account information which might lead somewhere."

"I'm all ears."

"While they were still married, they had a joint checking account at First Citizens Bank. Nothing surprising about that. Hannah would bank with her employer. The account was closed out when the divorce was filed. Hannah has an individual account now. For obvious reasons, the jilted ex-husband took his banking business elsewhere. Hannah still has an IRA with the bank. Harrison closed out his IRA with a balance of more than one hundred fifty thousand dollars. Presumably he transferred it to his new bank, Second National Bank."

"Makes perfect sense," Jax concluded.

"I'm not finished," Leonard interrupted. "Here's the intriguing part. I was able to latch onto a money trail that led me to a bank in the Cayman Islands. Your typical offshore account which is still open in the joint names of Hannah and Harrison Gilbert. The account was opened while they were still married. There is still major activity on the account."

Jax was getting more intrigued by the minute. "What sort of activity?"

Leonard pushed a stack of bank statements across the desk. "Starting more than a year ago, there has been a deposit of ten thousand dollars into the account every Friday without fail, with one exception. There was no deposit the week before Judy Kaplan's murder. The Friday after her death, the deposits resumed on schedule. The current balance is more than six hundred thousand dollars. There have been no withdrawals from the account, just the weekly deposits." Leonard continued, "I'm trying to trace the source of the deposits, but it's complicated when dealing with a foreign bank. I'll find out, but I need a few days."

Jax reviewed the bank statements before commenting, "We have a bank account with well over sixty deposits made like clockwork. The only interruption occurred just a week before Judy Kaplan was killed. This can't be coincidental. It's going to be key to discovering the identity of the killer, I can feel it. Keep digging, Leo."

Leonard moved the file aside before reminding Jax, "Hey, it's what I do best."

The following afternoon, the city was caught in a deluge of thunderstorms racing across the sky, brightening it with lightning strikes. He resolved two pending cases in court during pretrial conferences. He met with two new clients in the afternoon. Leaning back in his chair while Bailey napped in his lap, he took the deepest breath he had taken all week. The Ramsey trial, the gunfire after the verdict, and Kevin Wilson's drama had drained his energy. *But things are looking up. At least, nobody has shot at me today. So far.*

Locking the door to his office for the day, he threw his suit jacket in the rear seat of his car and drove to the bar at the Manor Hotel. He missed his evening chats with Frank, the bartender. Earlier in the day, he and Rick arranged to meet for cocktails.

Jax was immersed in conversation with Frank when Rick entered the bar. Frank poured Rick his usual cocktail without asking. Rick raised his glass in salute before taking the first sip.

Rick sat back in his bar stool, a sly smile on his face. "Quite the day you had yesterday, Chief. I saw it on the news last night. It sounds like something straight out of a gangster movie."

Setting his glass on the bar, Jax answered, "It was quite the day. But it didn't just end with the gunfire." Jax gave him the highlights of his evening with Kevin Wilson.

"You always know how to pack a lot of action into a day," he sighed as he ordered another round of drinks. "But yesterday breaks all previous records. Are you sure you're okay?"

Raising his second drink in the air in a silent toast, he said, "I'm fine. I think I'm fine. Once you actually get shot at, you'd think it would get easier the second time. Trust me, pal, it doesn't. Not at all." He savored a long, slow sip. "Let's talk about something else. I have some news and an invitation for you."

"Give it to me."

"I'm getting married, and I want you to be my best man."

Rick took a drink before quipping, "Wasn't I your best man the first time? Is it bad luck to have the same best man for the next wedding?"

Jax burst out laughing. "Yes, you were my best man the first time, smart-ass. No, I don't think it's bad luck for you to do it again. I'll make sure this is the last time."

After enjoying the frivolity of the moment, Jax gave him a brief rundown of the wedding plans. Rick and Olivia would be the only guests. While they finished their drinks, they went over the details.

Walking together in the hotel parking lot, Rick stopped in mid-stride. "Jax, all joking aside, I am truly happy for you. Julia seems terrific. Olivia is clearly happy about this. I'll be honored to stand up with you."

Shaking hands, they went their separate ways to their cars. Turning on the ignition, Jax reflected on the depth and breadth of his friendship with Rick. To know true friendship is to know truth, and to know truth is to know trust.

*****

Jax picked Olivia up from school on Friday afternoon and took her to their favorite ice-cream shop. She filled him in on the highlights of her day. School work, updates on her friends, and the details of the weekend soccer game were the topics of conversation.

Jax drove her to Catherine's house for her weekend parenting time. Turning onto the street as he approached the house, it occurred to him he had not laid eyes on his ex-wife since their divorce became final. He usually met Jenny when he dropped off Olivia or when Jenny would pick her up at Jax's house. He realized that not only the marriage but also all the feelings and emotions wrapped up in it were truly over. He did not miss Catherine. Not for a single moment. While traditional wisdom believes love and hate are on opposite ends of the emotional spectrum, Jax believed indifference was the true opposite of love. Other than having care and concern for Catherine as Olivia's mother, he rarely gave her any thought at all, despite the years they shared.

Turning into the driveway, he came upon an unexpected sight. Parked in front of the closed garage door was a black BMW. *They say good luck and bad luck come in threes,* thought Jax. First, there was the BMW shooting at Jax in the restaurant parking lot. Then there was the BMW Leonard discovered during his surveillance of Melissa Ramsey.

"Do you recognize that car?" Jax asked in a calm tone of voice.

"Oh, that's Charlie's car. Mommy said something about having plans for all of us together this weekend. That must be why he's here already."

Leaning over to kiss his daughter on the cheek, he said, "I'm sure your mother has lots of fun planned for you. Have a great time, sweetheart."

Watching Olivia as she let herself into the house, he jotted down the license plate number of Charlie's BMW and placed the note in his pocket. He would pass it along to Leonard.

CHAPTER 31

It was a hung jury. A damn hung jury. Jax was still seated at counsel table in the courtroom with his client. The jurors were dismissed after they were unable to reach a unanimous verdict. They had discussed and argued during three long days of deliberations. The shouting could be heard in the hallway outside the jury room.

The judge declared a mistrial and adjourned court.

It would prove to be a more disastrous outcome than an acquittal. Both sides of the case were consumed with a sense of justice denied. Jax could only imagine the repercussions brewing in the streets.

Kevin Wilson slumped in the front row of the gallery with his parents, Joe and Peggy Wilson. Like Jax, they were trying to predict their fate as well as that of the city.

The insufferable silence was broken when Leonard entered from a private door near the judge's chambers.

"Okay, folks, I've been able to assess the situation outside, and it's not good. Not good at all. In fact, I would go so far as to call it a shitstorm. My apologies for the language, Mrs. Wilson."

"No need to apologize, Mr. Kurtzman. I've lived in the same home with my husband and my sons for decades, so I've heard it all before," she replied in a vain attempt to inject a little levity into a very dark situation.

Smiling at her, Leonard explained, "There are protesters gathering outside in droves. When I last checked, there were more than a hundred. So far. It's only four o'clock. The crowd will grow after the sun goes down."

Jax stood up and asked, "What's our game plan? Court security can get us out of here."

"Getting out of the building isn't our problem," replied Leonard. "But once we're outside, we're no longer their problem. They'll wish us a good evening and good luck. Then they'll lock the door as quickly as they can without looking like cowards."

"Mr. Wilson," Jax said, turning toward Kevin and his parents, "how did you get to the courthouse this morning?"

"I employ a private security company, and they provided transportation every day during the trial. We've been traveling in an unmarked black SUV. There's room for you and Leonard if you want us to take you to your office."

Jax responded as he gathered his files, "Your choice of transportation will certainly blend in with all the other black SUVs. Leo, what's our game plan?"

Leonard sat down heavily in the front row of the gallery. "I'll walk back to the office. Maybe I can be of some use if the shit hits the fan out there."

"I'll go with you. Thanks for your offer, but we'll take our chances. Kevin, give me a call in the morning to discuss the next steps in this case."

Kevin, still seated next to his parents, nodded. "First thing tomorrow."

Mrs. Wilson asked, "Can you tell us quickly what the options are, Mr. Berman?"

"Please call me Jax."

"Only if you call me Peggy."

Jax explained, "Peggy, it depends largely on what the final jury vote was. If an overwhelming majority voted guilty, I'm sure the prosecution will want a new trial. However, if it was a majority vote for acquittal, he may think long and hard about whether to ask for another trial or instead dismiss the charges."

"But if he would just dismiss the charges, while that would be good for my son, it could spark a new whole outbreak of violence in the city, right?" asked Peggy.

"It's certainly a factor Mr. Dawson will consider. He will and should focus on the jury vote, the strength of his evidence, and how to present his case differently than he did in the first trial. He doesn't want another hung jury."

"When will you know the jury vote?" Mr. Wilson asked.

"I'll talk to Mr. Dawson in the morning. I'll have the information when your son and I talk tomorrow. Right now, though, I'd be much more comfortable knowing you're home safely. Let's not waste time."

The scene felt choreographed. The courtroom doors opened and three men, dressed in black suits with earpieces visible, signaled to the Wilson family to head to the waiting vehicle. Kevin and his parents followed the security detail.

Jax and Leonard packed up their files, tucked them into Jax's briefcase, and stored them in a cabinet tucked in the corner of the courtroom. The judge's bailiff, planning in advance for unrest on the streets, offered the use of the cabinet. This allowed them to return to the office without having to carry their files.

They made their way down the back staircase. They emerged as the late-afternoon sunshine cast a bright light on the gathering crowd.

More than a hundred protesters packed the steps at the main entrance. Dozens of homemade signs spewing messages of hate for the police were visible throughout the crowd. The protesters were chanting, "Justice for Henry," as they spilled down the steps and onto the sidewalk. Many were blocking traffic. Jax saw hundreds more marching toward the crowd, carrying more signs bearing hate speech. Some were there for the sake of the cause; others were there for the sake of the violence.

"Let's head south toward Main Street and circle back to the office," shouted Leonard above the din, "because it should be quieter for a while! We've got to get back to the office before sunset. That's when this party will really get started."

"I'm right behind you." The pair set off at jogging speed.

They were three blocks away from the courthouse when they rounded the corner and came upon an unexpected sight. The restaurant and shopping districts were under siege. Throngs of angry mobsters were throwing bricks and rocks through the plate-glass windows of cafés and stores. At the other end of the block, Jax could see a wave of people all dressed alike in tan khaki shirts and pants. The Sentinels had arrived.

"Leo!" Jax yelled. "This is going to end very badly very quickly. Let's get the hell out of here. Now!"

They accelerated their pace from jogging to run-for-your-life speed. The Sentinels were armed with baseball bats and tire irons. Heading for an alleyway, Jax and Leo ran past Harold's Deli. Harold was standing in his doorway, examining the damage. The windows were shattered. The tables and chairs that had been window seating were thrown into the street. Harold was pressing a towel to his forehead. Jax stopped to help him.

"It's just a little cut, Jax. It happened when the glass blew into the restaurant. It won't even need stitches. Get the hell out of here while you can. Don't stop till you're safe!" He gave Jax a forceful but friendly shove to send him on his way. Jax quickly caught up with Leonard, who stopped to wait for him.

The pair ran away from the standoff between the Sentinels and the protesters. The noise was deafening. The protesters were still chanting for justice for Henry, and the Sentinels responded with obscene racial slurs. The sound of shattering glass mingled with the shouting.

They wound through the alleyway and came out on the block parallel to the not-so-peaceful protest they had averted. They found themselves in the same precarious situation on Elm Street. Another gathering of protesters and another large group of Sentinels were squaring off to do battle. Just as they began to run, Jax felt a hand grip him firmly on his shoulder. Jax screamed when he turned to see who stopped him.

It was Kevin Wilson.

"Holy shit! What the hell are you doing? You're supposed to be with your parents."

Kevin yelled, "They're fine! They've got security. They don't need me. I couldn't leave you without protection."

"Kevin, if anyone recognizes you, things could get much worse than they already are."

He soberly replied, "I thought of that. But I wouldn't be able to live with myself if something happened to you."

Leonard interjected, "Okay, boys, this soap opera is over. Let's get the hell out of here!"

The trio ran through another narrow alley to avoid the gathering storm on Elm Street. The scene they encountered on Walnut Street was almost as chaotic. The crowds were assembling, but they had not yet taken over the streets. Traffic was crawling, but at least, it was moving.

Kevin was in the lead, with Jax following and Leonard bringing up the rear. They were a hundred feet ahead of another roving band of protesters and were closing in on Jax's office. They leaped over and around piles of shattered glass and splintered wood. It was a bleak accumulation of broken tables, chairs, and countertops tossed from the restaurants and shops. Rioters—not protesters—were inside the businesses, stealing anything they could carry and destroying anything they couldn't. While they were stuffing their pockets with beer cans and liquor bottles, they were smashing furniture.

Kevin signaled to follow him across the street, where the looting and destruction were not so rampant. Kevin let them run ahead of him into the street. Jax followed Leonard. They almost made it safely across the street when a silver sedan with dark tinted windows headed toward them. Jax felt Kevin push him with both hands in the middle of his back, propelling him onto the sidewalk. He regained his balance as he heard the sickening thud of Kevin Wilson's body colliding with the car. He flew through the air and landed on the pavement. Kevin's head struck the curb. The massive head trauma and the broken neck killed him instantly.

Leonard crawled to Kevin to check for a pulse while Jax called 911. Jax was cradling Kevin's head in his lap when the first responders arrived. Paramedics tended to Kevin, and they conducted a cursory examination of Jax and Leonard. As Kevin's lifeless body was loaded into the ambulance, Leonard provided police officers with the make and model of the vehicle and the license plate number. It would not take them long to find his killer.

Officer Kevin Wilson was laid to rest in his family's cemetery plot near their estate. His parents dispensed with a full police officer's memorial, in light of the events surrounding his death. Jax and Leonard were among the mourners at the private service.

Leaving the gravesite, Jax reflected on the similarities between Kevin Wilson and Matthew Spencer. Both were raised in a lifestyle of comfort and privilege, yet both had spent much of their young lives warding off demons who tortured their souls. Their lives came to an end suddenly, leaving so many unwritten chapters.

Driving home from the funeral, Leonard observed, "It's times like these that remind us how fragile life is. We've got to live each day to the fullest."

"Words to live by, my friend. Words to live by."

CHAPTER 32

Satellite trucks from every news network lined up around the courthouse, circling in for the kill. Reporters and videographers congregated around the trucks, sipping coffee and eating donuts while untangling cables or scrolling through their notepads. It reminded Jax of an outdoor festival, except the news trucks were not food trucks, and nobody was dancing as musicians strutted their sound on stage. Nobody seemed to be having any fun at all. He knew they were preparing to shove one another out of the way in their quest to get the best image of Miles Kaplan.

What they did not know was that Leonard had escorted Miles and his daughters into the courthouse more than an hour ago, before the media hounds showed up. They were able to escape reporters' questions and videographers descending upon them.

Jax entered the building without any fanfare. The press did not recognize him as a key player in this unfolding drama. The Kaplan murder trial had been a headline story for the past few months. It was a gripping real-life saga. There was the gruesome murder of a beloved socialite, and her husband was on trial for her death. The plot was set against the backdrop of wealth and privilege. The Kaplans' two beautiful and fashionable daughters in the front row of the courtroom added another dimension to the docudrama anticipated by a nationwide audience.

He found his client seated at counsel table. His daughters were in the front row of the gallery, sitting as close to their father as possible. Leonard was beside them, at the end of the pew closest to the aisle, to keep the press at bay.

Judge Myra Atkins had issued an order allowing one camera crew to be present in the courtroom. The other news networks would be entitled to share the video recordings for daily newsfeeds. Two videographers and one reporter were tucked in a rear corner of the courtroom. Judge Atkins included in her order a strict prohibition against filming anyone called to serve as jurors.

The silence was broken when dozens of potential jurors entered the gallery. Looking at their faces, it was evenly divided between those who wanted desperately to escape jury duty and those who hoped they would be called to serve on this high-profile case. The members of the press remained seated, and the videographers kept their cameras turned off. The show would begin when the jury was selected and the attorneys presented opening statements.

After two days, the judge swore in twelve jurors and two alternate jurors. Because of the headlines this crime captured, one would have to have lived under a rock not to know something about the case. The questions asked by Charlotte Petrie, the assistant prosecutor trying the case alongside Prosecutor John Dawson, as well as Jax's questions were focused on pretrial publicity and whether it would have any impact on their ability to serve without any preconceived ideas or opinions. After more than twelve hours of questions and answers, the prosecution and the defense were satisfied they selected five men and seven women who could and would listen to the evidence and disregard anything they had heard or read previously.

The prosecution's first witness was the patrol officer who first responded to the scene. Charlotte Petrie took him step by step, minute by minute, through his arrival at the house and what he found when entering through the garage door. He explained in excruciating detail the process of securing the crime scene as the paramedics arrived. Jax had already shared with the Kaplans the physical evidence to be introduced at trial. They had already dealt with the shock and horror of the crime-scene photos. Jenna and Madison huddled together on the sofa in Jax's office with their father. They sobbed together, looking through the colored photos of the bloody corpse who had been the loving matriarch of their family. They made it through the autopsy photos but not without more heartache. Jax explained it would be easier to get a first look at the pictures in the privacy of his office rather than on the oversize television monitor in the courtroom.

During her questions of the police officer, Charlotte cautioned the jury the images would be extremely disturbing. She cast a quick glance at the Kaplan girls. When the first photo was shown, depicting Judy Kaplan lying on her kitchen floor in a pool of blood, some jurors could not help but gasp and look away or close their eyes. Many looked toward Jenna and Madison, either out of compassion or curiosity. The girls were still visibly emotional, but having already seen the pictures, the shock value was diminished. Miles did his best to maintain his composure, but he was unable to stop the flow of tears.

Jax asked a few questions to the officer. He clarified that Miles was the only one home when he arrived. The officer described Miles Kaplan as highly emotional but very cooperative. Shortly after the officer encountered him, Miles rushed to the guest bathroom to vomit. No, said the officer, he did not take a formal statement from Mr. Kaplan, but he did ask some preliminary questions to try to establish a time line of events and a possible time of death. The paramedics tended to Mr. Kaplan after his trip to the bathroom, doing a quick assessment of his vital signs, which confirmed that he was in shock.

The county coroner was next to testify. Given the notoriety of the victim and the intense media coverage, the county coroner herself performed the autopsy rather than delegating it to an assistant. John Dawson questioned her, spending more than an hour asking the necessary technical questions to establish time and cause of death. The jurors had that glazed look that usually signals a lack of interest in the testimony. They were brought back to full alertness when photos taken during the autopsy flashed on the screen. It was a stark and eerie contrast to the crime-scene photos. The jurors had already absorbed a gruesome image of Judy Kaplan, who, just minutes earlier, had been a living and breathing soul, a dedicated wife and mother. They saw her dead on her kitchen floor, her clothing in disarray, and her hair matted with her own blood. The autopsy photos showed her lying on a cold stainless-steel table. Her body had been cleansed of blood. Her hair had been partially shaved because she had been stabbed twice in the head. The jurors examined the photos as the coroner explained each of the twenty-two stab wounds on her body. The coroner gave her opinion as to cause of death: while the slashing of a knife across her throat, nearly decapitating her, would have been the logical fatal wound, it was actually the knife wound to her chest that was the fatal injury because it severed her aorta. The coroner explained, in her professional opinion, Judy Kaplan was already dead when her throat was slashed by her assailant. Although she did not express this observation through her testimony, the jurors had the distinct impression the killer wanted to make certain she did not survive.

When Prosecutor Dawson completed his questioning, Jax advised the judge and jury he had no questions for the coroner. Judge Atkins recessed the courtroom for lunch.

Miles and his daughters joined Jax and Leonard in a small conference room. Leonard arranged for the delivery of lunch from Harold's Deli, who was operating out of a food truck in front of his store while the damage from the riot was repaired. Jax and Leo were the only ones with an appetite. Miles and his girls nibbled potato chips and sipped iced tea.

When the trial reconvened for the afternoon session, the jury heard from the lead detective, Mike Richardson. He confirmed Mr. Kaplan was still in a state of extreme emotional distress, but he was able to answer the detective's questions in a coherent manner. In answer to Jax's questions, the jury gained a clear understanding of his stress level and his cooperation to find his wife's murderer.

Moving in for the kill shot, Jax asked Detective Richardson, "This conversation with Mr. Kaplan took place in a room near the kitchen, correct?"

"Correct, sir."

"This was not a custodial interrogation, which is why you didn't read Mr. Kaplan his rights, including his right to remain silent. Is that correct?"

Sensing where this line of questioning was headed, the detective hesitated before answering, "That is correct."

"In fact, just hours after this conversation, you're aware I had made arrangements with Mr. Dawson"—Jax pointed to John Dawson seated at his table—"to meet with him and you the following day for a formal interview, are you not?"

"Yes, Mr. Dawson advised me of the meeting with you and Mr. Kaplan."

Jax approached the detective when he asked, "But that meeting didn't take place, did it?"

"No, sir, it did not."

Moving away from the podium and toward the jury box, Jax looked directly at the witness. "Detective Richardson, tell the ladies and gentlemen of the jury why the meeting did not take place."

"Because I arrested Mr. Kaplan at his home for the murder of his wife."

Jax paused while the jury absorbed this information. He continued his attack. "You didn't just arrest him, did you? You had a dozen officers, the SWAT team, and a local news station deployed to his home, didn't you?"

The detective gave Jax an icy stare. "We were arresting a suspected murderer. We didn't want to jeopardize the safety of the arresting officer."

"The arresting officer was you."

"Correct."

"Were you worried about jeopardizing the safety of the local media? Surely, they, unlike you, were not armed. Weren't you concerned for their well-being?"

"We had them covered."

"No, Detective, they had you covered. You were going to be the lead story on the news."

John Dawson rose from his seat and shouted, "Objection, your Honor. That was not a question. It was a declaration by defense counsel!"

Before Judge Atkins could rule on the objection, Jax turned toward her. "Mr. Dawson is correct, Judge. It was not a question. It was a declaration. I withdraw my declaration." But he had created the implied message that Miles Kaplan was a means to an end for Detective Richardson. It was possible Miles might have been the target of the killer. He could be a pawn in some power game being played by Detective Richardson. Painting the defendant as the victim is always good for poking holes in the State's case. "I have no further questions of this witness."

The reporter in the rear corner of the courtroom, an attractive and nationally known face on a major cable news network, smiled at Jax as he returned to counsel table. She sensed Jackson Berman himself would become a major player in this drama. She shifted her focus to Jax.

After the jury was excused for the day and the spectators departed, Jax and Leonard sat with Miles at counsel table. The only ones remaining were Jenna and Madison. Jax answered their questions about the testimony presented that day. Jax was careful not to make predictions about the jury's response to the evidence. He avoided making any forecast of what would happen the next day. During the lunch recess, Jax had reviewed the updated list of witnesses for the prosecution. There was only one name on the list that was a surprise. Hannah Gilbert.

The following morning, Miles and his daughters were again secreted into the courthouse by Leonard. The jury was seated in anticipation of more witnesses and evidence. Jenna and Madison appeared to be slightly less anxious than the previous day. Jax had assured them the sensational aspect of the crime scene and the autopsy photos would not be repeated.

The morning was filled with more technical testimony. Most of their information involved establishing a chain of custody of the physical evidence gathered at the scene—bloody clothing, photos of blood spatter on the kitchen walls and cabinets, and broken dishware toppled from the kitchen island during Judy's struggle with her attacker. As for the actual murder weapon, the jury knew it had not been found in the kitchen. A thorough search of the indoor and outdoor trash bins revealed no discarded weapon. The killer must have taken it when he fled the scene. A complete inventory of the cutlery in the Kaplan kitchen established all knives were accounted for. The killer must have brought the knife to the house. The killer came to the Kaplan home for the sole purpose of using the knife on someone. *This had to help the defense,* thought Jax. *How would his client have gotten rid of the weapon?*

Charlotte Petrie, through her questions, laid out a logical explanation for the absence of the murder weapon. While all the knives had been inventoried, they could not rule out the possibility that one of those knives was indeed the murder weapon. It was quite possible the killer used one of the knives and then thoroughly cleansed it, returning it to the drawer. The coroner had previously testified the time of death was within a range of two hours. Miles could have done something with the murder weapon before he placed his 911 call.

Jax continued this line of questioning on cross-examination. None of the witnesses could say with any reasonable certainty that the killer came to the house with the intention of killing Mrs. Kaplan. The witnesses could not rule out the possibility that Miles Kaplan was the target, and Judy Kaplan was in the wrong place at the wrong time. Jax scored one for the home team. The jury might view his client as the intended victim rather than the perpetrator of the murder.

Following another quick lunch in the conference room, Jax and Leonard returned to the courtroom with the Kaplans. When the jury filed into their seats, Jax noticed the women jurors glancing at Miles. *Perhaps,* he thought, *the seedling of reasonable doubt was taking root after the morning testimony.* If Miles Kaplan was supposed to be the murder victim, who would want him dead? Jax didn't have to provide the answer. He just had to keep the question alive.

The judge instructed John Dawson to call his next witness. The double doors opened, and Hannah Gilbert strolled up the aisle and took a seat on the witness stand. Looking at the jury, she swore to tell the truth, so help her God. Dressed in a stylish business suit with a pencil skirt, she had her hair pulled back in a sleek ponytail. *Is she channeling Melissa Ramsey?* wondered Jax. *Is there a tutorial on how to look pure and angelic when testifying in a criminal trial? There's probably an app for that.*

John Dawson took his place at the podium. His questions established basic background information. Born in Indianapolis, Hannah Gilbert, formerly Hannah Nicholas, was a graduate of the

Indiana University Business School. She was hired by a regional bank headquartered in Indy. She worked there for two years before being recruited by First Citizens Bank for a branch manager's position. She moved to Cincinnati almost ten years ago and had worked for First Citizens since then. Earning a master's degree in finance, she was promoted to vice president of wealth and asset management. She currently managed more than two dozen investment bankers in the First Citizens network.

She married Harrison Gilbert seven years ago. They had no children. Harrison was in the construction business. He was a construction manager for a national home-building corporation. She reached for a tissue in the box on the witness stand as she told of her marriage ending.

"We were probably too young when we got married," she began. "We just grew in different directions. It was an amicable split."

"Is your divorce final, Hannah?" John Dawson asked as he shuffled through his notes.

Dabbing at her eyes with the tissue, she shook her head. "Not yet, sir."

Miles scribbled a note to Jax—*she told me the divorce was final six months ago!*

John changed the direction of his questions. "Can you describe for the jury your relationship with Miles Kaplan?"

Jax leaned forward in his chair, scrutinizing her eye movements and her body language. She visibly tensed up. She avoided looking at Miles. "When I was promoted to VP, I worked more closely with Miles—I mean, Mr. Kaplan—than when I was a branch manager. There were weekly executive committee meetings, and he and I had one-on-one meetings too. It was one of his five-year goals to double the assets on hand in my division.

"The more we worked together, the more my professional admiration of him transformed into respect and admiration on a personal level. I was pretty sure he felt the same way. About two years ago, after a late meeting at the office, he invited me out for a drink. One thing led to another, and within a week, we were secretly meeting two or three times a month."

"Ms. Gilbert," inquired John, "when you say one thing led to another, can you be more specific?"

Shrugging her shoulders and smiling coyly, she replied, "We fell in love. We met in hotels for a while. Then Miles—uh, Mr. Kaplan—rented an apartment on the north side of the city for us. Once my husband moved out, he got rid of the apartment and came to my house instead."

"Did your husband know about your relationship with Mr. Kaplan?"

"Not at first. After we separated, I guess he was kind of stalking me. He saw Mr. Kaplan come to the house a few times. When he confronted me about it, I told him it was none of his business who I was seeing."

"Did you and the defendant ever talk about plans for the future?"

"Of course, we did. He loved me as much as I loved him. We weren't concerned about our age difference. After all, I'm not much older than his daughters." She looked at Jenna and Madison but quickly turned her gaze back to the prosecutor.

"Did your divorce have an impact on your plans?"

Glancing quickly at Miles, she responded, "Yes, but not in a good way. I thought once I was single, he would divorce his wife and we could get on with our life together. But the opposite happened instead. Miles—oh, there I go again, I mean, Mr. Kaplan—would conveniently change the subject whenever I tried to ask when he was going to leave his wife."

"Did anything significant happen?" asked John.

"Yes," Hannah answered emphatically. Without looking anywhere in the direction of Miles, she elaborated. "We had an argument about it one evening at my house. We had a wonderful time, making dinner together and drinking wine and talking about the future. But when I tried to pin him down on just when *exactly* he was going to divorce his wife, he again deflected the conversation. It was the worst argument we ever had. It was probably the only argument we ever had. Eventually I pulled myself together and apologized for starting the fight."

"Ms. Gilbert, when did this occur?"

Looking Miles straight in the eye, she stated, "Two days before his wife was murdered."

Jax could hear Jenna and Madison's collective gasp.

"Your witness, Mr. Berman," said the prosecutor. John was convinced he had proven the motive for Miles Kaplan to kill his wife.

"Court will be in recess for fifteen minutes," announced Judge Atkins. "Ms. Gilbert, you will retake the witness stand when we reconvene. You will still be under oath. Mr. Berman will then have the opportunity to ask you questions."

I have questions for you, Hannah Gilbert.

*****

Jax was waiting at the podium when Hannah took the witness stand. He felt like a cat ready to pounce.

"Mrs. Gilbert, let me introduce myself. I'm Jackson Berman. I represent Miles Kaplan."

"I know who you are, Mr. Berman. And I am *Ms. Nicholas,* not Mrs. Gilbert."

Jax approached her as he replied, "My apologies, but since you're still married, I assumed you were still Mrs. Gilbert. You are still married to your husband, correct?"

"Only technically. The divorce decree is still in the hands of our lawyers, but it will be filed soon."

"Didn't you tell Mr. Kaplan six months ago that your divorce was final and the decree was filed?"

Squirming in her seat, she searched for a plausible answer. *The cat has its prey in its sights.* "I don't remember. Maybe I was confused when I told him my divorce was final."

"It is possible you did, in fact, tell him, incorrectly, that you were divorced. It could be as simple as your having been 'confused,' to use your words, right?"

"Sure, yes, I suppose so."

"Are there any points of confusion about your relationship with my client?"

A perplexed look crossed her face. "What do you mean?"

"You just told us how your relationship began. Tell me if I have it right. When you earned your promotion, it meant a closer working relationship with Mr. Kaplan. The working relationship eventually became a romantic relationship. You and he have been in a romantic relationship for about two years. Did I get it right, Mrs. Gilbert?"

"Pretty much so."

"Here is where I need your help, Mrs. Gilbert. You told us today you were in love with each other. Mr. Kaplan had the same feelings for you as you did for him, right?"

"Yes. We often said 'I love you' to each other."

"You were together two years. When did 'love' enter into it?"

Hannah gave some thought before answering the question. "Probably after we'd been together for maybe six months."

"Who said 'I love you' first?"

Hannah was visibly annoyed. "What difference does it make?"

Judge Atkins interrupted and advised Hannah to answer any question unless a formal objection was made by the prosecutor.

Sighing heavily, she explained, "I guess I was the first to say those words. Eventually Miles said it back to me."

"Eventually? Give me a time frame."

"Maybe a couple months later."

The cat is stalking its prey. "All right, Mrs. Gilbert. Based upon what you told us, would you agree you were the first to move this relationship from a casual one to a relationship with the added component of 'love'?"

She looked briefly in Miles's direction before responding, "Yes."

"Were you the first one in the relationship to suggest divorcing your current spouses so you could be together?"

She was pissed off. "What are you getting at?"

"What I'm getting at, Mrs. Gilbert, is fairly straightforward. You were the one to take the relationship to the next level. You were the first one to say those three magic words, 'I love you.' What I now want to know is, which one of you initiated the idea of getting divorced and having a life together. Take your time, Mrs. Gilbert. I don't want you to be confused when you answer."

Hannah contemplated the question while glaring contemptuously at Jax. "I suppose I was the one to bring up the subject the first time."

"The first time? 'The first time' suggests the subject of divorce came up, at least, one time after that. Was it brought up again by you, or do you want to tell us it was brought up by Mr. Kaplan? Again, please take your time because I don't want to confuse you."

The prey is now aware the cat is ready to attack, and it knows it has no way to escape.

John Dawson stood up and objected to the question, arguing the information was not relevant.

"Your Honor," countered Jax, "it is not only relevant but crucial. The State's theory is that my client murdered his wife to be free to marry Mrs. Gilbert. Whether or not my client made any promises to Mrs. Gilbert is crucial information for the jury when it considers my client's motive."

"Objection overruled, Mr. Dawson," ruled Judge Atkins. "Mrs. Gilbert, you are directed to answer."

Having hoped for a reprieve from this battery of questions, Hannah sunk down in her chair and murmured, "It was me who always brought it up."

Attack time!

Jax paced in front of the jury box and asked, "Then is it correct it was you, and only you, who ever talked about you having a public life together?"

"Yes."

"What was Mr. Kaplan's response whenever you brought up the topic of marriage?"

Sinking even deeper into her chair, she muttered, "He always said it wasn't possible. While he was in love with me, he and Judy had been together for so long and had so much history together. He said he would never leave her."

"Again, Mrs. Gilbert, to make sure there's no confusion, Mr. Kaplan never promised to leave his wife, he never promised to marry you. Am I correct?"

And the prey has fallen.

"Yes," Hannah snarled.

"Thank you, Mrs. Gilbert. Judge, I'm finished with this witness."

Despite follow-up questions from the prosecutor, the expressions on the jurors' faces were unmistakable. Hannah Gilbert was young and naive but, at the same time, manipulative. She harbored hopes of elevating herself personally and professionally as Mrs. Miles Kaplan. While Miles Kaplan might have stumbled in their opinion due to his infidelity, Hannah's answers to Jax's questions cast a serious shadow on the prosecution's theory of motive to kill.

The jury was restless and losing focus. Judge Atkins recessed the trial an hour earlier than usual. A grateful jury exited the jury box before she could change her mind.

Jax and Leonard shepherded the Kaplan family through a side door to avoid the media. Their timing could not have been more perfect. Jax and Leonard emerged first, with the Kaplans following behind them. Moving toward the street, they saw a black BMW sedan pass at a quick pace. Jax and Leonard recognized the occupants. Hannah Gilbert was riding in the front passenger seat of the car, and behind the wheel was Harrison Gilbert.

"What the hell, Leo? Go to the clerk's office. Get a subpoena and serve Mr. Gilbert this evening."

"I'm on it, boss. I know where he lives and works. I'll track him down."

"Check the file on the Gilbert's divorce too. We need to find out exactly what is going on with them."

Leonard gave a thumbs-up and turned back into the courthouse. Jax walked with Miles and his daughters. Still reeling from seeing the Gilberts leaving together, Jax was startled by a tap on his shoulder. He turned around to face Candace Simon, the news reporter who had been observing the trial from the courtroom.

"Mr. Berman, my name is—"

"Candace Simon," Jax interrupted. "No need for introductions. What can I do for you?"

Smiling, she stated, "I've enjoyed watching you in the courtroom. We have a nationwide audience tuning in daily to watch this trial. My network would like to get some more information about you because you're getting a lot of positive comments from our viewers on our Facebook page and Twitter."

The trajectory of the trial shifted. While the story of the murder was intriguing, attorney Jackson Berman was becoming a leading character.

CHAPTER 33

The morning greeted Jax with a penetrating drizzle. It was not strong enough to require an umbrella, but the moisture clung to his suit as he neared the courthouse. Miles and his daughters again escaped the prying eyes of the media, thanks to Leonard. However, this morning held a different feeling in the air when Jax approached the media encampment.

A handful of reporters, their camera crew in tow, rushed toward him. It took a moment before he realized he was the object of their pursuit. They shouted questions at him. He wasn't getting past without answers. He came to a stop and waited for them to surround him. Having been on the receiving end of gunshots twice in the past few months, being rushed by reporters was a breeze.

"Thanks for your questions. You're here because this case has piqued the curiosity of your national audience. All I can and will say to you is Miles Kaplan steadfastly maintains his innocence. He has the unwavering support of his children. While we cannot offer up the true killer, we're not obligated to do so. When Mr. Kaplan is acquitted, I can assure you he and his daughters won't rest until they have identified the perpetrator and brought him or her to justice. Thanks."

This seemed to satisfy the press for the moment because they cleared a path for him to make his way into the courthouse.

His brief interview was broadcast live on the local news stations. He arrived at the courtroom when he received a text from Olivia: *Just saw you on the news, Dad. You sounded really great! But straighten your tie. Love you!*

"Dad"? When did she stop calling me "Daddy"? he shuddered as he adjusted his tie.

The prosecution called its final witness. The lead crime-scene technician explained in minute detail the work he performed at the Kaplan home. He identified the dozens of exhibits that were labeled. The jurors would have another, and closer, review of the items when they would go to the jury room. This was one more opportunity for them to view them in the courtroom. Again, the jury saw the bloody items of clothing worn by Judy Kaplan on the last night of her life. Again, they reviewed dozens of photos of the shards of broken glass, the shattered tavern stool, and blood on the floor and the walls and cabinets.

The crime-scene techie explained there was no sign of forced entry into the home. All windows and doors were in perfect order, free of any evidence of an intruder forcing his or her way inside.

The witness answered Charlotte Petrie's questions about fingerprints. He explained Mr. Kaplan provided his fingerprints on the night of the murder. Yes, he testified, Mr. Kaplan's fingerprints were found in the kitchen. Yes, Mrs. Kaplan's fingerprints were identified as well. Other fingerprints were later identified as belonging to the two full-time housekeepers.

There was one set of fingerprints, found on the counter of the kitchen island, which remained unidentified. The crime-scene analysis team ran it through every national fingerprint database with no positive match.

In an effort to plug the hole in the prosecution's case, Charlotte asked, "Explain the significance of this, please."

The technician straightened up in his chair and expounded, "It means whoever belongs to those fingerprints has not been accounted for in the databases. It means it's likely he or she has no serious criminal record. It means it's likely he or she has never had a job or applied for a job requiring fingerprints for the purpose of running a record check."

Charlotte continued her quest to seal any leak in her case. "Just so we all know this for certain, is there any way to tell the age of a fingerprint? In other words, is there any way to establish an approximate time when the fingerprint was left on the surface of the kitchen island?"

The techie shook his head with a wry smile. "Of course not. It's possible it had been there for days."

"Then all we really know is, Mr. and Mrs. Kaplan had been in the kitchen, as had the housekeepers and some unidentified person," Jax asked as his first question on cross-examination. He stood in front of the witness stand without any notes.

"That is correct."

"And while you just told the jury the fingerprint could have been there for days, isn't it also possible it could have been there for only minutes?"

"That would be correct."

"Thank you. No further questions of this witness, Your Honor."

John Dawson announced the State had no further witnesses to present in its case in chief. The exhibits were quickly inventoried and admitted into evidence. Judge Atkins recessed the court for lunch. When the courtroom was empty and Jax was organizing his notes, Leonard hurried into the courtroom.

"Mr. Gilbert is waiting in the hallway. He's not one bit happy about being subpoenaed to testify for the defense," Leonard said with a sly grin on his face. Leonard loved his job.

"Good work, Leo, as always. Did you get the information on the Gilberts' divorce?"

"Got everything you wanted," Leonard replied, handing over a blue file. "I got more than you asked for. It's all in there. There's a copy for the prosecution. Consider it an early birthday present." Giving a mock salute to Jax, Leonard left the courtroom.

Opening the defense case, Jax called a handful of witnesses to set the stage. Two vice presidents of the bank as well as Judy Kaplan's closest friend painted for the jurors a portrait of Miles Kaplan as a leader in the banking industry and as a husband and family man. The jurors who had been looking at him throughout the trial as an accused murderer were able to see him as a person not unlike themselves. He had worked hard, had established himself professionally, and was devoted to his family. Charlotte Petrie asked no questions.

"Your Honor, the defense calls Harrison Gilbert to the stand." Jax had already advised John Dawson of this new addition to his witness list and had given him the copy of Leonard's report. It was no surprise to the prosecution.

The bailiff escorted Harrison to the witness stand and administered the oath. Harrison sat down gingerly, his eyes darting back and forth between the jury and Jax.

"Good afternoon, Mr. Gilbert, I'm Jackson Berman, attorney for Miles Kaplan. Thank you for being here today."

Harrison made the mistake of thinking he could get the best of Jax by being clever. "Did I have a choice, Mr. Berman? Your investigator showed up at my house yesterday evening and served me with a subpoena."

"Yes, he did, Mr. Gilbert. I was just trying to break the ice."

Jax continued breaking the ice with basic background questions. Harrison Gilbert's testimony was consistent with his wife's. They had been married for seven years. He held a degree in construction management and was employed by a national homebuilder until he opened his own construction company. He earned approximately three hundred thousand dollars per year.

Harrison explained to the jury he and his wife separated almost a year ago, and the divorce was pending. It was not until after they separated that he found out his wife was sleeping with her boss. Any chance of reconciliation was destroyed when the affair came to light.

"There's no hope of saving your marriage?" asked Jax.

Harrison, annoyed at having to repeat his answer, grumbled, "That's what I just told you."

Marking a document with an exhibit label, Jax walked to the witness stand and handed it to Harrison. "Then could you identify this paper for the jury?"

Harrison's cheeks turned fiery red as he reviewed the paper. "It's an agreed entry of dismissal."

"A dismissal of what, Mr. Gilbert?"

"Our divorce."

"Whose signatures are on the document?"

He paused before responding, "Mine and Hannah's."

Still standing next to the witness stand, Jax pressed the issue. "Mr. Gilbert, do you see the date stamp on the paper indicating when the dismissal was filed?"

"Yes."

"Would you agree with me this dismissal was filed and your divorce was officially dismissed almost two months before Judy Kaplan was killed?"

Pretending to review the document closely, Harrison acknowledged his divorce was dismissed well before her death.

"Thank you, Mr. Gilbert. Take a look at this photo marked as an exhibit. Would you describe for the jury what this photo depicts?"

He looked closely at the photo. "It's a picture of my garage."

"What is the date stamp on the photo, Mr. Gilbert?"

"Today at seven a.m."

"The picture shows two cars parked in your garage. The black BMW is yours, correct?"

"Yes, it is."

"There is a red Toyota Camry parked next to your BMW. Is that also your car?"

"No."

"Who owns the Camry?"

Harrison paused for several seconds before saying, "It belongs to Hannah."

Jax returned to the podium. "I want to make sure I understand what you've told us. Your divorce was dismissed several months ago, and Hannah Gilbert's car was parked in your garage this morning. Have you resumed your marriage, or did she just need a place to park her car?"

"Objection, Your Honor!" shouted Charlotte Petrie. "Mr. Berman is badgering his own witness."

"Overruled," Judge Atkins ruled. "Mr. Gilbert, you are directed to answer the question."

"We're married and living together," sighed the witness as he looked toward the floor, shaking his head.

Jax was unrelenting. "When your wife told us the divorce was pending and the final decree was going to be filed, she was confused?"

"I wasn't here when she testified, so I don't know what she said or what she was thinking."

Jax smiled and said, "That's fair. The jury heard her testimony, and we'll let them decide whether she was confused." Two of the jurors failed to stifle a smile.

Harrison made the mistake of thinking this would be the end of the questioning and his witty retort would shut down Jackson Berman.

"Let me ask you questions you will be able to answer based on your own recollection. You and Hannah held a joint account at First Citizens Bank, but it was closed several months ago, right?"

"Yes, that's right. When we split up, we opened individual checking accounts. Mine is with Second National Bank."

Jax, still at the podium, stated, "That makes sense to me. I'm sure, at the time, you didn't want to have your money in an account at your wife's bank. Right?"

Harrison started to relax a bit. "Right. I also transferred my IRA to my new bank too." *Perfect*, thought Jax, *he's not only answering my questions; he's giving me extra information.*

"Your IRA has a sizeable balance for a young man like you. It's impressive."

Growing more confident, Harrison Gilbert replied in a boastful tone, "I'm good at money management. The balance is more than one hundred fifty thousand dollars."

"You have the two accounts at Second National Bank. Hannah still has her checking account and her IRA at First Citizens. Now that you and she have reconciled, are you going to reopen a joint checking account?"

"We haven't really discussed it. Right now, it seems best to keep our accounts separate."

Time for the kill shot. "What about your joint account in the Cayman Islands?"

Harrison's cheeks, which were bloodred when asked about the divorce, now drained of all color. It looked like he might collapse on the witness stand. Harrison stammered, "What are you talking about?"

Approaching him with a stack of papers in a binder marked with an exhibit label, Jax handed it to Harrison. "This is what I'm talking about. A joint account in the names of Harrison Gilbert and Hannah Gilbert opened almost eighteen months ago at the Strident Bank and Trust located in George Town, which is the capital city of the Cayman Islands. Take a few minutes to go through the account statements."

While Harrison fumbled through the paperwork with trembling hands, Jax poured water from the pitcher on counsel table into a disposable plastic cup and placed it in front of the witness. "Help yourself to a drink, Mr. Gilbert, while you look at the paperwork." Harrison warily picked up the cup and took a few sips. He shakily placed the binder on the witness stand.

Jax continued his pursuit. "This joint account has a fairly simple history, wouldn't you agree? The account was opened with an initial deposit of ten thousand dollars. Since then, there have been weekly deposits of ten thousand dollars. There have been no withdrawals. Am I correct?"

Harrison flipped through the binder again before nodding his head in assent.

"Mr. Gilbert, there is only one source of those weekly deposits, right?"

"Right."

"What is that source, Mr. Gilbert? Who has been depositing ten thousand dollars a week into your account?"

Harrison decided to try to fight back when he shouted at Judge Atkins, "Do I have to answer the question?"

Leaning toward him, the judge simply said, "Yes, you do. Answer the question."

Looking around the courtroom in a vain attempt to find someone or something to prevent him from answering, he answered, "Miles Kaplan." Harrison, deciding his best hope was full disclosure, continued his answer. "Hannah found out he was involved in a pretty sophisticated bank-fraud scheme. I'm not a banker. All I know about it is, he was skimming money, a lot of money, from pension funds. When Hannah let him know she had told me about it, he offered to pay us ten thousand dollars a week in exchange for our silence." Now it was Miles Kaplan's turn to start squirming in his seat.

"The account now has almost seven hundred thousand dollars in it, correct?"

"I guess so," said Harrison.

"With that arrangement, it certainly was in your and Hannah's best interest for Miles Kaplan to live a long and healthy life. Am I correct?"

"Sure. Did you think I wanted to kill him?"

Jax approached the witness stand. "It had occurred to me. He was sleeping with your wife. That would be enough to drive some people to murder. But that was before you told me Miles Kaplan was your golden goose."

Harrison relaxed and said, "You're right. I sure wouldn't want anything to happen to him."

"Answer this, Mr. Gilbert," Jax asked as he picked up the binder and opened it, "there was one week where there was no deposit at all. It was the week before Judy Kaplan was murdered."

Harrison tensed up again and stuttered, "I-I don't understand."

"It's right here in this bank statement. Inexplicably, out of months and months of regular deposits, there was no deposit that week. However, after Judy Kaplan's death, the deposits resumed like clockwork. Do you have an explanation?"

The witness took a handkerchief out of his pocket and wiped away the perspiration beading on his forehead. "No, I don't."

"Is it perhaps because somehow Mrs. Kaplan interfered with this financial arrangement?"

Feeling like a caged animal, Harrison Gilbert stood up in the witness stand and shouted, "I'm not answering any more questions without a lawyer!"

Jax smiled at him and said, "That's fine. You've answered my questions. Your witness, Ms. Petrie."

Charlotte Petrie and John Dawson, stunned by this turn of events, conferred between themselves. John Dawson then went to the podium. "Judge, in light of Mr. Gilbert's exercise of his right to remain silent, we will ask no questions."

The courtroom was buzzing after Judge Atkins recessed for the day. When the jury left, Jax went to the witness stand, took his handkerchief out of the inside pocket of his suit jacket, and picked up the water cup Harrison Gilbert had used. Still wrapped in his handkerchief, he brought it to John and Charlotte.

"Take good care of this. I'm willing to bet the fingerprints on this cup will be a match with the unidentified prints in the Kaplans' kitchen."

John Dawson placed the cup embedded in the handkerchief in his briefcase. "Do you believe he killed Judy Kaplan?"

"Think about it, John. It makes perfect sense. My hunch is somehow Judy figured out what was going on, and she demanded her husband quit paying the hush money. When there was no deposit that week, Harrison decided to eliminate the problem, which was Judy Kaplan. Whether or not Hannah knew what Harrison was planning, I couldn't say. Assuming I'm right and his fingerprints were left in the kitchen, he'll tell you everything you want to know in the hope that you go easy on him."

John thought about Jax's theory. "Your reasoning is plausible, no doubt about it. But I don't have enough to dismiss the charge against your client."

"I understand. I'm not going to put my client on the stand. Tomorrow morning, I'll rest my case. Assuming you have no rebuttal evidence to present, we can head straight into closing arguments."

The two attorneys and occasional drinking buddies shook hands and left the courtroom together.

Jax was again surrounded by the media when he stepped outside. He gave them a brief statement, which assuaged them for the moment, and made his way back to his office. Leonard was there, a Scotch on the rocks waiting on his desk. Together, they quietly celebrated what they believed had been a great day for the defense, and Jax worked on a rough draft of his closing argument. The words flowed onto the paper. Jax finished his cocktail. After Leonard left, he called Rick to meet for dinner.

*****

The jury returned their verdict of not guilty after thirty minutes. The judge thanked them for their service and excused them. Afterward Miles and his daughters hugged one another and cried tears of joy for Miles's vindication but also grief over the loss of Judy. After several minutes, when the courtroom was empty, Miles gave Jax a hug.

Wiping his eyes, Miles remarked, "It looks like I might have more legal battles on the horizon. It seems pretty certain the authorities will be interested in Mr. Gilbert's revelations about bank fraud."

Jax nodded. "That's a safe bet, Miles. I'm sorry it had to be brought to light the way it did. But dealing with bank fraud seems like a breath of fresh air compared to facing a murder charge."

Miles shook Jax's hand and replied, "I've already thought of that. Can I call you after the dust from this trial settles? There's nobody else I would trust to represent me."

"Count on me. For the moment, though, rejoice in your acquittal and spend some time with your girls. They are lovely young women, and they've been faithful to you. Count your blessings."

"Great advice." Miles turned and met Jenna and Madison in the hallway. The family left the courthouse together, escorted by Leonard.

Jax was not as lucky. Slipping out through a side door, he was again surrounded by the news cameras. He spent the next fifteen minutes of his life answering questions before he put an end to the makeshift press conference.

Finally back at his office, Marion was working with Bailey asleep in her lap. She offered Jax a heartfelt congratulations on his victory. Bailey awoke and wound her way around his legs, begging for attention. He picked up the cat, rubbed her head, and carried her into his office. Leonard was waiting. They discussed the turn of events in the case. They made preliminary plans for the inevitable bank-fraud charges in Miles's future.

The evening sun settled over the skyline when they walked to their cars. Jax opened his door and reached into his pocket for his keys when he pulled out a piece of notepaper.

Jax tapped on his car window. Leonard rolled it down. "What's up?"

Handing the paper to him, Jax said, "I meant to give this to you before the trial began. The last time I took Olivia to Catherine's house, there was a black BMW parked in the driveway. Olivia said it belongs to Charlie, who apparently is Catherine's boyfriend. Olivia doesn't know his last name. I wrote down his license number. See what you can find out about the guy."

"What's the deal with black BMWs? I'll get right on it. I'll have the information for you tomorrow."

Jax grinned. "Relax and enjoy the evening, Leo. I won't have time then. Remember? I'm getting married tomorrow!"

CHAPTER 34

Jackson Berman was often described by other lawyers as a hard charger. To those who had been on the receiving end of his brutal cross-examination in trial, he was a ruthless son of a bitch.

However, on his wedding day, there was a serenity to him that even took him by surprise. He could not recall ever being as joyful as he was on this day. He was marrying the love of his life, and rejoicing with him were his best friend and his daughter. He was celebrating with the three most important people in his life. Julia, Rick, and Olivia were all, in different ways, the very essence of his being.

The weather cooperated to make the day spectacular. The wedding party gathered at the gazebo in a beautifully landscaped park overlooking the river. Jax had reserved the gazebo; he wanted this moment of his life to be perfect. He did not want to risk any disruption from skateboarders and joggers.

Julia threw her energy into wedding decor. The gazebo was adorned with blooming jasmine vines woven through the lattice work. Oversize ceramic urns held white hydrangeas.

Julia and Olivia spent the previous night at her home. It was their idea of a bachelorette party. They cooked dinner and watched movies and music videos selected by Olivia. The next morning, they shared a light breakfast before their appointment at the salon. They left with perfect hair and makeup—just a light application of makeup for Olivia—and returned home to dress for the ceremony.

Jax arranged for a limo to deliver them promptly at six o'clock. Jax and Rick were waiting at the gazebo. Olivia exited first, dressed in a lilac sleeveless dress embellished with lace and tiny pearls. She wore shoes dyed to match the dress, and she carried a small bouquet of white roses and baby's breath. Jax was overwhelmed with emotion.

Here was his little girl, the only person in the world who called him Daddy and who seemed to have grown into a young lady overnight. He was reminded of her text she sent during the Kaplan trial: *Just saw you on the news, Dad.* Yes, Olivia had grown up right before his eyes. When she arrived at the gazebo, without saying a word, she reached up and put her arms around her father's neck. After a long and heartfelt hug, Olivia kissed him on the cheek and took her place next to Rick.

The door to the limo opened. Jax stared in absolute wonder. There was the woman of his dreams, the one who had taught him the meaning of true and unconditional love. She was the most beautiful woman he had ever seen. He was thankful he hired a photographer to capture this day. The photographer had been waiting as the limo arrived and had been chronicling every moment.

Julia was dressed in an off-white satin sheath that was calf-length. The scoop neck and the three-quarter-length sleeves hugged the contour of her body. The strand of pearls draping her neck was a wedding gift from Jax. She carried white roses and lilies. Walking toward the gazebo, her eyes never left Jax. She, too, was moments away from marrying the love of her life.

The wedding was officiated by a local judge who graduated from law school with Jax and Rick. This added another personal touch to the wedding. Jax had met with the judge; together they added another segment to the ceremony. After Julia and Jax exchanged their vows, the judge turned to Olivia.

"Olivia," he began, "this marriage means the beginning of a new family for you. Do you, Olivia, accept Julia as a member of your family to honor and respect her and to love her?"

Olivia had not expected to be anything more than the maid of honor. She looked at Jax, then she looked at Julia. "Oh yes, Your Honor, I do. I really do." She smiled her happiest smile.

The judge grinned, amused at her reference to him as Your Honor. He continued, "Julia, do you accept Olivia as a member of your new family, and do you promise to honor and respect her and to love her?"

Julia was also surprised at this part of the ceremony. "I do," she stated, taking Olivia's hand and giving it a gentle squeeze.

Jax took the opportunity to wipe happy tears from his eyes. Rick, despite his pronouncements about marriage versus bachelorhood, was visibly moved.

They exchanged rings, the judge pronounced them husband and wife, and the next several minutes were filled with hugs and kisses. The photographer captured the moment, and after several posed photos of the bride and groom plus the wedding party, she wished them well and took her leave.

The exuberant wedding party continued the celebration at an exclusive restaurant famous for its commanding view of the skyline and the river. Jax had reserved a small private dining room for the special occasion.

Jax, sipping his flute of champagne, delighted in listening to Julia and Rick in conversation. While Rick had joined them for dinner a handful of times, this evening seemed to be the perfect time for them to forge a meaningful friendship. Rick and Julia talked about everything from politics to favorite vacation destinations. Jax and Olivia sipped their champagne—nonalcoholic champagne for Olivia—standing at the full-length window. His arm draped around her shoulders, he looked at his daughter.

"You look beautiful tonight, Princess. This has been an incredible day."

Olivia sipped her faux champagne. "Today's been so much fun. The whole weekend has been a blast. Spending the night with Julia last night was awesome. You picked a real winner, Dad."

Fortunately, Jax had not yet taken another sip of his drink or it would have been running down his shirtfront. *The things this kid says. She's a grown-up in a child's body.* He pulled Olivia even more closely to him.

The following evening, Mr. and Mrs. Jackson Berman made themselves comfortable in first class on a nonstop flight to Paris. A weeklong honeymoon in the most romantic city in the world was the perfect way to begin their life together. Marion had given them perhaps the best wedding gift ever. Tucked inside a Waterford crystal ice bucket, wrapped in gold foil, was a burner phone. The card gave him specific instructions: it was only to be used to keep in touch with Olivia and Jenny Graham, who would be staying at the house with her. They were the only living souls who knew the phone number. Marion had a list of attorneys whom she could call to cover an arraignment or a bond hearing while he was away. Marion was more than capable of conducting initial interviews with new clients and fielding phone calls from current ones. Jax, settled in his seat, sipping champagne with his bride, knew his office would be in good hands. He could eliminate all thoughts about pending cases for the next week.

The weather in Paris was another wedding gift. They enjoyed seven days of blue skies and moderate temperatures, instead of the misty, gloomy Paris romanticized in movies. They strolled the Champs-Élysées, wandered through the Louvre, and marveled at the Monet murals in the Musée de l'Orangerie. They sampled local cuisine at the outdoor cafés and bistros. Window-shopping in the arrondissements on the Left Bank, walking hand in hand through the narrow streets, and listening to sidewalk musicians were all captured moment by moment in Jax's memory. He would treasure this first step in his life's journey with Julia.

They celebrated their last night in the City of Lights with dinner at the Jules Verne atop the Eiffel Tower. They spent three hours watching the sunset over the skyline, enjoying a tasting menu featuring an assortment of French delicacies. Foie gras, caviar, langoustine ravioli, duck confit, and roasted lamb with cream of mustard seed were the perfect complement to their conversation about life, love, and their future. The evening culminated with chocolate soufflé and a glass of tawny port. Convinced they had never had such an exquisite meal, they opted to walk back to their hotel to work off what had to have been a five-thousand-calorie dining experience.

*****

Leonard received the results of the license plate search Jax had given him the day before the wedding. The black BMW in

Catherine's driveway was registered to Patrick C. Gross. Without Jax to give him any assignments for the week, he used his free time to find out more about Mr. Gross. He learned Mr. Gross was actually Dr. Patrick Charles Gross, a local psychiatrist. Dr. Gross had to be Charlie. Leonard spent the next few days uncovering everything he could find about Dr. "Charlie" Gross. When he finished, he had a rather thick file of very interesting information to present to Jax when he returned.

CHAPTER 35

The newlyweds navigated through customs at the Cincinnati airport. Despite every effort of the airport security and airports everywhere to make air travel a miserable experience—dealing with surly employees, delays, and schedule changes—Mr. and Mrs. Berman arrived at the terminal exit in under an hour.

Waiting for them were Jenny and Olivia, who were holding an oversize sign. "Welcome Home, Family!" was spelled out in bold gold letters and embellished with a border of fluorescent flowers.

The reunion brought smiles to the faces of travelers passing by. Olivia first embraced her father, then she gave her new stepmother an equally affectionate hug. Jenny followed, planting a kiss on their cheeks. After several minutes of conversation about the wonders of Paris as well as Jenny and Olivia catching them up on everything they did during the week, Jenny said goodbye and headed to her car.

Olivia helped with the luggage when the threesome located Jax's car in long-term parking. Sitting in the back seat, Olivia asked question after question about Paris.

"It sounds like a fabulous trip!" Olivia sighed. "Maybe someday we can go there together."

Julia held Jax's hand in the front seat and replied, "That's a wonderful idea. Let's talk about a trip to celebrate your thirteenth birthday. What a great way to begin your teenage years."

I'll either be commemorating the teenage years or bracing myself for them, thought Jax.

They pulled into the garage and unloaded the car. They carried the luggage into the kitchen through the door leading from the garage. Jax and Julia, with Olivia's help, took everything upstairs and stacked the suitcases in the dressing area of the master bedroom. Julia announced she would unpack in the morning. Jax, thrilled at the reprieve from the mundane task of returning everything to its rightful place, led the way downstairs to the kitchen.

Conversation about Paris continued while the new family devoured the deli tray and side salads prepared by Jenny. After an entire day of airplane food, anything would have been a gourmet meal.

Olivia helped Julia clean the dishes and store the leftovers, then she bounded up the back stairs to her bedroom. She yelled, "I'll give you two time to be alone. I'll be back later, and we can watch something on TV!"

Jax wrapped his arms around Julia and laughed, "She's quite something, isn't she?"

Smiling back at him, Julia replied, "She's absolutely adorable. I swear she's a grown-up wrapped in a child's body."

"I wish I could keep her wrapped up in her childhood forever."

She planted a kiss on his lips. "You've done a marvelous job. Despite the divorce, she's full of the pure happiness and innocence every child should experience. She knows how lucky she is to have two parents who love her and support her."

"And now she has you on the team."

Giving him another kiss, she whispered, "Yes, she does, and she always will. She and I made vows to each other in our wedding ceremony, remember?"

The moment was interrupted by a voice unknown to Julia but all too familiar to Jax. Standing in the breakfast nook was Catherine. She had entered through the French doors from the rear terrace. The door was still ajar, letting a cool breeze into the room. The breeze should have been refreshing, but a sense of foreboding permeated Jax instead.

"Welcome home, lovebirds. Congratulations to the new Mrs. Jackson Berman," Catherine said in a low, raspy voice. "Actually, the congratulations go to you, Jax. Good job! You traded in the original for a younger model."

Catherine was holding a gun in both hands, aimed in their direction. She was standing less than twenty feet away.

Jax tried to determine if Catherine was sober before he said or did anything. Unable to assess his ex-wife's current mental state, he opted for the slow and cautious route.

"Catherine, what do you want? What do you need?" Jax asked in the calmest voice he could muster at the moment.

Julia was motionless, never taking her eyes off Catherine.

"What I need, Jax," Catherine answered, inching closer, "is for you and your new little wife to fall off the face of the earth."

Jax, careful not to make any sudden movement, asked, "Why?"

Moving closer, she let out a loud, frustrated sigh. "Because you destroyed me, Jax. You robbed me of my independence and my identity from the first day of our marriage. Be careful, Mrs. Berman," she said turning to Julia. "He'll do it to you next." Returning her attention to Jax, she continued, her voice getting louder with each word.

"You ended the marriage with no regard for me or my feelings. I was a good and faithful wife to you. I gave you your daughter, Jax. *Our daughter*, Jax. And if divorcing me wasn't enough, you stole *our daughter* from me. Do you honestly think Julia can replace me as Olivia's mother?"

"I don't want that, Catherine. I've never wanted that, Catherine. Nor does Julia." Jax struggled to maintain a calm voice.

Julia wanted to nod in agreement but was too frightened to move.

Jax continued his efforts to diffuse the situation. "I never, never wanted this to be an ugly divorce. Take a moment to reflect on what you just said. It was you, not me, who filed for divorce. It was your accusations that I was a child abuser which resulted in the psychological evaluations. It is what led us to where we are now. Yes, I do have legal custody of Olivia, but I have never and will never do anything to keep you from being her mother. She loves you. She loves me. She's fond of Julia but has never wanted to replace you with Julia. She seems to be fond of Charlie. She's told me about the fun you have together. I know Charlie can't replace me as Olivia's dad. Just as Julia can't replace you as her mother."

Keeping the gun aimed at them, Catherine laughed. Jax knew from bitter experience that laugh meant Catherine was teetering on the brink and that an explosion was looming. He had been able to diffuse the situations in the past, but she had never been holding a gun.

"Brilliant closing argument, Mr. Berman. But this one-person jury isn't buying a word of it."

Catherine pointed the gun at Julia and fired, hitting Julia in her upper left arm. The impact of the shot knocked Julia to the floor. The sound of the gunshot reverberated throughout the room, piercing Jax's ears.

"Stay down!" Jax yelled to Julia. He turned toward Catherine, who was now standing less than ten feet away.

"Catherine," he pleaded, "think about what you're doing. This is not what you want. Think about what this will do to Olivia."

"I am thinking about her, Jax. She needs two parents, no more than that. She needs a nice, neat, little family unit. And I'm going to be the person who gives it to her. Not you."

Catherine leveled the gun at his chest.

He heard the gun discharge. He had heard gunshots before. Hell, he had just experienced it moments ago. But he had never been shot. *What's it like to be shot? Am I supposed to feel something? Searing heat as the bullet pierces my body? A coldness? Blinding pain? Why am I feeling nothing?*

With these thoughts racing, he looked at Catherine. She was still holding the gun, but her face had an unnatural expression. She seemed to be catatonic. *Was she in shock, in numb disbelief at what she had just done?* This was another question swirling in his mind.

Catherine dropped the gun and fell to her knees. When she sank to the floor, Jax could see standing directly behind her was Olivia.

Olivia held in her child-size hands the pistol from his night table in his bedroom. The shot was fired from that gun, not Catherine's gun. Olivia shot her mother.

Julia, blood trickling down her arm, crawled to Catherine. Jax, kicking Catherine's gun across the kitchen floor, rushed to Olivia.

Julia said, "Catherine, you'll be fine. You have been," Julia hesitated, not wanting to say that Olivia had *shot* her, "struck in the shoulder, but it's a clean entry wound. You and I both need medical attention. But we'll be okay." Julia, holding her wounded arm close to her side, stood and grabbed her cell phone from the counter. She dialed 911, explaining there had been an accident and two people needed emergency medical care. She deliberately failed to report they were gunshot wounds.

Jax held Olivia in his arms, rocking slowly back and forth, while she sobbed uncontrollably. She was still holding the gun. Without letting go of his daughter, he gently pried it from her grasp.

"I saw Mom in the backyard when I went upstairs. She was sneaking around in the dark. I knew something bad was going to happen. When I was at her house last week, she was acting even stranger than usual, Daddy. I was scared, so I got the gun from your room. I know I'm not supposed to touch it, but I couldn't let her hurt you. Or Julia." Olivia wept, and Jax hugged her until she ran out of tears.

CHAPTER 36

"Your arraignment is scheduled to begin promptly at nine o'clock," Jax said to his client seated across the desk. "We'd better leave now to avoid the media circus."

He paused to reflect on the events of the past month. Had he not been there to witness it, he probably would still be living in a state of denial. A broad spectrum of emotions overwhelmed him whenever he relived the scene in his memory.

Julia was correct in her assessment of her and Catherine's gunshot wounds. Julia suffered only a minor wound to her upper arm. The bullet had entered and exited without shattering the bone. Her injuries were treated by the emergency room physicians. She was released a few hours later.

Catherine's wound to her shoulder required a minor surgical procedure to extract the bullet and repair muscle damage. She was admitted to the hospital, where she remained for two days. When she was discharged, she was transported to the Summerfield Center for Hope. Summerfield, located an hour north of the city, was a nationally acclaimed mental-health treatment center dedicated to long-term inpatient and outpatient care. Dr. Harper's diagnosis of narcissistic personality disorder, made during the divorce proceedings, was enough for Catherine to be admitted for assessment and treatment. The fact that she shot one person and fully intended to shoot another was further proof that she was in need of intensive therapy. The initial treatment plan was for her to remain there for ninety days, followed by intensive outpatient counseling.

Thanks to Jax's long-standing friendship with Prosecutor John Dawson, Catherine would not face criminal charges. He and Julia were adamant. Catherine's issues must be addressed in the treatment community. Subjecting her to criminal prosecution would only prolong her recovery.

Jax called John while the paramedics were escorting Julia and Catherine to the ambulance in his driveway. "John, I need your help and friendship like I never have before." He gave him the details of the shooting. "I need Catherine to get well, not get arrested. She's the mother of my daughter. Olivia needs her. Olivia's going to need her own intensive therapy to deal with the reality of shooting her own mother. Seeing Catherine getting well and not behind bars will go a long way toward her recovery."

Jax waited for what seemed like hours for a response. The sound of the gunshot was still ringing in his ears; he thought maybe he just hadn't heard his reply. John, who had been relaxing at home watching a baseball game on television when Jax called, was trying to recreate the scene in his mind. John breathed out a long, slow whistle.

"Holy shit, Jax, I'm trying to wrap my head around everything you told me. What a nightmare. Sure, I understand your position. I must say, though, if my wife took a shot at me, I hope I could be half as forgiving as you."

"Before you elevate me to sainthood, please understand my focus is on Olivia."

"I understand. Don't worry. Do anything and everything to see Olivia through this ordeal. You have my word. No charges will be filed against your ex-wife. Please let me know if there is anything else I can do."

"If you keep this mess out of court, you will have done plenty for me."

The day after the shooting, the bandages on her arm concealed under her suit jacket, Julia took Olivia with her to Children's Hospital. It had taken one phone call from Dr. Julia Winston, now Julia Berman, to the chief of the children's psychiatric unit. After learning the details of the shooting, she promised to personally accept Olivia as her patient. The counseling would commence that day and would continue twice a week for the next few months. Following an assessment of Olivia, the psychiatrist and Olivia's family would together make decisions concerning ongoing counseling. They would develop a plan for Olivia to visit Catherine while she was in the treatment center, in an effort to rebuild a mother-daughter relationship.

After more kisses and hugs than usual, the new yet traumatized family left the house together. Julia and Olivia drove to the hospital, and Jax went to his office. When he arrived, Leonard was sitting in Marion's office, stroking Bailey's head as she slept in his lap. Jax had called Leonard when he finished his call with John Dawson the night before. After giving Leonard the details of the shooting, he asked him to call Marion. Jax was simply too exhausted to do it himself. He went upstairs to bed where Julia was waiting. They spent their first night at home as a married couple staring at the ceiling instead of enjoying a sound sleep.

Without saying a word, Marion rose from her chair and embraced Jax. Feeling tears running down his face, he reached for a tissue on her desk without breaking her hold on him. Leonard was having a hard time hiding his emotions. Bailey kept sleeping.

Marion sat down and made her best attempt to be professional at the same time wiping her own tears.

"Waiting for you on your desk is a summary of everything that happened while you were away: new clients and preliminary info on them and their charges, their court dates, plus old clients and updates on their cases. None of it requires any immediate action. Take your time this morning. Leonard has been waiting for you because he has some information." She turned back to her desk to answer an incoming call.

Extricating Bailey from his lap and placing her on Marion's desk, Leonard followed Jax into his office.

Sitting in his usual chair, he placed a thick blue file folder on the desk. He had made copies of the documents; he pushed them across the desk.

"Let's start from the beginning. After you left town, I had plenty of time to do some digging into Catherine's friend Charlie." Leonard focused on the first document in the file while Jax did the same with his copy. "If I had had any idea Catherine was capable of what she pulled at your home last night, I would have been waiting for you at the airport with this information." He shook his head. "Then maybe none of this would have happened." Leonard, his voice cracking with emotion, paused and gazed out the window.

"Leo, you can't beat yourself up over this. Hell, I was married to the woman for almost fifteen years, and I had no idea she could have done it. So why should you?"

"You're right, but it's going to take a while for me to shake these pains of guilt. I'll be okay, but not for a while. Let's move through this file."

Reading the reports together, Leonard provided a running commentary.

Charlie was Dr. Patrick C. Gross, a psychiatrist in Cincinnati. He had offices in two locations. His patients were children and adults. One of his fields of expertise was hypnotherapy.

"Hypnotherapy?" asked Jax while reviewing the report on Charlie's education and professional background. "Is it what it sounds like? Hypnosis?"

"Flip to the next page. I have some basic information on hypnotherapy. Yes, it is hypnosis. The therapist uses what they call guided relaxation as well as intense concentration and focused attention, all in order, to achieve a heightened state of awareness. We, normal people, would refer to it as a trance."

Jax kept reading. "A trance, just like in the movies? Do they wave a swinging chain watch in front of the subject and chant 'you're getting sleepy' until he falls into this trance?"

Leonard could not hold back a grin. "I don't think it's that corny. But the more I kept reading, the more things started to make sense to me."

"How so?" asked Jax, leaning forward with his elbows on his desk.

"Keep reading. This so-called trance means the subject's attention is so focused that anything going on around him is temporarily blocked or ignored. This continues until the therapist brings the subject out of the trance. Because of this intense focus, the subject is open to any and all suggestions planted by the therapist. This treatment is much more effective with children than adults. It's very useful in patients of all ages to deal with phobias."

"I'm with you so far. But what do you mean about things starting to make sense to you?"

"Well, it started as a hunch, but the more I uncovered about the eminent Dr. Gross, the more my hunch turned into a solid lead on everything that has occurred over the past few months." Leonard paused before continuing. "Let me start with hard facts. Patrick C. Gross grew up in the same swanky part of Chicago as your ex-wife. Their parents were best friends. Catherine and Charlie went to school together; they vacationed together with their families when they were kids. They started casually dating when they reached high school, just a normal teenage romance. They were heavy into the party scene at school—drinking, smoking weed. Again, just more typical teen behavior. They both found themselves in juvenile court when they were arrested for shoplifting. This must be the reason why Catherine was packed off to boarding school. Her parents tried to separate her from Charlie. But it didn't work."

"What do you mean?" Jax wasn't sure he wanted to hear the rest of this story.

"Catherine graduated from boarding school, and Charlie graduated from his private school the same year. Although they attended different colleges, they apparently remained in constant communication. They visited each other, at least, once a month; she would travel to his school, or he would visit her on her campus. They never were arrested again, but they kept partying."

"When did he move to Cincinnati?" inquired Jax.

Leonard explained, "About three or four years before you met Catherine, which would explain why she didn't hesitate to move to Cincinnati when you popped the question. She knew she already had one friendly face waiting for her in her new hometown."

Jax ran his fingers through his hair. Trying to digest all this on zero sleep was challenging. "Are you suggesting she continued her relationship with him while we were together?"

"Not at all," Leonard was quick to say. "There's nothing I could find to suggest that. In fact, from everything I found, there was really no contact between them after Charlie moved here from Chicago. It seems to be nothing more than a freak coincidence that they both ended up here in Cincinnati. But we do know from Olivia that Charlie started visiting the house after you moved out."

"I'll buy that. Obviously, I don't know Catherine as well as I should because I never, for a moment, contemplated her breaking into my house to kill me. But I never suspected, during our marriage, that she was cheating on me."

Leo replied, "I have no reason to suspect it either. But we do know for a fact the lines of communication were reopened after your separation. Now here's where the saga gets really interesting."

"I don't think I can handle too much more interesting info."

"You're going to have to bear up under the pressure."

Jax settled in and listened without interrupting.

The black BMW registered to Patrick "Charlie" Gross was a perfect match to the one captured on the security camera after the shots were fired in the restaurant parking lot. More research into hypnotherapy led Leonard to surmise that, when Charlie would tell his bedtime stories to Olivia, he was actually engaging her in hypnotherapy without her knowing it. It was during these trance periods that he planted the suggestion that Jax had been sexually abusing her. He put her into a trance before she talked to the police and the caseworker. It also explained why, once she was brought out of the trance, Olivia had no recollection of the accusations she made to the authorities. It explained why she never acted uncomfortable or anxious when she was with her father.

"If I'm correct, she has no memory of accusing you of anything. And she never will."

It was with this hard information plus his theory of the case that convinced the police to bring Dr. Gross in for questioning about the shooting in the parking lot. Leonard observed the interrogation through a two-way mirror.

Leaning back in his chair, Leonard continued. "The good doctor caved less than five minutes into the interrogation. He folded like a house of cards."

"What did he tell the detectives?"

Leonard gave Jax a detailed account of the questioning that lasted more than two hours.

Charlie Gross started dating Catherine shortly after she and Jax separated. Catherine initiated the contact, but he was so excited about seeing her again that he arranged to meet her later the same day. He was so horrified and disgusted at the way Jax had treated her throughout their marriage—according to Catherine's version of the marriage. He jumped at the chance to get even with the person who caused his precious Catherine so much unhappiness.

He drove her to Jax's office to break the window. He drove her to Jax's house to damage his landscaping. After that, everything he did was on his own, without Catherine's knowledge.

"He remarked that the petty acts of vandalism seemed to do nothing to alarm you, so he decided to step up the game."

Jax, shaking his head, said, "I didn't know I was playing a game with anyone."

"Well, my friend, you were. The game became almost an obsession with the eminent headshrinker. Hold on to your seat because I haven't gotten to the good part yet."

Jax inhaled deeply. "I'm ready."

Leonard provided every detail Charlie Gross admitted during the interrogation. He was the one who started the fire at Jax's office building. He was the one who fired the shots at Jax in the restaurant parking lot. He saw Julia and Olivia with him but chose to carry out his plan anyway.

"Then," Leonard stated, "after spilling his guts about committing arson and attempted murder, he decided he needed a lawyer and invoked his right to remain silent. A little late for that, don't you agree? What a complete and total idiot. Naturally the detectives honored his request, but they had enough from his statement to take him into custody. He's in jail on a million-dollar bond. He retained some hotshot defense attorney from Chicago. He's convinced all of the local criminal defense lawyers will be prejudiced against him because of your involvement in the case. He may have a good point. But it's going to take a miracle for him to get out of this mess. He can practice his voodoo hypnotherapy on his cellmate in prison."

*****

Jax was leading Miles Kaplan past Marion's office to head to the federal courthouse for his arraignment on bank-fraud charges. Marion stopped him.

"Well, Jackson Berman, the first Kaplan trial is starting to pay off in a big way for you," Marion said with a smile.

Jax, looking confused, asked, "How so, Marion?"

She handed him her handwritten notes. "I know you've been otherwise distracted these past few weeks, but your performance on national television has captured a lot of media attention. Don't forget the exclusive interview with Candace Simon, the reporter who covered the trial from inside the courtroom."

"Are you telling me people actually pay attention to that kind of story?"

"That's what I'm telling you. I took a call from a potential client in Philadelphia who wants you to represent him on racketeering and tax-evasion charges. A few minutes ago, I was on the phone with a woman in Atlanta who is probably going to be charged with murdering her husband. Both of these potential clients have the funds to pay your fee and all travel expenses."

Jax was dumbfounded.

"My dear," Marion pronounced, "you're in the national spotlight. Don't worry. I told these new clients your schedule is too busy for you to talk today. They're willing to wait. Both offered to travel here for their first meeting. You are in high demand." Marion stood up and gave him a quick hug. "Malcolm Lamping taught you well."

Jax smiled as he took in this news. This was a game changer for his career.

"Thanks, Marion. I'm glad to have you along for what promises to be a very interesting ride."

Giving her his biggest smile, he left her office to return to his client.

"Okay, Miles, it's showtime. Again."

ABOUT THE AUTHOR

Stephanie Wyler has been a juvenile court judge for more than thirty years. She is an assistant professor of criminal justice at the University of Cincinnati. She began her legal career as an assistant prosecutor, followed by more than a decade as a criminal-defense attorney. She is active in charitable organizations devoted to serving children. She is a graduate of the University of Cincinnati School of Criminal Justice and the College of Law. She and her husband live in Cincinnati and Northern Michigan. They have four children and three grandchildren.

CPSIA information can be obtained
at www.ICGtesting.com
Printed in the USA
BVHW061013190122.
626601BV00013B/912